EDGAR WALLACE

COLLECTION

(VOL 1)

This text from these three novels was originally published between 1918.and 1922.
The text is in the public domain.
The unique cover has been designed with the aid of Canva AI.
The edits and layout of this version are Copyright © 2024
by Beauvale Publishing

This publication has no affiliation with the original Author or publication company.

The publishers have made all reasonable efforts to ensure this book is indeed in the Public Domain in any and all territories it has been published, and apologise for any omissions or errors made. Corrections may be made to future printings or electronic publications.

Printed or published to the highest ethical standard

EDGAR WALLACE COLLECTION
(VOL 1)

THE CLUE OF THE TWISTED CANDLE

THE MAN WHO KNEW

THE ANGEL OF TERROR

United Kingdom
1918-1922

CONTENTS

THE CLUE OF THE TWISTED CANDLE

CHAPTER I 1
CHAPTER II 15
CHAPTER III 20
CHAPTER IV 27
CHAPTER V 31
CHAPTER VI 35
CHAPTER VII 40
CHAPTER VIII 44
CHAPTER IX 57
CHAPTER X 64
CHAPTER XI 68
CHAPTER XII 75
CHAPTER XIII 78
CHAPTER XIV 82
CHAPTER XV 85
CHAPTER XVI 93
CHAPTER XVII 100
CHAPTER XVIII 111
CHAPTER XIX 113
CHAPTER XX 118
CHAPTER XXI 119
CHAPTER XXII 127
CHAPTER XXIII 135

THE MAN WHO KNEW

CHAPTER I 139
CHAPTER II 148
CHAPTER III 154

CHAPTER IV	162
CHAPTER V	168
CHAPTER VI	178
CHAPTER VII	182
CHAPTER VIII	193
CHAPTER IX	202
CHAPTER X	211
CHAPTER XI	221
CHAPTER XII	228
CHAPTER XIII	238
CHAPTER XIV	245
CHAPTER XV	252
CHAPTER XVI	258
CHAPTER XVII	269

THE ANGEL OF TERROR

CHAPTER I	281
CHAPTER II	285
CHAPTER III	290
CHAPTER IV	296
CHAPTER V	300
CHAPTER VI	304
CHAPTER VII	307
CHAPTER VIII	313
CHAPTER IX	317
CHAPTER X	321
CHAPTER XI	326
CHAPTER XII	329
CHAPTER XIII	334
CHAPTER XIV	339
CHAPTER XV	342
CHAPTER XVI	346

CHAPTER XVII ... 349
CHAPTER XVIII ... 354
CHAPTER XIX ... 357
CHAPTER XX ... 361
CHAPTER XXI ... 366
CHAPTER XXII ... 368
CHAPTER XXIII ... 372
CHAPTER XXIV ... 376
CHAPTER XXV ... 380
CHAPTER XXVI ... 383
CHAPTER XXVII ... 385
CHAPTER XXVIII ... 390
CHAPTER XXIX ... 396
CHAPTER XXX ... 402
CHAPTER XXXI ... 406
CHAPTER XXXII ... 411
CHAPTER XXXIII ... 415
CHAPTER XXXIV ... 420
CHAPTER XXXV ... 424
CHAPTER XXXVI ... 428
CHAPTER XXXVII ... 430
CHAPTER XXXVIII ... 435
CHAPTER XXXIX ... 441
CHAPTER XL ... 445
CHAPTER XLI ... 448

THE CLUE OF THE TWISTED CANDLE

CHAPTER I

The 4.15 from Victoria to Lewes had been held up at Three Bridges in consequence of a derailment and, though John Lexman was fortunate enough to catch a belated connection to Beston Tracey, the wagonette which was the sole communication between the village and the outside world had gone.

"If you can wait half an hour, Mr. Lexman," said the station-master, "I will telephone up to the village and get Briggs to come down for you."

John Lexman looked out upon the dripping landscape and shrugged his shoulders.

"I'll walk," he said shortly and, leaving his bag in the station-master's care and buttoning his mackintosh to his chin, he stepped forth resolutely into the rain to negotiate the two miles which separated the tiny railway station from Little Tracey.

The downpour was incessant and likely to last through the night. The high hedges on either side of the narrow road were so many leafy cascades; the road itself was in places ankle deep in mud. He stopped under the protecting cover of a big tree to fill and light his pipe and with its bowl turned downwards continued his walk. But for the driving rain which searched every crevice and found every chink in his waterproof armor, he preferred, indeed welcomed, the walk.

The road from Beston Tracey to Little Beston was associated in his mind with some of the finest situations in his novels. It was on this road that he had conceived "The Tilbury Mystery." Between the station and the house he had woven the plot which had made "Gregory Standish" the most popular detective story of the year. For John Lexman was a maker of cunning plots.

If, in the literary world, he was regarded by superior persons as a writer of "shockers," he had a large and increasing public who were fascinated by the wholesome and thrilling stories he wrote, and who held on breathlessly to the skein of mystery until they came to the denouement he had planned.

But no thought of books, or plots, or stories filled his troubled mind as he strode along the deserted road to Little Beston. He had had two interviews in London, one of which under ordinary circumstances would have filled him with joy: He had seen T. X. and "T. X." was T. X. Meredith, who would one day be Chief of the Criminal Investigation Department and was now an Assistant Commissioner of Police, engaged in the more delicate work of that department.

In his erratic, tempestuous way, T. X. had suggested the greatest idea for a plot that any author could desire. But it was not of T. X. that John Lexman thought as he breasted the hill, on the slope of which was the tiny habitation known by the somewhat magnificent title of Beston Priory.

It was the interview he had had with the Greek on the previous day which filled his mind, and he frowned as he recalled it. He opened the little wicket gate and went through the plantation to the house, doing his best to shake off the recollection of the remarkable and unedifying discussion he had had with the moneylender.

Beston Priory was little more than a cottage, though one of its walls was an indubitable relic of that establishment which a pious Howard had erected in the thirteenth century. A small and unpretentious building, built in the Elizabethan style with quaint gables and high chimneys, its latticed windows and sunken gardens, its rosary and its tiny meadow, gave it a certain manorial completeness which was a source of great pride to its owner.

He passed under the thatched porch, and stood for a moment in the broad hallway as he stripped his drenching mackintosh.

The hall was in darkness. Grace would probably be changing for dinner, and he decided that in his present mood he would not disturb her. He passed through the long passage which led to the big study at the back of the house. A fire burnt redly in the old-fashioned grate and the snug comfort of the room brought a sense of ease and relief. He changed his shoes, and lit the table lamp.

The room was obviously a man's den. The leather-covered chairs, the big and well-filled bookcase which covered one wall of the room, the huge, solid-oak writing-desk, covered with books and half-finished manuscripts, spoke unmistakably of its owner's occupation.

After he had changed his shoes, he refilled his pipe, walked over to the fire, and stood looking down into its glowing heart.

He was a man a little above medium height, slimly built, with a breadth of shoulder which was suggestive of the athlete. He had indeed rowed 4 in his boat, and had fought his way into the semi-finals of the amateur boxing championship of England. His face was strong, lean, yet well-moulded. His eyes were grey and deep, his eyebrows straight and a little forbidding. The clean-shaven mouth was big and generous, and the healthy tan of his cheek told of a life lived in the open air.

There was nothing of the recluse or the student in his appearance. He was in fact a typical, healthy-looking Britisher, very much like any other man of his class whom one would meet in the mess-room of the British army, in the wardrooms of the fleet, or in the far-off posts of the Empire, where the administrative cogs of the great machine are to be seen at work.

There was a little tap at the door, and before he could say "Come in" it was pushed open and Grace Lexman entered.

If you described her as brave and sweet you might secure from that brief description both her manner and her charm. He half crossed the room to meet her, and kissed her tenderly.

"I didn't know you were back until—" she said; linking her arm in his.

"Until you saw the horrible mess my mackintosh has made," he smiled. "I know your methods, Watson!"

She laughed, but became serious again.

"I am very glad you've come back. We have a visitor," she said.

He raised his eyebrows.

"A visitor? Whoever came down on a day like this?"

She looked at him a little strangely.

"Mr. Kara," she said.

"Kara? How long has he been here?"

"He came at four."

There was nothing enthusiastic in her tone.

"I can't understand why you don't like old Kara," rallied her husband.

"There are very many reasons," she replied, a little curtly for her.

"Anyway," said John Lexman, after a moment's thought, "his arrival is rather opportune. Where is he?"

"He is in the drawing-room."

The Priory drawing-room was a low-ceilinged, rambling apartment, "all old print and chrysanthemums," to use Lexman's description. Cosy armchairs, a grand piano, an almost medieval open grate, faced with dull-green tiles, a well-worn but cheerful carpet and two big silver candelabras were the principal features which attracted the newcomer.

There was in this room a harmony, a quiet order and a soothing quality which made it a haven of rest to a literary man with jagged nerves. Two big bronze bowls were filled with early violets, another blazed like a pale sun with primroses, and the early woodland flowers filled the room with a faint fragrance.

A man rose to his feet, as John Lexman entered and crossed the room with an easy carriage. He was a man possessed of singular beauty of face and of figure. Half a head taller than the author, he carried himself with such a grace as to conceal his height.

"I missed you in town," he said, "so I thought I'd run down on the off chance of seeing you."

He spoke in the well-modulated tone of one who had had a long acquaintance with the public schools and universities of England. There was no trace of any foreign accent, yet Remington Kara was a Greek and had been born and partly educated in the more turbulent area of Albania.

The two men shook hands warmly.

"You'll stay to dinner?"

Kara glanced round with a smile at Grace Lexman. She sat uncomfortably upright, her hands loosely folded on her lap, her face devoid of encouragement.

"If Mrs. Lexman doesn't object," said the Greek.

"I should be pleased, if you would," she said, almost mechanically; "it is a horrid night and you won't get anything worth eating this side of London and I doubt very much," she smiled a little, "if the meal I can give you will be worthy of that description."

"What you can give me will be more than sufficient," he said, with a little bow, and turned to her husband.

In a few minutes they were deep in a discussion of books and places, and Grace seized the opportunity to make her escape. From books in general to Lexman's books in particular the conversation flowed.

"I've read every one of them, you know," said Kara.

John made a little face. "Poor devil," he said sardonically.

"On the contrary," said Kara, "I am not to be pitied. There is a great criminal lost in you, Lexman."

"Thank you," said John.

"I am not being uncomplimentary, am I?" smiled the Greek. "I am merely referring to the ingenuity of your plots. Sometimes your books baffle and annoy me. If I cannot see the solution of your mysteries before the book is half through, it angers me a little. Of course in the majority of cases I know the solution before I have reached the fifth chapter."

John looked at him in surprise and was somewhat piqued.

"I flatter myself it is impossible to tell how my stories will end until the last chapter," he said.

Kara nodded.

"That would be so in the case of the average reader, but you forget that I am a student. I follow every little thread of the clue which you leave exposed."

"You should meet T. X.," said John, with a laugh, as he rose from his chair to poke the fire.

"T. X.?"

"T. X. Meredith. He is the most ingenious beggar you could meet. We were at Caius together, and he is by way of being a great pal of mine. He is in the Criminal Investigation Department."

Kara nodded. There was the light of interest in his eyes and he would have pursued the discussion further, but at the moment dinner was announced.

It was not a particularly cheerful meal because Grace did not as usual join in the conversation, and it was left to Kara and to her husband to supply the deficiencies. She was experiencing a curious sense of depression, a premonition of evil which she could not define. Again and again in the course of the dinner she took her mind back to the events of the day to discover the reason for her unease.

Usually when she adopted this method she came upon the trivial causes in which apprehension was born, but now she was puzzled to find that a solution was denied her. Her letters of the morning had been pleasant, neither the house nor the servants had given her any trouble. She was well herself, and though she knew John had a little money trouble, since his unfortunate speculation in Roumanian gold shares, and she half suspected that he had had to borrow money to make good his losses, yet his prospects were so excellent and the success of his last book so promising that she, probably seeing with a clearer vision the unimportance of those money worries, was less concerned about the problem than he.

"You will have your coffee in the study, I suppose," said Grace, "and I know you'll excuse me; I have to see Mrs. Chandler on the mundane subject of laundry."

She favoured Kara with a little nod as she left the room and touched John's shoulder lightly with her hand in passing.

Kara's eyes followed her graceful figure until she was out of view, then:

"I want to see you, Kara," said John Lexman, "if you will give me five minutes."

"You can have five hours, if you like," said the other, easily.

They went into the study together; the maid brought the coffee and liqueur, and placed them on a little table near the fire and disappeared.

For a time the conversation was general. Kara, who was a frank admirer of the comfort of the room and who lamented his own inability to secure with money the cosiness which John had obtained at little cost, went on a foraging expedition whilst his host applied himself to a proof which needed correcting.

"I suppose it is impossible for you to have electric light here," Kara asked.

"Quite," replied the other.

"Why?"

"I rather like the light of this lamp."

"It isn't the lamp," drawled the Greek and made a little grimace; "I hate these candles."

He waved his hand to the mantle-shelf where the six tall, white, waxen candles stood out from two wall sconces.

"Why on earth do you hate candles?" asked the other in surprise.

Kara made no reply for the moment, but shrugged his shoulders. Presently he spoke.

"If you were ever tied down to a chair and by the side of that chair was a small keg of black powder and stuck in that powder was a small candle that burnt lower and lower every minute—my God!"

John was amazed to see the perspiration stand upon the forehead of his guest.

"That sounds thrilling," he said.

The Greek wiped his forehead with a silk handkerchief and his hand shook a little.

"It was something more than thrilling," he said.

"And when did this occur?" asked the author curiously.

"In Albania," replied the other; "it was many years ago, but the devils are always sending me reminders of the fact."

He did not attempt to explain who the devils were or under what circumstances he was brought to this unhappy pass, but changed the subject definitely.

Sauntering round the cosy room he followed the bookshelf which filled one wall and stopped now and again to examine some title. Presently he drew forth a stout volume.

"'Wild Brazil'," he read, "by George Gathercole-do you know Gathercole?"

John was filling his pipe from a big blue jar on his desk and nodded.

"Met him once—a taciturn devil. Very short of speech and, like all men who have seen and done things, less inclined to talk about himself than any man I know."

Kara looked at the book with a thoughtful pucker of brow and turned the leaves idly.

"I've never seen him," he said as he replaced the book, "yet, in a sense, his new journey is on my behalf."

The other man looked up.

"On your behalf?"

"Yes—you know he has gone to Patagonia for me. He believes there is gold there—you will learn as much from his book on the mountain systems of South America. I was interested in his theories and corresponded with him. As a result of that correspondence he undertook to make a geological survey for me. I sent him money for his expenses, and he went off."

"You never saw him?" asked John Lexman, surprised.

Kara shook his head.

"That was not—?" began his host.

"Not like me, you were going to say. Frankly, it was not, but then I realized that he was an unusual kind of man. I invited him to dine with me before he left London, and in reply received a wire from Southampton intimating that he was already on his way."

Lexman nodded.

"It must be an awfully interesting kind of life," he said. "I suppose he will be away for quite a long time?"

"Three years," said Kara, continuing his examination of the bookshelf.

"I envy those fellows who run round the world writing books," said John, puffing reflectively at his pipe. "They have all the best of it."

Kara turned. He stood immediately behind the author and the other could not see his face. There was, however, in his voice an unusual earnestness and an unusual quiet vehemence.

"What have you to complain about!" he asked, with that little drawl of his. "You have your own creative work—the most fascinating branch of labour that comes to a man. He, poor beggar, is bound to actualities. You have the full range of all the worlds which your imagination gives to you. You can create men and destroy them, call into existence fascinating problems, mystify and baffle ten or twenty thousand people, and then, at a word, elucidate your mystery."

John laughed.

"There is something in that," he said.

"As for the rest of your life," Kara went on in a lower voice, "I think you have that which makes life worth living—an incomparable wife."

Lexman swung round in his chair, and met the other's gaze, and there was something in the set of the other's handsome face which took his breath away.

"I do not see—" he began.

Kara smiled.

"That was an impertinence, wasn't it!" he said, banteringly. "But then you mustn't forget, my dear man, that I was very anxious to marry your wife. I don't suppose it is secret. And when I lost her, I had ideas about you which are not pleasant to recall."

He had recovered his self-possession and had continued his aimless stroll about the room.

"You must remember I am a Greek, and the modern Greek is no philosopher. You must remember, too, that I am a petted child of fortune, and have had everything I wanted since I was a baby."

"You are a fortunate devil," said the other, turning back to his desk, and taking up his pen.

For a moment Kara did not speak, then he made as though he would say something, checked himself, and laughed.

"I wonder if I am," he said.

And now he spoke with a sudden energy.

"What is this trouble you are having with Vassalaro?"

John rose from his chair and walked over to the fire, stood gazing down into its depths, his legs wide apart, his hands clasped behind him, and Kara took his attitude to supply an answer to the question.

"I warned you against Vassalaro," he said, stooping by the other's side to light his cigar with a spill of paper. "My dear Lexman, my fellow countrymen are unpleasant people to deal with in certain moods."

"He was so obliging at first," said Lexman, half to himself.

"And now he is so disobliging," drawled Kara. "That is a way which moneylenders have, my dear man; you were very foolish to go to him at all. I could have lent you the money."

"There were reasons why I should not borrow money from you,", said John, quietly, "and I think you yourself have supplied the principal reason when you told me just now, what I already knew, that you wanted to marry Grace."

"How much is the amount?" asked Kara, examining his well-manicured finger-nails.

"Two thousand five hundred pounds," replied John, with a short laugh, "and I haven't two thousand five hundred shillings at this moment."

"Will he wait?"

John Lexman shrugged his shoulders.

"Look here, Kara," he said, suddenly, "don't think I want to reproach you, but it was through you that I met Vassalaro so that you know the kind of man he is."

Kara nodded.

"Well, I can tell you he has been very unpleasant indeed," said John, with a frown, "I had an interview with him yesterday in London and it is clear that he is going to make a lot of trouble. I depended upon the success of my play in town giving me enough to pay him off, and I very foolishly made a lot of promises of repayment which I have been unable to keep."

"I see," said Kara, and then, "does Mrs. Lexman know about this matter?"

"A little," said the other.

He paced restlessly up and down the room, his hands behind him and his chin upon his chest.

"Naturally I have not told her the worst, or how beastly unpleasant the man has been."

He stopped and turned.

"Do you know he threatened to kill me?" he asked.

Kara smiled.

"I can tell you it was no laughing matter," said the other, angrily, "I nearly took the little whippersnapper by the scruff of the neck and kicked him."

Kara dropped his hand on the other's arm.

"I am not laughing at you," he said; "I am laughing at the thought of Vassalaro threatening to kill anybody. He is the biggest coward in the world. What on earth induced him to take this drastic step?"

"He said he is being hard pushed for money," said the other, moodily, "and it is possibly true. He was beside himself with anger and anxiety, otherwise I might have given the little blackguard the thrashing he deserved."

Kara who had continued his stroll came down the room and halted in front of the fireplace looking at the young author with a paternal smile.

"You don't understand Vassalaro," he said; "I repeat he is the greatest coward in the world. You will probably discover he is full of firearms and threats of slaughter, but you have only to click a revolver to see him collapse. Have you a revolver, by the way?"

"Oh, nonsense," said the other, roughly, "I cannot engage myself in that kind of melodrama."

"It is not nonsense," insisted the other, "when you are in Rome, et cetera, and when you have to deal with a low-class Greek you must use methods which will at least impress him. If you thrash him, he will never forgive you and will probably stick a knife into you or your wife. If you meet his melodrama with melodrama and at the psychological moment produce your revolver; you will secure the effect you require. Have you a revolver?"

John went to his desk and, pulling open a drawer, took out a small Browning.

"That is the extent of my armory," he said, "it has never been fired and was sent to me by an unknown admirer last Christmas."

"A curious Christmas present," said the other, examining the weapon.

"I suppose the mistaken donor imagined from my books that I lived in a veritable museum of revolvers, sword sticks and noxious drugs," said Lexman, recovering some of his good humour; "it was accompanied by a card."

"Do you know how it works?" asked the other.

"I have never troubled very much about it," replied Lexman, "I know that it is loaded by slipping back the cover, but as my admirer did not send ammunition, I never even practised with it."

There was a knock at the door.

"That is the post," explained John.

The maid had one letter on the salver and the author took it up with a frown.

"From Vassalaro," he said, when the girl had left the room.

The Greek took the letter in his hand and examined it.

"He writes a vile fist," was his only comment as he handed it back to John.

He slit open the thin, buff envelope and took out half a dozen sheets of yellow paper, only a single sheet of which was written upon. The letter was brief:

> "I must see you to-night without fail," ran the scrawl; "meet me at the crossroads between Beston Tracey and the Eastbourne Road. I shall be there at eleven o'clock, and, if you want to preserve your life, you had better bring me a substantial instalment."

It was signed "Vassalaro."

John read the letter aloud. "He must be mad to write a letter like that," he said; "I'll meet the little devil and teach him such a lesson in politeness as he is never likely to forget."

He handed the letter to the other and Kara read it in silence.

"Better take your revolver," he said as he handed it back.

John Lexman looked at his watch.

"I have an hour yet, but it will take me the best part of twenty minutes to reach the Eastbourne Road."

"Will you see him?" asked Kara, in a tone of surprise.

"Certainly," Lexman replied emphatically: "I cannot have him coming up to the house and making a scene and that is certainly what the little beast will do."

"Will you pay him?" asked Kara softly.

John made no answer. There was probably 10 pounds in the house and a cheque which was due on the morrow would bring him another 30 pounds. He looked at the letter again. It was written on paper of an unusual texture. The surface was rough almost like blotting paper and in some places the ink absorbed by the porous surface had run. The blank sheets had evidently been inserted by a man in so violent a hurry that he had not noticed the extravagance.

"I shall keep this letter," said John.

"I think you are well advised. Vassalaro probably does not know that he transgresses a law in writing threatening letters and that should be a very strong weapon in your hand in certain eventualities."

There was a tiny safe in one corner of the study and this John opened with a key which he took from his pocket. He pulled open one of the steel drawers, took out the papers which were in it and put in their place the letter, pushed the drawer to, and locked it.

All the time Kara was watching him intently as one who found more than an ordinary amount of interest in the novelty of the procedure.

He took his leave soon afterwards.

"I would like to come with you to your interesting meeting," he said, "but unfortunately I have business elsewhere. Let me enjoin you to take your revolver and at the first sign of any bloodthirsty intention on the part of my admirable compatriot, produce it and click it once or twice, you won't have to do more."

Grace rose from the piano as Kara entered the little drawing-room and murmured a few conventional expressions of regret that the visitor's stay had been so short. That there was no sincerity in that regret Kara, for one, had no doubt. He was a man singularly free from illusions.

They stayed talking a little while.

"I will see if your chauffeur is asleep," said John, and went out of the room.

There was a little silence after he had gone.

"I don't think you are very glad to see me," said Kara. His frankness was a little embarrassing to the girl and she flushed slightly.

"I am always glad to see you, Mr. Kara, or any other of my husband's friends," she said steadily.

He inclined his head.

"To be a friend of your husband is something," he said, and then as if remembering something, "I wanted to take a book away with me—I wonder if your husband would mind my getting it?"

"I will find it for you."

"Don't let me bother you," he protested, "I know my way."

Without waiting for her permission he left the girl with the unpleasant feeling that he was taking rather much for granted. He was gone less than a minute and returned with a book under his arm.

"I have not asked Lexman's permission to take it," he said, "but I am rather interested in the author. Oh, here you are," he turned to John who came in at that moment. "Might I take this book on Mexico?" he asked. "I will return it in the morning."

They stood at the door, watching the tail light of the motor disappear down the drive; and returned in silence to the drawing room.

"You look worried, dear," she said, laying her hand on his shoulder.

He smiled faintly.

"Is it the money?" she asked anxiously.

For a moment he was tempted to tell her of the letter. He stifled the temptation realizing that she would not consent to his going out if she knew the truth.

"It is nothing very much," he said. "I have to go down to Beston Tracey to meet the last train. I am expecting some proofs down."

He hated lying to her, and even an innocuous lie of this character was repugnant to him.

"I'm afraid you have had a dull evening," he said, "Kara was not very amusing."

She looked at him thoughtfully.

"He has not changed very much," she said slowly.

"He's a wonderfully handsome chap, isn't he?" he asked in a tone of admiration. "I can't understand what you ever saw in a fellow like me, when you had a man who was not only rich, but possibly the best-looking man in the world."

She shivered a little.

"I have seen a side of Mr. Kara that is not particularly beautiful," she said. "Oh, John, I am afraid of that man!"

He looked at her in astonishment.

"Afraid?" he asked. "Good heavens, Grace, what a thing to say! Why I believe he'd do anything for you."

"That is exactly what I am afraid of," she said in a low voice.

She had a reason which she did not reveal. She had first met Remington Kara in Salonika two years before. She had been doing a tour through the Balkans with her father—it was the last tour the famous archeologist made—and had met the man who was fated to have such an influence upon her life at a dinner given by the American Consul.

Many were the stories which were told about this Greek with his Jove-like face, his handsome carriage and his limitless wealth. It was said that his mother was an American lady who had been captured by Albanian brigands and was sold to one of the Albanian chiefs who fell in love with her, and for her sake became a Protestant. He had been educated at Yale and at Oxford, and was known to be the possessor of vast wealth, and was virtually king of a hill district forty miles out of Durazzo. Here he reigned supreme, occupying a beautiful house which he had built by an Italian architect, and the fittings and appointments of which had been imported from the luxurious centres of the world.

In Albania they called him "Kara Rumo," which meant "The Black Roman," for no particular reason so far as any one could judge, for his skin was as fair as a Saxon's, and his close-cropped curls were almost golden.

He had fallen in love with Grace Terrell. At first his attentions had amused her, and then there came a time when they frightened her, for the man's fire and passion had been unmistakable. She had made it plain to him that he could base no hopes upon her returning his love, and, in a scene which she even now shuddered to recall, he had revealed something of his wild and reckless nature. On the following day she did not see him, but two days later, when returning through the Bazaar from a dance which had been given by the Governor General, her carriage was stopped, she was forcibly dragged from its interior, and her cries were stifled with a cloth impregnated with a scent of a peculiar aromatic sweetness. Her assailants were about to thrust her into another carriage, when a party of British bluejackets who had been on leave came upon the scene, and, without knowing anything of the nationality of the girl, had rescued her.

In her heart of hearts she did not doubt Kara's complicity in this medieval attempt to gain a wife, but of this adventure she had told her husband nothing. Until her marriage she was constantly receiving valuable presents which she as constantly returned to the only address she knew—Kara's estate at Lemazo. A few months after her marriage she had learned through the newspapers that this "leader of Greek society" had purchased a big house near Cadogan Square, and then, to her amazement and to her dismay, Kara had scraped an acquaintance with her husband even before the honeymoon was over.

His visits had been happily few, but the growing intimacy between John and this strange undisciplined man had been a source of constant distress to her.

Should she, at this, the eleventh hour, tell her husband all her fears and her suspicions?

She debated the point for some time. And never was she nearer taking him into her complete confidence than she was as he sat in the big armchair by the side of the piano, a little drawn of face, more than a little absorbed in his own meditations. Had he been less worried she might have spoken. As it was, she turned the conversation to his last work, the big mystery story which, if it would not make his fortune, would mean a considerable increase to his income.

At a quarter to eleven he looked at his watch, and rose. She helped him on with his coat. He stood for some time irresolutely.

"Is there anything you have forgotten?" she asked.

He asked himself whether he should follow Kara's advice. In any circumstance it was not a pleasant thing to meet a ferocious little man who had threatened his life, and to meet him unarmed was tempting Providence. The whole thing was of course ridiculous, but it was ridiculous that he should have borrowed, and it was ridiculous that the borrowing should have been necessary, and yet he had speculated on the best of advice—it was Kara's advice.

The connection suddenly occurred to him, and yet Kara had not directly suggested that he should buy Roumanian gold shares, but had merely spoken glowingly of their prospects. He thought a moment, and then walked back slowly into the study, pulled open the drawer of his desk, took out the sinister little Browning, and slipped it into his pocket.

"I shan't be long, dear," he said, and kissing the girl he strode out into the darkness.

Kara sat back in the luxurious depths of his car, humming a little tune, as the driver picked his way cautiously over the uncertain road. The rain was still falling, and Kara had to rub the windows free of the mist which had gathered on them to discover where he was. From time to time he looked out as though he expected to see somebody, and then with a little smile he remembered that he had changed his original plan, and that he had fixed the waiting room of Lewes junction as his rendezvous.

Here it was that he found a little man muffled up to the ears in a big top coat, standing before the dying fire. He started as Kara entered and at a signal followed him from the room.

The stranger was obviously not English. His face was sallow and peaked, his cheeks were hollow, and the beard he wore was irregular-almost unkempt.

Kara led the way to the end of the dark platform, before he spoke.

"You have carried out my instructions?" he asked brusquely.

The language he spoke was Arabic, and the other answered him in that language.

"Everything that you have ordered has been done, Effendi," he said humbly.

"You have a revolver?"

The man nodded and patted his pocket.

"Loaded?"

"Excellency," asked the other, in surprise, "what is the use of a revolver, if it is not loaded?"

"You understand, you are not to shoot this man," said Kara. "You are merely to present the pistol. To make sure, you had better unload it now."

Wonderingly the man obeyed, and clicked back the ejector.

"I will take the cartridges," said Kara, holding out his hand.

He slipped the little cylinders into his pocket, and after examining the weapon returned it to its owner.

"You will threaten him," he went on. "Present the revolver straight at his heart. You need do nothing else."

The man shuffled uneasily.

"I will do as you say, Effendi," he said. "But—"

"There are no 'buts,'" replied the other harshly. "You are to carry out my instructions without any question. What will happen then you shall see. I shall be at hand. That I have a reason for this play be assured."

"But suppose he shoots?" persisted the other uneasily.

"He will not shoot," said Kara easily. "Besides, his revolver is not loaded. Now you may go. You have a long walk before you. You know the way?"

The man nodded.

"I have been over it before," he said confidently.

Kara returned to the big limousine which had drawn up some distance from the station. He spoke a word or two to the chauffeur in Greek, and the man touched his hat.

CHAPTER II

Assistant Commissioner of Police T. X. Meredith did not occupy offices in New Scotland Yard. It is the peculiarity of public offices that they are planned with the idea of supplying the margin of space above all requirements and that on their completion they are found wholly inadequate to house the various departments which mysteriously come into progress coincident with the building operations.

"T. X.," as he was known by the police forces of the world, had a big suite of offices in Whitehall. The house was an old one facing the Board of Trade and the inscription on the ancient door told passers-by that this was the "Public Prosecutor, Special Branch."

The duties of T. X. were multifarious. People said of him—and like most public gossip, this was probably untrue—that he was the head of the "illegal" department of Scotland Yard. If by chance you lost the keys of your safe, T. X. could supply you (so popular rumour ran) with a burglar who would open that safe in half an hour.

If there dwelt in England a notorious individual against whom the police could collect no scintilla of evidence to justify a prosecution, and if it was necessary for the good of the community that that person should be deported, it was T. X. who arrested the obnoxious person, hustled him into a cab and did not loose his hold upon his victim until he had landed him on the indignant shores of an otherwise friendly power.

It is very certain that when the minister of a tiny power which shall be nameless was suddenly recalled by his government and brought to trial in his native land for putting into circulation spurious bonds, it was somebody from the department which T. X. controlled, who burgled His Excellency's house, burnt the locks from his safe and secured the necessary incriminating evidence.

I say it is fairly certain and here I am merely voicing the opinion of very knowledgeable people indeed, heads of public departments who speak behind their hands, mysterious under-secretaries of state who discuss things in whispers in the remote corners of their clubrooms and the more frank views of American correspondents who had no hesitation in putting those views into print for the benefit of their readers.

That T. X. had a more legitimate occupation we know, for it was that flippant man whose outrageous comment on the Home Office Administration is popularly supposed to have sent one Home Secretary to his grave, who traced the Deptford murderers through a labyrinth of perjury and who brought to book Sir Julius Waglite though he had covered his trail of defalcation through the balance sheets of thirty-four companies.

On the night of March 3rd, T. X. sat in his inner office interviewing a disconsolate inspector of metropolitan police, named Mansus.

In appearance T. X. conveyed the impression of extreme youth, for his face was almost boyish and it was only when you looked at him closely and saw the little creases about his eyes, the setting of his straight mouth, that you guessed he was on the way to forty. In his early days he had been something of a poet, and had written a slight volume of "Woodland Lyrics," the mention of which at this later stage was sufficient to make him feel violently unhappy.

In manner he was tactful but persistent, his language was at times marked by a violent extravagance and he had had the distinction of having provoked, by certain correspondence which had seen the light, the comment of a former Home Secretary that "it was unfortunate that Mr. Meredith did not take his position with the seriousness which was expected from a public official."

His language was, as I say, under great provocation, violent and unusual. He had a trick of using words which never were on land or sea, and illustrating his instruction or his admonition with the quaintest phraseology.

Now he was tilted back in his office chair at an alarming angle, scowling at his distressed subordinate who sat on the edge of a chair at the other side of his desk.

"But, T. X.," protested the Inspector, "there was nothing to be found."

It was the outrageous practice of Mr. Meredith to insist upon his associates calling him by his initials, a practice which had earnt disapproval in the highest quarters.

"Nothing is to be found!" he repeated wrathfully. "Curious Mike!"

He sat up with a suddenness which caused the police officer to start back in alarm.

"Listen," said T. X., grasping an ivory paperknife savagely in his hand and tapping his blotting-pad to emphasize his words, "you're a pie!"

"I'm a policeman," said the other patiently.

"A policeman!" exclaimed the exasperated T. X. "You're worse than a pie, you're a slud! I'm afraid I shall never make a detective of you," he shook his head sorrowfully at the smiling Mansus who had been in the police force when T. X. was a small boy at school, "you are neither Wise nor Wily; you combine the innocence of a Baby with the grubbiness of a County Parson—you ought to be in the choir."

At this outrageous insult Mr. Mansus was silent; what he might have said, or what further provocation he might have received may be never known, for at that moment, the Chief himself walked in.

The Chief of the Police in these days was a grey man, rather tired, with a hawk nose and deep eyes that glared under shaggy eyebrows and he was a terror to all men of his department save to T. X. who respected nothing on earth and very little elsewhere. He nodded curtly to Mansus.

"Well, T. X.," he said, "what have you discovered about our friend Kara?"

He turned from T. X. to the discomforted inspector.

"Very little," said T. X. "I've had Mansus on the job."

"And you've found nothing, eh?" growled the Chief.

"He has found all that it is possible to find," said T. X. "We do not perform miracles in this department, Sir George, nor can we pick up the threads of a case at five minutes' notice."

Sir George Haley grunted.

"Mansus has done his best," the other went on easily, "but it is rather absurd to talk about one's best when you know so little of what you want."

Sir George dropped heavily into the arm-chair, and stretched out his long thin legs.

"What I want," he said, looking up at the ceiling and putting his hands together, "is to discover something about one Remington Kara, a wealthy Greek who has taken a house in Cadogan Square, who has no particular position in London society and therefore has no reason for coming here, who openly expresses his detestation of the climate, who has a magnificent estate in some wild place in the Balkans, who is an excellent horseman, a magnificent shot and a passable aviator."

T. X. nodded to Mansus and with something of gratitude in his eyes the inspector took his leave.

"Now Mansus has departed," said T. X., sitting himself on the edge of his desk and selecting with great care a cigarette from the case he took from his pocket, "let me know something of the reason for this sudden interest in the great ones of the earth."

Sir George smiled grimly.

"I have the interest which is the interest of my department," he said. "That is to say I want to know a great deal about abnormal people. We have had an application from him," he went on, "which is rather unusual. Apparently he is in fear of his life from some cause or other and wants to know if he can have a private telephone connection between his house and the central office. We told him that he could always get the nearest Police Station on the 'phone, but that doesn't satisfy him. He has made bad friends with some gentleman of his own country who sooner or later, he thinks, will cut his throat."

T. X. nodded.

"All this I know," he said patiently, "if you will further unfold the secret dossier, Sir George, I am prepared to be thrilled."

"There is nothing thrilling about it," growled the older man, rising, "but I remember the Macedonian shooting case in South London and I don't want a repetition of that sort of thing. If people want to have blood feuds, let them take them outside the metropolitan area."

"By all means," said T. X., "let them. Personally, I don't care where they go. But if that is the extent of your information I can supplement it. He has had extensive alterations made to the house he bought in Cadogan Square; the room in which he lives is practically a safe."

Sir George raised his eyebrows.

"A safe," he repeated.

T. X. nodded.

"A safe," he said; "its walls are burglar proof, floor and roof are reinforced concrete, there is one door which in addition to its ordinary lock is closed by a sort of steel latch which he lets fall when he retires for the night and which he opens himself personally in the morning. The window is unreachable, there are no communicating doors, and altogether the room is planned to stand a siege."

The Chief Commissioner was interested.

"Any more?" he asked.

"Let me think," said T. X., looking up at the ceiling. "Yes, the interior of his room is plainly furnished, there is a big fireplace, rather an ornate bed, a steel safe built into the wall and visible from its outer side to the policeman whose beat is in that neighborhood."

"How do you know all this?" asked the Chief Commissioner.

"Because I've been in the room," said T. X. simply, "having by an underhand trick succeeded in gaining the misplaced confidence of Kara's housekeeper, who by the way"—he turned round to his desk and scribbled a name on the blotting-pad—"will be discharged to-morrow and must be found a place."

"Is there any—er—?" began the Chief.

"Funny business?" interrupted T. X., "not a bit. House and man are quite normal save for these eccentricities. He has announced his intention of spending three months of the year in England and nine months abroad. He is very rich, has no relations, and has a passion for power."

"Then he'll be hung," said the Chief, rising.

"I doubt it," said the other, "people with lots of money seldom get hung. You only get hung for wanting money."

"Then you're in some danger, T. X.," smiled the Chief, "for according to my account you're always more or less broke."

"A genial libel," said T. X., "but talking about people being broke, I saw John Lexman to-day—you know him!"

The Chief Commissioner nodded.

"I've an idea he's rather hit for money. He was in that Roumanian gold swindle, and by his general gloom, which only comes to a man when he's in love (and he can't possibly be in love since he's married) or when he's in debt, I fear that he is still feeling the effect of that rosy adventure."

A telephone bell in the corner of the room rang sharply, and T. X. picked up the receiver. He listened intently.

"A trunk call," he said over his shoulder to the departing commissioner, "it may be something interesting."

A little pause; then a hoarse voice spoke to him. "Is that you, T. X.?"

"That's me," said the Assistant Commissioner, commonly.

"It's John Lexman speaking."

"I shouldn't have recognized your voice," said T. X., "what is wrong with you, John, can't you get your plot to went?"

"I want you to come down here at once," said the voice urgently, and even over the telephone T. X. recognized the distress. "I have shot a man, killed him!"

T. X. gasped.

"Good Lord," he said, "you are a silly ass!"

CHAPTER III

In the early hours of the morning a tragic little party was assembled in the study at Beston Priory. John Lexman, white and haggard, sat on the sofa with his wife by his side. Immediate authority as represented by a village constable was on duty in the passage outside, whilst T. X. sitting at the table with a writing pad and a pencil was briefly noting the evidence.

The author had sketched the events of the day. He had described his interview with the money-lender the day before and the arrival of the letter.

"You have the letter!" asked T. X.

John Lexman nodded.

"I am glad of that," said the other with a sigh of relief, "that will save you from a great deal of unpleasantness, my poor old chap. Tell me what happened afterward."

"I reached the village," said John Lexman, "and passed through it. There was nobody about, the rain was still falling very heavily and indeed I didn't meet a single soul all the evening. I reached the place appointed about five minutes before time. It was the corner of Eastbourne Road on the station side and there I found Vassalaro waiting. I was rather ashamed of myself at meeting him at all under these conditions, but I was very keen on his not coming to the house for I was afraid it would upset Grace. What made it all the more ridiculous was this infernal pistol which was in my pocket banging against my side with every step I took as though to nudge me to an understanding of my folly."

"Where did you meet Vassalaro?" asked T. X.

"He was on the other side of the Eastbourne Road and crossed the road to meet me. At first he was very pleasant though a little agitated but afterward he began to behave in a most extraordinary manner as though he was lashing himself up into a fury which he didn't feel. I promised him a substantial amount on account, but he grew worse and worse and then, suddenly, before I realised what he was doing, he was brandishing a revolver in my face and uttering the most extraordinary threats. Then it was I remembered Kara's warning."

"Kara," said T. X. quickly.

"A man I know and who was responsible for introducing me to Vassalaro. He is immensely wealthy."

"I see," said T. X., "go on."

"I remembered this warning," the other proceeded, "and I thought it worth while trying it out to see if it had any effect upon the little man. I pulled the pistol from my pocket and pointed it at him, but that only seemed to make it— and then I pressed the trigger...."

"To my horror four shots exploded before I could recover sufficient self-possession to loosen my hold of the butt. He fell without a word. I dropped the revolver and knelt by his side. I could tell he was dangerously wounded, and indeed I knew at that moment that nothing would save him. My pistol had been pointed in the region of his heart...."

He shuddered, dropping his face in his hands, and the girl by his side, encircling his shoulder with a protecting arm, murmured something in his ear. Presently he recovered.

"He wasn't quite dead. I heard him murmur something but I wasn't able to distinguish what he said. I went straight to the village and told the constable and had the body removed."

T. X. rose from the table and walked to the door and opened it.

"Come in, constable," he said, and when the man made his appearance, "I suppose you were very careful in removing this body, and you took everything which was lying about in the immediate vicinity'?"

"Yes, sir," replied the man, "I took his hat and his walkingstick, if that's what you mean."

"And the revolver!" asked T. X.

The man shook his head.

"There warn't any revolver, sir, except the pistol which Mr. Lexman had."

He fumbled in his pocket and pulled it out gingerly, and T. X. took it from him.

"I'll look after your prisoner; you go down to the village, get any help you can and make a most careful search in the place where this man was killed and bring me the revolver which you will discover. You'll probably find it in a ditch by the side of the road. I'll give a sovereign to the man who finds it."

The constable touched his hat and went out.

"It looks rather a weird case to me," said T. X., as he came back to the table, "can't you see the unusual features yourself, Lexman! It isn't unusual for you to owe money and it isn't unusual for the usurer to demand the return of that money, but in this case he is asking for it before it was due, and further than that he was demanding it with threats. It is not the practice of the average money lender to go after his clients with a loaded revolver. Another peculiar thing is that if he wished to blackmail you, that is to say, bring you into contempt in the eyes of your friends, why did he choose to meet you in a dark and unfrequented road, and not in your house where the moral pressure would be greatest? Also, why did he write you a threatening letter which would certainly bring him into the grip of the law and would have saved you a great deal of unpleasantness if he had decided upon taking action!"

He tapped his white teeth with the end of his pencil and then suddenly,

"I think I'll see that letter," he said.

John Lexman rose from the sofa, crossed to the safe, unlocked it and was unlocking the steel drawer in which he had placed the incriminating document. His hand was on the key when T. X. noticed the look of surprise on his face.

"What is it!" asked the detective suddenly.

"This drawer feels very hot," said John,—he looked round as though to measure the distance between the safe and the fire.

T. X. laid his hand upon the front of the drawer. It was indeed warm.

"Open it," said T. X., and Lexman turned the key and pulled the drawer open.

As he did so, the whole contents burst up in a quick blaze of flame. It died down immediately and left only a little coil of smoke that flowed from the safe into the room.

"Don't touch anything inside," said T. X. quickly.

He lifted the drawer carefully and placed it under the light. In the bottom was no more than a few crumpled white ashes and a blister of paint where the flame had caught the side.

"I see," said T. X. slowly.

He saw something more than that handful of ashes, he saw the deadly peril in which his friend was standing. Here was one half of the evidence in Lexman's favour gone, irredeemably.

"The letter was written on a paper which was specially prepared by a chemical process which disintegrated the moment the paper was exposed to the air. Probably if you delayed putting the letter in the drawer another five minutes, you would have seen it burn before your eyes. As it was, it was smouldering before you had turned the key of the box. The envelope!"

"Kara burnt it," said Lexman in a low voice, "I remember seeing him take it up from the table and throw it in the fire."

T. X. nodded.

"There remains the other half of the evidence," he said grimly, and when an hour later, the village constable returned to report that in spite of his most careful search he had failed to discover the dead man's revolver, his anticipations were realized.

The next morning John Lexman was lodged in Lewes gaol on a charge of wilful murder.

A telegram brought Mansus from London to Beston Tracey, and T. X. received him in the library.

"I sent for you, Mansus, because I suffer from the illusion that you have more brains than most of the people in my department, and that's not saying much."

"I am very grateful to you, sir, for putting me right with Commissioner," began Mansus, but T. X. stopped him.

"It is the duty of every head of departments," he said oracularly, "to shield the incompetence of his subordinates. It is only by the adoption of some such method that the decencies of the public life can be observed. Now get down to this." He gave a sketch of the case from start to finish in as brief a space of time as possible.

"The evidence against Mr. Lexman is very heavy," he said. "He borrowed money from this man, and on the man's body were found particulars of the very Promissory Note which Lexman signed. Why he should have brought it with him, I cannot say. Anyhow I doubt very much whether Mr. Lexman will get a jury to accept his version. Our only chance is to find the Greek's revolver—I don't think there's any very great chance, but if we are to be successful we must make a search at once."

Before he went out he had an interview with Grace. The dark shadows under her eyes told of a sleepless night. She was unusually pale and surprisingly calm.

"I think there are one or two things I ought to tell you," she said, as she led the way into the drawing room, closing the door behind him.

"And they concern Mr. Kara, I think," said T. X.

She looked at him startled.

"How did you know that?"

"I know nothing."

He hesitated on the brink of a flippant claim of omniscience, but realizing in time the agony she must be suffering he checked his natural desire.

"I really know nothing," he continued, "but I guess a lot," and that was as near to the truth as you might expect T. X. to reach on the spur of the moment.

She began without preliminary.

"In the first place I must tell you that Mr. Kara once asked me to marry him, and for reasons which I will give you, I am dreadfully afraid of him."

She described without reserve the meeting at Salonika and Kara's extravagant rage and told of the attempt which had been made upon her.

"Does John know this?" asked T. X.

She shook her head sadly.

"I wish I had told him now," she said. "Oh, how I wish I had!" She wrung her hands in an ecstasy of sorrow and remorse.

T. X. looked at her sympathetically. Then he asked,

"Did Mr. Kara ever discuss your husband's financial position with you?"

"Never."

"How did John Lexman happen to meet Vassalaro?"

"I can tell you that," she answered, "the first time we met Mr. Kara in England was when we were staying at Babbacombe on a summer holiday—which was really a prolongation of our honeymoon. Mr. Kara came to stay at the same hotel. I think Mr. Vassalaro must have been there before; at any rate they knew one another and after Kara's introduction to my husband the rest was easy.

"Can I do anything for John!" she asked piteously.

T. X. shook his head.

"So far as your story is concerned, I don't think you will advantage him by telling it," he said. "There is nothing whatever to connect Kara with this business and you would only give your husband a great deal of pain. I'll do the best I can."

He held out his hand and she grasped it and somehow at that moment there came to T. X. Meredith a new courage, a new faith and a greater determination than ever to solve this troublesome mystery.

He found Mansus waiting for him in a car outside and in a few minutes they were at the scene of the tragedy. A curious little knot of spectators had gathered, looking with morbid interest at the place where the body had been found. There was a local policeman on duty and to him was deputed the ungracious task of warning his fellow villagers to keep their distance. The ground had already been searched very carefully. The two roads crossed almost at right angles and at the corner of the cross thus formed, the hedges were broken, admitting to a field which had evidently been used as a pasture by an adjoining dairy farm. Some rough attempt had been made to close the gap with barbed wire, but it was possible to step over the drooping strands with little or no difficulty. It was to this gap that T. X. devoted his principal attention. All the fields had been carefully examined without result, the four drains which were merely the connecting pipes between ditches at the sides of the crossroads had been swept out and only the broken hedge and its tangle of bushes behind offered any prospect of the new search being rewarded.

"Hullo!" said Mansus, suddenly, and stooping down he picked up something from the ground.

T. X. took it in his hand.

It was unmistakably a revolver cartridge. He marked the spot where it had been found by jamming his walking stick into the ground and continued his search, but without success.

"I am afraid we shall find nothing more here," said T. X., after half an hour's further search. He stood with his chin in his hand, a frown on his face.

"Mansus," he said, "suppose there were three people here, Lexman, the money lender and a third witness. And suppose this third person for some reason unknown was interested in what took place between the two men and he wanted to watch unobserved. Isn't it likely that if he, as I think, instigated the meeting, he would have chosen this place because this particular hedge gave him a chance of seeing without being seen?"

Mansus thought.

"He could have seen just as well from either of the other hedges, with less chance of detection," he said, after a long pause.

T. X. grinned.

"You have the makings of a brain," he said admiringly. "I agree with you. Always remember that, Mansus. That there was one occasion in your life when T. X. Meredith and you thought alike."

Mansus smiled a little feebly.

"Of course from the point of view of the observer this was the worst place possible, so whoever came here, if they did come here, dropping revolver bullets about, must have chosen the spot because it was get-at-able from another direction. Obviously he couldn't come down the road and climb in without attracting the attention of the Greek who was waiting for Mr. Lexman. We may suppose there is a gate farther along the road, we may suppose that he entered that gate, came along the field by the side of the hedge and that somewhere between here and the gate, he threw away his cigar."

"His cigar!" said Mansus in surprise.

"His cigar," repeated T. X., "if he was alone, he would keep his cigar alight until the very last moment."

"He might have thrown it into the road," said Mansus.

"Don't jibber," said T. X., and led the way along the hedge. From where they stood they could see the gate which led on to the road about a hundred yards further on. Within a dozen yards of that gate, T. X. found what he had been searching for, a half-smoked cigar. It was sodden with rain and he picked it up tenderly.

"A good cigar, if I am any judge," he said, "cut with a penknife, and smoked through a holder."

They reached the gate and passed through. Here they were on the road again and this they followed until they reached another cross road that to the left inclining southward to the new Eastbourne Road and that to the westward looking back to the Lewes-Eastbourne railway. The rain had obliterated much that T. X. was looking for, but presently he found a faint indication of a car wheel.

"This is where she turned and backed," he said, and walked slowly to the road on the left, "and this is where she stood. There is the grease from her engine."

He stooped down and moved forward in the attitude of a Russian dancer, "And here are the wax matches which the chauffeur struck," he counted, "one, two, three, four, five, six, allow three for each cigarette on a boisterous night like last night, that makes three cigarettes. Here is a cigarette end, Mansus, Gold Flake brand," he said, as he examined it carefully, "and a Gold Flake brand smokes for twelve minutes in normal weather, but about eight minutes in gusty weather. A car was here for about twenty-four minutes—what do you think of that, Mansus?"

"A good bit of reasoning, T. X.," said the other calmly, "if it happens to be the car you're looking for."

"I am looking for any old car," said T. X.

He found no other trace of car wheels though he carefully followed up the little lane until it reached the main road. After that it was hopeless to search because rain had fallen in the night and in the early hours of the morning. He drove his assistant to the railway station in time to catch the train at one o'clock to London.

"You will go straight to Cadogan Square and arrest the chauffeur of Mr. Kara," he said.

"Upon what charge!" asked Mansus hurriedly.

When it came to the step which T. X. thought fit to take in the pursuance of his duty, Mansus was beyond surprise.

"You can charge him with anything you like," said T. X., with fine carelessness, "probably something will occur to you on your way up to town. As a matter of fact the chauffeur has been called unexpectedly away to Greece and has probably left by this morning's train for the Continent. If that is so, we can do nothing, because the boat will have left Dover and will have landed him at Boulogne, but if by any luck you get him, keep him busy until I get back."

T. X. himself was a busy man that day, and it was not until night was falling that he again turned to Beston Tracey to find a telegram waiting for him. He opened it and read,

"Chauffeur's name, Goole. Formerly waiter English Club, Constantinople. Left for east by early train this morning, his mother being ill."

"His mother ill," said T. X. contemptuously, "how very feeble,—I should have thought Kara could have gone one better than that."

He was in John Lexman's study as the door opened and the maid announced, "Mr. Remington Kara."

CHAPTER IV

T. X. folded the telegram very carefully and slipped it into his waistcoat pocket.

He favoured the newcomer with a little bow and taking upon himself the honours of the establishment, pushed a chair to his visitor.

"I think you know my name," said Kara easily, "I am a friend of poor Lexman's."

"So I am told," said T. X., "but don't let your friendship for Lexman prevent your sitting down."

For a moment the Greek was nonplussed and then, with a little smile and bow, he seated himself by the writing table.

"I am very distressed at this happening," he went on, "and I am more distressed because I feel that as I introduced Lexman to this unfortunate man, I am in a sense responsible."

"If I were you," said T. X., leaning back in the chair and looking half questioningly and half earnestly into the face of the other, "I shouldn't let that fact keep me awake at night. Most people are murdered as a result of an introduction. The cases where people murder total strangers are singularly rare. That I think is due to the insularity of our national character."

Again the other was taken back and puzzled by the flippancy of the man from whom he had expected at least the official manner.

"When did you see Mr. Vassalaro last?" asked T. X. pleasantly.

Kara raised his eyes as though considering.

"I think it must have been nearly a week ago."

"Think again," said T. X.

For a second the Greek started and again relaxed into a smile.

"I am afraid," he began.

"Don't worry about that," said T. X., "but let me ask you this question. You were here last night when Mr. Lexman received a letter. That he did receive a letter, there is considerable evidence," he said as he saw the other hesitate, "because we have the supporting statements of the servant and the postman."

"I was here," said the other, deliberately, "and I was present when Mr. Lexman received a letter."

T. X. nodded.

"A letter written on some brownish paper and rather bulky," he suggested.

Again there was that momentary hesitation.

"I would not swear to the color of the paper or as to the bulk of the letter," he said.

"I should have thought you would," suggested T. X., "because you see, you burnt the envelope, and I presumed you would have noticed that."

"I have no recollection of burning any envelope," said the other easily.

"At any rate," T. X. went on, "when Mr. Lexman read this letter out to you..."

"To which letter are you referring?" asked the other, with a lift of his eyebrows.

"Mr. Lexman received a threatening letter," repeated T. X. patiently, "which he read out to you, and which was addressed to him by Vassalaro. This letter was handed to you and you also read it. Mr. Lexman to your knowledge put the letter in his safe—in a steel drawer."

The other shook his head, smiling gently.

"I am afraid you've made a great mistake," he said almost apologetically, "though I have a recollection of his receiving a letter, I did not read it, nor was it read to me."

The eyes of T. X. narrowed to the very slits and his voice became metallic and hard.

"And if I put you into the box, will you swear, that you did not see that letter, nor read it, nor have it read to you, and that you have no knowledge whatever of such a letter having been received by Mr. Lexman?"

"Most certainly," said the other coolly.

"Would you swear that you have not seen Vassalaro for a week?"

"Certainly," smiled the Greek.

"That you did not in fact see him last night," persisted T. X., "and interview him on the station platform at Lewes, that you did not after leaving him continue on your way to London and then turn your car and return to the neighbourhood of Beston Tracey?"

The Greek was white to the lips, but not a muscle of his face moved.

"Will you also swear," continued T. X. inexorably, "that you did not stand at the corner of what is known as Mitre's Lot and re-enter a gate near to the side where your car was, and that you did not watch the whole tragedy?"

"I'd swear to that," Kara's voice was strained and cracked.

"Would you also swear as to the hour of your arrival in London?"

"Somewhere in the region of ten or eleven," said the Greek.

T. X. smiled.

"Would you swear that you did not go through Guilford at half-past twelve and pull up to replenish your petrol?"

The Greek had now recovered his self-possession and rose.

"You are a very clever man, Mr. Meredith—I think that is your name?"

"That is my name," said T. X. calmly. "There has been, no need for me to change it as often as you have found the necessity."

He saw the fire blazing in the other's eyes and knew that his shot had gone home.

"I am afraid I must go," said Kara. "I came here intending to see Mrs. Lexman, and I had no idea that I should meet a policeman."

"My dear Mr. Kara," said T. X., rising and lighting a cigarette, "you will go through life enduring that unhappy experience."

"What do you mean?"

"Just what I say. You will always be expecting to meet one person, and meeting another, and unless you are very fortunate indeed, that other will always be a policeman."

His eyes twinkled for he had recovered from the gust of anger which had swept through him.

"There are two pieces of evidence I require to save Mr. Lexman from very serious trouble," he said, "the first of these is the letter which was burnt, as you know."

"Yes," said Kara.

T. X. leant across the desk.

"How did you know?" he snapped.

"Somebody told me, I don't know who it was."

"That's not true," replied T. X.; "nobody knows except myself and Mrs. Lexman."

"But my dear good fellow," said Kara, pulling on his gloves, "you have already asked me whether I didn't burn the letter."

"I said envelope," said T. X., with a little laugh.

"And you were going to say something about the other clue?"

"The other is the revolver," said T. X.

"Mr. Lexman's revolver!" drawled the Greek.

"That we have," said T. X. shortly. "What we want is the weapon which the Greek had when he threatened Mr. Lexman."

"There, I'm afraid I cannot help you."

Kara walked to the door and T. X. followed.

"I think I will see Mrs. Lexman."

"I think not," said T. X.

The other turned with a sneer.

"Have you arrested her, too?" he asked.

"Pull yourself together!" said T. X. coarsely. He escorted Kara to his waiting limousine.

"You have a new chauffeur to-night, I observe," he said.

Kara towering with rage stepped daintily into the car.

"If you are writing to the other you might give him my love," said T. X., "and make most tender enquiries after his mother. I particularly ask this."

Kara said nothing until the car was out of earshot then he lay back on the down cushions and abandoned himself to a paroxysm of rage and blasphemy.

CHAPTER V

Six months later T. X. Meredith was laboriously tracing an elusive line which occurred on an ordnance map of Sussex when the Chief Commissioner announced himself.

Sir George described T. X. as the most wholesome corrective a public official could have, and never missed an opportunity of meeting his subordinate (as he said) for this reason.

"What are you doing there?" he growled.

"The lesson this morning," said T. X. without looking up, "is maps."

Sir George passed behind his assistant and looked over his shoulder.

"That is a very old map you have got there," he said.

"1876. It shows the course of a number of interesting little streams in this neighbourhood which have been lost sight of for one reason or the other by the gentleman who made the survey at a later period. I am perfectly sure that in one of these streams I shall find what I am seeking."

"You haven't given up hope, then, in regard to Lexman?"

"I shall never give up hope," said T. X., "until I am dead, and possibly not then."

"Let me see, what did he get—fifteen years!"

"Fifteen years," repeated T. X., "and a very fortunate man to escape with his life."

Sir George walked to the window and stared out on to busy Whitehall.

"I am told you are quite friendly with Kara again."

T. X. made a noise which might be taken to indicate his assent to the statement.

"I suppose you know that gentleman has made a very heroic attempt to get you fired," he said.

"I shouldn't wonder," said T. X. "I made as heroic an attempt to get him hung, and one good turn deserves another. What did he do? See ministers and people?"

"He did," said Sir George.

"He's a silly ass," responded T. X.

"I can understand all that"—the Chief Commissioner turned round—"but what I cannot understand is your apology to him."

"There are so many things you don't understand, Sir George," said T. X. tartly, "that I despair of ever cataloguing them."

"You are an insolent cub," growled his Chief. "Come to lunch."

"Where will you take me?" asked T. X. cautiously.

"To my club."

"I'm sorry," said the other, with elaborate politeness, "I have lunched once at your club. Need I say more?"

He smiled, as he worked after his Chief had gone, at the recollection of Kara's profound astonishment and the gratification he strove so desperately to disguise.

Kara was a vain man, immensely conscious of his good looks, conscious of his wealth. He had behaved most handsomely, for not only had he accepted the apology, but he left nothing undone to show his desire to create a good impression upon the man who had so grossly insulted him.

T. X. had accepted an invitation to stay a weekend at Kara's "little place in the country," and had found there assembled everything that the heart could desire in the way of fellowship, eminent politicians who might conceivably be of service to an ambitious young Assistant Commissioner of Police, beautiful ladies to interest and amuse him. Kara had even gone to the length of engaging a theatrical company to play "Sweet Lavender," and for this purpose the big ballroom at Hever Court had been transformed into a theatre.

As he was undressing for bed that night T. X. remembered that he had mentioned to Kara that "Sweet Lavender" was his favorite play, and he realized that the entertainment was got up especially for his benefit.

In a score of other ways Kara had endeavoured to consolidate the friendship. He gave the young Commissioner advice about a railway company which was operating in Asia Minor, and the shares of which stood a little below par. T. X. thanked him for the advice, and did not take it, nor did he feel any regret when the shares rose 3 pounds in as many weeks.

T. X. had superintended the disposal of Beston Priory. He had the furniture removed to London, and had taken a flat for Grace Lexman.

She had a small income of her own, and this, added to the large royalties which came to her (as she was bitterly conscious) in increasing volume as the result of the publicity of the trial, placed her beyond fear of want.

"Fifteen years," murmured T. X., as he worked and whistled.

There had been no hope for John Lexman from the start. He was in debt to the man he killed. His story of threatening letters was not substantiated. The revolver which he said had been flourished at him had never been found. Two people believed implicitly in the story, and a sympathetic Home Secretary had assured T. X. personally that if he could find the revolver and associate it with the murder beyond any doubt, John Lexman would be pardoned.

Every stream in the neighbourhood had been dragged. In one case a small river had been dammed, and the bed had been carefully dried and sifted, but there was no trace of the weapon, and T. X. had tried methods more effective and certainly less legal.

A mysterious electrician had called at 456 Cadogan Square in Kara's absence, and he was armed with such indisputable authority that he was permitted to penetrate to Kara's private room, in order to examine certain fitments.

Kara returning next day thought no more of the matter when it was reported to him, until going to his safe that night he discovered that it had been opened and ransacked.

As it happened, most of Kara's valuable and confidential possessions were at the bank. In a fret of panic and at considerable cost he had the safe removed and another put in its place of such potency that the makers offered to indemnify him against any loss from burglary.

T. X. finished his work, washed his hands, and was drying them when Mansus came bursting into the room. It was not usual for Mansus to burst into anywhere. He was a slow, methodical, painstaking man, with a deliberate and an official, manner.

"What's the matter?" asked T. X. quickly.

"We didn't search Vassalaro's lodgings," cried Mansus breathlessly. "It just occurred to me as I was coming over Westminster Bridge. I was on top of a bus—"

"Wake up!" said T. X. "You're amongst friends and cut all that 'bus' stuff out. Of course we searched Vassalaro's lodgings!"

"No, we didn't, sir," said the other triumphantly. "He lived in Great James Street."

"He lived in the Adelphi," corrected T. X.

"There were two places where he lived," said Mansus.

"When did you learn this?" asked his Chief, dropping his flippancy.

"This morning. I was on a bus coming across Westminster Bridge, and there were two men in front of me, and I heard the word 'Vassalaro' and naturally I pricked up my ears."

"It was very unnatural, but proceed," said T. X.

"One of the men—a very respectable person—said, 'That chap Vassalaro used to lodge in my place, and I've still got a lot of his things. What do you think I ought to do?'"

"And you said," suggested the other.

"I nearly frightened his life out of him," said Mansus. "I said, 'I am a police officer and I want you to come along with me.'"

"And of course he shut up and would not say another word," said T. X.

"That's true, sir," said Mansus, "but after awhile I got him to talk. Vassalaro lived in Great James Street, 604, on the third floor. In fact, some of his furniture is there still. He had a good reason for keeping two addresses by all accounts."

T. X. nodded wisely.

"What was her name?" he asked.

"He had a wife," said the other, "but she left him about four months before he was killed. He used the Adelphi address for business purposes and apparently he slept two or three nights of the week at Great James Street. I have told the man to leave everything as it is, and that we will come round."

Ten minutes later the two officers were in the somewhat gloomy apartments which Vassalaro had occupied.

The landlord explained that most of the furniture was his, but that there were certain articles which were the property of the deceased man. He added, somewhat unnecessarily, that the late tenant owed him six months' rent.

The articles which had been the property of Vassalaro included a tin trunk, a small writing bureau, a secretaire bookcase and a few clothes. The secretaire was locked, as was the writing bureau. The tin box, which had little or nothing of interest, was unfastened.

The other locks needed very little attention. Without any difficulty Mansus opened both. The leaf of the bureau, when let down, formed the desk, and piled up inside was a whole mass of letters opened and unopened, accounts, note-books and all the paraphernalia which an untidy man collects.

Letter by letter, T. X. went through the accumulation without finding anything to help him. Then his eye was attracted by a small tin case thrust into one of the oblong pigeon holes at the back of the desk. This he pulled out and opened and found a small wad of paper wrapped in tin foil.

"Hello, hello!" said T. X., and he was pardonably exhilarated.

CHAPTER VI

A Man stood in the speckless courtyard before the Governor's house at Dartmoor gaol. He wore the ugly livery of shame which marks the convict. His head was clipped short, and there was two days' growth of beard upon his haggard face. Standing with his hands behind him, he waited for the moment when he would be ordered to his work.

John Lexman—A. O. 43—looked up at the blue sky as he had looked so many times from the exercise yard, and wondered what the day would bring forth. A day to him was the beginning and the end of an eternity. He dare not let his mind dwell upon the long aching years ahead. He dare not think of the woman he left, or let his mind dwell upon the agony which she was enduring. He had disappeared from the world, the world he loved, and the world that knew him, and all that there was in life; all that was worth while had been crushed and obliterated into the granite of the Princetown quarries, and its wide horizon shrunken by the gaunt moorland with its menacing tors.

New interests made up his existence. The quality of the food was one. The character of the book he would receive from the prison library another. The future meant Sunday chapel; the present whatever task they found him. For the day he was to paint some doors and windows of an outlying cottage. A cottage occupied by a warder who, for some reason, on the day previous, had spoken to him with a certain kindness and a certain respect which was unusual.

"Face the wall," growled a voice, and mechanically he turned, his hands still behind him, and stood staring at the grey wall of the prison storehouse.

He heard the shuffling feet of the quarry gang, his ears caught the clink of the chains which bound them together. They were desperate men, peculiarly interesting to him, and he had watched their faces furtively in the early period of his imprisonment.

He had been sent to Dartmoor after spending three months in Wormwood Scrubbs. Old hands had told him variously that he was fortunate or unlucky. It was usual to have twelve months at the Scrubbs before testing the life of a convict establishment. He believed there was some talk of sending him to Parkhurst, and here he traced the influence which T. X. would exercise, for Parkhurst was a prisoner's paradise.

He heard his warder's voice behind him.

"Right turn, 43, quick march."

He walked ahead of the armed guard, through the great and gloomy gates of the prison, turned sharply to the right, and walked up the village street toward the moors, beyond the village of Princetown, and on the Tavistock Road where were two or three cottages which had been lately taken by the prison staff; and it was to the decoration of one of these that A. O. 43 had been sent.

The house was as yet without a tenant.

A paper-hanger under the charge of another warder was waiting for the arrival of the painter. The two warders exchanged greetings, and the first went off leaving the other in charge of both men.

For an hour they worked in silence under the eyes of the guard. Presently the warder went outside, and John Lexman had an opportunity of examining his fellow sufferer.

He was a man of twenty-four or twenty-five, lithe and alert. By no means bad looking, he lacked that indefinable suggestion of animalism which distinguished the majority of the inhabitants at Dartmoor.

They waited until they heard the warder's step clear the passage, and until his iron-shod boots were tramping over the cobbled path which led from the door, through the tiny garden to the road, before the second man spoke.

"What are you in for?" he asked, in a low voice.

"Murder," said John Lexman, laconically.

He had answered the question before, and had noticed with a little amusement the look of respect which came into the eyes of the questioner.

"What have you got!"

"Fifteen years," said the other.

"That means 11 years and 9 months," said the first man. "You've never been here before, I suppose?"

"Hardly," said Lexman, drily.

"I was here when I was a kid," confessed the paper-hanger. "I am going out next week."

John Lexman looked at him enviously. Had the man told him that he had inherited a great fortune and a greater title his envy would not have been so genuine.

Going out!

The drive in the brake to the station, the ride to London in creased, but comfortable clothing, free as the air, at liberty to go to bed and rise when he liked, to choose his own dinner, to answer no call save the call of his conscience, to see—he checked himself.

"What are you in for?" he asked in self-defence.

"Conspiracy and fraud," said the other cheerfully. "I was put away by a woman after three of us had got clear with 12,000 pounds. Damn rough luck, wasn't it?"

John nodded.

It was curious, he thought, how sympathetic one grows with these exponents of crimes. One naturally adopts their point of view and sees life through their distorted vision.

"I bet I'm not given away with the next lot," the prisoner went on. "I've got one of the biggest ideas I've ever had, and I've got a real good man to help me."

"How?" asked John, in surprise.

The man jerked his head in the direction of the prison.

"Larry Green," he said briefly. "He's coming out next month, too, and we are all fixed up proper. We are going to get the pile and then we're off to South America, and you won't see us for dust."

Though he employed all the colloquialisms which were common, his tone was that of a man of education, and yet there was something in his address which told John as clearly as though the man had confessed as much, that he had never occupied any social position in life.

The warder's step on the stones outside reduced them to silence. Suddenly his voice came up the stairs.

"Forty-three," he called sharply, "I want you down here."

John took his paint pot and brush and went clattering down the uncarpeted stairs.

"Where's the other man?" asked the warder, in a low voice.

"He's upstairs in the back room."

The warder stepped out of the door and looked left and right. Coming up from Princetown was a big, grey car.

"Put down your paint pot," he said.

His voice was shaking with excitement.

"I am going upstairs. When that car comes abreast of the gate, ask no questions and jump into it. Get down into the bottom and pull a sack over you, and do not get up until the car stops."

The blood rushed to John Lexman's head, and he staggered.

"My God!" he whispered.

"Do as I tell you," hissed the warder.

Like an automaton John put down his brushes, and walked slowly to the gate. The grey car was crawling up the hill, and the face of the driver was half enveloped in a big rubber mask. Through the two great goggles John could see little to help him identify the man. As the machine came up to the gate, he leapt into the tonneau and sank instantly to the bottom. As he did so he felt the car leap forward underneath him. Now it was going fast, now faster, now it rocked and swayed as it gathered speed. He felt it sweeping down hill and up hill, and once he heard a hollow rumble as it crossed a wooden bridge.

He could not detect from his hiding place in what direction they were going, but he gathered they had switched off to the left and were making for one of the wildest parts of the moor. Never once did he feel the car slacken its pace, until, with a grind of brakes, it stopped suddenly.

"Get out," said a voice.

John Lexman threw off the cover and leapt out and as he did so the car turned and sped back the way it had come.

For a moment he thought he was alone, and looked around. Far away in the distance he saw the grey bulk of Princetown Gaol. It was an accident that he should see it, but it so happened that a ray of the sun fell athwart it and threw it into relief.

He was alone on the moors! Where could he go?

He turned at the sound of a voice.

He was standing on the slope of a small tor. At the foot there was a smooth stretch of green sward. It was on this stretch that the people of Dartmoor held their pony races in the summer months. There was no sign of horses; but only a great bat-like machine with out-stretched pinions of taut white canvas, and by that machine a man clad from head to foot in brown overalls.

John stumbled down the slope. As he neared the machine he stopped and gasped.

"Kara," he said, and the brown man smiled.

"But, I do not understand. What are you going to do!" asked Lexman, when he had recovered from his surprise.

"I am going to take you to a place of safety," said the other.

"I have no reason to be grateful to you, as yet, Kara," breathed Lexman. "A word from you could have saved me."

"I could not lie, my dear Lexman. And honestly, I had forgotten the existence of the letter; if that is what you are referring to, but I am trying to do what I can for you and for your wife."

"My wife!"

"She is waiting for you," said the other.

He turned his head, listening.

Across the moor came the dull sullen boom of a gun.

"You haven't time for argument. They discovered your escape," he said. "Get in."

John clambered up into the frail body of the machine and Kara followed.

"This is a self-starter," he said, "one of the newest models of monoplanes."

He clicked over a lever and with a roar the big three-bladed tractor screw spun.

The aeroplane moved forward with a jerk, ran with increasing gait for a hundred yards, and then suddenly the jerky progress ceased. The machine swayed gently from side to side, and looking over, the passenger saw the ground recede beneath him.

Up, up, they climbed in one long sweeping ascent, passing through drifting clouds till the machine soared like a bird above the blue sea.

John Lexman looked down. He saw the indentations of the coast and recognized the fringe of white houses that stood for Torquay, but in an incredibly short space of time all signs of the land were blotted out.

Talking was impossible. The roar of the engines defied penetration.

Kara was evidently a skilful pilot. From time to time he consulted the compass on the board before him, and changed his course ever so slightly. Presently he released one hand from the driving wheel, and scribbling on a little block of paper which was inserted in a pocket at the side of the seat he passed it back.

John Lexman read:

"If you cannot swim there is a life belt under your seat."

John nodded.

Kara was searching the sea for something, and presently he found it. Viewed from the height at which they flew it looked no more than a white speck in a great blue saucer, but presently the machine began to dip, falling at a terrific rate of speed, which took away the breath of the man who was hanging on with both hands to the dangerous seat behind.

He was deadly cold, but had hardly noticed the fact. It was all so incredible, so impossible. He expected to wake up and wondered if the prison was also part of the dream.

Now he saw the point for which Kara was making.

A white steam yacht, long and narrow of beam, was steaming slowly westward. He could see the feathery wake in her rear, and as the aeroplane fell he had time to observe that a boat had been put off. Then with a jerk the monoplane flattened out and came like a skimming bird to the surface of the water; her engines stopped.

"We ought to be able to keep afloat for ten minutes," said Kara, "and by that time they will pick us up."

His voice was high and harsh in the almost painful silence which followed the stoppage of the engines.

In less than five minutes the boat had come alongside, manned, as Lexman gathered from a glimpse of the crew, by Greeks. He scrambled aboard and five minutes later he was standing on the white deck of the yacht, watching the disappearing tail of the monoplane. Kara was by his side.

"There goes fifteen hundred pounds," said the Greek, with a smile, "add that to the two thousand I paid the warder and you have a tidy sum-but some things are worth all the money in the world!"

CHAPTER VII

T. X. came from Downing Street at 11 o'clock one night, and his heart was filled with joy and gratitude.

He swung his stick to the common danger of the public, but the policeman on point duty at the end of the street, who saw him, recognized and saluted him, did not think it fit to issue any official warning.

He ran up the stairs to his office, and found Mansus reading the evening paper.

"My poor, dumb beast," said T. X. "I am afraid I have kept you waiting for a very long time, but tomorrow you and I will take a little journey to Devonshire. It will be good for you, Mansus—where did you get that ridiculous name, by the way!"

"M. or N.," replied Mansus, laconically.

"I repeat that there is the dawn of an intellect in you," said T. X., offensively.

He became more serious as he took from a pocket inside his waistcoat a long blue envelope containing the paper which had cost him so much to secure.

"Finding the revolver was a master-stroke of yours, Mansus," he said, and he was in earnest as he spoke.

The man coloured with pleasure for the subordinates of T. X. loved him, and a word of praise was almost equal to promotion. It was on the advice of Mansus that the road from London to Lewes had been carefully covered and such streams as passed beneath that road had been searched.

The revolver had been found after the third attempt between Gatwick and Horsley. Its identification was made easier by the fact that Vassalaro's name was engraved on the butt. It was rather an ornate affair and in its earlier days had been silver plated; the handle was of mother-o'-pearl.

"Obviously the gift of one brigand to another," was T. X.'s comment.

Armed with this, his task would have been fairly easy, but when to this evidence he added a rough draft of the threatening letter which he had found amongst Vassalaro's belongings, and which had evidently been taken down at dictation, since some of the words were misspelt and had been corrected by another hand, the case was complete.

But what clinched the matter was the finding of a wad of that peculiar chemical paper, a number of sheets of which T. X. had ignited for the information of the Chief Commissioner and the Home Secretary by simply exposing them for a few seconds to the light of an electric lamp.

Instantly it had filled the Home Secretary's office with a pungent and most disagreeable smoke, for which he was heartily cursed by his superiors. But it had rounded off the argument.

He looked at his watch.

"I wonder if it is too late to see Mrs. Lexman," he said.

"I don't think any hour would be too late," suggested Mansus.

"You shall come and chaperon me," said his superior.

But a disappointment awaited. Mrs. Lexman was not in and neither the ringing at her electric bell nor vigorous applications to the knocker brought any response. The hall porter of the flats where she lived was under the impression that Mrs. Lexman had gone out of town. She frequently went out on Saturdays and returned on the Monday and, he thought, occasionally on Tuesdays.

It happened that this particular night was a Monday night and T. X. was faced with a dilemma. The night porter, who had only the vaguest information on the subject, thought that the day porter might know more, and aroused him from his sleep.

Yes, Mrs. Lexman had gone. She went on the Sunday, an unusual day to pay a week-end visit, and she had taken with her two bags. The porter ventured the opinion that she was rather excited, but when asked to define the symptoms relapsed into a chaos of incoherent "you-knows" and "what-I-means."

"I don't like this," said T. X., suddenly. "Does anybody know that we have made these discoveries?"

"Nobody outside the office," said Mansus, "unless, unless..."

"Unless what?" asked the other, irritably. "Don't be a jimp, Mansus. Get it off your mind. What is it?"

"I am wondering," said Mansus slowly, "if the landlord at Great James Street said anything. He knows we have made a search."

"We can easily find that out," said T. X.

They hailed a taxi and drove to Great James Street. That respectable thoroughfare was wrapped in sleep and it was some time before the landlord could be aroused. Recognizing T. X. he checked his sarcasm, which he had prepared for a keyless lodger, and led the way into the drawing room.

"You didn't tell me not to speak about it, Mr. Meredith," he said, in an aggrieved tone, "and as a matter of fact I have spoken to nobody except the gentleman who called the same day."

"What did he want?" asked T. X.

"He said he had only just discovered that Mr. Vassalaro had stayed with me and he wanted to pay whatever rent was due," replied the other.

"What like of man was he?" asked T. X.

The brief description the man gave sent a cold chill to the Commissioner's heart.

"Kara for a ducat!" he said, and swore long and variously.

"Cadogan Square," he ordered.

His ring was answered promptly. Mr. Kara was out of town, had indeed been out of town since Saturday. This much the man-servant explained with a suspicious eye upon his visitors, remembering that his predecessor had lost his job from a too confiding friendliness with spurious electric fitters. He did not know when Mr. Kara would return, perhaps it would be a long time and perhaps a short time. He might come back that night or he might not.

"You are wasting your young life," said T. X. bitterly. "You ought to be a fortune teller."

"This settles the matter," he said, in the cab on the way back. "Find out the first train for Tavistock in the morning and wire the George Hotel to have a car waiting."

"Why not go to-night?" suggested the other. "There is the midnight train. It is rather slow, but it will get you there by six or seven in the morning."

"Too late," he said, "unless you can invent a method of getting from here to Paddington in about fifty seconds."

The morning journey to Devonshire was a dispiriting one despite the fineness of the day. T. X. had an uncomfortable sense that something distressing had happened. The run across the moor in the fresh spring air revived him a little.

As they spun down to the valley of the Dart, Mansus touched his arm.

"Look at that," he said, and pointed to the blue heavens where, a mile above their heads, a white-winged aeroplane, looking no larger than a very distant dragon fly, shimmered in the sunlight.

"By Jove!" said T. X. "What an excellent way for a man to escape!"

"It's about the only way," said Mansus.

The significance of the aeroplane was borne in upon T. X. a few minutes later when he was held up by an armed guard. A glance at his card was enough to pass him.

"What is the matter?" he asked.

"A prisoner has escaped," said the sentry.

"Escaped—by aeroplane?" asked T. X.

"I don't know anything about aeroplanes, sir. All I know is that one of the working party got away."

The car came to the gates of the prison and T. X. sprang out, followed by his assistant. He had no difficulty in finding the Governor, a greatly perturbed man, for an escape is a very serious matter.

The official was inclined to be brusque in his manner, but again the magic card produced a soothing effect.

"I am rather rattled," said the Governor. "One of my men has got away. I suppose you know that?"

"And I am afraid another of your men is going away, sir," said T. X., who had a curious reverence for military authority. He produced his paper and laid it on the governor's table.

"This is an order for the release of John Lexman, convicted under sentence of fifteen years penal servitude."

The Governor looked at it.

"Dated last night," he said, and breathed a long sigh of relief. "Thank the Lord!—that is the man who escaped!"

CHAPTER VIII

Two years after the events just described, T. X. journeying up to London from Bath was attracted by a paragraph in the Morning Post. It told him briefly that Mr. Remington Kara, the influential leader of the Greek Colony, had been the guest of honor at a dinner of the Hellenic Society.

T. X. had only seen Kara for a brief space of time following that tragic morning, when he had discovered not only that his best friend had escaped from Dartmoor prison and disappeared, as it were, from the world at a moment when his pardon had been signed, but that that friend's wife had also vanished from the face of the earth.

At the same time—it might, as even T. X. admitted, have been the veriest coincidence that Kara had also cleared out of London to reappear at the end of six months. Any question addressed to him, concerning the whereabouts of the two unhappy people, was met with a bland expression of ignorance as to their whereabouts.

John Lexman was somewhere in the world, hiding as he believed from justice, and with him was his wife. T. X. had no doubt in his mind as to this solution of the puzzle. He had caused to be published the story of the pardon and the circumstances under which that pardon had been secured, and he had, moreover, arranged for an advertisement to be inserted in the principal papers of every European country.

It was a moot question amongst the departmental lawyers as to whether John Lexman was not guilty of a technical and punishable offence for prison breaking, but this possibility did not keep T. X. awake at nights. The circumstances of the escape had been carefully examined. The warder responsible had been discharged from the service, and had almost immediately purchased for himself a beer house in Falmouth, for a sum which left no doubt in the official mind that he had been the recipient of a heavy bribe.

Who had been the guiding spirit in that escape—Mrs. Lexman, or Kara?

It was impossible to connect Kara with the event. The motor car had been traced to Exeter, where it had been hired by a "foreign-looking gentleman," but the chauffeur, whoever he was, had made good his escape. An inspection of Kara's hangars at Wembley showed that his two monoplanes had not been removed, and T. X. failed entirely to trace the owner of the machine he had seen flying over Dartmoor on the fatal morning.

T. X. was somewhat baffled and a little amused by the disinclination of the authorities to believe that the escape had been effected by this method at all. All the events of the trial came back to him, as he watched the landscape spinning past.

He set down the newspaper with a little sigh, put his feet on the cushions of the opposite seat and gave himself up to reverie. Presently he returned to his journals and searched them idly for something to interest him in the final stretch of journey between Newbury and Paddington.

Presently he found it in a two column article with the uninspiring title, "The Mineral Wealth of Tierra del Fuego." It was written brightly with a style which was at once easy and informative. It told of adventures in the marshes behind St. Sebastian Bay and journeys up the Guarez Celman river, of nights spent in primeval forests and ended in a geological survey, wherein the commercial value of syenite, porphyry, trachite and dialite were severally canvassed.

The article was signed "G. G." It is said of T. X. that his greatest virtue was his curiosity. He had at the tip of his fingers the names of all the big explorers and author-travellers, and for some reason he could not place "G. G." to his satisfaction, in fact he had an absurd desire to interpret the initials into "George Grossmith." His inability to identify the writer irritated him, and his first act on reaching his office was to telephone to one of the literary editors of the Times whom he knew.

"Not my department," was the chilly reply, "and besides we never give away the names of our contributors. Speaking as a person outside the office I should say that 'G. G.' was 'George Gathercole' the explorer you know, the fellow who had an arm chewed off by a lion or something."

"George Gathercole!" repeated T. X. "What an ass I am."

"Yes," said the voice at the other end the wire, and he had rung off before T. X. could think of something suitable to say.

Having elucidated this little side-line of mystery, the matter passed from the young Commissioner's mind. It happened that morning that his work consisted of dealing with John Lexman's estate.

With the disappearance of the couple he had taken over control of their belongings. It had not embarrassed him to discover that he was an executor under Lexman's will, for he had already acted as trustee to the wife's small estate, and had been one of the parties to the ante-nuptial contract which John Lexman had made before his marriage.

The estate revenues had increased very considerably. All the vanished author's books were selling as they had never sold before, and the executor's work was made the heavier by the fact that Grace Lexman had possessed an aunt who had most inconsiderately died, leaving a considerable fortune to her "unhappy niece."

"I will keep the trusteeship another year," he told the solicitor who came to consult him that morning. "At the end of that time I shall go to the court for relief."

"Do you think they will ever turn up?" asked the solicitor, an elderly and unimaginative man.

"Of course, they'll turn up!" said T. X. impatiently; "all the heroes of Lexman's books turn up sooner or later. He will discover himself to us at a suitable moment, and we shall be properly thrilled."

That Lexman would return he was sure. It was a faith from which he did not swerve.

He had as implicit a confidence that one day or other Kara, the magnificent, would play into his hands.

There were some queer stories in circulation concerning the Greek, but on the whole they were stories and rumours which were difficult to separate from the malicious gossip which invariably attaches itself to the rich and to the successful.

One of these was that Kara desired something more than an Albanian chieftainship, which he undoubtedly enjoyed. There were whispers of wider and higher ambitions. Though his father had been born a Greek, he had indubitably descended in a direct line from one of those old Mprets of Albania, who had exercised their brief authority over that turbulent land.

The man's passion was for power. To this end he did not spare himself. It was said that he utilized his vast wealth for this reason, and none other, and that whatever might have been the irregularities of his youth—and there were adduced concrete instances—he was working toward an end with a singleness of purpose, from which it was difficult to withhold admiration.

T. X. kept in his locked desk a little red book, steel bound and triple locked, which he called his "Scandalaria." In this he inscribed in his own irregular writing the titbits which might not be published, and which often helped an investigator to light upon the missing threads of a problem. In truth he scorned no source of information, and was conscienceless in the compilation of this somewhat chaotic record.

The affairs of John Lexman recalled Kara, and Kara's great reception. Mansus would have made arrangements to secure a verbatim report of the speeches which were made, and these would be in his hands by the night. Mansus did not tell him that Kara was financing some very influential people indeed, that a certain Under-secretary of State with a great number of very influential relations had been saved from bankruptcy by the timely advances which Kara had made. This T. X. had obtained through sources which might be hastily described as discreditable. Mansus knew of the baccarat establishment in Albemarle Street, but he did not know that the neurotic wife of a very great man indeed, no less than the Minister of Justice, was a frequent visitor to that establishment, and that she had lost in one night some 6,000 pounds. In these circumstances it was remarkable, thought T. X., that she should report to the police so small a matter as the petty pilfering of servants. This, however, she had done and whilst the lesser officers of Scotland Yard were interrogating pawnbrokers, the men higher up were genuinely worried by the lady's own lapses from grace.

It was all sordid but, unfortunately, conventional, because highly placed people will always do underbred things, where money or women are concerned, but it was necessary, for the proper conduct of the department which T. X. directed, that, however sordid and however conventional might be the errors which the great ones of the earth committed, they should be filed for reference.

The motto which T. X. went upon in life was, "You never know."

The Minister of Justice was a very important person, for he was a personal friend of half the monarchs of Europe. A poor man, with two or three thousand a year of his own, with no very definite political views and uncommitted to the more violent policies of either party, he succeeded in serving both, with profit to himself, and without earning the obloquy of either. Though he did not pursue the blatant policy of the Vicar of Bray, yet it is fact which may be confirmed from the reader's own knowledge, that he served in four different administrations, drawing the pay and emoluments of his office from each, though the fundamental policies of those four governments were distinct.

Lady Bartholomew, the wife of this adaptable Minister, had recently departed for San Remo. The newspapers announced the fact and spoke vaguely of a breakdown which prevented the lady from fulfilling her social engagements.

T. X., ever a Doubting Thomas, could trace no visit of nerve specialist, nor yet of the family practitioner, to the official residence in Downing Street, and therefore he drew conclusions. In his own "Who's Who" T. X. noted the hobbies of his victims which, by the way, did not always coincide with the innocent occupations set against their names in the more pretentious volume. Their follies and their weaknesses found a place and were recorded at a length (as it might seem to the uninformed observer) beyond the limit which charity allowed.

Lady Mary Bartholomew's name appeared not once, but many times, in the erratic records which T. X. kept. There was a plain matter-of-fact and wholly unobjectionable statement that she was born in 1874, that she was the seventh daughter of the Earl of Balmorey, that she had one daughter who rejoiced in the somewhat unpromising name of Belinda Mary, and such further information as a man might get without going to a great deal of trouble.

T. X., refreshing his memory from the little red book, wondered what unexpected tragedy had sent Lady Bartholomew out of London in the middle of the season. The information was that the lady was fairly well off at this moment, and this fact made matters all the more puzzling and almost induced him to believe that, after all, the story was true, and a nervous breakdown really was the cause of her sudden departure. He sent for Mansus.

"You saw Lady Bartholomew off at Charing Cross, I suppose?"

Mansus nodded.

"She went alone?"

"She took her maid, but otherwise she was alone. I thought she looked ill."

"She has been looking ill for months past," said T. X., without any visible expression of sympathy.

"Did she take Belinda Mary?"

Mansus was puzzled. "Belinda Mary?" he repeated slowly. "Oh, you mean the daughter. No, she's at a school somewhere in France."

T. X. whistled a snatch of a popular song, closed the little red book with a snap and replaced it in his desk.

"I wonder where on earth people dig up names like Belinda Mary?" he mused. "Belinda Mary must be rather a weird little animal—the Lord forgive me for speaking so about my betters! If heredity counts for anything she ought to be something between a head waiter and a pack of cards. Have you lost anything'?"

Mansus was searching his pockets.

"I made a few notes, some questions I wanted to ask you about and Lady Bartholomew was the subject of one of them. I have had her under observation for six months; do you want it kept up?"

T. X. thought awhile, then shook his head.

"I am only interested in Lady Bartholomew in so far as Kara is interested in her. There is a criminal for you, my friend!" he added, admiringly.

Mansus busily engaged in going through the bundles of letters, slips of paper and little notebooks he had taken from his pocket, sniffed audibly.

"Have you a cold?" asked T. X. politely.

"No, sir," was the reply, "only I haven't much opinion of Kara as a criminal. Besides, what has he got to be a criminal about? He has all that he requires in the money department, he's one of the most popular people in London, and certainly one of the best-looking men I've ever seen in my life. He needs nothing."

T. X. regarded him scornfully.

"You're a poor blind brute," he said, shaking his head; don't you know that great criminals are never influenced by material desires, or by the prospect of concrete gains? The man, who robs his employer's till in order to give the girl of his heart the 25-pearl and ruby brooch her soul desires, gains nothing but the glow of satisfaction which comes to the man who is thought well of. The majority of crimes in the world are committed by people for the same reason— they want to be thought well of. Here is Doctor X. who murdered his wife because she was a drunkard and a slut, and he dared not leave her for fear the neighbours would have doubts as to his respectability. Here is another gentleman who murders his wives in their baths in order that he should keep up some sort of position and earn the respect of his friends and his associates. Nothing roused him more quickly to a frenzy of passion than the suggestion that he was not respectable. Here is the great financier, who has embezzled a million and a quarter, not because he needed money, but because people looked up to him. Therefore, he must build great mansions, submarine pleasure courts and must lay out huge estates—because he wished that he should be thought well of.

Mansus sniffed again.

"What about the man who half murders his wife, does he do that to be well thought of?" he asked, with a tinge of sarcasm.

T. X. looked at him pityingly.

"The low-brow who beats his wife, my poor Mansus," he said, "does so because she doesn't think well of him. That is our ruling passion, our national characteristic, the primary cause of most crimes, big or little. That is why Kara is a bad criminal and will, as I say, end his life very violently."

He took down his glossy silk hat from the peg and slipped into his overcoat.

"I am going down to see my friend Kara," he said. "I have a feeling that I should like to talk with him. He might tell me something."

His acquaintance with Kara's menage had been mere hearsay. He had interviewed the Greek once after his return, but since all his efforts to secure information concerning the whereabouts of John Lexman and his wife—the main reason for his visit—had been in vain, he had not repeated his visit.

The house in Cadogan Square was a large one, occupying a corner site. It was peculiarly English in appearance with its window boxes, its discreet curtains, its polished brass and enamelled doorway. It had been the town house of Lord Henry Gratham, that eccentric connoisseur of wine and follower of witless pleasure. It had been built by him "round a bottle of port," as his friends said, meaning thereby that his first consideration had been the cellarage of the house, and that when those cellars had been built and provision made for the safe storage of his priceless wines, the house had been built without the architect's being greatly troubled by his lordship. The double cellars of Gratham House had, in their time, been one of the sights of London. When Henry Gratham lay under eight feet of Congo earth (he was killed by an elephant whilst on a hunting trip) his executors had been singularly fortunate in finding an immediate purchaser. Rumour had it that Kara, who was no lover of wine, had bricked up the cellars, and their very existence passed into domestic legendary.

The door was opened by a well-dressed and deferential man-servant and T. X. was ushered into the hall. A fire burnt cheerily in a bronze grate and T. X. had a glimpse of a big oil painting of Kara above the marble mantle-piece.

"Mr. Kara is very busy, sir," said the man.

"Just take in my card," said T. X. "I think he may care to see me."

The man bowed, produced from some mysterious corner a silver salver and glided upstairs in that manner which well-trained servants have, a manner which seems to call for no bodily effort. In a minute he returned.

"Will you come this way, sir," he said, and led the way up a broad flight of stairs.

At the head of the stairs was a corridor which ran to the left and to the right. From this there gave four rooms. One at the extreme end of the passage on the right, one on the left, and two at fairly regular intervals in the centre.

When the man's hand was on one of the doors, T. X. asked quietly, "I think I have seen you before somewhere, my friend."

The man smiled.

"It is very possible, sir. I was a waiter at the Constitutional for some time."

T. X. nodded.

"That is where it must have been," he said.

The man opened the door and announced the visitor.

T. X. found himself in a large room, very handsomely furnished, but just lacking that sense of cosiness and comfort which is the feature of the Englishman's home.

Kara rose from behind a big writing table, and came with a smile and a quick step to greet the visitor.

"This is a most unexpected pleasure," he said, and shook hands warmly.

T. X. had not seen him for a year and found very little change in this strange young man. He could not be more confident than he had been, nor bear himself with a more graceful carriage. Whatever social success he had achieved, it had not spoiled him, for his manner was as genial and easy as ever.

"I think that will do, Miss Holland," he said, turning to the girl who, with notebook in hand, stood by the desk.

"Evidently," thought T. X., "our Hellenic friend has a pretty taste in secretaries."

In that one glance he took her all in—from the bronze-brown of her hair to her neat foot.

T. X. was not readily attracted by members of the opposite sex. He was self-confessed a predestined bachelor, finding life and its incidence too absorbing to give his whole mind to the serious problem of marriage, or to contract responsibilities and interests which might divert his attention from what he believed was the greater game. Yet he must be a man of stone to resist the freshness, the beauty and the youth of this straight, slender girl; the pink-and-whiteness of her, the aliveness and buoyancy and the thrilling sense of vitality she carried in her very presence.

"What is the weirdest name you have ever heard?" asked Kara laughingly. "I ask you, because Miss Holland and I have been discussing a begging letter addressed to us by a Maggie Goomer."

The girl smiled slightly and in that smile was paradise, thought T. X.

"The weirdest name?" he repeated, "why I think the worst I have heard for a long time is Belinda Mary."

"That has a familiar ring," said Kara.

T. X. was looking at the girl.

She was staring at him with a certain languid insolence which made him curl up inside. Then with a glance at her employer she swept from the room.

"I ought to have introduced you," said Kara. "That was my secretary, Miss Holland. Rather a pretty girl, isn't she?"

"Very," said T. X., recovering his breath.

"I like pretty things around me," said Kara, and somehow the complacency of the remark annoyed the detective more than anything that Kara had ever said to him.

The Greek went to the mantlepiece, and taking down a silver cigarette box, opened and offered it to his visitor. Kara was wearing a grey lounge suit; and although grey is a very trying colour for a foreigner to wear, this suit fitted his splendid figure and gave him just that bulk which he needed.

"You are a most suspicious man, Mr. Meredith," he smiled.

"Suspicious! I?" asked the innocent T. X.

Kara nodded.

"I am sure you want to enquire into the character of all my present staff. I am perfectly satisfied that you will never be at rest until you learn the antecedents of my cook, my valet, my secretary—"

T. X. held up his hand with a laugh.

"Spare me," he said. "It is one of my failings, I admit, but I have never gone much farther into your domestic affairs than to pry into the antecedents of your very interesting chauffeur."

A little cloud passed over Kara's face, but it was only momentary.

"Oh, Brown," he said, airily, with just a perceptible pause between the two words.

"It used to be Smith," said T. X., "but no matter. His name is really Poropulos."

"Oh, Poropulos," said Kara gravely, "I dismissed him a long time ago."

"Pensioned hire, too, I understand," said T. X.

The other looked at him awhile, then, "I am very good to my old servants," he said slowly and, changing the subject; "to what good fortune do I owe this visit?"

T. X. selected a cigarette before he replied.

"I thought you might be of some service to me," he said, apparently giving his whole attention to the cigarette.

"Nothing would give me greater pleasure," said Kara, a little eagerly. "I am afraid you have not been very keen on continuing what I hoped would have ripened into a valuable friendship, more valuable to me perhaps," he smiled, "than to you."

"I am a very shy man," said the shameless T. X., "difficult to a fault, and rather apt to underrate my social attractions. I have come to you now because you know everybody—by the way, how long have you had your secretary!" he asked abruptly.

Kara looked up at the ceiling for inspiration.

"Four, no three months," he corrected, "a very efficient young lady who came to me from one of the training establishments. Somewhat uncommunicative, better educated than most girls in her position—for example, she speaks and writes modern Greek fairly well."

"A treasure!" suggested T. X.

"Unusually so," said Kara. "She lives in Marylebone Road, 86a is the address. She has no friends, spends most of her evenings in her room, is eminently respectable and a little chilling in her attitude to her employer."

T. X. shot a swift glance at the other.

"Why do you tell me all this?" he asked.

"To save you the trouble of finding out," replied the other coolly. "That insatiable curiosity which is one of the equipments of your profession, would, I feel sure, induce you to conduct investigations for your own satisfaction."

T. X. laughed.

"May I sit down?" he said.

The other wheeled an armchair across the room and T. X. sank into it. He leant back and crossed his legs, and was, in a second, the personification of ease.

"I think you are a very clever man, Monsieur Kara," he said.

The other looked down at him this time without amusement.

"Not so clever that I can discover the object of your visit," he said pleasantly enough.

"It is very simply explained," said T. X. "You know everybody in town. You know, amongst other people, Lady Bartholomew."

"I know the lady very well indeed," said Kara, readily,—too readily in fact, for the rapidity with which answer had followed question, suggested to T. X. that Kara had anticipated the reason for the call.

"Have you any idea," asked T. X., speaking with deliberation, "as to why Lady Bartholomew has gone out of town at this particular moment?"

Kara laughed.

"What an extraordinary question to ask me—as though Lady Bartholomew confided her plans to one who is little more than a chance acquaintance!"

"And yet," said T. X., contemplating the burning end of his cigarette, "you know her well enough to hold her promissory note."

"Promissory note?" asked the other.

His tone was one of involuntary surprise and T. X. swore softly to himself for now he saw the faintest shade of relief in Kara's face. The Commissioner realized that he had committed an error—he had been far too definite.

"When I say promissory note," he went on easily, as though he had noticed nothing, "I mean, of course, the securities which the debtor invariably gives to one from whom he or she has borrowed large sums of money."

Kara made no answer, but opening a drawer of his desk he took out a key and brought it across to where T. X. was sitting.

"Here is the key of my safe," he said quietly. "You are at liberty to go carefully through its contents and discover for yourself any promissory note which I hold from Lady Bartholomew. My dear fellow, you don't imagine I'm a moneylender, do you?" he said in an injured tone.

"Nothing was further from my thoughts," said T. X., untruthfully.

But the other pressed the key upon him.

"I should be awfully glad if you would look for yourself," he said earnestly. "I feel that in some way you associate Lady Bartholomew's illness with some horrible act of usury on my part—will you satisfy yourself and in doing so satisfy me?"

Now any ordinary man, and possibly any ordinary detective, would have made the conventional answer. He would have protested that he had no intention of doing anything of the sort; he would have uttered, if he were a man in the position which T. X. occupied, the conventional statement that he had no authority to search the private papers, and that he would certainly not avail himself of the other's kindness. But T. X. was not an ordinary person. He took the key and balanced it lightly in the palm of his hand.

"Is this the key of the famous bedroom safe?" he said banteringly.

Kara was looking down at him with a quizzical smile. "It isn't the safe you opened in my absence, on one memorable occasion, Mr. Meredith," he said. "As you probably know, I have changed that safe, but perhaps you don't feel equal to the task?"

"On the contrary," said T. X., calmly, and rising from the chair, "I am going to put your good faith to the test."

For answer Kara walked to the door and opened it.

"Let me show you the way," he said politely.

He passed along the corridor and entered the apartment at the end. The room was a large one and lighted by one big square window which was protected by steel bars. In the grate which was broad and high a huge fire was burning and the temperature of the room was unpleasantly close despite the coldness of the day.

"That is one of the eccentricities which you, as an Englishman, will never excuse in me," said Kara.

Near the foot of the bed, let into, and flush with, the wall, was a big green door of the safe.

"Here you are, Mr. Meredith," said Kara. "All the precious secrets of Remington Kara are yours for the seeking."

"I am afraid I've had my trouble for nothing," said T. X., making no attempt to use the key.

"That is an opinion which I share," said Kara, with a smile.

"Curiously enough," said T. X. "I mean just what you mean."

He handed the key to Kara.

"Won't you open it?" asked the Greek.

T. X. shook his head.

"The safe as far as I can see is a Magnus, the key which you have been kind enough to give me is legibly inscribed upon the handle 'Chubb.' My experience as a police officer has taught me that Chubb keys very rarely open Magnus safes."

Kara uttered an exclamation of annoyance.

"How stupid of me!" he said, "yet now I remember, I sent the key to my bankers, before I went out of town—I only came back this morning, you know. I will send for it at once."

"Pray don't trouble," murmured T. X. politely. He took from his pocket a little flat leather case and opened it. It contained a number of steel implements of curious shape which were held in position by a leather loop along the centre of the case. From one of these loops he extracted a handle, and deftly fitted something that looked like a steel awl to the socket in the handle. Looking in wonder, and with no little apprehension, Kara saw that the awl was bent at the head.

"What are you going to do?" he asked, a little alarmed.

"I'll show you," said T. X. pleasantly.

Very gingerly he inserted the instrument in the small keyhole and turned it cautiously first one way and then the other. There was a sharp click followed by another. He turned the handle and the door of the safe swung open.

"Simple, isn't it!" he asked politely.

In that second of time Kara's face had undergone a transformation. The eyes which met T. X. Meredith's blazed with an almost insane fury. With a quick stride Kara placed himself before the open safe.

"I think this has gone far enough, Mr. Meredith," he said harshly. "If you wish to search my safe you must get a warrant."

T. X. shrugged his shoulders, and carefully unscrewing the instrument he had employed and replacing it in the case, he returned it to his inside pocket.

"It was at your invitation, my dear Monsieur Kara," he said suavely. "Of course I knew that you were putting a bluff up on me with the key and that you had no more intention of letting me see the inside of your safe than you had of telling me exactly what happened to John Lexman."

The shot went home.

The face which was thrust into the Commissioner's was ridged and veined with passion. The lips were turned back to show the big white even teeth, the eyes were narrowed to slits, the jaw thrust out, and almost every semblance of humanity had vanished from his face.

"You—you—" he hissed, and his clawing hands moved suspiciously backward.

"Put up your hands," said T. X. sharply, "and be damned quick about it!"

In a flash the hands went up, for the revolver which T. X. held was pressed uncomfortably against the third button of the Greek's waistcoat.

"That's not the first time you've been asked to put up your hands, I think," said T. X. pleasantly.

His own left hand slipped round to Kara's hip pocket. He found something in the shape of a cylinder and drew it out from the pocket. To his surprise it was not a revolver, not even a knife; it looked like a small electric torch, though instead of a bulb and a bull's-eye glass, there was a pepper-box perforation at one end.

He handled it carefully and was about to press the small nickel knob when a strangled cry of horror broke from Kara.

"For God's sake be careful!" he gasped. "You're pointing it at me! Do not press that lever, I beg!"

"Will it explode!" asked T. X. curiously.

"No, no!"

T. X. pointed the thing downward to the carpet and pressed the knob cautiously. As he did so there was a sharp hiss and the floor was stained with the liquid which the instrument contained. Just one gush of fluid and no more. T. X. looked down. The bright carpet had already changed colour, and was smoking. The room was filled with a pungent and disagreeable scent. T. X. looked from the floor to the white-faced man.

"Vitriol, I believe," he said, shaking his head admiringly. "What a dear little fellow you are!"

The man, big as he was, was on the point of collapse and mumbled something about self-defence, and listened without a word, whilst T. X., labouring under an emotion which was perfectly pardonable, described Kara, his ancestors and the possibilities of his future estate.

Very slowly the Greek recovered his self-possession.

"I didn't intend using it on you, I swear I didn't," he pleaded. "I'm surrounded by enemies, Meredith. I had to carry some means of protection. It is because my enemies know I carry this that they fight shy of me. I'll swear I had no intention of using it on you. The idea is too preposterous. I am sorry I fooled you about the safe."

"Don't let that worry you," said T. X. "I am afraid I did all the fooling. No, I cannot let you have this back again," he said, as the Greek put out his hand to take the infernal little instrument. "I must take this back to Scotland Yard; it's quite a long time since we had anything new in this shape. Compressed air, I presume."

Kara nodded solemnly.

"Very ingenious indeed," said T. X. "If I had a brain like yours," he paused, "I should do something with it—with a gun," he added, as he passed out of the room.

CHAPTER IX

"My dear Mr. Meredith,

"I cannot tell you how unhappy and humiliated I feel that my little joke with you should have had such an uncomfortable ending. As you know, and as I have given you proof, I have the greatest admiration in the world for one whose work for humanity has won such universal recognition.

"I hope that we shall both forget this unhappy morning and that you will give me an opportunity of rendering to you in person, the apologies which are due to you. I feel that anything less will neither rehabilitate me in your esteem, nor secure for me the remnants of my shattered self-respect.

"I am hoping you will dine with me next week and meet a most interesting man, George Gathercole, who has just returned from Patagonia,—I only received his letter this morning— having made most remarkable discoveries concerning that country.

"I feel sure that you are large enough minded and too much a man of the world to allow my foolish fit of temper to disturb a relationship which I have always hoped would be mutually pleasant. If you will allow Gathercole, who will be unconscious of the part he is playing, to act as peacemaker between yourself and myself, I shall feel that his trip, which has cost me a large sum of money, will not have been wasted.

"I am, dear Mr. Meredith,

"Yours very sincerely,

"REMINGTON KARA."

Kara folded the letter and inserted it in its envelope. He rang a bell on his table and the girl who had so filled T. X. with a sense of awe came from an adjoining room.

"You will see that this is delivered, Miss Holland."

She inclined her head and stood waiting. Kara rose from his desk and began to pace the room.

"Do you know T. X. Meredith?" he asked suddenly.

"I have heard of him," said the girl.

"A man with a singular mind," said Kara; "a man against whom my favourite weapon would fail."

She looked at him with interest in her eyes.

"What is your favourite weapon, Mr. Kara?" she asked.

"Fear," he said.

If he expected her to give him any encouragement to proceed he was disappointed. Probably he required no such encouragement, for in the presence of his social inferiors he was somewhat monopolizing.

"Cut a man's flesh and it heals," he said. "Whip a man and the memory of it passes, frighten him, fill him with a sense of foreboding and apprehension and let him believe that something dreadful is going to happen either to himself or to someone he loves—better the latter—and you will hurt him beyond forgetfulness. Fear is a tyrant and a despot, more terrible than the rack, more potent than the stake. Fear is many-eyed and sees horrors where normal vision only sees the ridiculous."

"Is that your creed?" she asked quietly.

"Part of it, Miss Holland," he smiled.

She played idly with the letter she held in her hand, balancing it on the edge of the desk, her eyes downcast.

"What would justify the use of such an awful weapon?" she asked.

"It is amply justified to secure an end," he said blandly. "For example—I want something—I cannot obtain that something through the ordinary channel or by the employment of ordinary means. It is essential to me, to my happiness, to my comfort, or my amour-propre, that that something shall be possessed by me. If I can buy it, well and good. If I can buy those who can use their influence to secure this thing for me, so much the better. If I can obtain it by any merit I possess, I utilize that merit, providing always, that I can secure my object in the time, otherwise—"

He shrugged his shoulders.

"I see," she said, nodding her head quickly. "I suppose that is how blackmailers feel."

He frowned.

"That is a word I never use, nor do I like to hear it employed," he said. "Blackmail suggests to me a vulgar attempt to obtain money."

"Which is generally very badly wanted by the people who use it," said the girl, with a little smile, "and, according to your argument, they are also justified."

"It is a matter of plane," he said airily. "Viewed from my standpoint, they are sordid criminals—the sort of person that T. X. meets, I presume, in the course of his daily work. T. X.," he went on somewhat oracularly, "is a man for whom I have a great deal of respect. You will probably meet him again, for he will find an opportunity of asking you a few questions about myself. I need hardly tell you—"

He lifted his shoulders with a deprecating smile.

"I shall certainly not discuss your business with any person," said the girl coldly.

"I am paying you 3 pounds a week, I think," he said. "I intend increasing that to 5 pounds because you suit me most admirably."

"Thank you," said the girl quietly, "but I am already being paid quite sufficient."

She left him, a little astonished and not a little ruffled.

To refuse the favours of Remington Kara was, by him, regarded as something of an affront. Half his quarrel with T. X. was that gentleman's curious indifference to the benevolent attitude which Kara had persistently adopted in his dealings with the detective.

He rang the bell, this time for his valet.

"Fisher," he said, "I am expecting a visit from a gentleman named Gathercole—a one-armed gentleman whom you must look after if he comes. Detain him on some pretext or other because he is rather difficult to get hold of and I want to see him. I am going out now and I shall be back at 6.30. Do whatever you can to prevent him going away until I return. He will probably be interested if you take him into the library."

"Very good, sir," said the urbane Fisher, "will you change before you go out?"

Kara shook his head.

"I think I will go as I am," he said. "Get me my fur coat. This beastly cold kills me," he shivered as he glanced into the bleak street. "Keep my fire going, put all my private letters in my bedroom, and see that Miss Holland has her lunch."

Fisher followed him to his car, wrapped the fur rug about his legs, closed the door carefully and returned to the house. From thence onward his behaviour was somewhat extraordinary for a well-bred servant. That he should return to Kara's study and set the papers in order was natural and proper.

That he should conduct a rapid examination of all the drawers in Kara's desk might be excused on the score of diligence, since he was, to some extent, in the confidence of his employer.

Kara was given to making friends of his servants—up to a point. In his more generous moments he would address his bodyguard as "Fred," and on more occasions than one, and for no apparent reason, had tipped his servant over and above his salary.

Mr. Fred Fisher found little to reward him for his search until he came upon Kara's cheque book which told him that on the previous day the Greek had drawn 6,000 pounds in cash from the bank. This interested him mightily and he replaced the cheque book with the tightened lips and the fixed gaze of a man who was thinking rapidly. He paid a visit to the library, where the secretary was engaged in making copies of Kara's correspondence, answering letters appealing for charitable donations, and in the hack words which fall to the secretaries of the great.

He replenished the fire, asked deferentially for any instructions and returned again to his quest. This time he made the bedroom the scene of his investigations. The safe he did not attempt to touch, but there was a small bureau in which Kara would have placed his private correspondence of the morning. This however yielded no result.

By the side of the bed on a small table was a telephone, the sight of which apparently afforded the servant a little amusement. This was the private 'phone which Kara had been instrumental in having fixed to Scotland Yard—as he had explained to his servants.

"Rum cove," said Fisher.

He paused for a moment before the closed door of the room and smilingly surveyed the great steel latch which spanned the door and fitted into an iron socket securely screwed to the framework. He lifted it gingerly—there was a little knob for the purpose—and let it fall gently into the socket which had been made to receive it on the door itself.

"Rum cove," he said again, and lifting the latch to the hook which held it up, left the room, closing the door softly behind him. He walked down the corridor, with a meditative frown, and began to descend the stairs to the hall.

He was less than half-way down when the one maid of Kara's household came up to meet him.

"There's a gentleman who wants to see Mr. Kara," she said, "here is his card."

Fisher took the card from the salver and read, "Mr. George Gathercole, Junior Travellers' Club."

"I'll see this gentleman," he said, with a sudden brisk interest.

He found the visitor standing in the hall.

He was a man who would have attracted attention, if only from the somewhat eccentric nature of his dress and his unkempt appearance. He was dressed in a well-worn overcoat of a somewhat pronounced check, he had a top-hat, glossy and obviously new, at the back of his head, and the lower part of his face was covered by a ragged beard. This he was plucking with nervous jerks, talking to himself the while, and casting a disparaging eye upon the portrait of Remington Kara which hung above the marble fireplace. A pair of pince-nez sat crookedly on his nose and two fat volumes under his arm completed the picture. Fisher, who was an observer of some discernment, noticed under the overcoat a creased blue suit, large black boots and a pair of pearl studs.

The newcomer glared round at the valet.

"Take these!" he ordered peremptorily, pointing to the books under his arm.

Fisher hastened to obey and noted with some wonder that the visitor did not attempt to assist him either by loosening his hold of the volumes or raising his hand. Accidentally the valet's hand pressed against the other's sleeve and he received a shock, for the forearm was clearly an artificial one. It was against a wooden surface beneath the sleeve that his knuckles struck, and this view of the stranger's infirmity was confirmed when the other reached round with his right hand, took hold of the gloved left hand and thrust it into the pocket of his overcoat.

"Where is Kara?" growled the stranger.

"He will be back very shortly, sir," said the urbane Fisher.

"Out, is he?" boomed the visitor. "Then I shan't wait. What the devil does he mean by being out? He's had three years to be out!"

"Mr. Kara expects you, sir. He told me he would be in at six o'clock at the latest."

"Six o'clock, ye gods'." stormed the man impatiently. "What dog am I that I should wait till six?"

He gave a savage little tug at his beard.

"Six o'clock, eh? You will tell Mr. Kara that I called. Give me those books."

"But I assure you, sir,—" stammered Fisher.

"Give me those books!" roared the other.

Deftly he lifted his left hand from the pocket, crooked the elbow by some quick manipulation, and thrust the books, which the valet most reluctantly handed to him, back to the place whence he had taken them.

"Tell Mr. Kara I will call at my own time—do you understand, at my own time. Good morning to you."

"If you would only wait, sir," pleaded the agonized Fisher.

"Wait be hanged," snarled the other. "I've waited three years, I tell you. Tell Mr. Kara to expect me when he sees me!"

He went out and most unnecessarily banged the door behind him. Fisher went back to the library. The girl was sealing up some letters as he entered and looked up.

"I am afraid, Miss Holland, I've got myself into very serious trouble."

"What is that, Fisher!" asked the girl.

"There was a gentleman coming to see Mr. Kara, whom Mr. Kara particularly wanted to see."

"Mr. Gathercole," said the girl quickly.

Fisher nodded.

"Yes, miss, I couldn't get him to stay though."

She pursed her lips thoughtfully.

"Mr. Kara will be very cross, but I don't see how you can help it. I wish you had called me."

"He never gave a chance, miss," said Fisher, with a little smile, "but if he comes again I'll show him straight up to you."

She nodded.

"Is there anything you want, miss?" he asked as he stood at the door.

"What time did Mr. Kara say he would be back?"

"At six o'clock, miss," the man replied.

"There is rather an important letter here which has to be delivered."

"Shall I ring up for a messenger?"

"No, I don't think that would be advisable. You had better take it yourself."

Kara was in the habit of employing Fisher as a confidential messenger when the occasion demanded such employment.

"I will go with pleasure, miss," he said.

It was a heaven-sent opportunity for Fisher, who had been inventing some excuse for leaving the house. She handed him the letter and he read without a droop of eyelid the superscription:

"T. X. Meredith, Esq., Special Service Dept., Scotland Yard, Whitehall."

He put it carefully in his pocket and went from the room to change. Large as the house was Kara did not employ a regular staff of servants. A maid and a valet comprised the whole of the indoor staff. His cook, and the other domestics, necessary for conducting an establishment of that size, were engaged by the day.

Kara had returned from the country earlier than had been anticipated, and, save for Fisher, the only other person in the house beside the girl, was the middle-aged domestic who was parlour-maid, serving-maid and housekeeper in one.

Miss Holland sat at her desk to all appearance reading over the letters she had typed that afternoon but her mind was very far from the correspondence before her. She heard the soft thud of the front door closing, and rising she crossed the room rapidly and looked down through the window to the street. She watched Fisher until he was out of sight; then she descended to the hall and to the kitchen.

It was not the first visit she had made to the big underground room with its vaulted roof and its great ranges—which were seldom used nowadays, for Kara gave no dinners.

The maid—who was also cook—arose up as the girl entered.

"It's a sight for sore eyes to see you in my kitchen, miss," she smiled.

"I'm afraid you're rather lonely, Mrs. Beale," said the girl sympathetically.

"Lonely, miss!" cried the maid. "I fairly get the creeps sitting here hour after hour. It's that door that gives me the hump."

She pointed to the far end of the kitchen to a soiled looking door of unpainted wood.

"That's Mr. Kara's wine cellar—nobody's been in it but him. I know he goes in sometimes because I tried a dodge that my brother—who's a policeman—taught me. I stretched a bit of white cotton across it an' it was broke the next morning."

"Mr. Kara keeps some of his private papers in there," said the girl quietly, "he has told me so himself."

"H'm," said the woman doubtfully, "I wish he'd brick it up—the same as he has the lower cellar—I get the horrors sittin' here at night expectin' the door to open an' the ghost of the mad lord to come out—him that was killed in Africa."

Miss Holland laughed.

"I want you to go out now," she said, "I have no stamps."

Mrs. Beale obeyed with alacrity and whilst she was assuming a hat—being desirous of maintaining her prestige as housekeeper in the eyes of Cadogan Square, the girl ascended to the upper floor.

Again she watched from the window the disappearing figure.

Once out of sight Miss Holland went to work with a remarkable deliberation and thoroughness. From her bag she produced a small purse and opened it. In that case was a new steel key. She passed swiftly down the corridor to Kara's room and made straight for the safe.

In two seconds it was open and she was examining its contents. It was a large safe of the usual type. There were four steel drawers fitted at the back and at the bottom of the strong box. Two of these were unlocked and contained nothing more interesting than accounts relating to Kara's estate in Albania.

The top pair were locked. She was prepared for this contingency and a second key was as efficacious as the first. An examination of the first drawer did not produce all that she had expected. She returned the papers to the drawer, pushed it to and locked it. She gave her attention to the second drawer. Her hand shook a little as she pulled it open. It was her last chance, her last hope.

There were a number of small jewel-boxes almost filling the drawer. She took them out one by one and at the bottom she found what she had been searching for and that which had filled her thoughts for the past three months.

It was a square case covered in red morocco leather. She inserted her shaking hand and took it out with a triumphant little cry.

"At last," she said aloud, and then a hand grasped her wrist and in a panic she turned to meet the smiling face of Kara.

CHAPTER X

She felt her knees shake under her and thought she was going to swoon. She put out her disengaged hand to steady herself, and if the face which was turned to him was pale, there was a steadfast resolution in her dark eyes.

"Let me relieve you of that, Miss Holland," said Kara, in his silkiest tones.

He wrenched rather than took the box from her hand, replaced it carefully in the drawer, pushed the drawer to and locked it, examining the key as he withdrew it. Then he closed the safe and locked that.

"Obviously," he said presently, "I must get a new safe."

He had not released his hold of her wrist nor did he, until he had led her from the room back to the library. Then he released the girl, standing between her and the door, with folded arms and that cynical, quiet, contemptuous smile of his upon his handsome face.

"There are many courses which I can adopt," he said slowly. "I can send for the police—when my servants whom you have despatched so thoughtfully have returned, or I can take your punishment into my own hands."

"So far as I am concerned," said the girl coolly, "you may send for the police."

She leant back against the edge of the desk, her hands holding the edge, and faced him without so much as a quaver.

"I do not like the police," mused Kara, when there came a knock at the door.

Kara turned and opened it and after a low strained conversation he returned, closing the door and laid a paper of stamps on the girl's table.

"As I was saying, I do not care for the police, and I prefer my own method. In this particular instance the police obviously would not serve me, because you are not afraid of them and in all probability you are in their pay—am I right in supposing that you are one of Mr. T. X. Meredith's accomplices!"

"I do not know Mr. T. X. Meredith," she replied calmly, "and I am not in any way associated with the police."

"Nevertheless," he persisted, "you do not seem to be very scared of them and that removes any temptation I might have to place you in the hands of the law. Let me see," he pursed his lips as he applied his mind to the problem.

She half sat, half stood, watching him without any evidence of apprehension, but with a heart which began to quake a little. For three months she had played her part and the strain had been greater than she had confessed to herself. Now the great moment had come and she had failed. That was the sickening, maddening thing about it all. It was not the fear of arrest or of conviction, which brought a sinking to her heart; it was the despair of failure, added to a sense of her helplessness against this man.

"If I had you arrested your name would appear in all the papers, of course," he said, narrowly, "and your photograph would probably adorn the Sunday journals," he added expectantly.

She laughed.

"That doesn't appeal to me," she said.

"I am afraid it doesn't," he replied, and strolled towards her as though to pass her on his way to the window. He was abreast of her when he suddenly swung round and catching her in his arms he caught her close to him. Before she could realise what he planned, he had stooped swiftly and kissed her full upon the mouth.

"If you scream, I shall kiss you again," he said, "for I have sent the maid to buy some more stamps—to the General Post Office."

"Let me go," she gasped.

Now for the first time he saw the terror in her eyes, and there surged within him that mad sense of triumph, that intoxication of power which had been associated with the red letter days of his warped life.

"You're afraid!" he bantered her, half whispering the words, "you're afraid now, aren't you? If you scream I shall kiss you again, do you hear?"

"For God's sake, let me go," she whispered.

He felt her shaking in his arms, and suddenly he released her with a little laugh, and she sank trembling from head to foot upon the chair by her desk.

"Now you're going to tell me who sent you here," he went on harshly, "and why you came. I never suspected you. I thought you were one of those strange creatures one meets in England, a gentlewoman who prefers working for her living to the more simple business of getting married. And all the time you were spying—clever—very clever!"

The girl was thinking rapidly. In five minutes Fisher would return. Somehow she had faith in Fisher's ability and willingness to save her from a situation which she realized was fraught with the greatest danger to herself. She was horribly afraid. She knew this man far better than he suspected, realized the treachery and the unscrupulousness of him. She knew he would stop short of nothing, that he was without honour and without a single attribute of goodness.

He must have read her thoughts for he came nearer and stood over her.

"You needn't shrink, my young friend," he said with a little chuckle. "You are going to do just what I want you to do, and your first act will be to accompany me downstairs. Get up."

He half lifted, half dragged her to her feet and led her from the room. They descended to the hall together and the girl spoke no word. Perhaps she hoped that she might wrench herself free and make her escape into the street, but in this she was disappointed. The grip about her arm was a grip of steel and she knew safety did not lie in that direction. She pulled back at the head of the stairs that led down to the kitchen.

"Where are you taking me?" she asked.

"I am going to put you into safe custody," he said. "On the whole I think it is best that the police take this matter in hand and I shall lock you into my wine cellar and go out in search of a policeman."

The big wooden door opened, revealing a second door and this Kara unbolted. She noticed that both doors were sheeted with steel, the outer on the inside, and the inner door on the outside. She had no time to make any further observations for Kara thrust her into the darkness. He switched on a light.

"I will not deny you that," he said, pushing her back as she made a frantic attempt to escape. He swung the outer door to as she raised her voice in a piercing scream, and clapping his hand over her mouth held her tightly for a moment.

"I have warned you," he hissed.

She saw his face distorted with rage. She saw Kara transfigured with devilish anger, saw that handsome, almost godlike countenance thrust into hers, flushed and seamed with malignity and a hatefulness beyond understanding and then her senses left her and she sank limp and swooning into his arms.

When she recovered consciousness she found herself lying on a plain stretcher bed. She sat up suddenly. Kara had gone and the door was closed. The cellar was dry and clean and its walls were enamelled white. Light was supplied by two electric lamps in the ceiling. There was a table and a chair and a small washstand, and air was evidently supplied through unseen ventilators. It was indeed a prison and no less, and in her first moments of panic she found herself wondering whether Kara had used this underground dungeon of his before for a similar purpose.

She examined the room carefully. At the farthermost end was another door and this she pushed gently at first and then vigorously without producing the slightest impression. She still had her bag, a small affair of black moire, which hung from her belt, in which was nothing more formidable than a penknife, a small bottle of smelling salts and a pair of scissors. The latter she had used for cutting out those paragraphs from the daily newspapers which referred to Kara's movements.

They would make a formidable weapon, and wrapping her handkerchief round the handle to give it a better grip she placed it on the table within reach. She was dimly conscious all the time that she had heard something about this wine cellar—something which, if she could recollect it, would be of service to her.

Then in a flash she remembered that there was a lower cellar, which according to Mrs. Beale was never used and was bricked up. It was approached from the outside, down a circular flight of stairs. There might be a way out from that direction and would there not be some connection between the upper cellar and the lower!

She set to work to make a closer examination of the apartment.

The floor was of concrete, covered with a light rush matting. This she carefully rolled up, starting at the door. One half of the floor was uncovered without revealing the existence of any trap. She attempted to pull the table into the centre of the room, better to roll the matting, but found it fixed to the wall, and going down on her knees, she discovered that it had been fixed after the matting had been laid.

Obviously there was no need for the fixture and, she tapped the floor with her little knuckle. Her heart started racing. The sound her knocking gave forth was a hollow one. She sprang up, took her bag from the table, opened the little penknife and cut carefully through the thin rushes. She might have to replace the matting and it was necessary she should do her work tidily.

Soon the whole of the trap was revealed. There was an iron ring, which fitted flush with the top and which she pulled. The trap yielded and swung back as though there were a counterbalance at the other end, as indeed there was. She peered down. There was a dim light below—the reflection of a light in the distance. A flight of steps led down to the lower level and after a second's hesitation she swung her legs over the cavity and began her descent.

She was in a cellar slightly smaller than that above her. The light she had seen came from an inner apartment which would be underneath the kitchen of the house. She made her way cautiously along, stepping on tip-toe. The first of the rooms she came to was well-furnished. There was a thick carpet on the floor, comfortable easy-chairs, a little bookcase well filled, and a reading lamp. This must be Kara's underground study, where he kept his precious papers.

A smaller room gave from this and again it was doorless. She looked in and after her eyes had become accustomed to the darkness she saw that it was a bathroom handsomely fitted.

The room she was in was also without any light which came from the farthermost chamber. As the girl strode softly across the well-carpeted room she trod on something hard. She stooped and felt along the floor and her fingers encountered a thin steel chain. The girl was bewildered-almost panic-stricken. She shrunk back from the entrance of the inner room, fearful of what she would see. And then from the interior came a sound that made her tingle with horror.

It was a sound of a sigh, long and trembling. She set her teeth and strode through the doorway and stood for a moment staring with open eyes and mouth at what she saw.

"My God!" she breathed, "London. . . . in the twentieth century. . . !"

CHAPTER XI

Superintendent Mansus had a little office in Scotland Yard proper, which, he complained, was not so much a private bureau, as a waiting-room to which repaired every official of the police service who found time hanging on his hands. On the afternoon of Miss Holland's surprising adventure, a plainclothes man of "D" Division brought to Mr. Mansus's room a very scared domestic servant, voluble, tearful and agonizingly penitent. It was a mood not wholly unfamiliar to a police officer of twenty years experience and Mr. Mansus was not impressed.

"If you will kindly shut up," he said, blending his natural politeness with his employment of the vernacular, "and if you will also answer a few questions I will save you a lot of trouble. You were Lady Bartholomew's maid weren't you?"

"Yes, sir," sobbed the red-eyed Mary Ann.

"And you have been detected trying to pawn a gold bracelet, the property of Lady Bartholomew?"

The maid gulped, nodded and started breathlessly upon a recital of her wrongs.

"Yes, sir—but she practically gave it to me, sir, and I haven't had my wages for two months, sir, and she can give that foreigner thousands and thousands of pounds at a time, sir, but her poor servants she can't pay—no, she can't. And if Sir William knew especially about my lady's cards and about the snuffbox, what would he think, I wonder, and I'm going to have my rights, for if she can pay thousands to a swell like Mr. Kara she can pay me and—"

Mansus jerked his head.

"Take her down to the cells," he said briefly, and they led her away, a wailing, woeful figure of amateur larcenist.

In three minutes Mansus was with T. X. and had reduced the girl's incoherence to something like order.

"This is important," said T. X.; "produce the Abigail."

"The—?" asked the puzzled officer.

"The skivvy—slavey—hired help—get busy," said T. X. impatiently.

They brought her to T. X. in a condition bordering upon collapse.

"Get her a cup of tea," said the wise chief. "Sit down, Mary Ann, and forget all your troubles."

"Oh, sir, I've never been in this position before," she began, as she flopped into the chair they put for her.

"Then you've had a very tiring time," said T. X. "Now listen—"

"I've been respectable—"

"Forget it!" said T. X., wearily. "Listen! If you'll tell me the whole truth about Lady Bartholomew and the money she paid to Mr. Kara—"

"Two thousand pounds—two separate thousand and by all accounts-"

"If you will tell me the truth, I'll compound a felony and let you go free."

It was a long time before he could prevail upon her to clear her speech of the ego which insisted upon intruding. There were gaps in her narrative which he bridged. In the main it was a believable story. Lady Bartholomew had lost money and had borrowed from Kara. She had given as security, the snuffbox presented to her husband's father, a doctor, by one of the Czars for services rendered, and was "all blue enamel and gold, and foreign words in diamonds." On the question of the amount Lady Bartholomew had borrowed, Abigail was very vague. All that she knew was that my lady had paid back two thousand pounds and that she was still very distressed ("in a fit" was the phrase the girl used), because apparently Kara refused to restore the box.

There had evidently been terrible scenes in the Bartholomew menage, hysterics and what not, the principal breakdown having occurred when Belinda Mary came home from school in France.

"Miss Bartholomew is home then. Where is she?" asked T. X.

Here the girl was more vague than ever. She thought the young lady had gone back again, anyway Miss Belinda had been very much upset. Miss Belinda had seen Dr. Williams and advised that her mother should go away for a change.

"Miss Belinda seems to be a precocious young person," said T. X. "Did she by any chance see Mr. Kara?"

"Oh, no," explained the girl. "Miss Belinda was above that sort of person. Miss Belinda was a lady, if ever there was one."

"And how old is this interesting young woman?" asked T. X. curiously.

"She is nineteen," said the girl, and the Commissioner, who had pictured Belinda in short plaid frocks and long pigtails, and had moreover visualised her as a freckled little girl with thin legs and snub nose, was abashed.

He delivered a short lecture on the sacred rights of property, paid the girl the three months' wages which were due to her—he had no doubt as to the legality of her claim—and dismissed her with instructions to go back to the house, pack her box and clear out.

After the girl had gone, T. X. sat down to consider the position. He might see Kara and since Kara had expressed his contrition and was probably in a more humble state of mind, he might make reparation. Then again he might not. Mansus was waiting and T. X. walked back with him to his little office.

"I hardly know what to make of it," he said in despair.

"If you can give me Kara's motive, sir, I can give you a solution," said Mansus.

T. X. shook his head.

"That is exactly what I am unable to give you," he said.

He perched himself on Mansus's desk and lit a cigar.

"I have a good mind to go round and see him," he said after a while.

"Why not telephone to him?" asked Mansus. "There is his 'phone straight into his boudoir."

He pointed to a small telephone in a corner of the room.

"Oh, he persuaded the Commissioner to run the wire, did he?" said T. X. interested, and walked over to the telephone.

He fingered the receiver for a little while and was about to take it off, but changed his mind.

"I think not," he said, "I'll go round and see him to-morrow. I don't hope to succeed in extracting the confidence in the case of Lady Bartholomew, which he denied me over poor Lexman."

"I suppose you'll never give up hope of seeing Mr. Lexman again," smiled Mansus, busily arranging a new blotting pad.

Before T. X. could answer there came a knock at the door, and a uniformed policeman, entered. He saluted T. X.

"They've just sent an urgent letter across from your office, sir. I said I thought you were here."

He handed the missive to the Commissioner. T. X. took it and glanced at the typewritten address. It was marked "urgent" and "by hand." He took up the thin, steel, paper-knife from the desk and slit open the envelope. The letter consisted of three or four pages of manuscript and, unlike the envelope, it was handwritten.

"My dear T. X.," it began, and the handwriting was familiar.

Mansus, watching the Commissioner, saw the puzzled frown gather on his superior's forehead, saw the eyebrows arch and the mouth open in astonishment, saw him hastily turn to the last page to read the signature and then:

"Howling apples!" gasped T. X. "It's from John Lexman!"

His hand shook as he turned the closely written pages. The letter was dated that afternoon. There was no other address than "London."

"My dear T. X.," it began, "I do not doubt that this letter will give you a little shock, because most of my friends will have believed that I am gone beyond return. Fortunately or unfortunately that is not so. For myself I could wish—but I am not going to take a very gloomy view since I am genuinely pleased at the thought that I shall be meeting you again. Forgive this letter if it is incoherent but I have only this moment returned and am writing at the Charing Cross Hotel. I am not staying here, but I will let you have my address later. The crossing has been a very severe one so you must forgive me if my letter sounds a little disjointed. You will be sorry to hear that my dear wife is dead. She died abroad about six months ago. I do not wish to talk very much about it so you will forgive me if I do not tell you any more.

"My principal object in writing to you at the moment is an official one. I suppose I am still amenable to punishment and I have decided to surrender myself to the authorities to-night. You used to have a most excellent assistant in Superintendent Mansus, and if it is convenient to you, as I hope it will be, I will report myself to him at 10.15. At any rate, my dear T. X., I do not wish to mix you up in my affairs and if you will let me do this business through Mansus I shall be very much obliged to you.

"I know there is no great punishment awaiting me, because my pardon was apparently signed on the night before my escape. I shall not have much to tell you, because there is not much in the past two years that I would care to recall. We endured a great deal of unhappiness and death was very merciful when it took my beloved from me.

"Do you ever see Kara in these days?

"Will you tell Mansus to expect me at between ten and half-past, and if he will give instructions to the officer on duty in the hall I will come straight up to his room.

"With affectionate regards, my dear fellow, I am,

"Yours sincerely,

"JOHN LEXMAN."

T. X. read the letter over twice and his eyes were troubled.

"Poor girl," he said softly, and handed the letter to Mansus. "He evidently wants to see you because he is afraid of using my friendship to his advantage. I shall be here, nevertheless."

"What will be the formality?" asked Mansus.

"There will be no formality," said the other briskly. "I will secure the necessary pardon from the Home Secretary and in point of fact I have it already promised, in writing."

He walked back to Whitehall, his mind fully occupied with the momentous events of the day. It was a raw February evening, sleet was falling in the street, a piercing easterly wind drove even through his thick overcoat. In such doorways as offered protection from the bitter elements the wreckage of humanity which clings to the West end of London, as the singed moth flutters about the flame that destroys it, were huddled for warmth.

T. X. was a man of vast human sympathies.

All his experience with the criminal world, all his disappointments, all his disillusions had failed to quench the pity for his unfortunate fellows. He made it a rule on such nights as these, that if, by chance, returning late to his office he should find such a shivering piece of jetsam sheltering in his own doorway, he would give him or her the price of a bed.

In his own quaint way he derived a certain speculative excitement from this practice. If the doorway was empty he regarded himself as a winner, if some one stood sheltered in the deep recess which is a feature of the old Georgian houses in this historic thoroughfare, he would lose to the extent of a shilling.

He peered forward through the semi-darkness as he neared the door of his offices.

"I've lost," he said, and stripped his gloves preparatory to groping in his pocket for a coin.

Somebody was standing in the entrance, but it was obviously a very respectable somebody. A dumpy, motherly somebody in a seal-skin coat and a preposterous bonnet.

"Hullo," said T. X. in surprise, "are you trying to get in here?"

"I want to see Mr. Meredith," said the visitor, in the mincing affected tones of one who excused the vulgar source of her prosperity by frequently reiterated claims to having seen better days.

"Your longing shall be gratified," said T. X. gravely.

He unlocked the heavy door, passed through the uncarpeted passage—there are no frills on Government offices—and led the way up the stairs to the suite on the first floor which constituted his bureau.

He switched on all the lights and surveyed his visitor, a comfortable person of the landlady type.

"A good sort," thought T. X., "but somewhat overweighted with lorgnettes and seal-skin."

"You will pardon my coming to see you at this hour of the night," she began deprecatingly, "but as my dear father used to say, 'Hopi soit qui mal y pense.'"

"Your dear father being in the garter business?" suggested T. X. humorously. "Won't you sit down, Mrs. ———"

"Mrs. Cassley," beamed the lady as she seated herself. "He was in the paper hanging business. But needs must, when the devil drives, as the saying goes."

"What particular devil is driving you, Mrs. Cassley?" asked T. X., somewhat at a loss to understand the object of this visit.

"I may be doing wrong," began the lady, pursing her lips, "and two blacks will never make a white."

"And all that glitters is not gold," suggested T. X. a little wearily. "Will you please tell me your business, Mrs. Cassley? I am a very hungry man."

"Well, it's like this, sir," said Mrs. Cassley, dropping her erudition, and coming down to bedrock homeliness; "I've got a young lady stopping with me, as respectable a gel as I've had to deal with. And I know what respectability is, I might tell you, for I've taken professional boarders and I have been housekeeper to a doctor."

"You are well qualified to speak," said T. X. with a smile. "And what about this particular young lady of yours! By the way what is your address?"

"86a Marylebone Road," said the lady.

T. X. sat up.

"Yes?" he said quickly. "What about your young lady?"

"She works as far as I can understand," said the loquacious landlady, "with a certain Mr. Kara in the typewriting line. She came to me four months ago."

"Never mind when she came to you," said T. X. impatiently. "Have you a message from the lady?"

"Well, it's like this, sir," said Mrs. Cassley, leaning forward confidentially and speaking in the hollow tone which she had decided should accompany any revelation to a police officer, "this young lady said to me, 'If I don't come any night by 8 o'clock you must go to T. X. and tell him—'!"

She paused dramatically.

"Yes, yes," said T. X. quickly, "for heaven's sake go on, woman."

"'Tell him,'" said Mrs. Cassley, "'that Belinda Mary—'"

He sprang to his feet.

"Belinda Mary!" he breathed, "Belinda Mary!" In a flash he saw it all. This girl with a knowledge of modern Greek, who was working in Kara's house, was there for a purpose. Kara had something of her mother's, something that was vital and which he would not part with, and she had adopted this method of securing that some thing. Mrs. Cassley was prattling on, but her voice was merely a haze of sound to him. It brought a strange glow to his heart that Belinda Mary should have thought of him.

"Only as a policeman, of course," said the still, small voice of his official self. "Perhaps!" said the human T. X., defiantly.

He got on the telephone to Mansus and gave a few instructions.

"You stay here," he ordered the astounded Mrs. Cassley; "I am going to make a few investigations."

Kara was at home, but was in bed. T. X. remembered that this extraordinary man invariably went to bed early and that it was his practice to receive visitors in this guarded room of his. He was admitted almost at once and found Kara in his silk dressing-gown lying on the bed smoking. The heat of the room was unbearable even on that bleak February night.

"This is a pleasant surprise," said Kara, sitting up; "I hope you don't mind my dishabille."

T. X. came straight to the point.

"Where is Miss Holland!" he asked.

"Miss Holland?" Kara's eyebrows advertised his astonishment. "What an extraordinary question to ask me, my dear man! At her home, or at the theatre or in a cinema palace—I don't know how these people employ their evenings."

"She is not at home," said T. X., "and I have reason to believe that she has not left this house."

"What a suspicious person you are, Mr. Meredith!" Kara rang the bell and Fisher came in with a cup of coffee on a tray.

"Fisher," drawled Kara. "Mr. Meredith is anxious to know where Miss Holland is. Will you be good enough to tell him, you know more about her movements than I do."

"As far as I know, sir," said Fisher deferentially, "she left the house about 5.30, her usual hour. She sent me out a little before five on a message and when I came back her hat and her coat had gone, so I presume she had gone also."

"Did you see her go?" asked T. X.

The man shook his head.

"No, sir, I very seldom see the lady come or go. There has been no restrictions placed upon the young lady and she has been at liberty to move about as she likes. I think I am correct in saying that, sir," he turned to Kara.

Kara nodded.

"You will probably find her at home."

He shook his finger waggishly at T. X.

"What a dog you are," he jibed, "I ought to keep the beauties of my household veiled, as we do in the East, and especially when I have a susceptible policeman wandering at large."

T. X. gave jest for jest. There was nothing to be gained by making trouble here. After a few amiable commonplaces he took his departure. He found Mrs. Cassley being entertained by Mansus with a wholly fictitious description of the famous criminals he had arrested.

"I can only suggest that you go home," said T. X. "I will send a police officer with you to report to me, but in all probability you will find the lady has returned. She may have had a difficulty in getting a bus on a night like this."

A detective was summoned from Scotland Yard and accompanied by him Mrs. Cassley returned to her domicile with a certain importance. T. X. looked at his watch. It was a quarter to ten.

"Whatever happens, I must see old Lexman," he said. "Tell the best men we've got in the department to stand by for eventualities. This is going to be one of my busy days."

CHAPTER XII

Kara lay back on his down pillows with a sneer on his face and his brain very busy. What started the train of thought he did not know, but at that moment his mind was very far away. It carried him back a dozen years to a dirty little peasant's cabin on the hillside outside Durazzo, to the livid face of a young Albanian chief, who had lost at Kara's whim all that life held for a man, to the hateful eyes of the girl's father, who stood with folded arms glaring down at the bound and manacled figure on the floor, to the smoke-stained rafters of this peasant cottage and the dancing shadows on the roof, to that terrible hour of waiting when he sat bound to a post with a candle flickering and spluttering lower and lower to the little heap of gunpowder that would start the trail toward the clumsy infernal machine under his chair. He remembered the day well because it was Candlemas day, and this was the anniversary. He remembered other things more pleasant. The beat of hoofs on the rocky roadway, the crash of the door falling in when the Turkish Gendarmes had battered a way to his rescue. He remembered with a savage joy the spectacle of his would-be assassins twitching and struggling on the gallows at Pezara and—he heard the faint tinkle of the front door bell.

Had T. X. returned! He slipped from the bed and went to the door, opened it slightly and listened. T. X. with a search warrant might be a source of panic especially if—he shrugged his shoulders. He had satisfied T. X. and allayed his suspicions. He would get Fisher out of the way that night and make sure.

The voice from the hall below was loud and gruff. Who could it be! Then he heard Fisher's foot on the stairs and the valet entered.

"Will you see Mr. Gathercole now!"

"Mr. Gathercole!"

Kara breathed a sigh of relief and his face was wreathed in smiles.

"Why, of course. Tell him to come up. Ask him if he minds seeing me in my room."

"I told him you were in bed, sir, and he used shocking language," said Fisher.

Kara laughed.

"Send him up," he said, and then as Fisher was going out of the room he called him back.

"By the way, Fisher, after Mr. Gathercole has gone, you may go out for the night. You've got somewhere to go, I suppose, and you needn't come back until the morning."

"Yes, sir," said the servant.

Such an instruction was remarkably pleasing to him. There was much that he had to do and that night's freedom would assist him materially.

"Perhaps" Kara hesitated, "perhaps you had better wait until eleven o'clock. Bring me up some sandwiches and a large glass of milk. Or better still, place them on a plate in the hall."

"Very good, sir," said the man and withdrew.

Down below, that grotesque figure with his shiny hat and his ragged beard was walking up and down the tesselated hallway muttering to himself and staring at the various objects in the hall with a certain amused antagonism.

"Mr. Kara will see you, sir," said Fisher.

"Oh!" said the other glaring at the unoffending Fisher, "that's very good of him. Very good of this person to see a scholar and a gentleman who has been about his dirty business for three years. Grown grey in his service! Do you understand that, my man!"

"Yes, sir," said Fisher.

"Look here!"

The man thrust out his face.

"Do you see those grey hairs in my beard?"

The embarrassed Fisher grinned.

"Is it grey!" challenged the visitor, with a roar.

"Yes, sir," said the valet hastily.

"Is it real grey?" insisted the visitor. "Pull one out and see!"

The startled Fisher drew back with an apologetic smile.

"I couldn't think of doing a thing like that, sir."

"Oh, you couldn't," sneered the visitor; "then lead on!"

Fisher showed the way up the stairs. This time the traveller carried no books. His left arm hung limply by his side and Fisher privately gathered that the hand had got loose from the detaining pocket without its owner being aware of the fact. He pushed open the door and announced, "Mr. Gathercole," and Kara came forward with a smile to meet his agent, who, with top hat still on the top of his head, and his overcoat dangling about his heels, must have made a remarkable picture.

Fisher closed the door behind them and returned to his duties in the hall below. Ten minutes later he heard the door opened and the booming voice of the stranger came down to him. Fisher went up the stairs to meet him and found him addressing the occupant of the room in his own eccentric fashion.

"No more Patagonia!" he roared, "no more Tierra del Fuego!" he paused.

"Certainly!" He replied to some question, "but not Patagonia," he paused again, and Fisher standing at the foot of the stairs wondered what had occurred to make the visitor so genial.

"I suppose your cheque will be honoured all right?" asked the visitor sardonically, and then burst into a little chuckle of laughter as he carefully closed the door.

He came down the corridor talking to himself, and greeted Fisher.

"Damn all Greeks," he said jovially, and Fisher could do no more than smile reproachfully, the smile being his very own, the reproach being on behalf of the master who paid him.

The traveller touched the other on the chest with his right hand.

"Never trust a Greek," he said, "always get your money in advance. Is that clear to you?"

"Yes, sir," said Fisher, "but I think you will always find that Mr. Kara is always most generous about money."

"Don't you believe it, don't you believe it, my poor man," said the other, "you—"

At that moment there came from Kara's room a faint "clang."

"What's that?" asked the visitor a little startled.

"Mr. Kara's put down his steel latch," said Fisher with a smile, "which means that he is not to be disturbed until—" he looked at his watch, "until eleven o'clock at any rate."

"He's a funk!" snapped the other, "a beastly funk!"

He stamped down the stairs as though testing the weight of every tread, opened the front door without assistance, slammed it behind him and disappeared into the night.

Fisher, his hands in his pockets, looked after the departing stranger, nodding his head in reprobation.

"You're a queer old devil," he said, and looked at his watch again.

It wanted five minutes to ten.

CHAPTER XIII

"IF you would care to come in, sir, I'm sure Lexman would be glad to see you," said T. X.; "it's very kind of you to take an interest in the matter."

The Chief Commissioner of Police growled something about being paid to take an interest in everybody and strolled with T. X. down one of the apparently endless corridors of Scotland Yard.

"You won't have any bother about the pardon," he said. "I was dining tonight with old man Bartholomew and he will fix that up in the morning."

"There will be no necessity to detain Lexman in custody?" asked T. X.

The Chief shook his head.

"None whatever," he said.

There was a pause, then,

"By the way, did Bartholomew mention Belinda Mary!"

The white-haired chief looked round in astonishment.

"And who the devil is Belinda Mary?" he asked.

T. X. went red.

"Belinda Mary," he said a little quickly, "is Bartholomew's daughter."

"By Jove," said the Commissioner, "now you mention it, he did—she is still in France."

"Oh, is she?" said T. X. innocently, and in his heart of hearts he wished most fervently that she was. They came to the room which Mansus occupied and found that admirable man waiting.

Wherever policemen meet, their conversation naturally drifts to "shop" and in two minutes the three were discussing with some animation and much difference of opinion, as far as T. X. was concerned, a series of frauds which had been perpetrated in the Midlands, and which have nothing to do with this story.

"Your friend is late," said the Chief Commissioner.

"There he is," cried T. X., springing up. He heard a familiar footstep on the flagged corridor, and sprung out of the room to meet the newcomer.

For a moment he stood wringing the hand of this grave man, his heart too full for words.

"My dear chap!" he said at last, "you don't know how glad I am to see you."

John Lexman said nothing, then,

"I am sorry to bring you into this business, T. X.," he said quietly.

"Nonsense," said the other, "come in and see the Chief."

He took John by the arm and led him into the Superintendent's room.

There was a change in John Lexman. A subtle shifting of balance which was not readily discoverable. His face was older, the mobile mouth a little more grimly set, the eyes more deeply lined. He was in evening dress and looked, as T. X. thought, a typical, clean, English gentleman, such an one as any self-respecting valet would be proud to say he had "turned out."

T. X. looking at him carefully could see no great change, save that down one side of his smooth shaven cheek ran the scar of an old wound; which could not have been much more than superficial.

"I must apologize for this kit," said John, taking off his overcoat and laying it across the back of a chair, "but the fact is I was so bored this evening that I had to do something to pass the time away, so I dressed and went to the theatre—and was more bored than ever."

T. X. noticed that he did not smile and that when he spoke it was slowly and carefully, as though he were weighing the value of every word.

"Now," he went on, "I have come to deliver myself into your hands."

"I suppose you have not seen Kara?" said T. X.

"I have no desire to see Kara," was the short reply.

"Well, Mr. Lexman," broke in the Chief, "I don't think you are going to have any difficulty about your escape. By the way, I suppose it was by aeroplane?"

Lexman nodded.

"And you had an assistant?"

Again Lexman nodded.

"Unless you press me I would rather not discuss the matter for some little time, Sir George," he said, "there is much that will happen before the full story of my escape is made known."

Sir George nodded.

"We will leave it at that," he said cheerily, "and now I hope you have come back to delight us all with one of your wonderful plots."

"For the time being I have done with wonderful plots," said John Lexman in that even, deliberate tone of his. "I hope to leave London next week for New York and take up such of the threads of life as remain. The greater thread has gone."

The Chief Commissioner understood.

The silence which followed was broken by the loud and insistent ringing of the telephone bell.

"Hullo," said Mansus rising quickly; "that's Kara's bell."

With two quick strides he was at the telephone and lifted down the receiver.

"Hullo," he cried. "Hullo," he cried again. There was no reply, only the continuous buzzing, and when he hung up the receiver again, the bell continued ringing.

The three policemen looked at one another.

"There's trouble there," said Mansus.

"Take off the receiver," said T. X., "and try again."

Mansus obeyed, but there was no response.

"I am afraid this is not my affair," said John Lexman gathering up his coat. "What do you wish me to do, Sir George?"

"Come along to-morrow morning and see us, Lexman," said Sir George, offering his hand.

"Where are you staying?" asked T. X.

"At the Great Midland," replied the other, "at least my bags have gone on there."

"I'll come along and see you to-morrow morning. It's curious this should have happened the night you returned," he said, gripping the other's shoulder affectionately.

John Lexman did not speak for the moment.

"If anything happened to Kara," he said slowly, "if the worst that was possible happened to him, believe me I should not weep."

T. X. looked down into the other's eyes sympathetically.

"I think he has hurt you pretty badly, old man," he said gently.

John Lexman nodded.

"He has, damn him," he said between his teeth.

The Chief Commissioner's motor car was waiting outside and in this T. X., Mansus, and a detective-sergeant were whirled off to Cadogan Square. Fisher was in the hall when they rung the bell and opened the door instantly.

He was frankly surprised to see his visitors. Mr. Kara was in his room he explained resentfully, as though T. X. should have been aware of the fact without being told. He had heard no bell ringing and indeed had not been summoned to the room.

"I have to see him at eleven o'clock," he said, "and I have had standing instructions not to go to him unless I am sent for."

T. X. led the way upstairs, and went straight to Kara's room. He knocked, but there was no reply. He knocked again and on this failing to evoke any response kicked heavily at the door.

"Have you a telephone downstairs?" he asked.

"Yes, sir," replied Fisher.

T. X. turned to the detective-sergeant.

"'Phone to the Yard," he said, "and get a man up with a bag of tools. We shall have to pick this lock and I haven't got my case with me."

"Picking the lock would be no good, sir," said Fisher, an interested spectator, "Mr. Kara's got the latch down."

"I forgot that," said T. X. "Tell him to bring his saw, we'll have to cut through the panel here."

While they were waiting for the arrival of the police officer T. X. strove to attract the attention of the inmates of the room, but without success.

"Does he take opium or anything!" asked Mansus.

Fisher shook his head.

"I've never known him to take any of that kind of stuff," he said.

T. X. made a rapid survey of the other rooms on that floor. The room next to Kara's was the library, beyond that was a dressing room which, according to Fisher, Miss Holland had used, and at the farthermost end of the corridor was the dining room.

Facing the dining room was a small service lift and by its side a storeroom in which were a number of trunks, including a very large one smothered in injunctions in three different languages to "handle with care." There was nothing else of interest on this floor and the upper and lower floors could wait. In a quarter of an hour the carpenter had arrived from Scotland Yard, and had bored a hole in the rosewood panel of Kara's room and was busily applying his slender saw.

Through the hole he cut T. X. could see no more than that the room was in darkness save for the glow of a blazing fire. He inserted his hand, groped for the knob of the steel latch, which he had remarked on his previous visit to the room, lifted it and the door swung open.

"Keep outside, everybody," he ordered.

He felt for the switch of the electric, found it and instantly the room was flooded with light. The bed was hidden by the open door. T. X. took one stride into the room and saw enough. Kara was lying half on and half off the bed. He was quite dead and the blood-stained patch above his heart told its own story.

T. X. stood looking down at him, saw the frozen horror on the dead man's face, then drew his eyes away and slowly surveyed the room. There in the middle of the carpet he found his clue, a bent and twisted little candle such as you find on children's Christmas trees.

CHAPTER XIV

It was Mansus who found the second candle, a stouter affair. It lay underneath the bed. The telephone, which stood on a fairly large-sized table by the side of the bed, was overturned and the receiver was on the floor. By its side were two books, one being the "Balkan Question," by Villari, and the other "Travels and Politics in the Near East," by Miller. With them was a long, ivory paper-knife.

There was nothing else on the bedside-table save a silver cigarette box. T. X. drew on a pair of gloves and examined the bright surface for finger-prints, but a superficial view revealed no such clue.

"Open the window," said T. X., "the heat here is intolerable. Be very careful, Mansus. By the way, is the window fastened?"

"Very well fastened," said the superintendent after a careful scrutiny.

He pushed back the fastenings, lifted the window and as he did, a harsh bell rang in the basement.

"That is the burglar alarm, I suppose," said T. X.; "go down and stop that bell."

He addressed Fisher, who stood with a troubled face at the door. When he had disappeared T. X. gave a significant glance to one of the waiting officers and the man sauntered after the valet.

Fisher stopped the bell and came back to the hall and stood before the hall fire, a very troubled man. Near the fire was a big, oaken writing table and on this there lay a small envelope which he did not remember having seen before, though it might have been there for some time, for he had spent a greater portion of the evening in the kitchen with the cook.

He picked up the envelope, and, with a start, recognised that it was addressed to himself. He opened it and took out a card. There were only a few words written upon it, but they were sufficient to banish all the colour from his face and set his hands shaking. He took the envelope and card and flung them into the fire.

It so happened that, at that moment, Mansus had called from upstairs, and the officer, who had been told off to keep the valet under observation, ran up in answer to the summons. For a moment Fisher hesitated, then hatless and coatless as he was, he crept to the door, opened it, leaving it ajar behind him and darting down the steps, ran like a hare from the house.

The doctor, who came a little later, was cautious as to the hour of death.

"If you got your telephone message at 10.25, as you say, that was probably the hour he was killed," he said. "I could not tell within half an hour. Obviously the man who killed him gripped his throat with his left hand—there are the bruises on his neck—and stabbed him with the right."

It was at this time that the disappearance of Fisher was noticed, but the cross-examination of the terrified Mrs. Beale removed any doubt that T. X. had as to the man's guilt.

"You had better send out an 'All Stations' message and pull him in," said T. X. "He was with the cook from the moment the visitor left until a few minutes before we rang. Besides which it is obviously impossible for anybody to have got into this room or out again. Have you searched the dead man?"

Mansus produced a tray on which Kara's belongings had been disposed. The ordinary keys Mrs. Beale was able to identify. There were one or two which were beyond her. T. X. recognised one of these as the key of the safe, but two smaller keys baffled him not a little, and Mrs. Beale was at first unable to assist him.

"The only thing I can think of, sir," she said, "is the wine cellar."

"The wine cellar?" said T. X. slowly. "That must be—" he stopped.

The greater tragedy of the evening, with all its mystifying aspects had not banished from his mind the thought of the girl—that Belinda Mary, who had called upon him in her hour of danger as he divined. Perhaps—he descended into the kitchen and was brought face to face with the unpainted door.

"It looks more like a prison than a wine cellar," he said.

"That's what I've always thought, sir," said Mrs. Beale, "and sometimes I've had a horrible feeling of fear."

He cut short her loquacity by inserting one of the keys in the lock—it did not turn, but he had more success with the second. The lock snapped back easily and he pulled the door back. He found the inner door bolted top and bottom. The bolts slipped back in their well-oiled sockets without any effort. Evidently Kara used this place pretty frequently, thought T. X.

He pushed the door open and stopped with an exclamation of surprise. The cellar apartment was brilliantly lit—but it was unoccupied.

"This beats the band," said T. X.

He saw something on the table and lifted it up. It was a pair of long-bladed scissors and about the handle was wound a handkerchief. It was not this fact which startled him, but that the scissors' blades were dappled with blood and blood, too, was on the handkerchief. He unwound the flimsy piece of cambric and stared at the monogram "B. M. B."

He looked around. Nobody had seen the weapon and he dropped it in his overcoat pocket, and walked from the cellar to the kitchen where Mrs. Beale and Mansus awaited him.

"There is a lower cellar, is there not!" he asked in a strained voice.

"That was bricked up when Mr. Kara took the house," explained the woman.

"There is nothing more to look for here," he said.

He walked slowly up the stairs to the library, his mind in a whirl. That he, an accredited officer of police, sworn to the business of criminal detection, should attempt to screen one who was conceivably a criminal was inexplicable. But if the girl had committed this crime, how had she reached Kara's room and why had she returned to the locked cellar!

He sent for Mrs. Beale to interrogate her. She had heard nothing and she had been in the kitchen all the evening. One fact she did reveal, however, that Fisher had gone from the kitchen and had been absent a quarter of an hour and had returned a little agitated.

"Stay here," said T. X., and went down again to the cellar to make a further search.

"Probably there is some way out of this subterranean jail," he thought and a diligent search of the room soon revealed it.

He found the iron trap, pulled it open, and slipped down the stairs. He, too, was puzzled by the luxurious character of the vault. He passed from room to room and finally came to the inner chamber where a light was burning.

The light, as he discovered, proceeded from a small reading lamp which stood by the side of a small brass bedstead. The bed had recently been slept in, but there was no sign of any occupant. T. X. conducted a very careful search and had no difficulty in finding the bricked up door. Other exits there were none.

The floor was of wood block laid on concrete, the ventilation was excellent and in one of the recesses which had evidently held at so time or other, a large wine bin, there was a prefect electrical cooking plant. In a small larder were a number of baskets, bearing the name of a well-known caterer, one of them containing an excellent assortment of cold and potted meats, preserves, etc.

T. X. went back to the bedroom and took the little lamp from the table by the side of the bed and began a more careful examination. Presently he found traces of blood, and followed an irregular trail to the outer room. He lost it suddenly at the foot of stairs leading down from the upper cellar. Then he struck it again. He had reached the end of his electric cord and was now depending upon an electric torch he had taken from his pocket.

There were indications of something heavy having been dragged across the room and he saw that it led to a small bathroom. He had made a cursory examination of this well-appointed apartment, and now he proceeded to make a close investigation and was well rewarded.

The bathroom was the only apartment which possess anything resembling a door—a two-fold screen and—as he pressed this back, he felt some thing which prevented its wider extension. He slipped into the room and flashed his lamp in the space behind the screen. There stiff in death with glazed eyes and lolling tongue lay a great gaunt dog, his yellow fangs exposed in a last grimace.

About the neck was a collar and attached to that, a few links of broken chain. T. X. mounted the steps thoughtfully and passed out to the kitchen.

Did Belinda Mary stab Kara or kill the dog? That she killed one hound or the other was certain. That she killed both was possible.

CHAPTER XV

After a busy and sleepless night he came down to report to the Chief Commissioner the next morning. The evening newspaper bills were filled with the "Chelsea Sensation" but the information given was of a meagre character.

Since Fisher had disappeared, many of the details which could have been secured by the enterprising pressmen were missing. There was no reference to the visit of Mr. Gathercole and in self-defence the press had fallen back upon a statement, which at an earlier period had crept into the newspapers in one of those chatty paragraphs which begin "I saw my friend Kara at Giros" and end with a brief but inaccurate summary of his hobbies. The paragraph had been to the effect that Mr. Kara had been in fear of his life for some time, as a result of a blood feud which existed between himself and another Albanian family. Small wonder, therefore, the murder was everywhere referred to as "the political crime of the century."

"So far," reported T. X. to his superior, "I have been unable to trace either Gathercole or the valet. The only thing we know about Gathercole is that he sent his article to The Times with his card. The servants of his Club are very vague as to his whereabouts. He is a very eccentric man, who only comes in occasionally, and the steward whom I interviewed says that it frequently happened that Gathercole arrived and departed without anybody being aware of the fact. We have been to his old lodgings in Lincoln's Inn, but apparently he sold up there before he went away to the wilds of Patagonia and relinquished his tenancy.

"The only clue I have is that a man answering to some extent to his description left by the eleven o'clock train for Paris last night."

"You have seen the secretary of course," said the Chief.

It was a question which T. X. had been dreading.

"Gone too," he answered shortly; "in fact she has not been seen since 5:30 yesterday evening."

Sir George leant back in his chair and rumpled his thick grey hair.

"The only person who seems to have remained," he said with heavy sarcasm, "was Kara himself. Would you like me to put somebody else on this case—it isn't exactly your job—or will you carry it on?"

"I prefer to carry it on, sir," said T. X. firmly.

"Have you found out anything more about Kara?"

T. X. nodded.

"All that I have discovered about him is eminently discreditable," he said. "He seems to have had an ambition to occupy a very important position in Albania. To this end he had bribed and subsidized the Turkish and Albanian officials and had a fairly large following in that country. Bartholomew tells me that Kara had already sounded him as to the possibility of the British Government recognising a fait accompli in Albania and had been inducing him to use his influence with the Cabinet to recognize the consequence of any revolution. There is no doubt whatever that Kara has engineered all the political assassinations which have been such a feature in the news from Albania during this past year. We also found in the house very large sums of money and documents which we have handed over to the Foreign Office for decoding."

Sir George thought for a long time.

Then he said, "I have an idea that if you find your secretary you will be half way to solving the mystery."

T. X. went out from the office in anything but a joyous mood. He was on his way to lunch when he remembered his promise to call upon John Lexman.

Could Lexman supply a key which would unravel this tragic tangle? He leant out of his taxi-cab and redirected the driver. It happened that the cab drove up to the door of the Great Midland Hotel as John Lexman was coming out.

"Come and lunch with me," said T. X. "I suppose you've heard all the news."

"I read about Kara being killed, if that's what you mean," said the other. "It was rather a coincidence that I should have been discussing the matter last night at the very moment when his telephone bell rang—I wish to heaven you hadn't been in this," he said fretfully.

"Why?" asked the astonished Assistant Commissioner, "and what do you mean by 'in it'?"

"In the concrete sense I wish you had not been present when I returned," said the other moodily, "I wanted to be finished with the whole sordid business without in any way involving my friends."

"I think you are too sensitive," laughed the other, clapping him on the shoulder. "I want you to unburden yourself to me, my dear chap, and tell me anything you can that will help me to clear up this mystery."

John Lexman looked straight ahead with a worried frown.

"I would do almost anything for you, T. X.," he said quietly, "the more so since I know how good you were to Grace, but I can't help you in this matter. I hated Kara living, I hate him dead," he cried, and there was a passion in his voice which was unmistakable; "he was the vilest thing that ever drew the breath of life. There was no villainy too despicable, no cruelty so horrid but that he gloried in it. If ever the devil were incarnate on earth he took the shape and the form of Remington Kara. He died too merciful a death by all accounts. But if there is a God, this man will suffer for his crimes in hell through all eternity."

T. X. looked at him in astonishment. The hate in the man's face took his breath away. Never before had he experienced or witnessed such a vehemence of loathing.

"What did Kara do to you?" he demanded.

The other looked out of the window.

"I am sorry," he said in a milder tone; "that is my weakness. Some day I will tell you the whole story but for the moment it were better that it were not told. I will tell you this," he turned round and faced the detective squarely, "Kara tortured and killed my wife."

T. X. said no more.

Half way through lunch he returned indirectly to the subject.

"Do you know Gathercole?" he asked.

T. X. nodded.

"I think you asked me that question once before, or perhaps it was somebody else. Yes, I know him, rather an eccentric man with an artificial arm."

"That's the cove," said T. X. with a little sigh; "he's one of the few men I want to meet just now."

"Why?"

"Because he was apparently the last man to see Kara alive."

John Lexman looked at the other with an impatient jerk of his shoulders.

"You don't suspect Gathercole, do you?" he asked.

"Hardly," said the other drily; "in the first place the man that committed this murder had two hands and needed them both. No, I only want to ask that gentleman the subject of his conversation. I also want to know who was in the room with Kara when Gathercole went in."

"H'm," said John Lexman.

"Even if I found who the third person was, I am still puzzled as to how they got out and fastened the heavy latch behind them. Now in the old days, Lexman," he said good humouredly, "you would have made a fine mystery story out of this. How would you have made your man escape?"

Lexman thought for a while.

"Have you examined the safe!" he asked.

"Yes," said the other.

"Was there very much in it?"

T. X. looked at him in astonishment.

"Just the ordinary books and things. Why do you ask?"

"Suppose there were two doors to that safe, one on the outside of the room and one on the inside, would it be possible to pass through the safe and go down the wall?"

"I have thought of that," said T. X.

"Of course," said Lexman, leaning back and toying with a salt-spoon, "in writing a story where one hasn't got to deal with the absolute possibilities, one could always have made Kara have a safe of that character in order to make his escape in the event of danger. He might keep a rope ladder stored inside, open the back door, throw out his ladder to a friend and by some trick arrangement could detach the ladder and allow the door to swing to again."

"A very ingenious idea," said T. X., "but unfortunately it doesn't work in this case. I have seen the makers of the safe and there is nothing very eccentric about it except the fact that it is mounted as it is. Can you offer another suggestion?"

John Lexman thought again.

"I will not suggest trap doors, or secret panels or anything so banal," he said, "nor mysterious springs in the wall which, when touched, reveal secret staircases."

He smiled slightly.

"In my early days, I must confess, I was rather keen upon that sort of thing, but age has brought experience and I have discovered the impossibility of bringing an architect to one's way of thinking even in so commonplace a matter as the position of a scullery. It would be much more difficult to induce him to construct a house with double walls and secret chambers."

T. X. waited patiently.

"There is a possibility, of course," said Lexman slowly, "that the steel latch may have been raised by somebody outside by some ingenious magnetic arrangement and lowered in a similar manner."

"I have thought about it," said T. X. triumphantly, "and I have made the most elaborate tests only this morning. It is quite impossible to raise the steel latch because once it is dropped it cannot be raised again except by means of the knob, the pulling of which releases the catch which holds the bar securely in its place. Try another one, John."

John Lexman threw back his head in a noiseless laugh.

"Why I should be helping you to discover the murderer of Kara is beyond my understanding," he said, "but I will give you another theory, at the same time warning you that I may be putting you off the track. For God knows I have more reason to murder Kara than any man in the world."

He thought a while.

"The chimney was of course impossible?"

"There was a big fire burning in the grate," explained T. X.; "so big indeed that the room was stifling."

John Lexman nodded.

"That was Kara's way," he said; "as a matter of fact I know the suggestion about magnetism in the steel bar was impossible, because I was friendly with Kara when he had that bar put in and pretty well know the mechanism, although I had forgotten it for the moment. What is your own theory, by the way?"

T. X. pursed his lips.

"My theory isn't very clearly formed," he said cautiously, "but so far as it goes, it is that Kara was lying on the bed probably reading one of the books which were found by the bedside when his assailant suddenly came upon him. Kara seized the telephone to call for assistance and was promptly killed."

Again there was silence.

"That is a theory," said John Lexman, with his curious deliberation of speech, "but as I say I refuse to be definite—have you found the weapon?"

T. X. shook his head.

"Were there any peculiar features about the room which astonished you, and which you have not told me?"

T. X. hesitated.

"There were two candles," he said, "one in the middle of the room and one under the bed. That in the middle of the room was a small Christmas candle, the one under the bed was the ordinary candle of commerce evidently roughly cut and probably cut in the room. We found traces of candle chips on the floor and it is evident to me that the portion which was cut off was thrown into the fire, for here again we have a trace of grease."

Lexman nodded.

"Anything further?" he asked.

"The smaller candle was twisted into a sort of corkscrew shape."

"The Clue of the Twisted Candle," mused John Lexman "that's a very good title—Kara hated candles."

"Why?"

Lexman leant back in his chair, selected a cigarette from a silver case.

"In my wanderings," he said, "I have been to many strange places. I have been to the country which you probably do not know, and which the traveller who writes books about countries seldom visits. There are queer little villages perched on the spurs of the bleakest hills you ever saw. I have lived with communities which acknowledge no king and no government. These have their laws handed down to them from father to son—it is a nation without a written language. They administer their laws rigidly and drastically. The punishments they award are cruel—inhuman. I have seen, the woman taken in adultery stoned to death as in the best Biblical traditions, and I have seen the thief blinded."

T. X. shivered.

"I have seen the false witness stand up in a barbaric market place whilst his tongue was torn from him. Sometimes the Turks or the piebald governments of the state sent down a few gendarmes and tried a sort of sporadic administration of the country. It usually ended in the representative of the law lapsing into barbarism, or else disappearing from the face of the earth, with a whole community of murderers eager to testify, with singular unanimity, to the fact that he had either committed suicide or had gone off with the wife of one of the townsmen.

"In some of these communities the candle plays a big part. It is not the candle of commerce as you know it, but a dip made from mutton fat. Strap three between the fingers of your hands and keep the hand rigid with two flat pieces of wood; then let the candles burn down lower and lower—can you imagine? Or set a candle in a gunpowder trail and lead the trail to a well-oiled heap of shavings thoughtfully heaped about your naked feet. Or a candle fixed to the shaved head of a man—there are hundreds of variations and the candle plays a part in all of them. I don't know which Kara had cause to hate the worst, but I know one or two that he has employed."

"Was he as bad as that?" asked T. X.

John Lexman laughed.

"You don't know how bad he was," he said.

Towards the end of the luncheon the waiter brought a note in to T. X. which had been sent on from his office.

"Dear Mr. Meredith,

"In answer to your enquiry I believe my daughter is in London, but I did not know it until this morning. My banker informs me that my daughter called at the bank this morning and drew a considerable sum of money from her private account, but where she has gone and what she is doing with the money I do not know. I need hardly tell you that I am very worried about this matter and I should be glad if you could explain what it is all about."

It was signed "William Bartholomew."

T. X. groaned.

"If I had only had the sense to go to the bank this morning, I should have seen her," he said. "I'm going to lose my job over this."

The other looked troubled.

"You don't seriously mean that."

"Not exactly," smiled T. X., "but I don't think the Chief is very pleased with me just now. You see I have butted into this business without any authority—it isn't exactly in my department. But you have not given me your theory about the candles."

"I have no theory to offer," said the other, folding up his serviette; "the candles suggest a typical Albanian murder. I do not say that it was so, I merely say that by their presence they suggest a crime of this character."

With this T. X. had to be content.

If it were not his business to interest himself in commonplace murder—though this hardly fitted such a description—it was part of the peculiar function which his department exercised to restore to Lady Bartholomew a certain very elaborate snuff-box which he discovered in the safe.

Letters had been found amongst his papers which made clear the part which Kara had played. Though he had not been a vulgar blackmailer he had retained his hold, not only upon this particular property of Lady Bartholomew, but upon certain other articles which were discovered, with no other object, apparently, than to compel influence from quarters likely to be of assistance to him in his schemes.

The inquest on the murdered man which the Assistant Commissioner attended produced nothing in the shape of evidence and the coroner's verdict of "murder against some person or persons unknown" was only to be expected.

T. X. spent a very busy and a very tiring week tracing elusive clues which led him nowhere. He had a letter from John Lexman announcing the fact that he intended leaving for the United States. He had received a very good offer from a firm of magazine publishers in New York and was going out to take up the appointment.

Meredith's plans were now in fair shape. He had decided upon the line of action he would take and in the pursuance of this he interviewed his Chief and the Minister of Justice.

"Yes, I have heard from my daughter," said that great man uncomfortably, "and really she has placed me in a most embarrassing position. I cannot tell you, Mr. Meredith, exactly in what manner she has done this, but I can assure you she has."

"Can I see her letter or telegram?" asked T. X.

"I am afraid that is impossible," said the other solemnly; "she begged me to keep her communication very secret. I have written to my wife and asked her to come home. I feel the constant strain to which I am being subjected is more than human can endure."

"I suppose," said T. X. patiently, "it is impossible for you to tell me to what address you have replied?"

"To no address," answered the other and corrected himself hurriedly; "that is to say I only received the telegram—the message this morning and there is no address—to reply to."

"I see," said T. X.

That afternoon he instructed his secretary.

"I want a copy of all the agony advertisements in to-morrow's papers and in the last editions of the evening papers—have them ready for me tomorrow morning when I come."

They were waiting for him when he reached the office at nine o'clock the next day and he went through them carefully. Presently he found the message he was seeking.

B. M. You place me awkward position. Very thoughtless. Have received package addressed your mother which have placed in mother's sitting-room. Cannot understand why you want me to go away week-end and give servants holiday but have done so. Shall require very full explanation. Matter gone far enough. Father.

"This," said T. X. exultantly, as he read the advertisement, "is where I get busy."

CHAPTER XVI

February as a rule is not a month of fogs, but rather a month of tempestuous gales, of frosts and snowfalls, but the night of February 17th, 19—, was one of calm and mist. It was not the typical London fog so dreaded by the foreigner, but one of those little patchy mists which smoke through the streets, now enshrouding and making the nearest object invisible, now clearing away to the finest diaphanous filament of pale grey.

Sir William Bartholomew had a house in Portman Place, which is a wide thoroughfare, filled with solemn edifices of unlovely and forbidding exterior, but remarkably comfortable within. Shortly before eleven on the night of February 17th, a taxi drew up at the junction of Sussex Street and Portman Place, and a girl alighted. The fog at that moment was denser than usual and she hesitated a moment before she left the shelter which the cab afforded.

She gave the driver a few instructions and walked on with a firm step, turning abruptly and mounting the steps of Number 173. Very quickly she inserted her key in the lock, pushed the door open and closed it behind her. She switched on the hall light. The house sounded hollow and deserted, a fact which afforded her considerable satisfaction. She turned the light out and found her way up the broad stairs to the first floor, paused for a moment to switch on another light which she knew would not be observable from the street outside and mounted the second flight.

Miss Belinda Mary Bartholomew congratulated herself upon the success of her scheme, and the only doubt that was in her mind now was whether the boudoir had been locked, but her father was rather careless in such matters and Jacks the butler was one of those dear, silly, old men who never locked anything, and, in consequence, faced every audit with a long face and a longer tale of the peculations of occasional servants.

To her immense relief the handle turned and the door opened to her touch. Somebody had had the sense to pull down the blinds and the curtains were drawn. She switched on the light with a sigh of relief. Her mother's writing table was covered with unopened letters, but she brushed these aside in her search for the little parcel. It was not there and her heart sank. Perhaps she had put it in one of the drawers. She tried them all without result.

She stood by the desk a picture of perplexity, biting a finger thoughtfully.

"Thank goodness!" she said with a jump, for she saw the parcel on the mantel shelf, crossed the room and took it down.

With eager hands she tore off the covering and came to the familiar leather case. Not until she had opened the padded lid and had seen the snuffbox reposing in a bed of cotton wool did she relapse into a long sigh of relief.

"Thank heaven for that," she said aloud.

"And me," said a voice.

She sprang up and turned round with a look of terror.

"Mr.—Mr. Meredith," she stammered.

T. X. stood by the window curtains from whence he had made his dramatic entry upon the scene.

"I say you have to thank me also, Miss Bartholomew," he said presently.

"How do you know my name?" she asked with some curiosity.

"I know everything in the world," he answered, and she smiled. Suddenly her face went serious and she demanded sharply,

"Who sent you after me—Mr. Kara?"

"Mr. Kara?" he repeated, in wonder.

"He threatened to send for the police," she went on rapidly, "and I told him he might do so. I didn't mind the police—it was Kara I was afraid of. You know what I went for, my mother's property."

She held the snuff-box in her outstretched hand.

"He accused me of stealing and was hateful, and then he put me downstairs in that awful cellar and—"

"And?" suggested T. X.

"That's all," she replied with tightened lips; "what are you going to do now?"

"I am going to ask you a few questions if I may," he said. "In the first place have you not heard anything about Mr. Kara since you went away?"

She shook her head.

"I have kept out of his way," she said grimly.

"Have you seen the newspapers?" he asked.

She nodded.

"I have seen the advertisement column—I wired asking Papa to reply to my telegram."

"I know—I saw it," he smiled; "that is what brought me here."

"I was afraid it would," she said ruefully; "father is awfully loquacious in print—he makes speeches you know. All I wanted him to say was yes or no. What do you mean about the newspapers?" she went on. "Is anything wrong with mother?"

He shook his head.

"So far as I know Lady Bartholomew is in the best of health and is on her way home."

"Then what do you mean by asking me about the newspapers!" she demanded; "why should I see the newspapers—what is there for me to see?"

"About Kara?" he suggested.

She shook her head in bewilderment.

"I know and want to know nothing about Kara. Why do you say this to me?"

"Because," said T. X. slowly, "on the night you disappeared from Cadogan Square, Remington Kara was murdered."

"Murdered," she gasped.

He nodded.

"He was stabbed to the heart by some person or persons unknown."

T. X. took his hand from his pocket and pulled something out which was wrapped in tissue paper. This he carefully removed and the girl watched with fascinated gaze, and with an awful sense of apprehension. Presently the object was revealed. It was a pair of scissors with the handle wrapped about with a small handkerchief dappled with brown stains. She took a step backward, raising her hands to her cheeks.

"My scissors," she said huskily; "you won't think—"

She stared up at him, fear and indignation struggling for mastery.

"I don't think you committed the murder," he smiled; "if that's what you mean to ask me, but if anybody else found those scissors and had identified this handkerchief you would have been in rather a fix, my young friend."

She looked at the scissors and shuddered.

"I did kill something," she said in a low voice, "an awful dog... I don't know how I did it, but the beastly thing jumped at me and I just stabbed him and killed him, and I am glad," she nodded many times and repeated, "I am glad."

"So I gather—I found the dog and now perhaps you'll explain why I didn't find you?"

Again she hesitated and he felt that she was hiding something from him.

"I don't know why you didn't find me," she said; "I was there."

"How did you get out?"

"How did you get out?" she challenged him boldly.

"I got out through the door," he confessed; "it seems a ridiculously commonplace way of leaving but that's the only way I could see."

"And that's how I got out," she answered, with a little smile.

"But it was locked."

She laughed.

"I see now," she said; "I was in the cellar. I heard your key in the lock and bolted down the trap, leaving those awful scissors behind. I thought it was Kara with some of his friends and then the voices died away and I ventured to come up and found you had left the door open. So—so I—"

These queer little pauses puzzled T. X. There was something she was not telling him. Something she had yet to reveal.

"So I got away you see," she went on. "I came out into the kitchen; there was nobody there, and I passed through the area door and up the steps and just round the corner I found a taxicab, and that is all."

She spread out her hands in a dramatic little gesture.

"And that is all, is it?" said T. X.

"That is all," she repeated; "now what are you going to do?"

T. X. looked up at the ceiling and stroked his chin.

"I suppose that I ought to arrest you. I feel that something is due from me. May I ask if you were sleeping in the bed downstairs?"

"In the lower cellar?" she demanded,—a little pause and then, "Yes, I was sleeping in the cellar downstairs."

There was that interval of hesitation almost between each word.

"What are you going to do?" she asked again.

She was feeling more sure of herself and had suppressed the panic which his sudden appearance had produced in her. He rumpled his hair, a gross imitation, did she but know it, of one of his chief's mannerisms and she observed that his hair was very thick and inclined to curl. She saw also that he was passably good looking, had fine grey eyes, a straight nose and a most firm chin.

"I think," she suggested gently, "you had better arrest me."

"Don't be silly," he begged.

She stared at him in amazement.

"What did you say?" she asked wrathfully.

"I said 'don't be silly,'" repeated the calm young man.

"Do you know that you're being very rude?" she asked.

He seemed interested and surprised at this novel view of his conduct.

"Of course," she went on carefully smoothing her dress and avoiding his eye, "I know you think I am silly and that I've got a most comic name."

"I have never said your name was comic," he replied coldly; "I would not take so great a liberty."

"You said it was 'weird' which was worse," she claimed.

"I may have said it was 'weird,'" he admitted, "but that's rather different to saying it was 'comic.' There is dignity in weird things. For example, nightmares aren't comic but they're weird."

"Thank you," she said pointedly.

"Not that I mean your name is anything approaching a nightmare." He made this concession with a most magnificent sweep of hand as though he were a king conceding her the right to remain covered in his presence. "I think that Belinda Ann—"

"Belinda Mary," she corrected.

"Belinda Mary, I was going to say, or as a matter of fact," he floundered, "I was going to say Belinda and Mary."

"You were going to say nothing of the kind," she corrected him.

"Anyway, I think Belinda Mary is a very pretty name."

"You think nothing of the sort."

She saw the laughter in his eyes and felt an insane desire to laugh.

"You said it was a weird name and you think it is a weird name, but I really can't be bothered considering everybody's views. I think it's a weird name, too. I was named after an aunt," she added in self-defence.

"There you have the advantage of me," he inclined his head politely; "I was named after my father's favourite dog."

"What does T. X. stand for?" she asked curiously.

"Thomas Xavier," he said, and she leant back in the big chair on the edge of which a few minutes before she had perched herself in trepidation and dissolved into a fit of immoderate laughter.

"It is comic, isn't it?" he asked.

"Oh, I am sorry I'm so rude," she gasped. "Fancy being called Tommy Xavier—I mean Thomas Xavier."

"You may call me Tommy if you wish—most of my friends do."

"Unfortunately I'm not your friend," she said, still smiling and wiping the tears from her eyes, "so I shall go on calling you Mr. Meredith if you don't mind."

She looked at her watch.

"If you are not going to arrest me I'm going," she said.

"I have certainly no intention of arresting you," said he, "but I am going to see you home!"

She jumped up smartly.

"You're not," she commanded.

She was so definite in this that he was startled.

"My dear child," he protested.

"Please don't 'dear child' me," she said seriously; "you're going to be a good little Tommy and let me go home by myself."

She held out her hand frankly and the laughing appeal in her eyes was irresistible.

"Well, I'll see you to a cab," he insisted.

"And listen while I give the driver instructions where he is to take me?"

She shook her head reprovingly.

"It must be an awful thing to be a policeman."

He stood back with folded arms, a stern frown on his face.

"Don't you trust me?" he asked.

"No," she replied.

"Quite right," he approved; "anyway I'll see you to the cab and you can tell the driver to go to Charing Cross station and on your way you can change your direction."

"And you promise you won't follow me?" she asked.

"On my honour," he swore; "on one condition though."

"I will make no conditions," she replied haughtily.

"Please come down from your great big horse," he begged, "and listen to reason. The condition I make is that I can always bring you to an appointed rendezvous whenever I want you. Honestly, this is necessary, Belinda Mary."

"Miss Bartholomew," she corrected, coldly.

"It is necessary," he went on, "as you will understand. Promise me that, if I put an advertisement in the agonies of either an evening paper which I will name or in the Morning Port, you will keep the appointment I fix, if it is humanly possible."

She hesitated a moment, then held out her hand.

"I promise," she said.

"Good for you, Belinda Mary," said he, and tucking her arm in his he led her out of the room switching off the light and racing her down the stairs.

If there was a lot of the schoolgirl left in Belinda Mary Bartholomew, no less of the schoolboy was there in this Commissioner of Police. He would have danced her through the fog, contemptuous of the proprieties, but he wasn't so very anxious to get her to her cab and to lose sight of her.

"Good-night," he said, holding her hand.

"That's the third time you've shaken hands with me to-night," she interjected.

"Don't let us have any unpleasantness at the last," he pleaded, "and remember."

"I have promised," she replied.

"And one day," he went on, "you will tell me all that happened in that cellar."

"I have told you," she said in a low voice.

"You have not told me everything, child."

He handed her into the cab. He shut the door behind her and leant through the open window.

"Victoria or Marble Arch?" he asked politely.

"Charing Cross," she replied, with a little laugh.

He watched the cab drive away and then suddenly it stopped and a figure lent out from the window beckoning him frantically. He ran up to her.

"Suppose I want you," she asked.

"Advertise," he said promptly, "beginning your advertisement 'Dear Tommy.'"

"I shall put 'T. X.,'" she said indignantly.

"Then I shall take no notice of your advertisement," he replied and stood in the middle of the street, his hat in his hand, to the intense annoyance of a taxi-cab driver who literally all but ran him down and in a figurative sense did so until T. X. was out of earshot.

CHAPTER XVII

Thomas Xavier Meredith was a shrewd young man. It was said of him by Signor Paulo Coselli, the eminent criminologist, that he had a gift of intuition which was abnormal. Probably the mystery of the twisted candle was solved by him long before any other person in the world had the dimmest idea that it was capable of solution.

The house in Cadogan Square was still in the hands of the police. To this house and particularly to Kara's bedroom T. X. from time to time repaired, and reproduced as far as possible the conditions which obtained on the night of the murder. He had the same stifling fire, the same locked door. The latch was dropped in its socket, whilst T. X., with a stop watch in his hand, made elaborate calculations and acted certain parts which he did not reveal to a soul.

Three times, accompanied by Mansus, he went to the house, three times went to the death chamber and was alone on one occasion for an hour and a half whilst the patient Mansus waited outside. Three times he emerged looking graver on each occasion, and after the third visit he called into consultation John Lexman.

Lexman had been spending some time in the country, having deferred his trip to the United States.

"This case puzzles me more and more, John," said T. X., troubled out of his usual boisterous self, "and thank heaven it worries other people besides me. De Mainau came over from France the other day and brought all his best sleuths, whilst O'Grady of the New York central office paid a flying visit just to get hold of the facts. Not one of them has given me the real solution, though they've all been rather ingenious. Gathercole has vanished and is probably on his way to some undiscoverable region, and our people have not yet traced the valet."

"He should be the easiest for you," said John Lexman, reflectively.

"Why Gathercole should go off I can't understand," T. X. continued. "According to the story which was told me by Fisher, his last words to Kara were to the effect that he was expecting a cheque or that he had received a cheque. No cheque has been presented or drawn and apparently Gathercole has gone off without waiting for any payment. An examination of Kara's books show nothing against the Gathercole account save the sum of 600 pounds which was originally advanced, and now to upset all my calculations, look at this."

He took from his pocketbook a newspaper cutting and pushed it across the table, for they were dining together at the Carlton. John Lexman picked up the slip and read. It was evidently from a New York paper:

"Further news has now come to hand by the Antarctic Trading Company's steamer, Cyprus, concerning the wreck of the City of the Argentine. It is believed that this ill-fated vessel, which called at South American ports, lost her propellor and drifted south out of the track of shipping. This theory is now confirmed.

Apparently the ship struck an iceberg on December 23rd and foundered with all aboard save a few men who were able to launch a boat and who were picked up by the Cyprus. The following is the passenger list."

John Lexman ran down the list until he came upon the name which was evidently underlined in ink by T. X. That name was George Gathercole and after it in brackets (Explorer).

"If that were true, then, Gathercole could not have come to London."

"He may have taken another boat," said T. X., "and I cabled to the Steamship Company without any great success. Apparently Gathercole was an eccentric sort of man and lived in terror of being overcrowded. It was a habit of his to make provisional bookings by every available steamer. The company can tell me no more than that he had booked, but whether he shipped on the City of the Argentine or not, they do not know."

"I can tell you this about Gathercole," said John slowly and thoughtfully, "that he was a man who would not hurt a fly. He was incapable of killing any man, being constitutionally averse to taking life in any shape. For this reason he never made collections of butterflies or of bees, and I believe has never shot an animal in his life. He carried his principles to such an extent that he was a vegetarian—poor old Gathercole!" he said, with the first smile which T. X. had seen on his face since he came back.

"If you want to sympathize with anybody," said T. X. gloomily, "sympathize with me."

On the following day T. X. was summoned to the Home Office and went steeled for a most unholy row. The Home Secretary, a large and worthy gentleman, given to the making of speeches on every excuse, received him, however, with unusual kindness.

"I've sent for you, Mr. Meredith," he said, "about this unfortunate Greek. I've had all his private papers looked into and translated and in some cases decoded, because as you are probably aware his diaries and a great deal of his correspondence were in a code which called for the attention of experts."

T. X. had not troubled himself greatly about Kara's private papers but had handed them over, in accordance with instructions, to the proper authorities.

"Of course, Mr. Meredith," the Home Secretary went on, beaming across his big table, "we expect you to continue your search for the murderer, but I must confess that your prisoner when you secure him will have a very excellent case to put to a jury."

"That I can well believe, sir," said T. X.

"Seldom in my long career at the bar," began the Home Secretary in his best oratorical manner, "have I examined a record so utterly discreditable as that of the deceased man."

Here he advanced a few instances which surprised even T. X.

"The man was a lunatic," continued the Home Secretary, "a vicious, evil man who loved cruelty for cruelty's sake. We have in this diary alone sufficient evidence to convict him of three separate murders, one of which was committed in this country."

T. X. looked his astonishment.

"You will remember, Mr. Meredith, as I saw in one of your reports, that he had a chauffeur, a Greek named Poropulos."

T. X. nodded.

"He went to Greece on the day following the shooting of Vassalaro," he said.

The Home Secretary shook his head.

"He was killed on the same night," said the Minister, "and you will have no difficulty in finding what remains of his body in the disused house which Kara rented for his own purpose on the Portsmouth Road. That he has killed a number of people in Albania you may well suppose. Whole villages have been wiped out to provide him with a little excitement. The man was a Nero without any of Nero's amiable weaknesses. He was obsessed with the idea that he himself was in danger of assassination, and saw an enemy even in his trusty servant. Undoubtedly the chauffeur Poropulos was in touch with several Continental government circles. You understand," said the Minister in conclusion, "that I am telling you this, not with the idea of expecting you, to relax your efforts to find the murderer and clear up the mystery, but in order that you may know something of the possible motive for this man's murder."

T. X. spent an hour going over the decoded diary and documents and left the Home Office a little shakily. It was inconceivable, incredible. Kara was a lunatic, but the directing genius was a devil.

T. X. had a flat in Whitehall Gardens and thither he repaired to change for dinner. He was half dressed when the evening paper arrived and he glanced as was his wont first at the news' page and then at the advertisement column. He looked down the column marked "Personal" without expecting to find anything of particular interest to himself, but saw that which made him drop the paper and fly round the room in a frenzy to complete his toilet.

"Tommy X.," ran the brief announcement, "most urgent, Marble Arch 8."

He had five minutes to get there but it seemed like five hours. He was held up at almost every crossing and though he might have used his authority to obtain right of way, it was a step which his curious sense of honesty prevented him taking. He leapt out of the cab before it stopped, thrust the fare into the driver's hands and looked round for the girl. He saw her at last and walked quickly towards her. As he approached her, she turned about and with an almost imperceptible beckoning gesture walked away. He followed her along the Bayswater Road and gradually drew level.

"I am afraid I have been watched," she said in a low voice. "Will you call a cab?"

He hailed a passing taxi, helped her in and gave at random the first place that suggested itself to him, which was Finsbury Park.

"I am very worried," she said, "and I don't know anybody who can help me except you."

"Is it money?" he asked.

"Money," she said scornfully, "of course it isn't money. I want to show you a letter," she said after a while.

She took it from her bag and gave it to him and he struck a match and read it with difficulty.

It was written in a studiously uneducated hand.

> "Dear Miss,
>
> "I know who you are. You are wanted by the police but I will not give you away. Dear Miss. I am very hard up and 20 pounds will be very useful to me and I shall not trouble you again. Dear Miss. Put the money on the window sill of your room. I know you sleep on the ground floor and I will come in and take it. And if not—well, I don't want to make any trouble.
>
> "Yours truly,
>
> "A FRIEND."

"When did you get this?" he asked.

"This morning," she replied. "I sent the Agony to the paper by telegram, I knew you would come."

"Oh, you did, did you?" he said.

Her assurance was very pleasing to him. The faith that her words implied gave him an odd little feeling of comfort and happiness.

"I can easily get you out of this," he added; "give me your address and when the gentleman comes—"

"That is impossible," she replied hurriedly. "Please don't think I'm ungrateful, and don't think I'm being silly—you do think I'm being silly, don't you!"

"I have never harboured such an unworthy thought," he said virtuously.

"Yes, you have," she persisted, "but really I can't tell you where I am living. I have a very special reason for not doing so. It's not myself that I'm thinking about, but there's a life involved."

This was a somewhat dramatic statement to make and she felt she had gone too far.

"Perhaps I don't mean that," she said, "but there is some one I care for—" she dropped her voice.

"Oh," said T. X. blankly.

He came down from his rosy heights into the shadow and darkness of a sunless valley.

"Some one you care for," he repeated after a while.

"Yes."

There was another long silence, then,

"Oh, indeed," said T. X.

Again the unbroken interval of quiet and after a while she said in a low voice, "Not that way."

"Not what way!" asked T. X. huskily, his spirits doing a little mountaineering.

"The way you mean," she said.

"Oh," said T. X.

He was back again amidst the rosy snows of dawn, was in fact climbing a dizzy escalier on the topmost height of hope's Mont Blanc when she pulled the ladder from under him.

"I shall, of course, never marry," she said with a certain prim decision.

T. X. fell with a dull sickening thud, discovering that his rosy snows were not unlike cold, hard ice in their lack of resilience.

"Who said you would?" he asked somewhat feebly, but in self defence.

"You did," she said, and her audacity took his breath away.

"Well, how am I to help you!" he asked after a while.

"By giving me some advice," she said; "do you think I ought to put the money there!"

"Indeed I do not," said T. X., recovering some of his natural dominance; "apart from the fact that you would be compounding a felony, you would merely be laying out trouble for yourself in the future. If he can get 20 pounds so easily, he will come for 40 pounds. But why do you stay away, why don't you return home? There's no charge and no breath of suspicion against you."

"Because I have something to do which I have set my mind to," she said, with determination in her tones.

"Surely you can trust me with your address," he urged her, "after all that has passed between us, Belinda Mary—after all the years we have known one another."

"I shall get out and leave you," she said steadily.

"But how the dickens am I going to help you?" he protested.

"Don't swear," she could be very severe indeed; "the only way you can help me is by being kind and sympathetic."

"Would you like me to burst into tears?" he asked sarcastically.

"I ask you to do nothing more painful or repugnant to your natural feelings than to be a gentleman," she said.

"Thank you very kindly," said T. X., and leant back in the cab with an air of supreme resignation.

"I believe you're making faces in the dark," she accused him.

"God forbid that I should do anything so low," said he hastily; "what made you think that?"

"Because I was putting my tongue out at you," she admitted, and the taxi driver heard the shrieks of laughter in the cab behind him above the wheezing of his asthmatic engine.

At twelve that night in a certain suburb of London an overcoated man moved stealthily through a garden. He felt his way carefully along the wall of the house and groped with hope, but with no great certainty, along the window sill. He found an envelope which his fingers, somewhat sensitive from long employment in nefarious uses, told him contained nothing more substantial than a letter.

He went back through the garden and rejoined his companion, who was waiting under an adjacent lamp-post.

"Did she drop?" asked the other eagerly.

"I don't know yet," growled the man from the garden.

He opened the envelope and read the few lines.

"She hasn't got the money," he said, "but she's going to get it. I must meet her to-morrow afternoon at the corner of Oxford Street and Regent Street."

"What time!" asked the other.

"Six o'clock," said the first man. "The chap who takes the money must carry a copy of the Westminster Gazette in his hand."

"Oh, then it's a plant," said the other with conviction.

The other laughed.

"She won't work any plants. I bet she's scared out of her life."

The second man bit his nails and looked up and down the road, apprehensively.

"It's come to something," he said bitterly; "we went out to make our thousands and we've come down to 'chanting' for 20 pounds."

"It's the luck," said the other philosophically, "and I haven't done with her by any means. Besides we've still got a chance of pulling of the big thing, Harry. I reckon she's good for a hundred or two, anyway."

At six o'clock on the following afternoon, a man dressed in a dark overcoat, with a soft felt hat pulled down over his eyes stood nonchalantly by the curb near where the buses stop at Regent Street slapping his hand gently with a folded copy of the Westminster Gazette.

That none should mistake his Liberal reading, he stood as near as possible to a street lamp and so arranged himself and his attitude that the minimum of light should fall upon his face and the maximum upon that respectable organ of public opinion. Soon after six he saw the girl approaching, out of the tail of his eye, and strolled off to meet her. To his surprise she passed him by and he was turning to follow when an unfriendly hand gripped him by the arm.

"Mr. Fisher, I believe," said a pleasant voice.

"What do you mean?" said the man, struggling backward.

"Are you going quietly!" asked the pleasant Superintendent Mansus, "or shall I take my stick to you'?"

Mr. Fisher thought awhile.

"It's a cop," he confessed, and allowed himself to be hustled into the waiting cab.

He made his appearance in T. X.'s office and that urbane gentleman greeted him as a friend.

"And how's Mr. Fisher!" he asked; "I suppose you are Mr. Fisher still and not Mr. Harry Gilcott, or Mr. George Porten."

Fisher smiled his old, deferential, deprecating smile.

"You will always have your joke, sir. I suppose the young lady gave me away."

"You gave yourself away, my poor Fisher," said T. X., and put a strip of paper before him; "you may disguise your hand, and in your extreme modesty pretend to an ignorance of the British language, which is not creditable to your many attainments, but what you must be awfully careful in doing in future when you write such epistles," he said, "is to wash your hands."

"Wash my hands!" repeated the puzzled Fisher.

T. X. nodded.

"You see you left a little thumb print, and we are rather whales on thumb prints at Scotland Yard, Fisher."

"I see. What is the charge now, sir!"

"I shall make no charge against you except the conventional one of being a convict under license and failing to report."

Fisher heaved a sigh.

"That'll only mean twelve months. Are you going to charge me with this business?" he nodded to the paper.

T. X. shook his head.

"I bear you no ill-will although you tried to frighten Miss Bartholomew. Oh yes, I know it is Miss Bartholomew, and have known all the time. The lady is there for a reason which is no business of yours or of mine. I shall not charge you with attempt to blackmail and in reward for my leniency I hope you are going to tell me all you know about the Kara murder. You wouldn't like me to charge you with that, would you by any chance!"

Fisher drew a long breath.

"No, sir, but if you did I could prove my innocence," he said earnestly. "I spent the whole of the evening in the kitchen."

"Except a quarter of an hour," said T. X.

The man nodded.

"That's true, sir, I went out to see a pal of mine."

"The man who is in this!" asked T. X.

Fisher hesitated.

"Yes, sir. He was with me in this but there was nothing wrong about the business—as far as we went. I don't mind admitting that I was planning a Big Thing. I'm not going to blow on it, if it's going to get me into trouble, but if you'll promise me that it won't, I'll tell you the whole story."

"Against whom was this coup of yours planned?"

"Against Mr. Kara, sir," said Fisher.

"Go on with your story," nodded T. X.

The story was a short and commonplace one. Fisher had met a man who knew another man who was either a Turk or an Albanian. They had learnt that Kara was in the habit of keeping large sums of money in the house and they had planned to rob him. That was the story in a nutshell. Somewhere the plan miscarried. It was when he came to the incidents that occurred on the night of the murder that T. X. followed him with the greatest interest.

"The old gentleman came in," said Fisher, "and I saw him up to the room. I heard him coming out and I went up and spoke to him while he was having a chat with Mr. Kara at the open door."

"Did you hear Mr. Kara speak?"

"I fancy I did, sir," said Fisher; "anyway the old gentleman was quite pleased with himself."

"Why do you say 'old gentleman'!" asked T. X.; "he was not an old man."

"Not exactly, sir," said Fisher, "but he had a sort of fussy irritable way that old gentlemen sometimes have and I somehow got it fixed in my mind that he was old. As a matter of fact, he was about forty-five, he may have been fifty."

"You have told me all this before. Was there anything peculiar about him!"

Fisher hesitated.

"Nothing, sir, except the fact that one of his arms was a game one."

"Meaning that it was—"

"Meaning that it was an artificial one, sir, so far as I can make out."

"Was it his right or his left arm that was game!" interrupted T. X.

"His left arm, sir."

"You're sure?"

"I'd swear to it, sir."

"Very well, go on."

"He came downstairs and went out and I never saw him again. When you came and the murder was discovered and knowing as I did that I had my own scheme on and that one of your splits might pinch me, I got a bit rattled. I went downstairs to the hall and the first thing I saw lying on the table was a letter. It was addressed to me."

He paused and T. X. nodded.

"Go on," he said again.

"I couldn't understand how it came to be there, but as I'd been in the kitchen most of the evening except when I was seeing my pal outside to tell him the job was off for that night, it might have been there before you came. I opened the letter. There were only a few words on it and I can tell you those few words made my heart jump up into my mouth, and made me go cold all over."

"What were they!" asked T. X.

"I shall not forget them, sir. They're sort of permanently fixed in my brain," said the man earnestly; "the note started with just the figures 'A. C. 274.'"

"What was that!" asked T. X.

"My convict number when I was in Dartmoor Prison, sir."

"What did the note say?"

"'Get out of here quick'—I don't know who had put it there, but I'd evidently been spotted and I was taking no chances. That's the whole story from beginning to end. I accidentally happened to meet the young lady, Miss Holland—Miss Bartholomew as she is—and followed her to her house in Portman Place. That was the night you were there."

T. X. found himself to his intense annoyance going very red.

"And you know no more?" he asked.

"No more, sir—and if I may be struck dead—"

"Keep all that sabbath talk for the chaplain," commended T. X., and they took away Mr. Fisher, not an especially dissatisfied man.

That night T. X. interviewed his prisoner at Cannon Row police station and made a few more enquiries.

"There is one thing I would like to ask you," said the girl when he met her next morning in Green Park.

"If you were going to ask whether I made enquiries as to where your habitation was," he warned her, "I beg of you to refrain."

She was looking very beautiful that morning, he thought. The keen air had brought a colour to her face and lent a spring to her gait, and, as she strode along by his side with the free and careless swing of youth, she was an epitome of the life which even now was budding on every tree in the park.

"Your father is back in town, by the way," he said, "and he is most anxious to see you."

She made a little grimace.

"I hope you haven't been round talking to father about me."

"Of course I have," he said helplessly; "I have also had all the reporters up from Fleet Street and given them a full description of your escapades."

She looked round at him with laughter in her eyes.

"You have all the manners of an early Christian martyr," she said. "Poor soul! Would you like to be thrown to the lions?"

"I should prefer being thrown to the demnition ducks and drakes," he said moodily.

"You're such a miserable man," she chided him, "and yet you have everything to make life worth living."

"Ha, ha!" said T. X.

"You have, of course you have! You have a splendid position. Everybody looks up to you and talks about you. You have got a wife and family who adore you—"

He stopped and looked at her as though she were some strange insect.

"I have a how much?" he asked credulously.

"Aren't you married?" she asked innocently.

He made a strange noise in his throat.

"Do you know I have always thought of you as married," she went on; "I often picture you in your domestic circle reading to the children from the Daily Megaphone those awfully interesting stories about Little Willie Waterbug."

He held on to the railings for support.

"May we sit down?" he asked faintly.

She sat by his side, half turned to him, demure and wholly adorable.

"Of course you are right in one respect," he said at last, "but you're altogether wrong about the children."

"Are you married!" she demanded with no evidence of amusement.

"Didn't you know?" he asked.

She swallowed something.

"Of course it's no business of mine and I'm sure I hope you are very happy."

"Perfectly happy," said T. X. complacently. "You must come out and see me one Saturday afternoon when I am digging the potatoes. I am a perfect devil when they let me loose in the vegetable garden."

"Shall we go on?" she said.

He could have sworn there were tears in her eyes and manlike he thought she was vexed with him at his fooling.

"I haven't made you cross, have I?" he asked.

"Oh no," she replied.

"I mean you don't believe all this rot about my being married and that sort of thing?"

"I'm not interested," she said, with a shrug of her shoulders, "not very much. You've been very kind to me and I should be an awful boor if I wasn't grateful. Of course, I don't care whether you're married or not, it's nothing to do with me, is it?"

"Naturally it isn't," he replied. "I suppose you aren't married by any chance?"

"Married," she repeated bitterly; "why, you will make my fourth!"

She had hardy got the words out of her mouth before she realized her terrible error. A second later she was in his arms and he was kissing her to the scandal of one aged park keeper, one small and dirty-faced little boy and a moulting duck who seemed to sneer at the proceedings which he watched through a yellow and malignant eye.

"Belinda Mary," said T. X. at parting, "you have got to give up your little country establishment, wherever it may be and come back to the discomforts of Portman Place. Oh, I know you can't come back yet. That 'somebody' is there, and I can pretty well guess who it is."

"Who?" she challenged.

"I rather fancy your mother has come back," he suggested.

A look of scorn dawned into her pretty face.

"Good lord, Tommy!" she said in disgust, "you don't think I should keep mother in the suburbs without her telling the world all about it!"

"You're an undutiful little beggar," he said.

They had reached the Horse Guards at Whitehall and he was saying good-bye to her.

"If it comes to a matter of duty," she answered, "perhaps you will do your duty and hold up the traffic for me and let me cross this road."

"My dear girl," he protested, "hold up the traffic?"

"Of course," she said indignantly, "you're a policeman."

"Only when I am in uniform," he said hastily, and piloted her across the road.

It was a new man who returned to the gloomy office in Whitehall. A man with a heart that swelled and throbbed with the pride and joy of life's most precious possession.

CHAPTER XVIII

T. X. sat at his desk, his chin in his hands, his mind remarkably busy. Grave as the matter was which he was considering, he rose with alacrity to meet the smiling girl who was ushered through the door by Mansus, preternaturally solemn and mysterious.

She was radiant that day. Her eyes were sparkling with an unusual brightness.

"I've got the most wonderful thing to tell you," she said, "and I can't tell you."

"That's a very good beginning," said T. X., taking her muff from her hand.

"Oh, but it's really wonderful," she cried eagerly, "more wonderful than anything you have ever heard about."

"We are interested," said T. X. blandly.

"No, no, you mustn't make fun," she begged, "I can't tell you now, but it is something that will make you simply—" she was at a loss for a simile.

"Jump out of my skin?" suggested T. X.

"I shall astonish you," she nodded her head solemnly.

"I take a lot of astonishing, I warn you," he smiled; "to know you is to exhaust one's capacity for surprise."

"That can be either very, very nice or very, very nasty," she said cautiously.

"But accept it as being very, very nice," he laughed. "Now come, out with this tale of yours."

She shook her head very vigorously.

"I can't possibly tell you anything," she said.

"Then why the dickens do you begin telling anything for?" he complained, not without reason.

"Because I just want you to know that I do know something."

"Oh, Lord!" he groaned. "Of course you know everything. Belinda Mary, you're really the most wonderful child."

He sat on the edge of her arm-chair and laid his hand on her shoulder.

"And you've come to take me out to lunch!"

"What were you worrying about when I came in?" she asked.

He made a little gesture as if to dismiss the subject.

"Nothing very much. You've heard me speak of John Lexman?"

She bent her head.

"Lexman's the writer of a great many mystery stories, but you've probably read his books."

She nodded again, and again T. X. noticed the suppressed eagerness in her eyes.

"You're not ill or sickening for anything, are you?" he asked anxiously; "measles, or mumps or something?"

"Don't be silly," she said; "go on and tell me something about Mr. Lexman."

"He's going to America," said T. X., "and before he goes he wants to give a little lecture."

"A lecture?"

"It sounds rum, doesn't it, but that's just what he wants to do."

"Why is he doing it!" she asked.

T. X. made a gesture of despair.

"That is one of the mysteries which may never be revealed to me, except—" he pursed his lips and looked thoughtfully at the girl. "There are times," he said, "when there is a great struggle going on inside a man between all the human and better part of him and the baser professional part of him. One side of me wants to hear this lecture of John Lexman's very much, the other shrinks from the ordeal."

"Let us talk it over at lunch," she said practically, and carried him off.

CHAPTER XIX

One would not readily associate the party of top-booted sewermen who descend nightly to the subterranean passages of London with the stout viceconsul at Durazzo. Yet it was one unimaginative man who lived in Lambeth and had no knowledge that there was such a place as Durazzo who was responsible for bringing this comfortable official out of his bed in the early hours of the morning causing him—albeit reluctantly and with violent and insubordinate language—to conduct certain investigations in the crowded bazaars.

At first he was unsuccessful because there were many Hussein Effendis in Durazzo. He sent an invitation to the American Consul to come over to tiffin and help him.

"Why the dickens the Foreign Office should suddenly be interested in Hussein Effendi, I cannot for the life of me understand."

"The Foreign Department has to be interested in something, you know," said the genial American. "I receive some of the quaintest requests from Washington; I rather fancy they only wire you to find if they are there."

"Why are you doing this!"

"I've seen Hakaat Bey," said the English official. "I wonder what this fellow has been doing? There is probably a wigging for me in the offing."

At about the same time the sewerman in the bosom of his own family was taking loud and noisy sips from a big mug of tea.

"Don't you be surprised," he said to his admiring better half, "if I have to go up to the Old Bailey to give evidence."

"Lord! Joe!" she said with interest, "what has happened!"

The sewer man filled his pipe and told the story with a wealth of rambling detail. He gave particulars of the hour he had descended the Victoria Street shaft, of what Bill Morgan had said to him as they were going down, of what he had said to Harry Carter as they splashed along the low-roofed tunnel, of how he had a funny feeling that he was going to make a discovery, and so on and so forth until he reached his long delayed climax.

T. X. waited up very late that night and at twelve o'clock his patience was rewarded, for the Foreign Office messenger brought a telegram to him. It was addressed to the Chief Secretary and ran:

"No. 847. Yours 63952 of yesterday's date. Begins. Hussein Effendi a prosperous merchant of this city left for Italy to place his daughter in convent Marie Theressa, Florence Hussein being Christian. He goes on to Paris. Apply Ralli Theokritis et Cie., Rue de l'Opera. Ends."

Half an hour later T. X. had a telephone connection through to Paris and was instructing the British police agent in that city. He received a further telephone report from Paris the next morning and one which gave him infinite satisfaction. Very slowly but surely he was gathering together the pieces of this baffling mystery and was fitting them together. Hussein Effendi would probably supply the last missing segments.

At eight o'clock that night the door opened and the man who represented T. X. in Paris came in carrying a travelling ulster on his arm. T. X. gave him a nod and then, as the newcomer stood with the door open, obviously waiting for somebody to follow him, he said,

"Show him in—I will see him alone."

There walked into his office, a tall man wearing a frock coat and a red fez. He was a man from fifty-five to sixty, powerfully built, with a grave dark face and a thin fringe of white beard. He salaamed as he entered.

"You speak French, I believe," said T. X. presently.

The other bowed.

"My agent has explained to you," said T. X. in French, "that I desire some information for the purpose of clearing up a crime which has been committed in this country. I have given you my assurance, if that assurance was necessary, that you would come to no harm as a result of anything you might tell me."

"That I understand, Effendi," said the tall Turk; "the Americans and the English have always been good friends of mine and I have been frequently in London. Therefore, I shall be very pleased to be of any help to you."

T. X. walked to a closed bookcase on one side of the room, unlocked it, took out an object wrapped in white tissue paper. He laid this on the table, the Turk watching the proceedings with an impassive face. Very slowly the Commissioner unrolled the little bundle and revealed at last a long, slim knife, rusted and stained, with a hilt, which in its untarnished days had evidently been of chased silver. He lifted the dagger from the table and handed it to the Turk.

"This is yours, I believe," he said softly.

The man turned it over, stepping nearer the table that he might secure the advantage of a better light. He examined the blade near the hilt and handed the weapon back to T. X.

"That is my knife," he said.

T. X. smiled.

"You understand, of course, that I saw 'Hussein Effendi of Durazzo' inscribed in Arabic near the hilt."

The Turk inclined his head.

"With this weapon," T. X. went on, speaking with slow emphasis, "a murder was committed in this town."

There was no sign of interest or astonishment, or indeed of any emotion whatever.

"It is the will of God," he said calmly; "these things happen even in a great city like London."

"It was your knife," suggested T. X.

"But my hand was in Durazzo, Effendi," said the Turk.

He looked at the knife again.

"So the Black Roman is dead, Effendi."

"The Black Roman?" asked T. X., a little puzzled.

"The Greek they call Kara," said the Turk; "he was a very wicked man."

T. X. was up on his feet now, leaning across the table and looking at the other with narrowed eyes.

"How did you know it was Kara?" he asked quickly.

The Turk shrugged his shoulders.

"Who else could it be?" he said; "are not your newspapers filled with the story?"

T. X. sat back again, disappointed and a little annoyed with himself.

"That is true, Hussein Effendi, but I did not think you read the papers."

"Neither do I, master," replied the other coolly, "nor did I know that Kara had been killed until I saw this knife. How came this in your possession!"

"It was found in a rain sewer," said T. X., "into which the murderer had apparently dropped it. But if you have not read the newspapers, Effendi, then you admit that you know who committed this murder."

The Turk raised his hands slowly to a level with his shoulders.

"Though I am a Christian," he said, "there are many wise sayings of my father's religion which I remember. And one of these, Effendi, was, 'the wicked must die in the habitations of the just, by the weapons of the worthy shall the wicked perish.' Your Excellency, I am a worthy man, for never have I done a dishonest thing in my life. I have traded fairly with Greeks, with Italians, have with Frenchmen and with Englishmen, also with Jews. I have never sought to rob them nor to hurt them. If I have killed men, God knows it was not because I desired their death, but because their lives were dangerous to me and to mine. Ask the blade all your questions and see what answer it gives. Until it speaks I am as dumb as the blade, for it is also written that 'the soldier is the servant of his sword,' and also, 'the wise servant is dumb about his master's affairs.'"

T. X. laughed helplessly.

"I had hoped that you might be able to help me, hoped and feared," he said; "if you cannot speak it is not my business to force you either by threat or by act. I am grateful to you for having come over, although the visit has been rather fruitless so far as I am concerned."

He smiled again and offered his hand.

"Excellency," said the old Turk soberly, "there are some things in life that are well left alone and there are moments when justice should be so blind that she does not see guilt; here is such a moment."

And this ended the interview, one on which T. X. had set very high hopes. His gloom carried to Portman Place, where he had arranged to meet Belinda Mary.

"Where is Mr. Lexman going to give this famous lecture of his?" was the question with which she greeted him, "and, please, what is the subject?"

"It is on a subject which is of supreme interest to me;" he said gravely; "he has called his lecture 'The Clue of the Twisted Candle.' There is no clearer brain being employed in the business of criminal detection than John Lexman's. Though he uses his genius for the construction of stories, were it employed in the legitimate business of police work, I am certain he would make a mark second to none in the world. He is determined on giving this lecture and he has issued a number of invitations. These include the Chiefs of the Secret Police of nearly all the civilized countries of the world. O'Grady is on his way from America, he wirelessed me this morning to that effect. Even the Chief of the Russian police has accepted the invitation, because, as you know, this murder has excited a great deal of interest in police circles everywhere. John Lexman is not only going to deliver this lecture," he said slowly, "but he is going to tell us who committed the murder and how it was committed."

She thought a moment.

"Where will it be delivered!"

"I don't know," he said in astonishment; "does that matter?"

"It matters a great deal," she said emphatically, "especially if I want it delivered in a certain place. Would you induce Mr. Lexman to lecture at my house?"

"At Portman Place!" he asked.

She shook her head.

"No, I have a house of my own. A furnished house I have rented at Blackheath. Will you induce Mr. Lexman to give the lecture there?"

"But why?" he asked.

"Please don't ask questions," she pleaded, "do this for me, Tommy."

He saw she was in earnest.

"I'll write to old Lexman this afternoon," he promised.

John Lexman telephoned his reply.

"I should prefer somewhere out of London," he said, "and since Miss Bartholomew has some interest in the matter, may I extend my invitation to her? I promise she shall not be any more shocked than a good woman need be."

And so it came about that the name of Belinda Mary Bartholomew was added to the selected list of police chiefs, who were making for London at that moment to hear from the man who had guaranteed the solution of the story of Kara and his killing; the unravelment of the mystery which surrounded his death, and the significance of the twisted candles, which at that moment were reposing in the Black Museum at Scotland Yard.

CHAPTER XX

The room was a big one and most of the furniture had been cleared out to admit the guests who had come from the ends of the earth to learn the story of the twisted candles, and to test John Lexman's theory by their own.

They sat around chatting cheerfully of men and crimes, of great coups planned and frustrated, of strange deeds committed and undetected. Scraps of their conversation came to Belinda Mary as she stood in the chintz-draped doorway which led from the drawing-room to the room she used as a study.

"... do you remember, Sir George, the Bolbrook case! I took the man at Odessa...."

"... the curious thing was that I found no money on the body, only a small gold charm set with a single emerald, so I knew it was the girl with the fur bonnet who had..."

"... Pinot got away after putting three bullets into me, but I dragged myself to the window and shot him dead—it was a real good shot...!"

They rose to meet her and T. X. introduced her to the men. It was at that moment that John Lexman was announced.

He looked tired, but returned the Commissioner's greeting with a cheerful mien. He knew all the men present by name, as they knew him. He had a few sheets of notes, which he laid on the little table which had been placed for him, and when the introductions were finished he went to this and with scarcely any preliminary began.

CHAPTER XXI

THE NARRATIVE OF JOHN LEXMAN

"I am, as you may all know, a writer of stories which depend for their success upon the creation and unravelment of criminological mysteries. The Chief Commissioner has been good enough to tell you that my stories were something more than a mere seeking after sensation, and that I endeavoured in the course of those narratives to propound obscure but possible situations, and, with the ingenuity that I could command, to offer to those problems a solution acceptable, not only to the general reader, but to the police expert.

"Although I did not regard my earlier work with any great seriousness and indeed only sought after exciting situations and incidents, I can see now, looking back, that underneath the work which seemed at the time purposeless, there was something very much like a scheme of studies.

"You must forgive this egotism in me because it is necessary that I should make this explanation and you, who are in the main police officers of considerable experience and discernment, should appreciate the fact that as I was able to get inside the minds of the fictitious criminals I portrayed, so am I now able to follow the mind of the man who committed this murder, or if not to follow his mind, to recreate the psychology of the slayer of Remington Kara.

"In the possession of most of you are the vital facts concerning this man. You know the type of man he was, you have instances of his terrible ruthlessness, you know that he was a blot upon God's earth, a vicious wicked ego, seeking the gratification of that strange blood-lust and pain-lust, which is to be found in so few criminals."

John Lexman went on to describe the killing of Vassalaro.

"I know now how that occurred," he said. "I had received on the previous Christmas eve amongst other presents, a pistol from an unknown admirer. That unknown admirer was Kara, who had planned this murder some three months ahead. He it was, who sent me the Browning, knowing as he did that I had never used such a weapon and that therefore I would be chary about using it. I might have put the pistol away in a cupboard out of reach and the whole of his carefully thought out plan would have miscarried.

"But Kara was systematic in all things. Three weeks after I received the weapon, a clumsy attempt was made to break into my house in the middle of the night. It struck me at the time it was clumsy, because the burglar made a tremendous amount of noise and disappeared soon after he began his attempt, doing no more damage than to break a window in my dining-room. Naturally my mind went to the possibility of a further attempt of this kind, as my house stood on the outskirts of the village, and it was only natural that I should take the pistol from one of my boxes and put it somewhere handy. To make doubly sure, Kara came down the next day and heard the full story of the outrage.

"He did not speak of pistols, but I remember now, though I did not remember at the time, that I mentioned the fact that I had a handy weapon. A fortnight later a second attempt was made to enter the house. I say an attempt, but again I do not believe that the intention was at all serious. The outrage was designed to keep that pistol of mine in a get-at-able place.

"And again Kara came down to see us on the day following the burglary, and again I must have told him, though I have no distinct recollection of the fact, of what had happened the previous night. It would have been unnatural if I had not mentioned the fact, as it was a matter which had formed a subject of discussion between myself, my wife and the servants.

"Then came the threatening letter, with Kara providentially at hand. On the night of the murder, whilst Kara was still in my house, I went out to find his chauffeur. Kara remained a few minutes with my wife and then on some excuse went into the library. There he loaded the pistol, placing one cartridge in the chamber, and trusting to luck that I did not pull the trigger until I had it pointed at my victim. Here he took his biggest chance, because, before sending the weapon to me, he had had the spring of the Browning so eased that the slightest touch set it off and, as you know, the pistol being automatic, the explosion of one cartridge, reloading and firing the next and so on, it was probably that a chance touch would have brought his scheme to nought—probably me also.

"Of what happened on that night you are aware."

He went on to tell of his trial and conviction and skimmed over the life he led until that morning on Dartmoor.

"Kara knew my innocence had been proved and his hatred for me being his great obsession, since I had the thing he had wanted but no longer wanted, let that be understood—he saw the misery he had planned for me and my dear wife being brought to a sudden end. He had, by the way, already planned and carried his plan into execution, a system of tormenting her.

"You did not know," he turned to T. X., "that scarcely a month passed, but some disreputable villain called at her flat, with a story that he had been released from Portland or Wormwood Scrubbs that morning and that he had seen me. The story each messenger brought was one sufficient to break the heart of any but the bravest woman. It was a story of ill-treatment by brutal officials, of my illness, of my madness, of everything calculated to harrow the feelings of a tender-hearted and faithful wife.

"That was Kara's scheme. Not to hurt with the whip or with the knife, but to cut deep at the heart with his evil tongue, to cut to the raw places of the mind. When he found that I was to be released,—he may have guessed, or he may have discovered by some underhand method; that a pardon was about to be signed,—he conceived his great plan. He had less than two days to execute it.

"Through one of his agents he discovered a warder who had been in some trouble with the authorities, a man who was avaricious and was even then on the brink of being discharged from the service for trafficking with prisoners. The bribe he offered this man was a heavy one and the warder accepted.

"Kara had purchased a new monoplane and as you know he was an excellent aviator. With this new machine he flew to Devon and arrived at dawn in one of the unfrequented parts of the moor.

"The story of my own escape needs no telling. My narrative really begins from the moment I put my foot upon the deck of the Mpret. The first person I asked to see was, naturally, my wife. Kara, however, insisted on my going to the cabin he had prepared and changing my clothes, and until then I did not realise I was still in my convict's garb. A clean change was waiting for me, and the luxury of soft shirts and well-fitting garments after the prison uniform I cannot describe.

"After I was dressed I was taken by the Greek steward to the larger stateroom and there I found my darling waiting for me."

His voice sank almost to a whisper, and it was a minute or two before he had mastered his emotions.

"She had been suspicious of Kara, but he had been very insistent. He had detailed the plans and shown her the monoplane, but even then she would not trust herself on board, and she had been waiting in a motor-boat, moving parallel with the yacht, until she saw the landing and realized, as she thought, that Kara was not playing her false. The motor-boat had been hired by Kara and the two men inside were probably as well-bribed as the warder.

"The joy of freedom can only be known to those who have suffered the horrors of restraint. That is a trite enough statement, but when one is describing elemental things there is no room for subtlety. The voyage was a fairly eventless one. We saw very little of Kara, who did not intrude himself upon us, and our main excitement lay in the apprehension that we should be held up by a British destroyer or, that when we reached Gibraltar, we should be searched by the Brit's authorities. Kara had foreseen that possibility and had taken in enough coal to last him for the run.

"We had a fairly stormy passage in the Mediterranean, but after that nothing happened until we arrived at Durazzo. We had to go ashore in disguise, because Kara told us that the English Consul might see us and make some trouble. We wore Turkish dresses, Grace heavily veiled and I wearing a greasy old kaftan which, with my somewhat emaciated face and my unshaven appearance, passed me without comment.

"Kara's home was and is about eighteen miles from Durazzo. It is not on the main road, but it is reached by following one of the rocky mountain paths which wind and twist among the hills to the south-east of the town. The country is wild and mainly uncultivated. We had to pass through swamps and skirt huge lagoons as we mounted higher and higher from terrace to terrace and came to the roads which crossed the mountains.

"Kara's, palace, you could call it no less, is really built within sight of the sea. It is on the Acroceraunian Peninsula near Cape Linguetta. Hereabouts the country is more populated and better cultivated. We passed great slopes entirely covered with mulberry and olive trees, whilst in the valleys there were fields of maize and corn. The palazzo stands on a lofty plateau. It is approached by two paths, which can be and have been well defended in the past against the Sultan's troops or against the bands which have been raised by rival villages with the object of storming and plundering this stronghold.

"The Skipetars, a blood-thirsty crowd without pity or remorse, were faithful enough to their chief, as Kara was. He paid them so well that it was not profitable to rob him; moreover he kept their own turbulent elements fully occupied with the little raids which he or his agents organized from time to time. The palazzo was built rather in the Moorish than in the Turkish style.

"It was a sort of Eastern type to which was grafted an Italian architecture—a house of white-columned courts, of big paved yards, fountains and cool, dark rooms.

"When I passed through the gates I realized for the first time something of Kara's importance. There were a score of servants, all Eastern, perfectly trained, silent and obsequious. He led us to his own room.

"It was a big apartment with divans running round the wall, the most ornate French drawing room suite and an enormous Persian carpet, one of the finest of the kind that has ever been turned out of Shiraz. Here, let me say, that throughout the trip his attitude to me had been perfectly friendly and towards Grace all that I could ask of my best friend, considerate and tactful.

"'We had hardly reached his room before he said to me with that bonhomie which he had observed throughout the trip, 'You would like to see your room?'

"I expressed a wish to that effect. He clapped his hands and a big Albanian servant came through the curtained doorway, made the usual salaam, and Kara spoke to him a few words in a language which I presume was Turkish.

"'He will show you the way,' said Kara with his most genial smile.

"I followed the servant through the curtains which had hardly fallen behind me before I was seized by four men, flung violently on the ground, a filthy tarbosch was thrust into my mouth and before I knew what was happening I was bound hand and foot.

"As I realised the gross treachery of the man, my first frantic thoughts were of Grace and her safety. I struggled with the strength of three men, but they were too many for me and I was dragged along the passage, a door was opened and I was flung into a bare room. I must have been lying on the floor for half an hour when they came for me, this time accompanied by a middle-aged man named Savolio, who was either an Italian or a Greek.

"He spoke English fairly well and he made it clear to me that I had to behave myself. I was led back to the room from whence I had come and found Kara sitting in one of those big armchairs which he affected, smoking a cigarette. Confronting him, still in her Turkish dress, was poor Grace. She was not bound I was pleased to see, but when on my entrance she rose and made as if to come towards me, she was unceremoniously thrown back by the guardian who stood at her side.

"'Mr. John Lexman,' drawled Kara, 'you are at the beginning of a great disillusionment. I have a few things to tell you which will make you feel rather uncomfortable.' It was then that I heard for the first time that my pardon had been signed and my innocence discovered.

"'Having taken a great deal of trouble to get you in prison,' said Kara, 'it isn't likely that I'm going to allow all my plans to be undone, and my plan is to make you both extremely uncomfortable.'

"He did not raise his voice, speaking still in the same conversational tone, suave and half amused.

"'I hate you for two things,' he said, and ticked them off on his fingers: 'the first is that you took the woman that I wanted. To a man of my temperament that is an unpardonable crime. I have never wanted women either as friends or as amusement. I am one of the few people in the world who are self-sufficient. It happened that I wanted your wife and she rejected me because apparently she preferred you.'

"He looked at me quizzically.

"'You are thinking at this moment,' he went on slowly, 'that I want her now, and that it is part of my revenge that I shall put her straight in my harem. Nothing is farther from my desires or my thoughts. The Black Roman is not satisfied with the leavings of such poor trash as you. I hate you both equally and for both of you there is waiting an experience more terrible than even your elastic imagination can conjure. You understand what that means!' he asked me still retaining his calm.

"I did not reply. I dared not look at Grace, to whom he turned.

"'I believe you love your husband, my friend,' he said; 'your love will be put to a very severe test. You shall see him the mere wreckage of the man he is. You shall see him brutalized below the level of the cattle in the field. I will give you both no joys, no ease of mind. From this moment you are slaves, and worse than slaves.'

"He clapped his hands. The interview was ended and from that moment I only saw Grace once."

John Lexman stopped and buried his face in his hands.

"They took me to an underground dungeon cut in the solid rock. In many ways it resembled the dungeon of the Chateau of Chillon, in that its only window looked out upon a wild, storm-swept lake and its floor was jagged rock. I have called it underground, as indeed it was on that side, for the palazzo was built upon a steep slope running down from the spur of the hills.

"They chained me by the legs and left me to my own devices. Once a day they gave me a little goat flesh and a pannikin of water and once a week Kara would come in and outside the radius of my chain he would open a little camp stool and sitting down smoke his cigarette and talk. My God! the things that man said! The things he described! The horrors he related! And always it was Grace who was the centre of his description. And he would relate the stories he was telling to her about myself. I cannot describe them. They are beyond repetition."

John Lexman shuddered and closed his eyes.

"That was his weapon. He did not confront me with the torture of my darling, he did not bring tangible evidence of her suffering—he just sat and talked, describing with a remarkable clarity of language which seemed incredible in a foreigner, the 'amusements' which he himself had witnessed.

"I thought I should go mad. Twice I sprang at him and twice the chain about my legs threw me headlong on that cruel floor. Once he brought the jailer in to whip me, but I took the whipping with such phlegm that it gave him no satisfaction. I told you I had seen Grace only once and this is how it happened.

"It was after the flogging, and Kara, who was a veritable demon in his rage, planned to have his revenge for my indifference. They brought Grace out upon a boat and rowed the boat to where I could see it from my window. There the whip which had been applied to me was applied to her. I can't tell you any more about that," he said brokenly, "but I wish, you don't know how fervently, that I had broken down and given the dog the satisfaction he wanted. My God! It was horrible!

"When the winter came they used to take me out with chains on my legs to gather in wood from the forest. There was no reason why I should be given this work, but the truth was, as I discovered from Salvolio, that Kara thought my dungeon was too warm. It was sheltered from the winds by the hill behind and even on the coldest days and nights it was not unbearable. Then Kara went away for some time. I think he must have gone to England, and he came back in a white fury. One of his big plans had gone wrong and the mental torture he inflicted upon me was more acute than ever.

"In the old days he used to come once a week; now he came almost every day. He usually arrived in the afternoon and I was surprised one night to be awakened from my sleep to see him standing at the door, a lantern in his hand, his inevitable cigarette in his mouth. He always wore the Albanian costume when he was in the country, those white kilted skirts and zouave jackets which the hillsmen affect and, if anything, it added to his demoniacal appearance. He put down the lantern and leant against the wall.

"'I'm afraid that wife of yours is breaking up, Lexman,' he drawled; 'she isn't the good, stout, English stuff that I thought she was.'

"I made no reply. I had found by bitter experience that if I intruded into the conversation, I should only suffer the more.

"'I have sent down to Durazzo to get a doctor,' he went on; 'naturally having taken all this trouble I don't want to lose you by death. She is breaking up,' he repeated with relish and yet with an undertone of annoyance in his voice; 'she asked for you three times this morning.'

"I kept myself under control as I had never expected that a man so desperately circumstanced could do.

"'Kara,' I said as quietly as I could, 'what has she done that she should deserve this hell in which she has lived?'

"He sent out a long ring of smoke and watched its progress across the dungeon.

"'What has she done?' he said, keeping his eye on the ring—I shall always remember every look, every gesture, and every intonation of his voice. 'Why, she has done all that a woman can do for a man like me. She has made me feel little. Until I had a rebuff from her, I had all the world at my feet, Lexman. I did as I liked. If I crooked my little finger, people ran after me and that one experience with her has broken me. Oh, don't think,' he went on quickly, 'that I am broken in love. I never loved her very much, it was just a passing passion, but she killed my self-confidence. After then, whenever I came to a crucial moment in my affairs, when the big manner, the big certainty was absolutely necessary for me to carry my way, whenever I was most confident of myself and my ability and my scheme, a vision of this damned girl rose and I felt that momentary weakening, that memory of defeat, which made all the difference between success and failure.

"'I hated her and I hate her still,' he said with vehemence; 'if she dies I shall hate her more because she will remain everlastingly unbroken to menace my thoughts and spoil my schemes through all eternity.'

"He leant forward, his elbows on his knees, his clenched fist under his chin—how well I can see him!—and stared at me.

"'I could have been king here in this land,' he said, waving his hand toward the interior, 'I could have bribed and shot my way to the throne of Albania. Don't you realize what that means to a man like me? There is still a chance and if I could keep your wife alive, if I could see her broken in reason and in health, a poor, skeleton, gibbering thing that knelt at my feet when I came near her I should recover the mastery of myself. Believe me,' he said, nodding his head, 'your wife will have the best medical advice that it is possible to obtain.'

"Kara went out and I did not see him again for a very long time. He sent word, just a scrawled note in the morning, to say my wife had died."

John Lexman rose up from his seat, and paced the apartment, his head upon his breast.

"From that moment," he said, "I lived only for one thing, to punish Remington Kara. And gentlemen, I punished him."

He stood in the centre of the room and thumped his broad chest with his clenched hand.

"I killed Remington Kara," he said, and there was a little gasp of astonishment from every man present save one. That one was T. X. Meredith, who had known all the time.

CHAPTER XXII

After a while Lexman resumed his story.

"I told you that there was a man at the palazzo named Salvolio. Salvolio was a man who had been undergoing a life sentence in one of the prisons of southern Italy. In some mysterious fashion he escaped and got across the Adriatic in a small boat. How Kara found him I don't know. Salvolio was a very uncommunicative person. I was never certain whether he was a Greek or an Italian. All that I am sure about is that he was the most unmitigated villain next to his master that I have ever met.

"He was a quick man with his knife and I have seen him kill one of the guards whom he had thought was favouring me in the matter of diet with less compunction than you would kill a rat.

"It was he who gave me this scar," John Lexman pointed to his cheek. "In his master's absence he took upon himself the task of conducting a clumsy imitation of Kara's persecution. He gave me, too, the only glimpse I ever had of the torture poor Grace underwent. She hated dogs, and Kara must have come to know this and in her sleeping room—she was apparently better accommodated than I—he kept four fierce beasts so chained that they could almost reach her.

"Some reference to my wife from this low brute maddened me beyond endurance and I sprang at him. He whipped out his knife and struck at me as I fell and I escaped by a miracle. He evidently had orders not to touch me, for he was in a great panic of mind, as he had reason to be, because on Kara's return he discovered the state of my face, started an enquiry and had Salvolio taken to the courtyard in the true eastern style and bastinadoed until his feet were pulp.

"You may be sure the man hated me with a malignity which almost rivalled his employer's. After Grace's death Kara went away suddenly and I was left to the tender mercy of this man. Evidently he had been given a fairly free hand. The principal object of Kara's hate being dead, he took little further interest in me, or else wearied of his hobby. Salvolio began his persecutions by reducing my diet. Fortunately I ate very little. Nevertheless the supplies began to grow less and less, and I was beginning to feel the effects of this starvation system when there happened a thing which changed the whole course of my life and opened to me a way to freedom and to vengeance.

"Salvolio did not imitate the austerity of his master and in Kara's absence was in the habit of having little orgies of his own. He would bring up dancing girls from Durazzo for his amusement and invite prominent men in the neighbourhood to his feasts and entertainments, for he was absolutely lord of the palazzo when Kara was away and could do pretty well as he liked. On this particular night the festivities had been more than usually prolonged, for as near as I could judge by the day-light which was creeping in through my window it was about four o'clock in the morning when the big steel-sheeted door was opened and Salvolio came in, more than a little drunk. He brought with him, as I judged, one of his dancing girls, who apparently was privileged to see the sights of the palace.

"For a long time he stood in the doorway talking incoherently in a language which I think must have been Turkish, for I caught one or two words.

"Whoever the girl was, she seemed a little frightened, I could see that, because she shrank back from him though his arm was about her shoulders and he was half supporting his weight upon her. There was fear, not only in the curious little glances she shot at me from time to time, but also in the averted face. Her story I was to learn. She was not of the class from whence Salvolio found the dancers who from time to time came up to the palace for his amusement and the amusement of his guests. She was the daughter of a Turkish merchant of Scutari who had been received into the Catholic Church.

"Her father had gone down to Durazzo during the first Balkan war and then Salvolio had seen the girl unknown to her parent, and there had been some rough kind of courtship which ended in her running away on this very day and joining her ill-favoured lover at the palazzo. I tell you this because the fact had some bearing on my own fate.

"As I say, the girl was frightened and made as though to go from the dungeon. She was probably scared both by the unkempt prisoner and by the drunken man at her side. He, however, could not leave without showing to her something of his authority. He came lurching over near where I lay, his long knife balanced in his hand ready for emergencies, and broke into a string of vituperations of the character to which I was quite hardened.

"Then he took a flying kick at me and got home in my ribs, but again I experienced neither a sense of indignity nor any great hurt. Salvolio had treated me like this before and I had survived it. In the midst of the tirade, looking past him, I was a new witness to an extraordinary scene.

"The girl stood in the open doorway, shrinking back against the door, looking with distress and pity at the spectacle which Salvolio's brutality afforded. Then suddenly there appeared beside her a tall Turk. He was grey-bearded and forbidding. She looked round and saw him, and her mouth opened to utter a cry, but with a gesture he silenced her and pointed to the darkness outside.

"Without a word she cringed past him, her sandalled feet making no noise. All this time Salvolio was continuing his stream of abuse, but he must have seen the wonder in my eyes for he stopped and turned.

"The old Turk took one stride forward, encircled his body with his left arm, and there they stood grotesquely like a couple who were going to start to waltz. The Turk was a head taller than Salvolio and, as I could see, a man of immense strength.

"They looked at one another, face to face, Salvolio rapidly recovering his senses... and then the Turk gave him a gentle punch in the ribs. That is what it seemed like to me, but Salvolio coughed horribly, went limp in the other's arms and dropped with a thud to the ground. The Turk leant down soberly and wiped his long knife on the other's jacket before he put it back in the sash at his waist.

"Then with a glance at me he turned to go, but stopped at the door and looked back thoughtfully. He said something in Turkish which I could not understand, then he spoke in French.

"'Who are you?' he asked.

"In as few words as possible I explained. He came over and looked at the manacle about my leg and shook his head.

"'You will never be able to get that undone,' he said.

"He caught hold of the chain, which was a fairly long one, bound it twice round his arm and steadying his arm across his thigh, he turned with a sudden jerk. There was a smart 'snap' as the chain parted. He caught me by the shoulder and pulled me to my feet. 'Put the chain about your waist, Effendi,' he said, and he took a revolver from his belt and handed it to me.

"'You may need this before we get back to Durazzo,' he said. His belt was literally bristling with weapons—I saw three revolvers beside the one I possessed—and he had, evidently come prepared for trouble. We made our way from the dungeon into the clean-smelling world without.

"It was the second time I had been in the open air for eighteen months and my knees were trembling under me with weakness and excitement. The old man shut the prison door behind us and walked on until we came up to the girl waiting for us by the lakeside. She was weeping softly and he spoke to her a few words in a low voice and her weeping ceased.

"'This daughter of mine will show us the way,' he said, 'I do not know this part of the country—she knows it too well.'

"To cut a long story short," said Lexman, "we reached Durazzo in the afternoon. There was no attempt made to follow us up and neither my absence nor the body of Salvolio were discovered until late in the afternoon. You must remember that nobody but Salvolio was allowed into my prison and therefore nobody had the courage to make any investigations.

"The old man got me to his house without being observed, and brought a brother-in-law or some relative of his to remove the anklet. The name of my host was Hussein Effendi.

"That same night we left with a little caravan to visit some of the old man's relatives. He was not certain what would be the consequence of his act, and for safety's sake took this trip, which would enable him if need be to seek sanctuary with some of the wilder Turkish tribes, who would give him protection.

"In that three months I saw Albania as it is—it was an experience never to be forgotten!

"If there is a better man in God's world than Hiabam Hussein Effendi, I have yet to meet him. It was he who provided me with money to leave Albania. I begged from him, too, the knife with which he had killed Salvolio. He had discovered that Kara was in England and told me something of the Greek's occupation which I had not known before. I crossed to Italy and went on to Milan. There it was that I learnt that an eccentric Englishman who had arrived a few days previously on one of the South American boats at Genoa, was in my hotel desperately ill.

"My hotel I need hardly tell you was not a very expensive one and we were evidently the only two Englishmen in the place. I could do no less than go up and see what I could do for the poor fellow who was pretty well gone when I saw him. I seemed to remember having seen him before and when looking round for some identification I discovered his name I readily recalled the circumstance.

"It was George Gathercole, who had returned from South America. He was suffering from malarial fever and blood poisoning and for a week, with an Italian doctor, I fought as hard as any man could fight for his life. He was a trying patient," John Lexman smiled suddenly at the recollection, "vitriolic in his language, impatient and imperious in his attitude to his friends. He was, for example, terribly sensitive about his lost arm and would not allow either the doctor or my-self to enter the room until he was covered to the neck, nor would he eat or drink in our presence. Yet he was the bravest of the brave, careless of himself and only fretful because he had not time to finish his new book. His indomitable spirit did not save him. He died on the 17th of January of this year. I was in Genoa at the time, having gone there at his request to save his belongings. When I returned he had been buried. I went through his papers and it was then that I conceived my idea of how I might approach Kara.

"I found a letter from the Greek, which had been addressed to Buenos Ayres, to await arrival, and then I remembered in a flash, how Kara had told me he had sent George Gathercole to South America to report upon possible gold formations. I was determined to kill Kara, and determined to kill him in such a way that I myself would cover every trace of my complicity.

"Even as he had planned my downfall, scheming every step and covering his trail, so did I plan to bring about his death that no suspicion should fall on me.

"I knew his house. I knew something of his habits. I knew the fear in which he went when he was in England and away from the feudal guards who had surrounded him in Albania. I knew of his famous door with its steel latch and I was planning to circumvent all these precautions and bring to him not only the death he deserved, but a full knowledge of his fate before he died.

"Gathercole had some money,—about 140 pounds—I took 100 pounds of this for my own use, knowing that I should have sufficient in London to recompense his heirs, and the remainder of the money with all such documents as he had, save those which identified him with Kara, I handed over to the British Consul.

"I was not unlike the dead man. My beard had grown wild and I knew enough of Gathercole's eccentricities to live the part. The first step I took was to announce my arrival by inference. I am a fairly good journalist with a wide general knowledge and with this, corrected by reference to the necessary books which I found in the British Museum library, I was able to turn out a very respectable article on Patagonia.

"This I sent to The Times with one of Gathercole's cards and, as you know, it was printed. My next step was to find suitable lodgings between Chelsea and Scotland Yard. I was fortunate in being able to hire a furnished flat, the owner of which was going to the south of France for three months. I paid the rent in advance and since I dropped all the eccentricities I had assumed to support the character of Gathercole, I must have impressed the owner, who took me without references.

"I had several suits of new clothes made, not in London," he smiled, "but in Manchester, and again I made myself as trim as possible to avoid after-identification. When I had got these together in my flat, I chose my day. In the morning I sent two trunks with most of my personal belongings to the Great Midland Hotel.

"In the afternoon I went to Cadogan Square and hung about until I saw Kara drive off. It was my first view of him since I had left Albania and it required all my self-control to prevent me springing at him in the street and tearing at him with my hands.

"Once he was out of sight I went to the house adopting all the style and all the mannerisms of poor Gathercole. My beginning was unfortunate for, with a shock, I recognised in the valet a fellow-convict who had been with me in the warder's cottage on the morning of my escape from Dartmoor. There was no mistaking him, and when I heard his voice I was certain. Would he recognise me I wondered, in spite of my beard and my eye-glasses?

"Apparently he did not. I gave him every chance. I thrust my face into his and on my second visit challenged him, in the eccentric way which poor old Gathercole had, to test the grey of my beard. For the moment however, I was satisfied with my brief experiment and after a reasonable interval I went away, returning to my place off Victoria Street and waiting till the evening.

"In my observation of the house, whilst I was waiting for Kara to depart, I had noticed that there were two distinct telephone wires running down to the roof. I guessed, rather than knew, that one of these telephones was a private wire and, knowing something of Kara's fear, I presumed that that wire would lead to a police office, or at any rate to a guardian of some kind or other. Kara had the same arrangement in Albania, connecting the palazzo with the gendarme posts at Alesso. This much Hussein told me.

"That night I made a reconnaissance of the house and saw Kara's window was lit and at ten minutes past ten I rang the bell and I think it was then that I applied the test of the beard. Kara was in his room, the valet told me, and led the way upstairs. I had come prepared to deal with this valet for I had an especial reason for wishing that he should not be interrogated by the police. On a plain card I had written the number he bore in Dartmoor and had added the words, 'I know you, get out of here quick.'

"As he turned to lead the way upstairs I flung the envelope containing the card on the table in the hall. In an inside pocket, as near to my body as I could put them, I had the two candles. How I should use them both I had already decided. The valet ushered me into Kara's room and once more I stood in the presence of the man who had killed my girl and blotted out all that was beautiful in life for me."

There was a breathless silence when he paused. T. X. leaned back in his chair, his head upon his breast, his arms folded, his eyes watching the other intently.

The Chief Commissioner, with a heavy frown and pursed lips, sat stroking his moustache and looking under his shaggy eyebrows at the speaker. The French police officer, his hands thrust deep in his pockets, his head on one side, was taking in every word eagerly. The sallow-faced Russian, impassive of face, might have been a carved ivory mask. O'Grady, the American, the stump of a dead cigar between his teeth, shifted impatiently with every pause as though he would hurry forward the denouement.

Presently John Lexman went on.

"He slipped from the bed and came across to meet me as I closed the door behind me.

"'Ah, Mr. Gathercole,' he said, in that silky tone of his, and held out his hand.

"I did not speak. I just looked at him with a sort of fierce joy in my heart the like of which I had never before experienced.

"'And then he saw in my eyes the truth and half reached for the telephone.

"But at that moment I was on him. He was a child in my hands. All the bitter anguish he had brought upon me, all the hardships of starved days and freezing nights had strengthened and hardened me. I had come back to London disguised with a false arm and this I shook free. It was merely a gauntlet of thin wood which I had had made for me in Paris.

"I flung him back on the bed and half knelt, half laid on him.

"'Kara,' I said, 'you are going to die, a more merciful death than my wife died.'

"He tried to speak. His soft hands gesticulated wildly, but I was half lying on one arm and held the other.

"I whispered in his ear:

"'Nobody will know who killed you, Kara, think of that! I shall go scot free—and you will be the centre of a fine mystery! All your letters will be read, all your life will be examined and the world will know you for what you are!'

"I released his arm for just as long as it took to draw my knife and strike. I think he died instantly," John Lexman said simply.

"I left him where he was and went to the door. I had not much time to spare. I took the candles from my pocket. They were already ductile from the heat of my body.

"I lifted up the steel latch of the door and propped up the latch with the smaller of the two candles, one end of which was on the middle socket and the other beneath the latch. The heat of the room I knew would still further soften the candle and let the latch down in a short time.

"I was prepared for the telephone by his bedside though I did not know to whither it led. The presence of the paper-knife decided me. I balanced it across the silver cigarette box so that one end came under the telephone receiver; under the other end I put the second candle which I had to cut to fit. On top of the paper-knife at the candle end I balanced the only two books I could find in the room, and fortunately they were heavy.

"I had no means of knowing how long it would take to melt the candle to a state of flexion which would allow the full weight of the books to bear upon the candle end of the paper-knife and fling off the receiver. I was hoping that Fisher had taken my warning and had gone. When I opened the door softly, I heard his footsteps in the hall below. There was nothing to do but to finish the play.

"I turned and addressed an imaginary conversation to Kara. It was horrible, but there was something about it which aroused in me a curious sense of humour and I wanted to laugh and laugh and laugh!

"I heard the man coming up the stairs and closed the door gingerly. What length of time would it take for the candle to bend!

"To completely establish the alibi I determined to hold Fisher in conversation and this was all the easier since apparently he had not seen the envelope I had left on the table downstairs. I had not long to wait for suddenly with a crash I heard the steel latch fall in its place. Under the effect of the heat the candle had bent sooner than I had expected. I asked Fisher what was the meaning of the sound and he explained. I passed down the stairs talking all the time. I found a cab at Sloane Square and drove to my lodgings. Underneath my overcoat I was partly dressed in evening kit.

"Ten minutes after I entered the door of my flat I came out a beardless man about town, not to be distinguished from the thousand others who would be found that night walking the promenade of any of the great music-halls. From Victoria Street I drove straight to Scotland Yard. It was no more than a coincidence that whilst I should have been speaking with you all, the second candle should have bent and the alarm be given in the very office in which I was sitting.

"I assure you all in all earnestness that I did not suspect the cause of that ringing until Mr. Mansus spoke.

"There, gentlemen, is my story!" He threw out his arms.

"You may do with me as you will. Kara was a murderer, dyed a hundred times in innocent blood. I have done all that I set myself to do—that and no more—that and no less. I had thought to go away to America, but the nearer the day of my departure approached, the more vivid became the memory of the plans which she and I had formed, my girl... my poor martyred girl!"

He sat at the little table, his hands clasped before him, his face lined and white.

"And that is the end!" he said suddenly, with a wry smile.

"Not quite!" T. X. swung round with a gasp. It was Belinda Mary who spoke.

"I can carry it on," she said.

She was wonderfully self-possessed, thought T. X., but then T. X. never thought anything of her but that she was "wonderfully" something or the other.

"Most of your story is true, Mr. Lexman," said this astonishing girl, oblivious of the amazed eyes that were staring at her, "but Kara deceived you in one respect."

"What do you mean?" asked John Lexman, rising unsteadily to his feet.

For answer she rose and walked back to the door with the chintz curtains and flung it open: There was a wait which seemed an eternity, and then through the doorway came a girl, slim and grave and beautiful.

"My God!" whispered T. X. "Grace Lexman!"

CHAPTER XXIII

They went out and left them alone, two people who found in this moment a heaven which is not beyond the reach of humanity, but which is seldom attained to. Belinda Mary had an eager audience all to her very self.

"Of course she didn't die," she said scornfully. "Kara was playing on his fears all the time. He never even harmed her—in the way Mr. Lexman feared. He told Mrs. Lexman that her husband was dead just as he told John Lexman his wife was gone. What happened was that he brought her back to England—"

"Who?" asked T. X., incredulously.

"Grace Lexman," said the girl, with a smile. "You wouldn't think it possible, but when you realize that he had a yacht of his own and that he could travel up from whatever landing place he chose to his house in Cadogan Square by motorcar and that he could take her straight away into his cellar without disturbing his household, you'll understand that the only difficulty he had was in landing her. It was in the lower cellar that I found her."

"You found her in the cellar?" demanded the Chief Commissioner.

The girl nodded.

"I found her and the dog—you heard how Kara terrified her—and I killed the dog with my own hands," she said a little proudly, and then shivered. "It was very beastly," she admitted.

"And she's been living with you all this time and you've said nothing!" asked T. X., incredulously. Belinda Mary nodded.

"And that is why you didn't want me to know where you were living?" She nodded again.

"You see she was very ill," she said, "and I had to nurse her up, and of course I knew that it was Lexman who had killed Kara and I couldn't tell you about Grace Lexman without betraying him. So when Mr. Lexman decided to tell his story, I thought I'd better supply the grand denouement."

The men looked at one another.

"What are you going to do about Lexman?" asked the Chief Commissioner, "and, by the way, T. X., how does all this fit your theories!"

"Fairly well," replied T. X. coolly; "obviously the man who committed the murder was the man introduced into the room as Gathercole and as obviously it was not Gathercole, although to all appearance, he had lost his left arm."

"Why obvious?" asked the Chief Commissioner.

"Because," answered T. X. Meredith, "the real Gathercole had lost his right arm—that was the one error Lexman made."

"H'm," the Chief pulled at his moustache and looked enquiringly round the room, "we have to make up our minds very quickly about Lexman," he said. "What do you think, Carlneau?"

The Frenchman shrugged his shoulders.

"For my part I should not only importune your Home Secretary to pardon him, but I should recommend him for a pension," he said flippantly.

"What do you think, Savorsky?"

The Russian smiled a little.

"It is a very impressive story," he said dispassionately; "it occurs to me that if you intend bringing your M. Lexman to judgment you are likely to expose some very pretty scandals. Incidentally," he said, stroking his trim little moustache, "I might remark that any exposure which drew attention to the lawless conditions of Albania would not be regarded by my government with favour."

The Chief Commissioner's eyes twinkled and he nodded.

"That is also my view," said the Chief of the Italian bureau; "naturally we are greatly interested in all that happens on the Adriatic littoral. It seems to me that Kara has come to a very merciful end and I am not inclined to regard a prosecution of Mr. Lexman with equanimity."

"Well, I guess the political aspect of the case doesn't affect us very much," said O'Grady, "but as one who was once mighty near asphyxiated by stirring up the wrong kind of mud, I should leave the matter where it is."

The Chief Commissioner was deep in thought and Belinda Mary eyed him anxiously.

"Tell them to come in," he said bluntly.

The girl went and brought John Lexman and his wife, and they came in hand in hand supremely and serenely happy whatever the future might hold for them. The Chief Commissioner cleared his throat.

"Lexman, we're all very much obliged to you," he said, "for a very interesting story and a most interesting theory. What you have done, as I understand the matter," he proceeded deliberately, "is to put yourself in the murderer's place and advance a theory not only as to how the murder was actually committed, but as to the motive for that murder. It is, I might say, a remarkable piece of reconstruction," he spoke very deliberately, and swept away John Lexman's astonished interruption with a stern hand, "please wait and do not speak until I am out of hearing," he growled. "You have got into the skin of the actual assassin and have spoken most convincingly. One might almost think that the man who killed Remington Kara was actually standing before us. For that piece of impersonation we are all very grateful;" he glared round over his spectacles at his understanding colleagues and they murmured approvingly.

He looked at his watch.

"Now I am afraid I must be off," he crossed the room and put out his hand to John Lexman. "I wish you good luck," he said, and took both Grace Lexman's hands in his. "One of these days," he said paternally, "I shall come down to Beston Tracey and your husband shall tell me another and a happier story."

He paused at the door as he was going out and looking back caught the grateful eyes of Lexman.

"By the way, Mr. Lexman," he said hesitatingly, "I don't think I should ever write a story called 'The Clue of the Twisted Candle,' if I were you."

John Lexman shook his head.

"It will never be written," he said, "—by me."

THE END

THE MAN WHO KNEW

CHAPTER I

THE MAN IN THE LABORATORY

The room was a small one, and had been chosen for its remoteness from the dwelling rooms. It had formed the billiard room, which the former owner of Weald Lodge had added to his premises, and John Minute, who had neither the time nor the patience for billiards, had readily handed over this damp annex to his scientific secretary.

Along one side ran a plain deal bench which was crowded with glass stills and test tubes. In the middle was as plain a table, with half a dozen books, a microscope under a glass shade, a little wooden case which was opened to display an array of delicate scientific instruments, a Bunsen burner, which was burning bluely under a small glass bowl half filled with a dark and turgid concoction of some kind.

The face of the man sitting at the table watching this unsavory stew was hidden behind a mica and rubber mask, for the fumes which were being given off by the fluid were neither pleasant nor healthy. Save for a shaded light upon the table and the blue glow of the Bunsen lamp, the room was in darkness. Now and again the student would take a glass rod, dip it for an instant into the boiling liquid, and, lifting it, would allow the liquid drop by drop to fall from the rod on to a strip of litmus paper. What he saw was evidently satisfactory, and presently he turned out the Bunsen lamp, walked to the window and opened it, and switched on an electric fan to aid the process of ventilation.

He removed his mask, revealing the face of a good-looking young man, rather pale, with a slight dark mustache and heavy, black, wavy hair. He closed the window, filled his pipe from the well-worn pouch which he took from his pocket, and began to write in a notebook, stopping now and again to consult some authority from the books before him.

In half an hour he had finished this work, had blotted and closed his book, and, pushing back his chair, gave himself up to reverie. They were not pleasant thoughts to judge by his face. He pulled from his inside pocket a leather case and opened it. From this he took a photograph. It was the picture of a girl of sixteen. It was a pretty face, a little sad, but attractive in its very weakness. He looked at it for a long time, shaking his head as at an unpleasant thought.

There came a gentle tap at the door, and quickly he replaced the photograph in his case, folded it, and returned it to his pocket as he rose to unlock the door.

John Minute, who entered, sniffed suspiciously.

"What beastly smells you have in here, Jasper!" he growled. "Why on earth don't they invent chemicals that are more agreeable to the nose?"

Jasper Cole laughed quietly.

"I'm afraid, sir, that nature has ordered it otherwise," he said.

"Have you finished?" asked his employer.

He looked at the still warm bowl of fluid suspiciously.

"It is all right, sir," said Jasper. "It is only noxious when it is boiling. That is why I keep the door locked."

"What is it?" asked John Minute, scowling down at the unoffending liquor.

"It is many things," said the other ruefully. "In point of fact, it is an experiment. The bowl contains one or two elements which will only mix with the others at a certain temperature, and as an experiment it is successful because I have kept the unmixable elements in suspension, though the liquid has gone cold."

"I hope you will enjoy your dinner, even though it has gone cold," grumbled John Minute.

"I didn't hear the bell, sir," said Jasper Cole. "I'm awfully sorry if I've kept you waiting."

They were the only two present in the big, black-looking dining room, and dinner was as usual a fairly silent meal. John Minute read the newspapers, particularly that portion of them which dealt with the latest fluctuations in the stock market.

"Somebody has been buying Gwelo Deeps," he complained loudly.

Jasper looked up.

"Gwelo Deeps?" he said. "But they are the shares—"

"Yes, yes," said the other testily; "I know. They were quoted at a shilling last week; they are up to two shillings and threepence. I've got five hundred thousand of them; to be exact," he corrected himself, "I've got a million of them, though half of them are not my property. I am almost tempted to sell."

"Perhaps they have found gold," suggested Jasper.

John Minute snorted.

"If there is gold in the Gwelo Deeps there are diamonds on the downs," he said scornfully. "By the way, the other five hundred thousand shares belong to May."

Jasper Cole raised his eyebrows as much in interrogation as in surprise.

John Minute leaned back in his chair and manipulated his gold toothpick.

"May Nuttall's father was the best friend I ever had," he said gruffly. "He lured me into the Gwelo Deeps against my better judgment We sank a bore three thousand feet and found everything except gold."

He gave one of his brief, rumbling chuckles.

"I wish that mine had been a success. Poor old Bill Nuttall! He helped me in some tight places."

"And I think you have done your best for his daughter, sir."

"She's a nice girl," said John Minute, "a dear girl. I'm not taken with girls." He made a wry face. "But May is as honest and as sweet as they make them. She's the sort of girl who looks you in the eye when she talks to you; there's no damned nonsense about May."

Jasper Cole concealed a smile.

"What the devil are you grinning at?" demanded John Minute.

"I also was thinking that there was no nonsense about her," he said.

John Minute swung round.

"Jasper," he said, "May is the kind of girl I would like you to marry; in fact, she *is* the girl I would like you to marry."

"I think Frank would have something to say about that," said the other, stirring his coffee.

"Frank!" snorted John Minute. "What the devil do I care about Frank? Frank has to do as he's told. He's a lucky young man and a bit of a rascal, too, I'm thinking. Frank would marry anybody with a pretty face. Why, if I hadn't interfered—"

Jasper looked up.

"Yes?"

"Never mind," growled John Minute.

As was his practice, he sat a long time over dinner, half awake and half asleep. Jasper had annexed one of the newspapers, and was reading it. This was the routine which marked every evening of his life save on those occasions when he made a visit to London. He was in the midst of an article by a famous scientist on radium emanation, when John Minute continued a conversation which he had broken off an hour ago.

"I'm worried about May sometimes."

Jasper put down his paper.

"Worried! Why?"

"I am worried. Isn't that enough?" growled the other. "I wish you wouldn't ask me a lot of questions, Jasper. You irritate me beyond endurance."

"Well, I'll take it that you're worried," said his confidential secretary patiently, "and that you've good reason."

"I feel responsible for her, and I hate responsibilities of all kinds. The responsibilities of children—"

He winced and changed the subject, nor did he return to it for several days.

Instead he opened up a new line.

"Sergeant Smith was here when I was out, I understand," he said.

"He came this afternoon—yes."

"Did you see him?"

Jasper nodded.

"What did he want?"

"He wanted to see you, as far as I could make out. You were saying the other day that he drinks."

"Drinks!" said the other scornfully. "He doesn't drink; he eats it. What do you think about Sergeant Smith?" he demanded.

"I think he is a very curious person," said the other frankly, "and I can't understand why you go to such trouble to shield him or why you send him money every week."

"One of these days you'll understand," said the other, and his prophecy was to be fulfilled. "For the present, it is enough to say that if there are two ways out of a difficulty, one of which is unpleasant and one of which is less unpleasant, I take the less unpleasant of the two. It is less unpleasant to pay Sergeant Smith a weekly stipend than it is to be annoyed, and I should most certainly be annoyed if I did not pay him."

He rose up slowly from the chair and stretched himself.

"Sergeant Smith," he said again, "is a pretty tough proposition. I know, and I have known him for years. In my business, Jasper, I have had to know some queer people, and I've had to do some queer things. I am not so sure that they would look well in print, though I am not sensitive as to what newspapers say about me or I should have been in my grave years ago; but Sergeant Smith and his knowledge touches me at a raw place. You are always messing about with narcotics and muck of all kinds, and you will understand when I tell you that the money I give Sergeant Smith every week serves a double purpose. It is an opiate and a prophy—"

"Prophylactic," suggested the other.

"That's the word," said John Minute. "I was never a whale at the long uns; when I was twelve I couldn't write my own name, and when I was nineteen I used to spell it with two n's."

He chuckled again.

"Opiate and prophylactic," he repeated, nodding his head. "That's Sergeant Smith. He is a dangerous devil because he is a rascal."

"Constable Wiseman—" began Jasper.

"Constable Wiseman," snapped John Minute, rubbing his hand through his rumpled gray hair, "is a dangerous devil because he's a fool. What has Constable Wiseman been here about?"

"He didn't come here," smiled Jasper. "I met him on the road and had a little talk with him."

"You might have been better employed," said John Minute gruffly. "That silly ass has summoned me three times. One of these days I'll get him thrown out of the force."

"He's not a bad sort of fellow," soothed Jasper Cole. "He's rather stupid, but otherwise he is a decent, well-conducted man with a sense of the law."

"Did he say anything worth repeating?" asked John Minute.

"He was saying that Sergeant Smith is a disciplinarian."

"I know of nobody more of a disciplinarian than Sergeant Smith," said the other sarcastically, "particularly when he is getting over a jag. The keenest sense of duty is that possessed by a man who has broken the law and has not been found out. I think I will go to bed," he added, looking at the clock on the mantelpiece. "I am going up to town to-morrow. I want to see May."

"Is anything worrying you?" asked Jasper.

"The bank is worrying me," said the old man.

Jasper Cole looked at him steadily.

"What's wrong with the bank?"

"There is nothing wrong with the bank, and the knowledge that my dear nephew, Frank Merrill, esquire, is accountant at one of its branches removes any lingering doubt in my mind as to its stability. And I wish to Heaven you'd get out of the habit of asking me 'why' this happens or 'why' I do that."

Jasper lit a cigar before replying:

"The only way you can find things out in this world is by asking questions."

"Well, ask somebody else," boomed John Minute at the door.

Jasper took up his paper, but was not to be left to the enjoyment its columns offered, for five minutes later John Minute appeared in the doorway, minus his tie and coat, having been surprised in the act of undressing with an idea which called for development.

"Send a cable in the morning to the manager of the Gwelo Deeps and ask him if there is any report. By the way, you are the secretary of the company. I suppose you know that?"

"Am I?" asked the startled Jasper.

"Frank was, and I don't suppose he has been doing the work now. You had better find out or you will be getting me into a lot of trouble with the registrar. We ought to have a board meeting."

"Am I the directors, too?" asked Jasper innocently.

"It is very likely," said John Minute. "I know I am chairman, but there has never been any need to hold a meeting. You had better find out from Frank when the last was held."

He went away, to reappear a quarter of an hour later, this time in his pajamas.

"That mission May is running," he began, "they are probably short of money. You might inquire of their secretary. *They* will have a secretary, I'll be bound! If they want anything send it on to them."

He walked to the sideboard and mixed himself a whisky and soda.

"I've been out the last three or four times Smith has called. If he comes to-morrow tell him I will see him when I return. Bolt the doors and don't leave it to that jackass, Wilkins."

Jasper nodded.

"You think I am a little mad, don't you, Jasper?" asked the older man, standing by the sideboard with the glass in his hand.

"That thought has never occurred to me," said Jasper. "I think you are eccentric sometimes and inclined to exaggerate the dangers which surround you."

The other shook his head.

"I shall die a violent death; I know it. When I was in Zululand an old witch doctor 'tossed the bones.' You have never had that experience?"

"I can't say that I have," said Jasper, with a little smile.

"You can laugh at that sort of thing, but I tell you I've got a great faith in it. Once in the king's kraal and once in Echowe it happened, and both witch doctors told me the same thing—that I'd die by violence. I didn't use to worry about it very much, but I suppose I'm growing old now, and living surrounded by the law, as it were, I am too law-abiding. A law-abiding man is one who is afraid of people who are not law-abiding, and I am getting to that stage. You laugh at me because I'm jumpy whenever I see a stranger hanging around the house, but I have got more enemies to the square yard than most people have to the county. I suppose you think I am subject to delusions and ought to be put under restraint. A rich man hasn't a very happy time," he went on, speaking half to himself and half to the young man. "I've met all sorts of people in this country and been introduced as John Minute, the millionaire, and do you know what they say as soon as my back is turned?"

Jasper offered no suggestion.

"They say this," John Minute went on, "whether they're young or old, good, bad, or indifferent: 'I wish he'd die and leave me some of his money.'"

Jasper laughed softly.

"You haven't a very good opinion of humanity."

"I have no opinion of humanity," corrected his chief, "and I am going to bed."

Jasper heard his heavy feet upon the stairs and the thud of them overhead. He waited for some time; then he heard the bed creak. He closed the windows, personally inspected the fastenings of the doors, and went to his little office study on the first floor.

He shut the door, took out the pocket case, and gave one glance at the portrait, and then took an unopened letter which had come that evening and which, by his deft handling of the mail, he had been able to smuggle into his pocket without John Minute's observance.

He slit open the envelope, extracted the letter, and read:

> DEAR SIR: Your esteemed favor is to hand. We have to thank you for the check, and we are very pleased that we have given you satisfactory service. The search has been a very long and, I am afraid, a very expensive one to yourself, but now that discovery has been made I trust you will feel rewarded for your energies.

The note bore no heading, and was signed "J. B. Fleming."

Jasper read it carefully, and then, striking a match, lit the paper and watched it burn in the grate.

CHAPTER II

THE GIRL WHO CRIED

The northern express had deposited its passengers at King's Cross on time. All the station approaches were crowded with hurrying passengers. Taxicabs and "growlers" were mixed in apparently inextricable confusion. There was a roaring babble of instruction and counter-instruction from police-men, from cab drivers, and from excited porters. Some of the passengers hurried swiftly across the broad asphalt space and disappeared down the stairs toward the underground station. Others waited for unpunctual friends with protesting and frequent examination of their watches.

One alone seemed wholly bewildered by the noise and commotion. She was a young girl not more than eighteen, and she struggled with two or three brown paper parcels, a hat-box, and a bulky hand-bag. She was among those who expected to be met at the station, for she looked helplessly at the clock and wandered from one side of the building to the other till at last she came to a standstill in the center, put down all her parcels carefully, and, taking a letter from a shabby little bag, opened it and read.

Evidently she saw something which she had not noticed before, for she hastily replaced the letter in the bag, scrambled together her parcels, and walked swiftly out of the station. Again she came to a halt and looked round the darkened courtyard.

"Here!" snapped a voice irritably. She saw a door of a taxicab open, and came toward it timidly.

"Come in, come in, for heaven's sake!" said the voice.

She put in her parcels and stepped into the cab. The owner of the voice closed the door with a bang, and the taxi moved on.

"I've been waiting here ten minutes," said the man in the cab.

"I'm so sorry, dear, but I didn't read—"

"Of course you didn't read," interrupted the other brusquely.

It was the voice of a young man not in the best of tempers, and the girl, folding her hands in her lap, prepared for the tirade which she knew was to follow her act of omission.

"You never seem to be able to do anything right," said the man. "I suppose it is your natural stupidity."

"Why couldn't you meet me inside the station?" she asked with some show of spirit.

"I've told you a dozen times that I don't want to be seen with you," said the man brutally. "I've had enough trouble over you already. I wish to Heaven I'd never met you."

The girl could have echoed that wish, but eighteen months of bullying had cowed and all but broken her spirit.

"You are a stone around my neck," said the man bitterly. "I have to hide you, and all the time I'm in a fret as to whether you will give me away or not. I am going to keep you under my eye now," he said. "You know a little too much about me."

"I should never say a word against you," protested the girl.

"I hope, for your sake, you don't," was the grim reply.

The conversation slackened from this moment until the girl plucked up courage to ask where they were going.

"Wait and see," snapped the man, but added later: "You are going to a much nicer home than you have ever had in your life, and you ought to be very thankful."

"Indeed I am, dear," said the girl earnestly.

"Don't call me 'dear,'" snarled her husband.

The cab took them to Camden Town, and they descended in front of a respectable-looking house in a long, dull street. It was too dark for the girl to take stock of her surroundings, and she had scarcely time to gather her parcels together before the man opened the door and pushed her in.

The cab drove off, and a motor cyclist who all the time had been following the taxi, wheeled his machine slowly from the corner of the street where he had waited until he came opposite the house. He let down the supports of his machine, went stealthily up the steps, and flashed a lamp upon the enamel numbers over the fanlight of the door. He jotted down the figures in a notebook, descended the steps again, and, wheeling his machine back a little way, mounted and rode off.

Half an hour later another cab pulled up at the door, and a man descended, telling the driver to wait. He mounted the steps, knocked, and after a short delay was admitted.

"Hello, Crawley!" said the man who had opened the door to him. "How goes it?"

"Rotten," said the newcomer. "What do you want me for?"

His was the voice of an uncultured man, but his tone was that of an equal.

"What do you think I want you for?" asked the other savagely.

He led the way to the sitting room, struck a match, and lit the gas. His bag was on the floor. He picked it up, opened it, and took out a flask of whisky which he handed to the other.

"I thought you might need it," he said sarcastically.

Crawley took the flask, poured out a stiff tot, and drank it at a gulp. He was a man of fifty, dark and dour. His face was lined and tanned as one who had lived for many years in a hot climate. This was true of him, for he had spent ten years of his life in the Matabeleland mounted police.

The young man pulled up a chair to the table.

"I've got an offer to make to you," he said.

"Is there any money in it?"

The other laughed.

"You don't suppose I should make any kind of offer to you that hadn't money in it?" he answered contemptuously.

Crawley, after a moment's hesitation, poured out another drink and gulped it down.

"I haven't had a drink to-day," he said apologetically.

"That is an obvious lie," said the younger man; "but now to get to business. I don't know what your game is in England, but I will tell you what mine is. I want a free hand, and I can only have a free hand if you take your daughter away out of the country."

"You want to get rid of her, eh?" asked the other, looking at him shrewdly.

The young man nodded.

"I tell you, she's a millstone round my neck," he said for the second time that evening, "and I am scared of her. At any moment she may do some fool thing and ruin me."

Crawley grinned.

"'For better or for worse,'" he quoted, and then, seeing the ugly look in the other man's face, he said: "Don't try to frighten me, Mr. Brown or Jones, or whatever you call yourself, because I can't be frightened. I have had to deal with worse men than you and I'm still alive. I'll tell you right now that I'm not going out of England. I've got a big game on. What did you think of offering me?"

"A thousand pounds," said the other.

"I thought it would be something like that," said Crawley coolly. "It is a flea-bite to me. You take my tip and find another way of keeping her quiet. A clever fellow like you, who knows more about dope than any other man I have met, ought to be able to do the trick without any assistance from me. Why, didn't you tell me that you knew a drug that sapped the will power of people and made them do just as you like? That's the knockout drop to give her. Take my tip and try it."

"You won't accept my offer?" asked the other.

Crawley shook his head.

"I've got a fortune in my hand if I work my cards right," he said. "I've managed to get a position right under the old devil's nose. I see him every day, and I have got him scared. What's a thousand pounds to me? I've lost more than a thousand on one race at Lewes. No, my boy, employ the resources of science," he said flippantly. "There's no sense in being a dope merchant if you can't get the right dope for the right case."

"The less you say about my doping, the better," snarled the other man. "I was a fool to take you so much into my confidence."

"Don't lose your temper," said the other, raising his hand in mock alarm. "Lord bless us, Mr. Wright or Robinson, who would have thought that the nice, mild-mannered young man who goes to church in Eastbourne could be such a fierce chap in London? I've often laughed, seeing you walk past me as though butter wouldn't melt in your mouth and everybody saying what a nice young man Mr. So-and-so is, and I have thought, if they only knew that this sleek lad—"

"Shut up!" said the other savagely. "You are getting as much of a danger as this infernal girl."

"You take things too much to heart," said the other. "Now I'll tell you what I'll do. I am not going out of England. I am going to keep my present menial job. You see, it isn't only the question of money, but I have an idea that your old man has got something up his sleeve for me, and the only way to prevent unpleasant happenings is to keep close to him."

"I have told you a dozen times he has nothing against you," said the other emphatically. "I know his business, and I have seen most of his private papers. If he could have caught you with the goods, he would have had you long ago. I told you that the last time you called at the house and I saw you. What! Do you think John Minute would pay blackmail if he could get out of it? You are a fool!"

"Maybe I am," said the other philosophically, "but I am not such a fool as you think me to be."

"You had better see her," said his host suddenly.

Crawley shook his head.

"A parent's feelings," he protested, "have a sense of decency, Reginald or Horace or Hector; I always forget your London name. No," he said, "I won't accept your suggestion, but I have got a proposition to make to you, and it concerns a certain relative of John Minute—a nice, young fellow who will one day secure the old man's swag."

"Will he?" said the other between his teeth.

They sat for two hours discussing the proposition, and then Crawley rose to leave.

"I leave my final jar for the last," he said pleasantly. He had finished the contents of the flask, and was in a very amiable frame of mind.

"You are in some danger, my young friend, and I, your guardian angel, have discovered it. You have a valet at one of your numerous addresses."

"A chauffeur," corrected the other; "a Swede, Jonsen."

Crawley nodded.

"I thought he was a Swede."

"Have you seen him?" asked the other quickly.

"He came down to make some inquiries in Eastbourne," said Crawley, "and I happened to meet him. One of those talkative fellows who opens his heart to a uniform. I stopped him from going to the house, so I saved you a shock—if John Minute had been there, I mean."

The other bit his lips, and his face showed his concern.

"That's bad," he said. "He has been very restless and rather impertinent lately, and has been looking for another job. What did you tell him?"

"I told him to come down next Wednesday," said Crawley. "I thought you'd like to make a few arrangements in the meantime."

He held out his hand, and the young man, who did not mistake the gesture, dived into his pockets with a scowl and handed four five-pound notes into the outstretched palm.

"It will just pay my taxi," said Crawley light-heartedly.

The other went upstairs. He found the girl sitting where he had left her in her bedroom.

"Clear out of here," he said roughly. "I want the room."

Meekly she obeyed. He locked the door behind her, lifted a suitcase on to the bed, and, opening it, took out a small Japanese box. From this he removed a tiny glass pestle and mortar, six little vials, a hypodermic syringe, and a small spirit lamp. Then from his pocket he took a cigarette case and removed two cigarettes which he laid carefully on the dressing table. He was busy for the greater part of the hour.

As for the girl, she spent that time in the cold dining room huddled up in a chair, weeping softly to herself.

CHAPTER III

FOUR IMPORTANT CHARACTERS

The writer pauses here to say that the story of "The Man Who Knew" is an unusual one. It is reconstructed partly from the reports of a certain trial, partly from the confidential matter which has come into the writer's hands from Saul Arthur Mann and his extraordinary bureau, and partly from the private diary which May Nuttall put at the writer's disposal.

Those practiced readers who begin this narrative with the weary conviction that they are merely to see the workings out of a conventional record of crime, of love, and of mystery may be urged to pursue their investigations to the end. Truth is stranger than fiction, and has need to be, since most fiction is founded on truth. There is a strangeness in the story of "The Man Who Knew" which brings it into the category of veracious history. It cannot be said in truth that any story begins at the beginning of the first chapter, since all stories began with the creation of the world, but this present story may be said to begin when we cut into the lives of some of the characters concerned, upon the seventeenth day of July, 19—.

There was a little group of people about the prostrate figure of a man who lay upon the sidewalk in Gray Square, Bloomsbury.

The hour was eight o'clock on a warm summer evening, and that the unusual spectacle attracted only a small crowd may be explained by the fact that Gray Square is a professional quarter given up to the offices of lawyers, surveyors, and corporation offices which at eight o'clock on a summer's day are empty of occupants. The unprofessional classes who inhabit the shabby streets impinging upon the Euston Road do not include Gray Square in their itinerary when they take their evening constitutionals abroad, and even the loud children find a less depressing environment for their games.

The gray-faced youth sprawled upon the pavement was decently dressed and was obviously of the superior servant type.

He was as obviously dead.

Death, which beautifies and softens the plainest, had failed entirely to dissipate the impression of meanness in the face of the stricken man. The lips were set in a little sneer, the half-closed eyes were small, the clean-shaven jaw was long and underhung, the ears were large and grotesquely prominent.

A constable stood by the body, waiting for the arrival of the ambulance, answering in monosyllables the questions of the curious. Ten minutes before the ambulance arrived there joined the group a man of middle age.

He wore the pepper-and-salt suit which distinguishes the country excursionist taking the day off in London. He had little side whiskers and a heavy brown mustache. His golf cap was new and set at a somewhat rakish angle on his head. Across his waistcoat was a large and heavy chain hung at intervals with small silver medals. For all his provincial appearance his movements were decisive and suggested authority. He elbowed his way through the little crowd, and met the constable's disapproving stare without faltering.

"Can I be of any help, mate?" he said, and introduced himself as Police Constable Wiseman, of the Sussex constabulary.

The London constable thawed.

"Thanks," he said; "you can help me get him into the ambulance when it comes."

"Fit?" asked the newcomer.

The policeman shook his head.

"He was seen to stagger and fall, and by the time I arrived he'd snuffed out. Heart disease, I suppose."

"Ah!" said Constable Wiseman, regarding the body with a proprietorial and professional eye, and retailed his own experiences of similar tragedies, not without pride, as though he had to some extent the responsibility for their occurrence.

On the far side of the square a young man and a girl were walking slowly. A tall, fair, good-looking youth he was, who might have attracted attention even in a crowd. But more likely would that attention have been focused, had he been accompanied by the girl at his side, for she was by every standard beautiful. They reached the corner of Tabor Street, and it was the fixed and eager stare of a little man who stood on the corner of the street and the intensity of his gaze which first directed their attention to the tragedy on the opposite side of the square.

The little man who watched was dressed in an ill-fitting frock coat, trousers which seemed too long, since they concertinaed over his boots, and a glossy silk hat set at the back of his head.

"What a funny old thing!" said Frank Merrill under his breath, and the girl smiled.

The object of their amusement turned sharply as they came abreast of him. His freckled, clean-shaven face looked strangely old, and the big, gold-rimmed spectacles bridged halfway down his nose added to his ludicrous appearance. He raised his eyebrows and surveyed the two young people.

"There's an accident over there," he said briefly and without any preliminary.

"Indeed," said the young man politely.

"There have been several accidents in Gray Square," said the strange old man meditatively. "There was one in 1875, when the corner house—you can see the end of it from here—collapsed and buried fourteen people, seven of whom were killed, four of whom were injured for life, and three of whom escaped with minor injuries."

He said this calmly and apparently without any sense that he was acting at all unconventionally in volunteering the information, and went on:

"There was another accident in 1881, on the seventeenth of October, a collision between two hansom cabs which resulted in the death of a driver whose name was Samuel Green. He lived at 14 Portington Mews, and had a wife and nine children."

The girl looked at the old man with a little apprehension, and Frank Merrill laughed.

"You have a very good memory for this kind of thing. Do you live here?" he asked.

"Oh, no!" The little man shook his head vigorously.

He was silent for a moment, and then:

"I think we had better go over and see what it is all about," he said with a certain gravity.

His assumption of leadership was a little staggering, and Frank turned to the girl.

"Do you mind?" he asked.

She shook her head, and the three passed over the road to the little group just as the ambulance came jangling into the square. To Merrill's surprise, the policeman greeted the little man respectfully, touching his helmet.

"I'm afraid nothing can be done, sir. He is—gone."

"Oh, yes, he's gone!" said the other quite calmly.

He stooped down, turned back the man's coat, and slipped his hand into the inside pocket, but drew blank; the pocket was empty. With an extraordinary rapidity of movement, he continued his search, and to the astonishment of Frank Merrill the policeman did not deny his right. In the top left-hand pocket of the waistcoat he pulled out a crumpled slip which proved to be a newspaper clipping.

"Ah!" said the little man. "An advertisement for a manservant cut out of this morning's *Daily Telegraph*; I saw it myself. Evidently a manservant who was on his way to interview a new employer. You see: 'Call at eight-thirty at Holborn Viaduct Hotel.' He was taking a short cut when his illness overcame him. I know who is advertising for the valet," he added gratuitously; "he is a Mr. T. Burton, who is a rubber factor from Penang. Mr. T. Burton married the daughter of the Reverend George Smith, of Scarborough, in 1889, and has four children, one of whom is at Winchester. Hum!"

He pursed his lips and looked down again at the body; then suddenly he turned to Frank Merrill.

"Do you know this man?" he demanded.

Frank looked at him in astonishment.

"No. Why do you ask?"

"You were looking at him as though you did," said the little man. "That is to say, you were not looking at his face. People who do not look at other people's faces under these circumstances know them."

"Curiously enough," said Frank, with a little smile, "there is some one here I know," and he caught the eye of Constable Wiseman.

That ornament of the Sussex constabulary touched his cap.

"I thought I recognized you, sir. I have often seen you at Weald Lodge," he said.

Further conversation was cut short as they lifted the body on to a stretcher and put it into the interior of the ambulance. The little group watched the white car disappear, and the crowd of idlers began to melt away.

Constable Wiseman took a professional leave of his comrade, and came back to Frank a little shyly.

"You are Mr. Minute's nephew, aren't you, sir?" he asked.

"Quite right," said Frank.

"I used to see you at your uncle's place."

"Uncle's name?"

It was the little man's pert but wholly inoffensive inquiry. He seemed to ask it as a matter of course and as one who had the right to be answered without equivocation.

Frank Merrill laughed.

"My uncle is Mr. John Minute," he said, and added, with a faint touch of sarcasm: "You probably know him."

"Oh, yes," said the other readily. "One of the original Rhodesian pioneers who received a concession from Lo Bengula and amassed a large fortune by the sale of gold-mining properties which proved to be of no especial value. He was tried at Salisbury in 1897 with the murder of two Mashona chiefs, and was acquitted.

He amassed another fortune in Johannesburg in the boom of '97, and came to this country in 1901, settling on a small estate between Polegate and Eastbourne. He has one nephew, his heir, Frank Merrill, the son of the late Doctor Henry Merrill, who is an accountant in the London and Western Counties Bank. He—"

Frank looked at him in undisguised amazement.

"You know my uncle?"

"Never met him in my life," said the little man brusquely. He took off his silk hat with a sweep.

"I wish you good afternoon," he said, and strode rapidly away.

The uniformed policeman turned a solemn face upon the group.

"Do you know that gentleman?" asked Frank.

The constable smiled.

"Oh, yes, sir; that is Mr. Mann. At the yard we call him 'The Man Who Knows!'"

"Is he a detective?"

The constable shook his head.

"From what I understand, sir, he does a lot of work for the commissioner and for the government. We have orders never to interfere with him or refuse him any information that we can give."

"The Man Who Knows?" repeated Frank, with a puzzled frown. "What an extraordinary person! What does he know?" he asked suddenly.

"Everything," said the constable comprehensively.

A few minutes later Frank was walking slowly toward Holborn.

"You seem to be rather depressed," smiled the girl.

"Confound that fellow!" said Frank, breaking his silence. "I wonder how he comes to know all about uncle?" He shrugged his shoulders. "Well, dear, this is not a very cheery evening for you. I did not bring you out to see accidents."

"Frank," the girl said suddenly, "I seem to know that man's face—the man who was on the pavement, I mean—"

She stopped with a shudder.

"It seemed a little familiar to me," said Frank thoughtfully.

"Didn't he pass us about twenty minutes ago?"

"He may have done," said Frank, "but I have no particular recollection of it. My impression of him goes much farther back than this evening. Now where could I have seen him?"

"Let's talk about something else," she said quickly. "I haven't a very long time. What am I to do about your uncle?"

He laughed.

"I hardly know what to suggest," he said. "I am very fond of Uncle John, and I hate to run counter to his wishes, but I am certainly not going to allow him to take my love affairs into his hands. I wish to Heaven you had never met him!"

She gave a little gesture of despair.

"It is no use wishing things like that, Frank. You see, I knew your uncle before I knew you. If it had not been for your uncle I should not have met you."

"Tell me what happened," he asked. He looked at his watch. "You had better come on to Victoria," he said, "or I shall lose my train."

He hailed a taxicab, and on the way to the station she told him of all that had happened.

"He was very nice, as he always is, and he said nothing really which was very horrid about you. He merely said he did not want me to marry you because he did not think you'd make a suitable husband. He said that Jasper had all the qualities and most of the virtues."

Frank frowned.

"Jasper is a sleek brute," he said viciously.

She laid her hand on his arm.

"Please be patient," she said. "Jasper has said nothing whatever to me and has never been anything but most polite and kind."

"I know that variety of kindness," growled the young man. "He is one of those sly, soft-footed sneaks you can never get to the bottom of. He is worming his way into my uncle's confidence to an extraordinary extent. Why, he is more like a son to Uncle John than a beastly secretary."

"He has made himself necessary," said the girl, "and that is halfway to making yourself wealthy."

The little frown vanished from Frank's brow, and he chuckled.

"That is almost an epigram," he said. "What did you tell uncle?"

"I told him that I did not think that his suggestion was possible and that I did not care for Mr. Cole, nor he for me. You see, Frank, I owe your Uncle John so much. I am the daughter of one of his best friends, and since dear daddy died

Uncle John has looked after me. He has given me my education—my income—my everything; he has been a second father to me."

Frank nodded

"I recognize all the difficulties," he said, "and here we are at Victoria."

She stood on the platform and watched the train pull out and waved her hand in farewell, and then returned to the pretty flat in which John Minute had installed her. As she said, her life had been made very smooth for her. There was no need for her to worry about money, and she was able to devote her days to the work she loved best. The East End Provident Society, of which she was president, was wholly financed by the Rhodesian millionaire.

May had a natural aptitude for charity work. She was an indefatigable worker, and there was no better known figure in the poor streets adjoining the West Indian Docks than Sister Nuttall. Frank was interested in the work without being enthusiastic. He had all the man's apprehension of infectious disease and of the inadvisability of a beautiful girl slumming without attendance, but the one visit he had made to the East End in her company had convinced him that there was no fear as to her personal safety.

He was wont to grumble that she was more interested in her work than she was in him, which was probably true, because her development had been a slow one, and it could not be said that she was greatly in love with anything in the world save her self-imposed mission.

She ate her frugal dinner, and drove down to the mission headquarters off the Albert Dock Road. Three nights a week were devoted by the mission to visitation work. Many women and girls living in this area spend their days at factories in the neighborhood, and they have only the evenings for the treatment of ailments which, in people better circumstanced, would produce the attendance of specialists. For the night work the nurses were accompanied by a volunteer male escort. May Nuttall's duties carried her that evening to Silvertown and to a network of mean streets to the east of the railway. Her work began at dusk, and was not ended until night had fallen and the stars were quivering in a hot sky.

The heat was stifling, and as she came out of the last foul dwelling she welcomed as a relief even the vitiated air of the hot night. She went back into the passageway of the house, and by the light of a paraffin lamp made her last entry in the little diary she carried.

"That makes eight we have seen, Thompson," she said to her escort. "Is there anybody else on the list?"

"Nobody else to-night, miss," said the young man, concealing a yawn.

"I'm afraid it is not very interesting for you, Thompson," said the girl sympathetically; "you haven't even the excitement of work. It must be awfully dull standing outside waiting for me."

"Bless you, miss," said the man. "I don't mind at all. If it is good enough for you to come into these streets, it is good enough for me to go round with you."

They stood in a little courtyard, a cul-de-sac cut off at one end by a sheer wall, and as the girl put back her diary into her little net bag a man came swiftly down from the street entrance of the court and passed her. As he did so the dim light of the lamp showed for a second his face, and her mouth formed an "O" of astonishment. She watched him until he disappeared into one of the dark doorways at the farther end of the court, and stood staring at the door as though unable to believe her eyes.

There was no mistaking the pale face and the straight figure of Jasper Cole, John Minute's secretary.

CHAPTER IV

THE ACCOUNTANT AT THE BANK

May Nuttall expressed her perplexity in a letter:

> DEAR FRANK: Such a remarkable thing happened last night. I was in Silvers Rents about eleven o'clock, and had just finished seeing the last of my patients, when a man passed me and entered one of the houses—it was, I thought at the time, either the last or the last but one on the left. I now know that it was the last but one. There is no doubt at all in my mind that it was Mr. Cole, for not only did I see his face, but he carried the snakewood cane which he always affects.
>
> I must confess I was curious enough to make inquiries, and I found that he is a frequent visitor here, but nobody quite knows why he comes. The last house is occupied by two families, very uninteresting people, and the last house but one is empty save for a room which is apparently the one Mr. Cole uses. None of the people in the Rents know Mr. Cole or have ever seen him. Apparently the downstairs room in the empty house is kept locked, and a woman who lives opposite told my informant, Thompson, whom you will remember as the man who always goes with me when I am slumming, that the gentleman sometimes comes, uses this room, and that he always sweeps it out for himself. It cannot be very well furnished, and apparently he never stays the night there.
>
> Isn't it very extraordinary? Please tell me what you make of it—

Frank Merrill put down the letter and slowly filled his pipe. He was puzzled, and found no solution either then or on his way to the office.

He was the accountant of the Piccadilly branch of the London and Western Counties Bank, and had very little time to give to outside problems. But the thought of Cole and his curious appearance in a London slum under circumstances which, to say the least, were mysterious came between him and his work more than once.

He was entering up some transactions when he was sent for by the manager. Frank Merrill, though he did not occupy a particularly imposing post in the bank, held nevertheless a very extraordinary position and one which insured for him more consideration than the average official receives at the hands of his superiors. His uncle was financially interested in the bank, and it was generally believed that Frank had been sent as much to watch his relative's interests as to prepare himself for the handling of the great fortune which John Minute would some day leave to his heir.

The manager nodded cheerily as Frank came in and closed the door behind him.

"Good morning, Mr. Merrill," said the chief. "I want to see you about Mr. Holland's account. You told me he was in the other day."

Frank nodded.

"He came in in the lunch hour."

"I wish I had been here," said the manager thoughtfully. "I would like to see this gentleman."

"Is there anything wrong with his account?"

"Oh, no," said the manager with a smile; "he has a very good balance. In fact, too large a balance for a floating account. I wish you would see him and persuade him to put some of this money on deposit. The head office does not like big floating balances which may be withdrawn at any moment and which necessitates the keeping here of a larger quantity of cash than I care to hold.

"Personally," he went on, "I do not like our method of doing business at all. Our head office being in Plymouth, it is necessary, by the peculiar rules of the bank, that the floating balances should be so covered, and I confess that your uncle is as great a sinner as any. Look at this?"

He pushed a check across the table.

"Here's a bearer check for sixty thousand pounds which has just come in. It is to pay the remainder of the purchase price due to Consolidated Mines. Why they cannot accept the ordinary crossed check Heavens knows!"

Frank looked at the sprawling signature and smiled.

"You see, uncle's got a reputation to keep up," he said good-humoredly; "one is not called 'Ready-Money Minute' for nothing."

The manager made a little grimace.

"That sort of thing may be necessary in South Africa," he said, "but here in the very heart of the money world cash payments are a form of lunacy. I do not want you to repeat this to your relative."

"I am hardly likely to do that," said Frank, "though I do think you ought to allow something for uncle's peculiar experiences in the early days of his career."

"Oh, I make every allowance," said the other; "only it is very inconvenient, but it was not to discuss your uncle's shortcomings that I brought you here."

He pulled out a pass book from a heap in front of him.

"'Mr. Rex Holland,'" he read. "He opened his account while I was on my holiday, you remember."

"I remember very well," said Frank, "and he opened it through me."

"What sort of man is he?" asked the manager.

"I am afraid I am no good at descriptions," replied Frank, "but I should describe him as a typical young man about town, not very brainy, very few ideas outside of his own immediate world—which begins at Hyde Park Corner—"

"And ends at the Hippodrome," interrupted the manager.

"Possibly," said Frank. "He seemed a very sound, capable man in spite of a certain languid assumption of ignorance as to financial matters, and he came very well recommended. What would you like me to do?"

The manager pushed himself back in his chair, thrust his hands in his trousers' pockets, and looked at the ceiling for inspiration.

"Suppose you go along and see him this afternoon and ask him as a favor to put some of his money on deposit. We will pay the usual interest and all that sort of thing. You can explain that he can get the money back whenever he wants it by giving us thirty days' notice. Will you do this for me?"

"Surely," said Frank heartily. "I will see him this afternoon. What is his address? I have forgotten."

"Albemarle Chambers, Knightsbridge," replied the manager. "He may be in town."

"And what is his balance?" asked Frank.

"Thirty-seven thousand pounds," said the other, "and as he is not buying Consolidated Mines I do not see what need he has for the money, the more so since we can always give him an overdraft on the security of his deposit. Suggest to him that he puts thirty thousand pounds with us and leaves seven thousand pounds floating. By the way, your uncle is sending his secretary here this afternoon to go into the question of his own account."

Frank looked up.

"Cole," he said quickly, "is he coming here? By Jove!"

He stood by the manager's desk, and a look of amusement came into his eyes.

"I want to ask Cole something," he said slowly. "What time do you expect him?"

"About four o'clock."

"After the bank closes?"

The manager nodded.

"Uncle has a weird way of doing business," said Frank, after a pause. "I suppose that means that I shall have to stay on?"

"It isn't necessary," said Mr. Brandon. "You see Mr. Cole is one of our directors."

Frank checked an exclamation of surprise.

"How long has this been?" he asked.

"Since last Monday. I thought I told you. At any rate, if you have not been told by your uncle, you had better pretend to know nothing about it," said Brandon hastily.

"You may be sure I shall keep my counsel," said Frank, a little amused by the other's anxiety. "You have been very good to me, Mr. Brandon, and I appreciate your kindness."

"Mr. Cole is a nominee of your uncle, of course," Brandon went on, with a little nod of acknowledgment for the other's thanks. "Your uncle makes a point of never sitting on boards if he can help it, and has never been represented except by his solicitor since he acquired so large an interest in the bank. As a matter of fact, I think Mr. Cole is coming here as much to examine the affairs of the branch as to look after your uncle's account. Cole is a very first-class man of business, isn't he?"

Frank's answer was a grim smile.

"Excellent!" he said dryly. "He has the scientific mind grafted to a singular business capacity."

"You don't like him?"

"I have no particular reason for not liking him," said the other. "Possibly I am being constitutionally uncharitable. He is not the type of man I greatly care for. He possesses all the virtues, according to uncle, spends his days and nights almost slavishly working for his employer. Oh, yes, I know what you are going to say; that is a very fine quality in a young man, and honestly I agree with you, only it doesn't seem natural. I don't suppose anybody works as hard as I or takes as much interest in his work, yet I have no particular anxiety to carry it on after business hours."

The manager rose.

"You are not even an idle apprentice," he said good-humoredly. "You will see Mr. Rex Holland for me?"

"Certainly," said Frank, and went back to his desk deep in thought.

It was four o'clock to the minute when Jasper Cole passed through the one open door of the bank at which the porter stood ready to close. He was well, but neatly, dressed, and had hooked to his wrist a thin snakewood cane attached to a crook handle.

He saw Frank across the counter and smiled, displaying two rows of even, white teeth.

"Hello, Jasper!" said Frank easily, extending his hand. "How is uncle?"

"He is very well indeed," replied the other. "Of course he is very worried about things, but then I think he is always worried about something or other."

"Anything in particular?" asked Frank interestedly.

Jasper shrugged his shoulders.

"You know him much better than I; you were with him longer. He is getting so horribly suspicious of people, and sees a spy or an enemy in every strange face. That is usually a bad sign, but I think he has been a little overwrought lately."

He spoke easily; his voice was low and modulated with the faintest suggestion of a drawl, which was especially irritating to Frank, who secretly despised the Oxford product, though he admitted—since he was a very well-balanced and on the whole good-humored young man—his dislike was unreasonable.

"I hear you have come to audit the accounts," said Frank, leaning on the counter and opening his gold cigarette case.

"Hardly that," drawled Jasper.

He reached out his hand and selected a cigarette.

"I just want to sort out a few things. By the way, your uncle had a letter from a friend of yours."

"Mine?"

"A Rex Holland," said the other.

"He is hardly a friend of mine; in fact, he is rather an infernal nuisance," said Frank. "I went down to Knightsbridge to see him to-day, and he was out. What has Mr. Holland to say?"

"Oh, he is interested in some sort of charity, and he is starting a guinea collection. I forget what the charity was."

"Why do you call him a friend of mine?" asked Frank, eying the other keenly.

Jasper Cole was halfway to the manager's office and turned.

"A little joke," he said. "I had heard you mention the gentleman. I have no other reason for supposing he was a friend of yours."

"Oh, by the way, Cole," said Frank suddenly, "were you in town last night?"

Jasper Cole shot a swift glance at him.

"Why?"

"Were you near Victoria Docks?"

"What a question to ask!" said the other, with his inscrutable smile, and, turning abruptly, walked in to the waiting Mr. Brandon.

Frank finished work at five-thirty that night and left Jasper Cole and a junior clerk to the congenial task of checking the securities. At nine o'clock the clerk went home, leaving Jasper alone in the bank. Mr. Brandon, the manager, was a bachelor and occupied a flat above the bank premises. From time to time he strode in, his big pipe in the corner of his mouth. The last of these occasions was when Jasper Cole had replaced the last ledger in Mr. Minute's private safe.

"Half past eleven," said the manager disapprovingly, "and you have had no dinner."

"I can afford to miss a dinner," laughed the other.

"Lucky man," said the manager.

Jasper Cole passed out into the street and called a passing taxi to the curb.

"Charing Cross Station," he said.

He dismissed the cab in the station courtyard, and after a while walked back to the Strand and hailed another.

"Victoria Dock Road," he said in a low voice.

CHAPTER V

JOHN MINUTE'S LEGACY

La Rochefoucauld has said that prudence and love are inconsistent. May Nuttall, who had never explored the philosophies of La Rochefoucauld, had nevertheless seen that quotation in the birthday book of an acquaintance, and the saying had made a great impression upon her. She was twenty-one years of age, at which age girls are most impressionable and are little influenced by the workings of pure reason. They are prepared to take their philosophies ready-made, and not disinclined to accept from others certain rigid standards by which they measure their own elastic temperaments.

Frank Merrill was at once a comfort and the cause of a certain half-ashamed resentment, since she was of the age which resents dependence. The woman who spends any appreciable time in the discussion with herself as to whether she does or does not love a man can only have her doubts set at rest by the discovery of somebody whom she loves better. She liked Frank, and liked him well enough to accept the little ring which marked the beginning of a new relationship which was not exactly an engagement, yet brought to her friendship a glamour which it had never before possessed.

She liked him well enough to want his love. She loved him little enough to find the prospect of an early marriage alarming. That she did not understand herself was not remarkable. Twenty-one has not the experience by which the complexities of twenty-one may be straightened out and made visible.

She sat at breakfast, puzzling the matter out, and was a little disturbed and even distressed to find, in contrasting the men, that of the two she had a warmer and a deeper feeling for Jasper Cole. Her alarm was due to the recollection of one of Frank's warnings, almost prophetic, it seemed to her now:

"That man has a fascination which I would be the last to deny. I find myself liking him, though my instinct tells me he is the worst enemy I have in the world."

If her attitude toward Frank was difficult to define, more remarkable was her attitude of mind toward Jasper Cole. There was something sinister—no, that was not the word—something "frightening" about him. He had a magnetism, an aura of personal power, which seemed to paralyze the will of any who came into conflict with him.

She remembered how often she had gone to the big library at Weald Lodge with the firm intention of "having it out with Jasper." Sometimes it was a question of domestic economy into which he had obtruded his views—when she was sixteen she was practically housekeeper to her adopted uncle—perhaps it was a matter of carriage arrangement. Once it had been much more serious, for after she had fixed up to go with a merry picnic party to the downs, Jasper, in her uncle's absence and on his authority, had firmly but gently forbidden her attendance. Was it an accident that Frank Merrill was one of the party, and that he was coming down from London for an afternoon's fun?

In this case, as in every other, Jasper had his way. He even convinced her that his view was right and hers was wrong. He had pooh-poohed on this occasion all suggestion that it was the presence of Frank Merrill which had induced him to exercise the veto which his extraordinary position gave to him. According to his version, it had been the inclusion in the party of two ladies whose names were famous in the theatrical world which had raised his delicate gorge.

May thought of this particular incident as she sat at breakfast, and with a feeling of exasperation she realized that whenever Jasper had set his foot down he had never been short of a plausible reason for opposing her.

For one thing, however, she gave him credit. Never once had he spoken depreciatingly of Frank.

She wondered what business brought Jasper to such an unsavory neighborhood as that in which she had seen him. She had all a woman's curiosity without a woman's suspicions, and, strangely enough, she did not associate his presence in this terrible neighborhood or his mysterious comings and goings with anything discreditable to himself. She thought it was a little eccentric in him, and wondered whether he, too, was running a "little mission" of his own, but dismissed that idea since she had received no confirmation of the theory from the people with whom she came into contact in that neighborhood.

She was halfway through her breakfast when the telephone bell rang, and she rose from the table and crossed to the wall. At the first word from the caller she recognized him.

"Why, uncle!" she said. "Whatever are you doing in town?"

The voice of John Minute bellowed through the receiver:

"I've an important engagement. Will you lunch with me at one-thirty at the Savoy?"

He scarcely waited for her to accept the invitation before he hung up his receiver.

The commissioner of police replaced the book which he had taken from the shelf at the side of his desk, swung round in his chair, and smiled quizzically at the perturbed and irascible visitor.

The man who sat at the other side of the desk might have been fifty-five. He was of middle height, and was dressed in a somewhat violent check suit, the fit of which advertised the skill of the great tailor who had ably fashioned so fine a creation from so unlovely a pattern.

He wore a low collar which would have displayed a massive neck but for the fact that a glaring purple cravat and a diamond as big as a hazelnut directed the observer's attention elsewhere. The face was an unusual one. Strong to a point of coarseness, the bulbous nose, the thick, irregular lips, the massive chin all spoke of the hard life which John Minute had spent. His eyes were blue and cold, his hair a thick and unruly mop of gray. At a distance he conveyed a curious illusion of refinement. Nearer at hand, his pink face repelled one by its crudities. He reminded the commissioner of a piece of scene painting that pleased from the gallery and disappointed from the boxes.

"You see, Mr. Minute," said Sir George suavely, "we are rather limited in our opportunities and in our powers. Personally, I should be most happy to help you, not only because it is my business to help everybody, but because you were so kind to my boy in South Africa; the letters of introduction you gave to him were most helpful."

The commissioner's son had been on a hunting trip through Rhodesia and Barotseland, and a chance meeting at a dinner party with the Rhodesian millionaire had produced these letters.

"But," continued the official, with a little gesture of despair, "Scotland Yard has its limitations. We cannot investigate the cause of intangible fears. If you are threatened we can help you, but the mere fact that you fancy there is come sort of vague danger would not justify our taking any action."

John Minute hitched about in his chair.

"What are the police for?" he asked impatiently. "I have enemies, Sir George. I took a quiet little place in the country, just outside Eastbourne, to get away from London, and all sorts of new people are prying round us. There was a new parson called the other day for a subscription to some boy scouts' movement or other. He has been hanging round my place for a month, and lives at a cottage near Polegate. Why should he have come to Eastbourne?"

"On a holiday trip?" suggested the commissioner.

"Bah!" said John Minute contemptuously. "There's some other reason. I've had him watched. He goes every day to visit a woman at a hotel—a confederate. They're never seen in public together. Then there's a peddler, one of those fellows who sell glass and repair windows; nobody knows anything about him. He doesn't do enough business to keep a fly alive. He's always hanging round Weald Lodge. Then there's a Miss Paines, who says she's a landscape gardener, and wants to lay out the grounds in some newfangled way. I sent her packing about her business, but she hasn't left the neighborhood."

"Have you reported the matter to the local police?" asked the commissioner.

Minute nodded.

"And they know nothing suspicious about them?"

"Nothing!" said Mr. Minute briefly.

"Then," said the other, smiling, "there is probably nothing known against them, and they are quite innocent people trying to get a living. After all, Mr. Minute, a man who is as rich as you are must expect to attract a number of people, each trying to secure some of your wealth in a more or less legitimate way. I suspect nothing more remarkable than this has happened."

He leaned back in his chair, his hands clasped, a sudden frown on his face.

"I hate to suggest that anybody knows any more than we, but as you are so worried I will put you in touch with a man who will probably relieve your anxiety."

Minute looked up.

"A police officer?" he asked.

Sir George shook his head.

"No, this is a private detective. He can do things for you which we cannot. Have you ever heard of Saul Arthur Mann? I see you haven't. Saul Arthur Mann," said the commissioner, "has been a good friend of ours, and possibly in recommending him to you I may be a good friend to both of you. He is 'The Man Who Knows.'"

"'The Man Who Knows,'" repeated Mr. Minute dubiously. "What does he know?"

"I'll show you," said the commissioner. He went to the telephone, gave a number, and while he was waiting for the call to be put through he asked: "What is the name of your boy-scout parson?"

"The Reverend Vincent Lock," replied Mr. Minute.

"I suppose you don't know the name of your glass peddler?"

Minute shook his head.

"They call him 'Waxy' in the village," he said.

"And the lady's name is Miss Paines, I think?" asked the commissioner, jotting down the names as he repeated them. "Well, we shall—Hello! Is that Saul Arthur Mann? This is Sir George Fuller. Connect me with Mr. Mann, will you?"

He waited a second, and then continued:

"Is that you, Mr. Mann? I want to ask you something. Will you note these three names? The Reverend Vincent Lock, a peddling glazier who is known as 'Waxy,' and a Miss Paines. Have you got them? I wish you would let me know something about them."

Mr. Minute rose.

"Perhaps you'll let me know, Sir George—" he began, holding out his hand.

"Don't go yet," replied the commissioner, waving him to his chair again. "You will obtain all the information you want in a few minutes."

"But surely he must make inquiries," said the other, surprised.

Sir George shook his head.

"The curious thing about Saul Arthur Mann is that he never has to make inquiries. That is why he is called 'The Man Who Knows.' He is one of the most remarkable people in the world of criminal investigation," he went on. "We tried to induce him to come to Scotland Yard. I am not so sure that the government would have paid him his price. At any rate, he saved me any embarrassment by refusing point-blank."

The telephone bell rang at that moment, and Sir George lifted the receiver. He took a pencil and wrote rapidly on his pad, and when he had finished he said, "Thank you," and hung up the receiver.

"Here is your information, Mr. Minute," he said. "The Reverend Vincent Lock, curate in a very poor neighborhood near Manchester, interested in the boy scouts' movement. His brother, George Henry Locke, has had some domestic trouble, his wife running away from him. She is now staying at the Grand Hotel, Eastbourne, and is visited every day by her brother-in-law, who is endeavoring to induce her to return to her home. That disposes of the reverend gentleman and his confederate. Miss Paines is a genuine landscape gardener, has been the plaintiff in two breach-of-promise cases, one of which came to the court. There is no doubt," the commissioner went on reading the paper, "that her *modus operandi* is to get elderly gentlemen to propose marriage and then to commence her action. That disposes of Miss Paines, and you now know why she is worrying you. Our friend 'Waxy' has another name—Thomas Cobbler—and he has been three times convicted of larceny."

The commissioner looked up with a grim little smile.

"I shall have something to say to our own record department for failing to trace 'Waxy,'" he said, and then resumed his reading.

"And that is everything! It disposes of our three," he said. "I will see that 'Waxy' does not annoy you any more."

"But how the dickens—" began Mr. Minute. "How the dickens does this fellow find out in so short a time?"

The commissioner shrugged his shoulders.

"He just knows," he said.

He took leave of his visitor at the door.

"If you are bothered any more," he said, "I should strongly advise you to go to Saul Arthur Mann. I don't know what your real trouble is, and you haven't told me exactly why you should fear an attack of any kind. You won't have to tell Mr. Mann," he said with a little twinkle in his eye.

"Why not?" asked the other suspiciously.

"Because he will know," said the commissioner.

"The devil he will!" growled John Minute, and stumped down the broad stairs on to the Embankment, a greatly mystified man. He would have gone off to seek an interview with this strange individual there and then, for his curiosity was piqued and he had also a little apprehension, one which, in his impatient way, he desired should be allayed, but he remembered that he had asked May to lunch with him, and he was already five minutes late.

He found the girl in the broad vestibule, waiting for him, and greeted her affectionately.

Whatever may be said of John Minute that is not wholly to his credit, it cannot be said that he lacked sincerity.

There are people in Rhodesia who speak of him without love. They describe him as the greatest land thief that ever rode a Zeedersburg coach from Port Charter to Salisbury to register land that he had obtained by trickery. They tell stories of those wonderful coach drives of his with relays of twelve mules waiting every ten miles. They speak of his gambling propensities, of ten-thousand-acre farms that changed hands at the turn of a card, and there are stories that are less printable. When M'Lupi, a little Mashona chief, found gold in '92, and refused to locate the reef, it was John Minute who staked him out and lit a grass fire on his chest until he spoke.

Many of the stories are probably exaggerated, but all Rhodesia agrees that John Minute robbed impartially friend and foe. The confidant of Lo'Ben and the Company alike, he betrayed both, and on that terrible day when it was a toss of a coin whether the concession seekers would be butchered in Lo'Ben's kraal, John Minute escaped with the only available span of mules and left his comrades to their fate.

Yet he had big, generous traits, and could on occasions be a tender and a kindly friend. He had married when a young man, and had taken his wife into the wilds.

There was a story that she had met a handsome young trader and had eloped with him, that John Minute had chased them over three hundred miles of hostile country from Victoria Falls to Charter, from Charter to Marandalas, from Marandalas to Massikassi, and had arrived in Biera so close upon their trail that he had seen the ship which carried them to the Cape steaming down the river.

He had never married again. Report said that the woman had died of malaria. A more popular version of the story was that John Minute had relentlessly followed his erring wife to Pieter Maritzburg and had shot her and had thereupon served seven years on the breakwater for his sin.

About a man who is rich, powerful, and wholly unpopular, hated by the majority, and feared by all, legends grow as quickly as toadstools on a marshy moor. Some were half true, some wholly apocryphal, deliberate, and malicious inventions. True or false, John Minute ignored them all, denying nothing, explaining nothing, and even refusing to take action against a Cape Town weekly which dealt with his career in a spirit of unpardonable frankness.

There was only one person in the world whom he loved more than the girl whose hand he held as they went down to the cheeriest restaurant in London.

"I have had a queer interview," he said in his gruff, quick way, "I have been to see the police."

"Oh, uncle!" she said reproachfully.

He jerked his shoulder impatiently.

"My dear, you don't know," he said. "I have got all sorts of people who—"

He stopped short.

"What was there remarkable in the interview? she asked, after he had ordered the lunch.

"Have you ever heard," he asked, "of Saul Arthur Mann?"

"Saul Arthur Mann?" she repeated, "I seem to know that name. Mann, Mann! Where have I heard it?"

"Well," said he, with that fierce and fleeting little smile which rarely lit his face for a second, "if you don't know him he knows you; he knows everybody."

"Oh, I remember! He is 'The Man Who Knows!'"

It was his turn to be astonished.

"Where in the world have you heard of him?"

Briefly she retailed her experience, and when she came to describe the omniscient Mr. Mann—"A crank," growled Mr. Minute. "I was hoping there was something in it."

"Surely, uncle, there must be something in it," said the girl seriously. "A man of the standing of the chief commissioner would not speak about him as Sir George did unless he had very excellent reason."

"Tell me some more about what you saw," he said. "I seem to remember the report of the inquest. The dead man was unknown and has not been identified."

She described, as well as she could remember, her meeting with the knowledgable Mr. Mann. She had to be tactful because she wished to tell the story without betraying the fact that she had been with Frank. But she might have saved herself the trouble, because when she was halfway through the narrative he interrupted her.

"I gather you were not by yourself," he grumbled. "Master Frank was somewhere handy, I suppose?"

She laughed.

"I met him quite by accident," she said demurely.

"Naturally," said John Minute.

"Oh, uncle, and there was a man whom Frank knew! You probably know him—Constable Wiseman."

John Minute unfolded his napkin, stirred his soup, and grunted.

"Wiseman is a stupid ass," he said briefly. "The mere fact that he was mixed up in the affair is sufficient explanation as to why the dead man remains unknown. I know Constable Wiseman very well," he said. "He has summoned me twice—once for doing a little pistol-shooting in the garden just as an object lesson to all tramps, and once—confound him!—for a smoking chimney. Oh, yes, I know Constable Wiseman."

Apparently the thought of Constable Wiseman filled his mind through two courses, for he did not speak until he set his fish knife and fork together and muttered something about a "silly, meddling jackass!"

He was very silent throughout the meal, his mind being divided between two subjects. Uppermost, though of least importance, was the personality of Saul Arthur Mann. Him he mentally viewed with suspicion and apprehension. It was an irritation even to suggest that there might be secret places in his own life which could be flooded with the light of this man's knowledge, and he resolved to beard "The Man Who Knows" in his den that afternoon and challenge him by inference to produce all the information he had concerning his past.

There was much which was public property. It was John Minute's boast that his life was a book which might be read, but in his inmost heart he knew of one dark place which baffled the outside world. He brought himself from the mental rehearsal of his interview to what was, after all, the first and more important business.

"May," he said suddenly, "have you thought any more about what I asked you?"

She made no attempt to fence with the question.

"You mean Jasper Cole?"

He nodded, and for the moment she made no reply, and sat with eyes downcast, tracing a little figure upon the tablecloth with her finger tip.

"The truth is, uncle," she said at last, "I am not keen on marriage at all just yet, and you are sufficiently acquainted with human nature to know that anything which savors of coercion will not make me predisposed toward Mr. Cole."

"I suppose the real truth is," he said gruffly, "that you are in love with Frank?"

She laughed.

"That is just what the real truth is not," she said. "I like Frank very much. He is a dear, bright, sunny boy."

Mr. Minute grunted.

"Oh, yes, he is!" the girl went on. "But I am not in love with him—really."

"I suppose you are not influenced by the fact that he is my—heir," he said, and eyed her keenly.

She met his glance steadily.

"If you were not the nicest man I know," she smiled, "I should be very offended. Of course, I don't care whether Frank is rich or poor. You have provided too well for me for mercenary considerations to weigh at all with me."

John Minute grunted again.

"I am quite serious about Jasper."

"Why are you so keen on Jasper?" she asked.

He hesitated.

"I know him," he said shortly. "He has proved to me in a hundred ways that he is a reliable, decent lad. He has become almost indispensable to me," he continued with his quick little laugh, "and that Frank has never been. Oh, yes, Frank's all right in his way, but he's crazy on things which cut no ice with me. Too fond of sports, too fond of loafing," he growled.

The girl laughed again.

"I can give you a little information on one point," John Minute went on, "and it was to tell you this that I brought you here to-day. I am a very rich man. You know that. I have made millions and lost them, but I have still enough to satisfy my heirs. I am leaving you two hundred thousand pounds in my will."

She looked at him with a startled exclamation.

"Uncle!" she said.

He nodded.

"It is not a quarter of my fortune," he went on quickly, "but it will make you comfortable after I am gone."

He rested his elbows on the table and looked at her searchingly.

"You are an heiress," he said, "for, whatever you did, I should never change my mind. Oh, I know you will do nothing of which I should disapprove, but there is the fact. If you marry Frank you would still get your two hundred thousand, though I should bitterly regret your marriage. No, my girl," he said more kindly than was his wont, "I only ask you this—that whatever else you do, you will not make your choice until the next fortnight has expired."

With a jerk of his head, John Minute summoned a waiter and paid his bill.

No more was said until he handed her into her cab in the courtyard.

"I shall be in town next week," he said.

He watched the cab disappear in the stream of traffic which flowed along the Strand, and, calling another taxi, he drove to the address with which the chief commissioner had furnished him.

CHAPTER VI

THE MAN WHO KNEW

Backwell Street, in the City of London, contains one palatial building which at one time was the headquarters of the South American Stock Exchange, a superior bucket shop which on its failure had claimed its fifty thousand victims. The ornate gold lettering on its great plate-glass window had long since been removed, and the big brass plate which announced to the passerby that here sat the spider weaving his golden web for the multitude of flies, had been replaced by a modest, oxidized scroll bearing the simple legend:

SAUL ARTHUR MANN

What Mr. Mann's business was few people knew. He kept an army of clerks. He had the largest collection of file cabinets possessed by any three business houses in the City, he had an enormous post bag, and both he and his clerks kept regulation business hours. His beginnings, however, were well known.

He had been a stockbroker's clerk, with a passion for collecting clippings mainly dealing with political, geographical, and meteorological conditions obtaining in those areas wherein the great Joint Stock Companies of the earth were engaged in operations. He had gradually built up a service of correspondence all over the world.

The first news of labor trouble on a gold field came to him, and his brokers indicated his view upon the situation in that particular area by "bearing" the stock of the affected company.

If his Liverpool agents suddenly descended upon the Cotton Exchange and began buying May cotton in enormous quantities, the initiated knew that Saul Arthur Mann had been awakened from his slumbers by a telegram describing storm havoc in the cotton belt of the United States of America. When a curious blight fell upon the coffee plantations of Ceylon, a six-hundred-word cablegram describing the habits and characteristics of the minute insect which caused the blight reached Saul Arthur Mann at two o'clock in the afternoon, and by three o'clock the price of coffee had jumped.

When, on another occasion, Señor Almarez, the President of Cacura, had thrown a glass of wine in the face of his brother-in-law, Captain Vassalaro, Saul Arthur Mann had jumped into the market and beaten down all Cacura stocks, which were fairly high as a result of excellent crops and secure government. He "beared" them because he knew that Vassalaro was a dead shot, and that the inevitable duel would deprive Cacura of the best president it had had for twenty years, and that the way would be open for the election of Sebastian Romelez, who had behind him a certain group of German financiers who desired to exploit the country in their own peculiar fashion.

He probably built up a very considerable fortune, and it is certain that he extended the range of his inquiries until the making of money by means of his curious information bureau became only a secondary consideration. He had a marvelous memory, which was supplemented by his system of filing. He would go to work patiently for months, and spend sums of money out of all proportion to the value of the information, to discover, for example, the reason why a district officer in some far-away spot in India had been obliged to return to England before his tour of duty had ended.

His thirst for facts was insatiable; his grasp of the politics of every country in the world, and his extraordinarily accurate information concerning the personality of all those who directed those policies, was the basis upon which he was able to build up theories of amazing accuracy.

A man of simple tastes, who lived in a rambling old house in Streatham, his work, his hobby, and his very life was his bureau. He had assisted the police times without number, and had been so fascinated by the success of this branch of his investigations that he had started a new criminal record, which had been of the greatest help to the police and had piqued Scotland Yard to emulation.

John Minute, descending from his cab at the door, looked up at the imposing facia with a frown. Entering the broad vestibule, he handed his card to the waiting attendant and took a seat in a well-furnished waiting room. Five minutes later he was ushered into the presence of "The Man Who Knew." Mr. Mann, a comical little figure at a very large writing table, jumped up and went halfway across the big room to meet his visitor. He beamed through his big spectacles as he waved John Minute to a deep armchair.

"The chief commissioner sent you, didn't he?" he said, pointing an accusing finger at the visitor. "I know he did, because he called me up this morning and asked me about three people who, I happen to know, have been bothering you. Now what can I do for you, Mr. Minute?"

John Minute stretched his legs and thrust his hands defiantly into his trousers' pockets.

"You can tell me all you know about me," he said.

Saul Arthur Mann trotted back to his big table and seated himself.

"I haven't time to tell you as much," he said breezily, "but I'll give you a few outlines."

He pressed a bell at his desk, opened a big index, and ran his finger down.

"Bring me 8874," he said impressively to the clerk who made his appearance.

To John Minute's surprise, it was not a bulky dossier with which the attendant returned, but a neat little book soberly bound in gray.

"Now," said Mr. Mann, wriggling himself comfortably back in his chair, "I will read a few things to you."

He held up the book.

"There are no names in this book, my friend; not a single, blessed name. Nobody knows who 8874 is except myself."

He patted the big index affectionately.

"The name is there. When I leave this office it will be behind three depths of steel; when I die it will be burned with me."

He opened the little book again and read. He read steadily for a quarter of an hour in a monotonous, singsong voice, and John Minute slowly sat himself erect and listened with tense face and narrow eyelids to the record. He did not interrupt until the other had finished.

"Half of your facts are lies," he said harshly. "Some of them are just common gossip; some are purely imaginary."

Saul Arthur Mann closed the book and shook his head.

"Everything here," he said, touching the book, "is true. It may not be the truth as you want it known, but it is the truth. If I thought there was a single fact in there which was not true my *raison d'être* would be lost. That is the truth, the whole truth, and nothing but the truth, Mr. Minute," he went on, and the good-natured little face was pink with annoyance.

"Suppose it were the truth," interrupted John Minute, "what price would you ask for that record and such documents as you say you have to prove its truth?"

The other leaned back in his chair and clasped his hands meditatively.

"How much do you think you are worth, Mr. Minute?"

"You ought to know," said the other with a sneer.

Saul Arthur Mann inclined his head.

"At the present price of securities, I should say about one million two hundred and seventy thousand pounds," he said, and John Minute opened his eyes in astonishment.

"Near enough," he reluctantly admitted.

"Well," the little man continued, "if you multiply that by fifty and you bring all that money into my office and place it on that table in ten-thousand-pound notes, you could not buy that little book or the records which support it."

He jumped up.

"I am afraid I am keeping you, Mr. Minute."

"You are not keeping me," said the other roughly. "Before I go I want to know what use you are going to make of your knowledge."

The little man spread out his hands in deprecation.

"What use? You have seen the use to which I have put it. I have told you what no other living soul will know."

"How do you know I am John Minute?" asked the visitor quickly.

"Some twenty-seven photographs of you are included in the folder which contains your record, Mr. Minute," said the little investigator calmly. "You see, you are quite a prominent personage—one of the two hundred and four really rich men in England. I am not likely to mistake you for anybody else, and, more than this, your history is so interesting a one that naturally I know much more about you than I should if you had lived the dull and placid life of a city merchant."

"Tell me one thing before I go," asked Minute. "Where is the person you refer to as 'X'?"

Saul Arthur Mann smiled and inclined his head never so slightly.

"That is a question which you have no right to ask," he said. "It is information which is available to the police or to any authorized person who wishes to get into touch with 'X.' I might add," he went on, "that there is much more I could tell you, if it were not that it would involve persons with whom you are acquainted."

John Minute left the bureau looking a little older, a little paler than when he had entered. He drove to his club with one thought in his mind, and that thought revolved about the identity and the whereabouts of the person referred to in the little man's record as "X."

CHAPTER VII

INTRODUCING MR. REX HOLLAND

Mr. Rex Holland stepped out of his new car, and, standing back a pace, surveyed his recent acquisition with a dispassionate eye.

"I think she will do, Feltham," he said.

The chauffeur touched his cap and grinned broadly.

"She did it in thirty-eight minutes, sir; not bad for a twenty-mile run—half of it through London."

"Not bad," agreed Mr. Holland, slowly stripping his gloves.

The car was drawn up at the entrance to the country cottage which a lavish expenditure of money had converted into a bijou palace.

He still lingered, and the chauffeur, feeling that some encouragement to conversation was called for, ventured the view that a car ought to be a good one if one spent eight hundred pounds on it.

"Everything that is good costs money," said Mr. Rex Holland sententiously, and then continued: "Correct me if I am mistaken, but as we came through Putney did I not see you nod to the driver of another car?"

"Yes, sir."

"When I engaged you," Mr. Holland went on in his even voice, "you told me that you had just arrived from Australia and knew nobody in England; I think my advertisement made it clear that I wanted a man who fulfilled these conditions?"

"Quite right, sir. I was as much surprised as you; the driver of that car was a fellow who traveled over to the old country on the same boat as me. It's rather rum that he should have got the same kind of job."

Mr. Holland smiled quietly.

"I hope his employer is not as eccentric as I and that he pays his servant on my scale."

With this shot he unlocked and passed through the door of the cottage.

Feltham drove his car to the garage which had been built at the back of the house, and, once free from observation, lit his pipe, and, seating himself on a box, drew from his pocket a little card which he perused with unusual care.

He read:

> One: To act as chauffeur and valet. Two: To receive ten pounds a week and expenses. Three: To make no friends or acquaintances. Four: Never under any circumstances to discuss my employer, his habits, or his business. Five: Never under any circumstances to go farther eastward into London than is represented by a line drawn from the Marble Arch to Victoria Station. Six: Never to recognize my employer if I see him in the street in company with any other person.

The chauffeur folded the card and scratched his chin reflectively.

"Eccentricity," he said.

It was a nice five-syllable word, and its employment was a comfort to this perturbed Australian. He cleaned his face and hands, and went into the tiny kitchen to prepare his master's dinner.

Mr. Holland's house was a remarkable one. It was filled with every form of labor-saving device which the ingenuity of man could devise. The furniture, if luxurious, was not in any great quantity. Vacuum tubes were to be found in every room, and by the attachment of hose and nozzle and the pressure of a switch each room could be dusted in a few minutes. From the kitchen, at the back of the cottage, to the dining room ran two endless belts electrically controlled, which presently carried to the table the very simple meal which his cook-chauffeur had prepared.

The remnants of dinner were cleared away, the chauffeur dismissed to his quarters, a little one-roomed building separated from the cottage, and the switch was turned over which heated the automatic coffee percolator which stood on the sideboard.

Mr. Holland sat reading, his feet resting on a chair.

He only interrupted his study long enough to draw off the coffee into a little white cup and to switch off the current.

He sat until the little silver clock on the mantelshelf struck twelve, and then he placed a card in the book to mark the place, closed it, and rose leisurely.

He slid back a panel in the wall, disclosing the steel door of a safe. This he opened with a key which he selected from a bunch. From the interior of the safe he removed a cedarwood box, also locked. He threw back the lid and removed one by one three check books and a pair of gloves of some thin, transparent fabric. These were obviously to guard against tell-tale finger prints.

He carefully pulled them on and buttoned them. Next he detached three checks, one from each book, and, taking a fountain pen from his pocket, he began filling in the blank spaces. He wrote slowly, almost laboriously, and he wrote without a copy. There are very few forgers in the criminal records who have ever accomplished the feat of imitating a man's signature from memory. Mr. Rex Holland was singularly exceptional to all precedent, for from the date to the flourishing signature these checks might have been written and signed by John Minute.

There were the same fantastic "E's," the same stiff-tailed "Y's." Even John Minute might have been in doubt whether he wrote the "Eight hundred and fifty" which appeared on one slip.

Mr. Holland surveyed his handiwork without emotion.

He waited for the ink to dry before he folded the checks and put them in his pocket. This was John Minute's way, for the millionaire never used blotting paper for some reason, probably not unconnected with an event in his earlier career. When the checks were in his pocket, Mr. Holland removed his gloves, replaced them with the check books in the box and in the safe, locked the steel door, drew the sliding panel, and went to bed.

Early the next morning he summoned his servant.

"Take the car back to town," he said. "I am going back by train. Meet me at the Holland Park tube at two o'clock; I have a little job for you which will earn you five hundred."

"That's my job, sir," said the dazed man when he recovered from the shock.

Frank sometimes accompanied May to the East End, and on the day Mr. Rex Holland returned to London he called for the girl at her flat to drive her to Canning Town.

"You can come in and have some tea," she invited.

"You're a luxurious beggar, May," he said, glancing round approvingly at the prettily furnished sitting room. "Contrast this with my humble abode in Bayswater."

"I don't know your humble abode in Bayswater," she laughed. "But why on earth you should elect to live at Bayswater I can't imagine."

He sipped his tea with a twinkle in his eye.

"Guess what income the heir of the Minute millions enjoys?" he asked ironically. "No, I'll save you the agony of guessing. I earn seven pounds a week at the bank, and that is the whole of my income."

"But doesn't uncle—" she began in surprise.

"Not a bob," replied Frank vulgarly; "not half a bob."

"But—"

"I know what you're going to say; he treats you generously, I know. He treats me justly. Between generosity and justice, give me generosity all the time. I will tell you something else. He pays Jasper Cole a thousand a year! It's very curious, isn't it?"

She leaned over and patted his arm.

"Poor boy," she said sympathetically, "that doesn't make it any easier—Jasper, I mean."

Frank indulged in a little grimace, and said:

"By the way, I saw the mysterious Jasper this morning—coming out of the Waterloo Station looking more mysterious than ever. What particular business has he in the country?"

She shook her head and rose.

"I know as little about Jasper as you," she answered.

She turned and looked at him thoughtfully.

"Frank," she said, "I am rather worried about you and Jasper. I am worried because your uncle does not seem to take the same view of Jasper as you take. It is not a very heroic position for either of you, and it is rather hateful for me."

Frank looked at her with a quizzical smile.

"Why hateful for you?"

She shook her head.

"I would like to tell you everything, but that would not be fair."

"To whom?" Frank asked quickly.

"To you, your uncle, or to Jasper."

He came nearer to her.

"Have you so warm a feeling for Jasper?" he asked.

"I have no warm feeling for anybody," she said candidly. "Oh, don't look so glum, Frank! I suppose I am slow to develop, but you cannot expect me to have any very decided views yet a while."

Frank smiled ruefully.

"That is my one big trouble, dear," he said quietly; "bigger than anything else in the world."

She stood with her hand on the door, hesitating, a look of perplexity upon her beautiful face. She was of the tall, slender type, a girl slowly ripening into womanhood. She might have been described as cold and a little repressive, but the truth was that she was as yet untouched by the fires of passion, and for all her twenty-one years she was still something of the healthy schoolgirl, with a schoolgirl's impatience of sentiment.

"I am the last to spin a hard-luck yarn," Frank went on, "but I have not had the best of everything, dear. I started wrong with uncle. He never liked my father nor any of my father's family. His treatment of his wife was infamous. My poor governor was one of those easy-going fellows who was always in trouble, and it was always John Minute's job to get him out. I don't like talking about him—" He hesitated.

She nodded.

"I know," she said sympathetically.

"Father was not the rotter that Uncle John thinks he was. He had his good points. He was careless, and he drank much more than was good for him, but all the scrapes he fell into were due to this latter failing."

The girl knew the story of Doctor Merrill. It had been sketched briefly but vividly by John Minute. She knew also some of those scrapes which had involved Doctor Merrill's ruin, material and moral.

"Frank," she said, "if I can help you in any way I would do it."

"You can help me absolutely," said the young man quietly, "by marrying me."

She gasped.

"When?" she asked, startled.

"Now, next week; at any rate, soon." He smiled, and, crossing to her, caught her hand in his.

"May, dear, you know I love you. You know there is nothing in the world I would not do for you, no sacrifice that I would not make."

She shook her head.

"You must give me some time to think about this, Frank," she said.

"Don't go," he begged. "You cannot know how urgent is my need of you. Uncle John has told you a great deal about me, but has he told you this—that my only hope of independence—independence of his millions and his influence—you cannot know how widespread or pernicious that influence is," he said, with an unaccustomed passion in his voice, "lies in my marriage before my twenty-fourth birthday?"

"Frank!"

"It is true. I cannot tell you any more, but John Minute knows. If I am married within the next ten days"—he snapped his fingers—"that for his millions. I am independent of his legacies, independent of his patronage."

She stared at him, open-eyed.

"You never told me this before."

He shook his head a little despairingly.

"There are some things I can never tell you, May, and some things which you can never know till we are married. I only ask you to trust me."

"But suppose," she faltered, "you are not married within ten days, what will happen?"

He shrugged his shoulders.

"'I am John's liege man of life and limb and of earthly regard,'" he quoted flippantly. "I shall wait hopefully for the only release that can come, the release which his death will bring. I hate saying that, for there is something about him that I like enormously, but that is the truth, and, May," he said, still holding her hand and looking earnestly into her face, "I don't want to feel like that about John Minute. I don't want to look forward to his end. I want to meet him without any sense of dependence. I don't want to be looking all the time for signs of decay and decrepitude, and hail each illness he may have with a feeling of pleasant anticipation. It is beastly of me to talk like this, I know, but if you were in my position—if you knew all that I know—you would understand."

The girl's mind was in a ferment. An ordinary meeting had developed so tumultuously that she had lost her command of the situation. A hundred thoughts ran riot through her mind. She felt as though she were an arbitrator deciding between two men, of both of whom she was fond, and, even at that moment, there intruded into her mental vision a picture of Jasper Cole, with his pale, intellectual face and his grave, dark eyes.

"I must think about this," she said again. "I don't think you had better come down to the mission with me."

He nodded.

"Perhaps you're right," he said.

Gently she released her hand and left him.

For her that day was one of supreme mental perturbation. What was the extraordinary reason which compelled his marriage by his twenty-fourth birthday? She remembered how John Minute had insisted that her thoughts about marriage should be at least postponed for the next fortnight. Why had John Minute suddenly sprung this story of her legacy upon her? For the first time in her life she began to regard her uncle with suspicion.

For Frank the day did not develop without its sensations. The Piccadilly branch of the London and Western Counties Bank occupies commodious premises, but Frank had never been granted the use of a private office. His big desk was in a corner remote from the counter, surrounded on three sides by a screen which was half glass and half teak paneling. From where he sat he could secure a view of the counter, a necessary provision, since he was occasionally called upon to identify the bearers of checks.

He returned a little before three o'clock in the afternoon, and Mr. Brandon, the manager, came hurriedly from his little sanctum at the rear of the premises and beckoned Frank into his office.

"You've taken an awful long time for lunch," he complained.

"I'm sorry," said Frank. "I met Miss Nuttall, and the time flew."

"Did you see Holland the other day?" the manager interrupted.

"I didn't see him on the day you sent me," replied Frank, "but I saw him on the following day."

"Is he a friend of your uncle's?"

"I don't think so. Why do you ask?"

The manager took up three checks which lay on the table, and Frank examined them. One was for eight hundred and fifty pounds six shillings, and was drawn upon the Liverpool Cotton Bank, one was for forty-one thousand one hundred and forty pounds, and was drawn upon the Bank of England, and the other was for seven thousand nine hundred and ninety-nine pounds fourteen shillings. They were all signed "John Minute," and they were all made payable to "Rex Holland, esquire," and were crossed.

Now John Minute had a very curious practice of splitting up payments so that they covered the three banking houses at which his money was deposited. The check for seven thousand nine hundred and ninety-nine pounds fourteen shillings was drawn upon the London and Western Counties Bank, and that would have afforded the manager some clew even if he had not been well acquainted with John Minute's eccentricity.

"Seven thousand nine hundred and ninety-nine pounds fourteen shillings from Mr. Minute's balance," said the manager, "leaves exactly fifty thousand pounds."

Mr. Brandon shook his head in despair at the unbusinesslike methods of his patron.

"Does he know your uncle?"

"Who?"

"Rex Holland."

Frank frowned in an effort of memory.

"I don't remember my uncle ever speaking of him, and yet, now I come to think of it, one of the first checks he put into the bank was on my uncle's account. Yes, now I remember," he exclaimed. "He opened the account on a letter of introduction which was signed by Mr. Minute. I thought at the time that they had probably had business dealings together, and as uncle never encourages the discussion of bank affairs outside of the bank, I have never mentioned it to him."

Again Mr. Brandon shook his head in doubt.

"I must say, Mr. Merrill," he said, "I don't like these mysterious depositors. What is he like in appearance?"

"Rather a tall, youngish man, exquisitely dressed."

"Clean shaven?"

"No, he has a closely trimmed black beard, though he cannot be much more than twenty-eight. In fact, when I saw him for the first time the face was familiar to me and I had an impression of having seen him before. I think he was wearing a gold-rimmed eyeglass when he came on the first occasion, but I have never met him in the street, and he hardly moves in my humble social circle." Frank smiled.

"I suppose it is all right," said the manager dubiously; "but, anyway, I'll see him to-morrow. As a precautionary measure we might get in touch with your uncle, though I know he'll raise Cain if we bother him about his account."

"He will certainly raise Cain if you get in touch with him to-day," smiled Frank, "for he is due to leave by the two-twenty this afternoon for Paris."

It wanted five minutes to the hour at which the bank closed when a clerk came through the swing door and laid a letter upon the counter which was taken in to Mr. Brandon, who came into the office immediately and crossed to where Frank sat.

"Look at this," he said.

Frank took the letter and read it. It was addressed to the manager, and ran:

> DEAR SIR: I am leaving for Paris to-night to join my partner, Mr. Minute. I shall be very glad, therefore, if you will arrange to cash the inclosed check.
>
> Yours faithfully,
>
> REX A. HOLLAND.

The "inclosed check" was for fifty-five thousand pounds and was within five thousand pounds of the amount standing to Mr. Holland's account in the bank. There was a postscript to the letter:

You will accept this, my receipt, for the sum, and hand it to my messenger, Sergeant George Graylin, of the corps of commissionaires, and this form of receipt will serve to indemnify you against loss in the event of mishap.

The manager walked to the counter.

"Who gave you this letter?" he asked.

"Mr. Holland, sir," said the man.

"Where is Mr. Holland?" asked Frank.

The sergeant shook his head.

"At his flat. My instructions were to take this letter to the bank and bring back the money."

The manager was in a quandary. It was a regular transaction, and it was by no means unusual to pay out money in this way. It was only the largeness of the sum which made him hesitate. He disappeared into his office and came back with two bundles of notes which he had taken from the safe. He counted them over, placed them in a sealed envelope, and received from the sergeant his receipt.

When the man had gone Brandon wiped his forehead.

"Phew!" he said. "I don't like this way of doing business very much, and I should be very glad indeed to be transferred back to the head office."

The words were hardly out of his mouth when a bell rang violently. The front doors of the bank had been closed with the departure of the commissioner, and one of the junior clerks, balancing up his day book, dropped his pen, and, at a sign from his chief, walking to the door, pulled back the bolts and admitted—John Minute.

Frank stared at him in astonishment.

"Hello, uncle," he said. "I wish you had come a few minutes before. I thought you were in Paris."

"The wire calling me to Paris was a fake," growled John Minute. "I wired for confirmation, and discovered my Paris people had not sent me any message. I only got the wire just before the train started. I have been spending all the afternoon getting on to the phone to Paris to untangle the muddle. Why did you wish I was here five minutes before?"

"Because," said Frank, "we have just paid out fifty-five thousand pounds to your friend, Mr. Holland."

"My friend?" John Minute stared from the manager to Frank and from Frank to the manager, who suddenly experienced a sinking feeling which accompanies disaster.

"What do you mean by 'my friend'?" asked John Minute. "I have never heard of the man before."

"Didn't you give Mr. Holland checks amounting to fifty-five thousand pounds this morning?" gasped the manager, turning suddenly pale.

"Certainly not!" roared John Minute. "Why the devil should I give him checks? I have never heard of the man."

The manager grasped the counter for support.

He explained the situation in a few halting words, and led the way to his office, Frank accompanying him.

John Minute examined the checks.

"That is my writing," he said. "I could swear to it myself, and yet I never wrote those checks or signed them. Did you note the commissionaire's number?"

"As it happens I jotted it down," said Frank.

By this time the manager was on the phone to the police. At seven o'clock that night the commissionaire was discovered. He had been employed, he said, by a Mr. Holland, whom he described as a slimmish man, clean shaven, and by no means answering to the description which Frank had given.

"I have lived for a long time in Australia," said the commissionaire, "and he spoke like an Australian. In fact, when I mentioned certain places I had been to he told me he knew them."

The police further discovered that the Knightsbridge flat had been taken, furnished, three months before by Mr. Rex Holland, the negotiations having been by letter. Mr. Holland's agent had assumed responsibility for the flat, and Mr. Holland's agent was easily discoverable in a clerk in the employment of a well-known firm of surveyors and auctioneers, who had also received his commission by letter.

When the police searched the flat they found only one thing which helped them in their investigations. The hall porter said that, as often as not, the flat was untenanted, and only occasionally, when he was off duty, had Mr. Holland put in an appearance, and he only knew this from statements which had been made by other tenants.

"It comes to this," said John Minute grimly; "that nobody has seen Mr. Holland but you, Frank."

Frank stiffened.

"I am not suggesting that you are in the swindle," said Minute gruffly. "As likely as not, the man you saw was not Mr. Holland, and it is probably the work of a gang, but I am going to find out who this man is, if I have to spend twice as much as I have lost."

The police were not encouraging.

Detective Inspector Nash, from Scotland Yard, who had handled some of the biggest cases of bank swindles, held out no hope of the money being recovered.

"In theory you can get back the notes if you have their numbers," he said, "but in practice it is almost impossible to recover them, because it is quite easy to change even notes for five hundred pounds, and probably you will find these in circulation in a week or two."

His speculation proved to be correct, for on the third day after the crime three of the missing notes made a curious appearance.

"Ready-Money Minute," true to his nickname, was in the habit of balancing his accounts as between bank and bank by cash payments. He had made it a practice for all his dividends to be paid in actual cash, and these were sent to the Piccadilly branch of the London and Western Counties Bank in bulk. After a payment of a very large sum on account of certain dividends accruing from his South African investments, three of the missing notes were discovered in the bank itself.

John Minute, apprised by telegram of the fact, said nothing; for the money had been paid in by his confidential secretary, Jasper Cole, and there was excellent reason why he did not desire to emphasize the fact.

CHAPTER VIII

SERGEANT SMITH CALLS

The big library of Weald Lodge was brilliantly lighted and nobody had pulled down the blinds. So that it was possible for any man who troubled to jump the low stone wall which ran by the road and push a way through the damp shrubbery to see all that was happening in the room.

Weald Lodge stands between Eastbourne and Wilmington, and in the winter months the curious, represented by youthful holiday makers, are few and far between. Constable Wiseman, of the Eastbourne constabulary, certainly was not curious. He paced his slow, moist way and merely noted, in passing, the fact that the flood of light reflected on the little patch of lawn at the side of the house.

The hour was nine o'clock on a June evening, and officially it was only the hour of sunset, though lowering rain clouds had so darkened the world that night had closed down upon the weald, had blotted out its pleasant villages and had hidden the green downs.

He continued to the end of his beat and met his impatient superior.

"Everything's all right, sergeant," he reported; "only old Minute's lights are blazing away and his windows are open."

"Better go and warn him," said the sergeant, pulling his bicycle into position for mounting.

He had his foot on the treadle, but hesitated.

"I'd warn him myself, but I don't think he'd be glad to see me."

He grinned to himself, then remarked: "Something queer about Minute—eh?"

"There is, indeed," agreed Constable Wiseman heartily. His beat was a lonely one, and he was a very bored man. If by agreement with his officer he could induce that loquacious gentleman to talk for a quarter of an hour, so much dull time might be passed. The fact that Sergeant Smith was loquacious indicated, too, that he had been drinking and was ready to quarrel with anybody.

"Come under the shelter of that wall," said the sergeant, and pushed his machine to the protection afforded by the side wall of a house.

It is possible that the sergeant was anxious to impress upon his subordinate's mind a point of view which might be useful to himself one day.

"Minute is a dangerous old man," he said.

"Don't I know it?" said Constable Wiseman, with the recollection of sundry "reportings" and inquiries.

"You've got to remember that, Wiseman," the sergeant went on; "and by 'dangerous' I mean that he's the sort of old fellow that would ask a constable to come in to have a drink and then report him."

"Good Lord!" said the shocked Mr. Wiseman at this revelation of the blackest treachery.

Sergeant Smith nodded.

"That's the sort of man he is," he said. "I knew him years ago—at least, I've seen him. I was in Matabeleland with him, and I tell you there's nothing too mean for 'Ready-Money Minute'—curse him!"

"I'll bet you have had a terrible life, sergeant," encouraged Constable Wiseman.

The other laughed bitterly.

"I have," he said.

Sergeant Smith's acquaintance with Eastbourne was a short one. He had only been four years in the town, and had, so rumor ran, owed his promotion to influence. What that influence was none could say. It had been suggested that John Minute himself had secured him his sergeant's stripes, but that was a theory which was pooh-poohed by people who knew that the sergeant had little that was good to say of his supposed patron.

Constable Wiseman, a profound thinker and a secret reader of sensational detective stories, had at one time made a report against John Minute for some technical offense, and had made it in fear and trembling, expecting his sergeant promptly to squash this attempt to persecute his patron; but, to his surprise and delight, Sergeant Smith had furthered his efforts and had helped to secure the conviction which involved a fine.

"You go on and finish your beat, Constable," said the sergeant suddenly, "and I'll ride up to the old devil's house and see what's doing."

He mounted his bicycle and trundled up the hill, dismounting before Weald Lodge, and propped his bicycle against the wall. He looked for a long time toward the open French windows, and then, jumping the wall, made his way slowly across the lawn, avoiding the gravel path which would betray his presence. He got to a point opposite the window which commanded a full view of the room.

Though the window was open, there was a fire in the grate. To the sergeant's satisfaction, John Minute was alone. He sat in a deep armchair in his favorite attitude, his hands pushed into his pockets, his head upon his chest. He heard the sergeant's foot upon the gravel and stood up as the rain-drenched figure appeared at the open window.

"Oh, it is you, is it?" growled John Minute. "What do you want?"

"Alone?" said the sergeant, and he spoke as one to his equal.

"Come in!"

Mr. Minute's library had been furnished by the Artistic Furniture Company, of Eastbourne, which had branches at Hastings, Bexhill, Brighton, and—it was claimed—at London. The furniture was of dark oak, busily carved. There was a large bookcase which half covered one wall. This was the "library," and it was filled with books of uniform binding which occupied the shelves. The books had been supplied by a great bookseller of London, and included—at Mr. Minute's suggestion—"The Hundred Best Books," "Books That Have Helped Me," "The Encyclopedia Brillonica," and twenty bound volumes of a certain weekly periodical of international reputation. John Minute had no literary leanings.

The sergeant hesitated, wiped his heavy boots on the sodden mat outside the window, and walked into the room.

"You are pretty cozy, John," he said.

"What do you want?" asked Minute, without enthusiasm.

"I thought I'd look you up. My constable reported your windows were open, and I felt it my duty to come along and warn you—there are thieves about, John."

"I know of one," said John Minute, looking at the other steadily. "Your constable, as you call him, is, I presume, that thick-headed jackass, Wiseman!"

"Got him first time," said the sergeant, removing his waterproof cape. "I don't often trouble you, but somehow I had a feeling I'd like to see you to-night. My constable revived old memories, John."

"Unpleasant for you, I hope," said John Minute ungraciously.

"There's a nice little gold farm four hundred miles north of Gwelo," said Sergeant Smith meditatively.

"And a nice little breakwater half a mile south of Cape Town," said John Minute, "where the Cape government keeps highwaymen who hold up the Salisbury coach and rob the mails."

Sergeant Smith smiled.

"You will have your little joke," he said; "but I might remind you that they have plenty of accommodation on the breakwater, John. They even take care of men who have stolen land and murdered natives."

"What do you want?" asked John Minute again.

The other grinned.

"Just a pleasant little friendly visit," he explained. "I haven't looked you up for twelve months. It is a hard life, this police work, even when you have got two or three pounds a week from a private source to add to your pay. It is nothing like the work we have in the Matabele mounted police, eh, John? But, Lord," he said, looking into the fire thoughtfully, "when I think how I stood up in the attorney's office at Salisbury and took my solemn oath that old John Gedding had transferred his Saibach gold claims to you on his death bed; when I think of the amount of perjury—me a uniformed servant of the British South African Company, and, so to speak, an official of the law—I blush for myself."

"Do you ever blush for yourself when you think of how you and your pals held up Hoffman's store, shot Hoffman, and took his swag?" asked John Minute. "I'd give a lot of money to see you blush, Crawley; and now, for about the fourteenth time, what do you want? If it is money, you can't have it. If it is more promotion, you are not fit to have it. If it is a word of advice—"

The other stopped him with a motion of his hand.

"I can't afford to have your advice, John," he said. "All I know is that you promised me my fair share over those Saibach claims. It is a paying mine now. They tell me that its capital is two millions."

"You were well paid," said John Minute shortly.

"Five hundred pounds isn't much for the surrender of your soul's salvation," said Sergeant Smith.

He slowly replaced his cape on his broad shoulders and walked to the window.

"Listen here, John Minute!" All the good nature had gone out of his voice, and it was Trooper Henry Crawley, the lawbreaker, who spoke. "You are not going to satisfy me much longer with a few pounds a week. You have got to do the right thing by me, or I am going to blow."

"Let me know when your blowing starts," said John Minute, "and I'll send you a bowl of soup to cool."

"You're funny, but you don't amuse me," were the last words of the sergeant as he walked into the rain.

As before, he avoided the drive and jumped over the low wall on to the road, and was glad that he had done so, for a motor car swung into the drive and pulled up before the dark doorway of the house. He was over the wall again in an instant, and crossing with swift, noiseless steps in the direction of the car. He got as close as he could and listened.

Two of the voices he recognized. The third, that of a man, was a stranger. He heard this third person called "inspector," and wondered who was the guest. His curiosity was not to be satisfied, for by the time he had reached the view place on the lawn which overlooked the library John Minute had closed the windows and pulled down the blinds.

The visitors to Weald Lodge were three—Jasper Cole, May Nuttall, and a stout, middle-aged man of slow speech but of authoritative tone. This was Inspector

Nash, of Scotland Yard, who was in charge of the investigations into the forgeries. Minute received them in the library. He knew the inspector of old.

Jasper had brought May down in response to the telegraphed instructions which John Minute had sent him.

"What's the news?" he asked.

"Well, I think I have found your Mr. Holland," said the inspector.

He took a fat case from his inside pocket, opened it, and extracted a snapshot photograph. It represented a big motor car, and, standing by its bonnet, a little man in chauffeur's uniform.

"This is the fellow who called himself 'Rex Holland' and who sent the commissionaire on his errand. The photograph came into my possession as the result of an accident. It was discovered in the flat and had evidently fallen out of the man's pocket. I made inquiries and found that it was taken by a small photographer in Putney, and that the man had called for the photographs about ten o'clock in the morning of the same day that he sent the commissionaire on his errand. He was probably examining them during the period of his waiting in the flat, and one of them slipped to the ground. At any rate, the commissionaire has no doubt that this was the man."

"Do you seriously suggest that this fellow is Rex Holland?"

The inspector shook his head.

"I think he is merely one of the gang," he said. "I don't believe you will ever find Rex Holland, for each of the gang took the name in turn to take the part, according to the circumstances in which they found themselves. I have been unable to identify him, except that he went by the name of Feltham and was an Australian. That was the name he gave to the photographer with whom he talked. You see, the photograph was taken in High Street, Putney. The only clew we have is that he has been seen several times on the Portsmouth Road, driving one or two cars in which was a man who is probably the nearest approach to Rex Holland we shall get.

"I put my men on to make further investigations, and the Haslemere police told them that it is believed that the car was the property of a gentleman who lived in a lockup cottage some distance from Haslemere—evidently rather a swagger affair, because its owner had an electric cable and telephone wires laid in, and the cottage was altered and renovated twelve months ago at a very considerable cost. I shall be able to tell you more about that to-morrow."

They spent the rest of the evening discussing the crime, and the girl was a silent listener. It was not until very late that John Minute was able to give her his undivided attention.

"I asked you to come down," he said, "because I am getting a little worried about you."

"Worried about me, uncle?" she said, in surprise.

He nodded.

The two men had gone off to Jasper's study, and she was alone with her uncle.

"When I lunched with you the other day at the Savoy," he said, "I spoke to you about your marriage, and I asked you to defer any action for a fortnight."

She nodded.

"I was coming down to see you on that very matter," she said. "Uncle, won't you tell me why you want me to delay my marriage for a fortnight, and why you think I am going to get married at all?"

He did not answer immediately, but paced up and down the room.

"May," he said, "you have heard a great deal about me which is not very flattering. I lived a very rough life in South Africa, and I only had one friend in the world in whom I had the slightest confidence. That friend was your father. He stood by me in my bad times. He never worried me when I was flush of money, never denied me when I was broke. Whenever he helped me, he was content with what reward I offered him. There was no 'fifty-fifty' with Bill Nuttall. He was a man who had no ambition, no avarice—the whitest man I have ever met. What I have not told you about him is this: He and I were equal partners in a mine, the Gwelo Deep. He had great faith in the mine, and I had none at all. I knew it to be one of those properties you sometimes get in Rhodesia, all pocket and outcrop. Anyway, we floated a company."

He stopped and chuckled as at an amusing memory.

"The pound shares were worth a little less than sixpence until a fortnight ago."

He looked at her with one of those swift, penetrating glances, as though he were anxious to discover her thoughts.

"A fortnight ago," he said, "I learned from my agent in Bulawayo that a reef had been struck on an adjoining mine, and that the reef runs through our property. If that is true, you will be a rich woman in your own right, apart from the money you get from me. I cannot tell whether it is true until I have heard from the engineers, who are now examining the property, and I cannot know that for a fortnight. May, you are a dear girl," he said, and laid his hand on her arm, "and I have looked after you as though you were my own daughter. It is a happiness to me to know that you will be a very rich woman, because your father's shares was the only property you inherited from him. There is, however, one curious thing about it that I cannot understand."

He walked over to the bureau, unlocked a drawer, and took out a letter.

"My agent says that he advised me two years ago that this reef existed, and wondered why I had never given him authority to bore. I have no recollection of his ever having told me anything of the sort. Now you know the position," he said, putting back the letter and closing the drawer with a bang.

"You want me to wait for a better match," said the girl.

He inclined his head.

"I don't want you to get married for a fortnight," he repeated.

May Nuttall went to bed that night full of doubt and more than a little unhappy. The story that John Minute told about her father—was it true? Was it a story invented on the spur of the moment to counter Frank's plan? She thought of Frank and his almost solemn entreaty. There had been no mistaking his earnestness or his sincerity. If he would only take her into his confidence—and yet she recognized and was surprised at the revelation that she did not want that confidence. She wanted to help Frank very badly, and it was not the romance of the situation which appealed to her. There was a large sense of duty, something of that mother sense which every woman possesses, which tempted her to the sacrifice. Yet was it a sacrifice?

She debated that question half the night, tossing from side to side. She could not sleep, and, rising before the dawn, slipped into her dressing gown and went to the window. The rain had ceased, the clouds had broken and stood in black bars against the silver light of dawn. She felt unaccountably hungry, and after a second's hesitation she opened the door and went down the broad stairs to the hall.

To reach the kitchen she had to pass her uncle's door, and she noticed that it was ajar. She thought possibly he had gone to bed and left the light on, and her hand was on the knob to investigate when she heard a voice and drew back hurriedly. It was the voice of Jasper Cole.

"I have been into the books very carefully with Mackensen, the accountant, and there seems no doubt," he said.

"You think—" demanded her uncle.

"I am certain," answered Jasper, in his even, passionless tone. "The fraud has been worked by Frank. He had access to the books. He was the only person who saw Rex Holland; he was the only official at the bank who could possibly falsify the entries and at the same time hide his trail."

The girl turned cold and for a moment swayed as though she would faint. She clutched the jamb of the door for support and waited.

"I am half inclined to your belief," said John Minute slowly. "It is awful to believe that Frank is a forger, as his father was—awful!"

"It is pretty ghastly," said Jasper's voice, "but it is true."

The girl flung open the door and stood in the doorway.

"It is a lie!" she cried wrathfully. "A horrible lie—and you know it is a lie, Jasper!"

Without another word, she turned, slamming the door behind her.

CHAPTER IX

FRANK MERRILL AT THE ALTAR

Frank Merrill stepped through the swing doors of the London and Western Counties Bank with a light heart and a smile in his eyes, and went straight to his chief's office.

"I shall want you to let me go out this afternoon for an hour," he said.

Brandon looked up wearily. He had not been without his sleepless moments, and the strain of the forgery and the audit which followed was telling heavily upon him. He nodded a silent agreement, and Frank went back to his desk, humming a tune.

He had every reason to be happy, for in his pocket was the special license which, for a consideration, had been granted to him, and which empowered him to marry the girl whose amazing telegram had arrived that morning while he was at breakfast. It had contained only four words:

    Marry you to-day. MAY.

He could not guess what extraordinary circumstances had induced her to take so definite a view, but he was a very contented and happy young man.

She was to arrive in London soon after twelve, and he had arranged to meet her at the station and take her to lunch. Perhaps then she would explain the reason for her action. He numbered among his acquaintances the rector of a suburban church, who had agreed to perform the ceremony and to provide the necessary witnesses.

It was a beaming young man that met the girl, but the smile left his face when he saw how wan and haggard she was.

"Take me somewhere," she said quickly.

"Are you ill?" he asked anxiously.

She shook her head.

They had the Pall Mall Restaurant to themselves, for it was too early for the regular lunchers.

"Now tell me, dear," he said, catching her hands over the table, "to what do I owe this wonderful decision?"

"I cannot tell you, Frank," she said breathlessly. "I don't want to think about it. All I know is that people have been beastly about you. I am going to do all I possibly can to make up for it."

She was a little hysterical and very much overwrought, and he decided not to press the question, though her words puzzled him.

"Where are you going to stay?" he asked.

"I am staying at the Savoy," she replied. "What am I to do?"

In as few words as possible he told her where the ceremony was to be performed, and the hour at which she must leave the hotel.

"We will take the night train for the Continent," he said.

"But your work, Frank?"

He laughed.

"Oh, blow work!" he cried hilariously. "I cannot think of work to-day."

At two-fifteen he was waiting in the vestry for the girl's arrival, chatting with his friend the rector. He had arranged for the ceremony to be performed at two-thirty; and the witnesses, a glum verger and a woman engaged in cleaning the church, sat in the pews of the empty building, waiting to earn the guinea which they had been promised.

The conversation was about nothing in particular—one of those empty, purposeless exchanges of banal thought and speech characteristic of such an occasion.

At two-thirty Frank looked at his watch and walked out of the church to the end of the road. There was no sign of the girl. At two-forty-five he crossed to a providential tobacconist and telephoned to the Savoy and was told that the lady had left half an hour before.

"She ought to be here very soon," he said to the priest. He was a little impatient, a little nervous, and terribly anxious.

As the church clock struck three, the rector turned to him.

"I am afraid I cannot marry you to-day, Mr. Merrill," he said.

Frank was very pale.

"Why not?" he asked quickly. "Miss Nuttall has probably been detained by the traffic or a burst tire. She will be here very shortly."

The minister shook his head and hung up his white surplice in the cupboard.

"The law of the land, my dear Mr. Merrill," he said, "does not allow weddings after three in the afternoon. You can come along to-morrow morning any time after eight."

There was a tap at the door, and Frank swung round. It was not the girl, but a telegraph boy. He snatched the buff envelope from the lad's hand and tore it open. It read simply:

> The wedding cannot take place.

It was unsigned.

At two-fifteen that afternoon May had passed through the vestibule of the hotel, and her foot was on the step of the taxicab when a hand fell upon her arm, and she turned in alarm to meet the searching eyes of Jasper Cole.

"Where are you off to in such a hurry, May?"

She flushed and drew her arm away with a decisive gesture.

"I have nothing to say to you, Jasper," she said coldly. "After your horrible charge against Frank, I never want to speak to you again."

He winced a little, then smiled.

"At least you can be civil to an old friend," he said good-humoredly, "and tell me where you are off to in such a hurry."

Should she tell him? A moment's indecision, and then she spoke.

"I am going to marry Frank Merrill," she said.

He nodded.

"I thought as much. In that case, I am coming down to the church to make a scene."

He said this with a smile on his lips; but there was no mistaking the resolution which showed in the thrust of his square jaw.

"What do you mean?" she said. "Don't be absurd, Jasper. My mind is made up."

"I mean," he said quietly, "that I have Mr. Minute's power of attorney to act for him, and Mr. Minute happens to be your legal guardian. You are, in point of fact, my dear May, more or less of a ward, and you cannot marry before you are twenty-one without your guardian's consent."

"I shall be twenty-one next week," she said defiantly.

"Then," smiled the other, "wait till next week before you marry. There is no very pressing hurry."

"You forced this situation upon me," said the girl hotly, "and I think it is very horrid of you. I am going to marry Frank to-day."

"Under those circumstances, I must come down and forbid the marriage; and when our parson asks if there is any just cause I shall step forward to the rails, gayly flourishing the power of attorney, and not even the most hardened parson could continue in the face of that legal instrument. It is a mandamus, a caveat, and all sorts of horrific things."

"Why are you doing this?" she asked.

"Because I have no desire that you shall marry a man who is certainly a forger, and possibly a murderer," said Jasper Cole calmly.

"I won't listen to you!" she cried, and stepped into the waiting taxicab.

Without a word, Jasper followed her.

"You can't turn me out," he said, "and I know where you are going, anyway, because you were giving directions to the driver when I stood behind you. You had better let me go with you. I like the suburbs."

She turned and faced him swiftly.

"And Silvers Rents?" she asked.

He went a shade paler.

"What do you know about Silvers Rents?" he demanded, recovering himself with an effort.

She did not reply.

The taxicab was halfway to its destination before the girl spoke again:

"Are you serious when you say you will forbid the marriage?"

"Quite serious," he replied; "so much so that I shall bring in a policeman to witness my act."

The girl was nearly in tears.

"It is monstrous of you! Uncle wouldn't—"

"Had you not better see your uncle?" he asked.

Something told her that he would keep his word. She had a horror of scenes, and, worst of all, she feared the meeting of the two men under these circumstances. Suddenly she leaned forward and tapped the window, and the taxi slowed down.

"Tell him to go back and call at the nearest telegraph office. I want to send a wire."

"If it is to Mr. Frank Merrill," said Jasper smoothly, "you may save yourself the trouble. I have already wired."

Frank came back to London in a pardonable fury. He drove straight to the hotel, only to learn that the girl had left again with her uncle. He looked at his watch. He had still some work to do at the bank, though he had little appetite for work.

Yet it was to the bank he went. He threw a glance over the counter to the table and the chair where he had sat for so long and at which he was destined never to sit again, for as he was passing behind the counter Mr. Brandon met him.

"Your uncle wishes to see you, Mr. Merrill," he said gravely.

Frank hesitated, then walked into the office, closing the door behind him, and he noticed that Mr. Brandon did not attempt to follow.

John Minute sat in the one easy chair and looked up heavily as Frank entered.

"Sit down, Frank," he said. "I have a lot of things to ask you."

"And I've one or two things to ask you, uncle," said Frank calmly.

"If it is about May, you can save yourself the trouble," said the other. "If it is about Mr. Rex Holland, I can give you a little information."

Frank looked at him steadily.

"I don't quite get your meaning, sir," he said, "though I gather there is something offensive behind what you have said."

John Minute twisted round in the chair and threw one leg over its padded arm.

"Frank," he said, "I want you to be perfectly straight with me, and I'll be as perfectly straight with you."

The young man made no reply.

"Certain facts have been brought to my attention, which leave no doubt in my mind as to the identity of the alleged Mr. Rex Holland," said John Minute slowly. "I don't relish saying this, because I have liked you, Frank, though I have sometimes stood in your way and we have not seen eye to eye together. Now, I want you to come down to Eastbourne to-morrow and have a heart-to-heart talk with me."

"What do you expect I can tell you?" asked Frank quietly.

"I want you to tell me the truth. I expect you won't," said John Minute.

A half smile played for a second upon Frank's lips.

"At any rate," he said, "you are being straight with me. I don't know exactly what you are driving at, uncle, but I gather that it is something rather unpleasant, and that somewhere in the background there is hovering an accusation against me. From the fact that you have mentioned Mr. Rex Holland or the gang which went by that name, I suppose that you are suggesting that I am an accomplice of that gentleman."

"I suggest more than that," said the other quickly. "I suggest that you are Rex Holland."

Frank laughed aloud.

"It is no laughing matter," said John Minute sternly.

"From your point of view it is not," said Frank, "but from my point of view it has certain humorous aspects, and unfortunately I am cursed with a sense of humor. I hardly know how I can go into the matter here"—he looked round—"for even if this is the time, it is certainly not the place, and I think I'll accept your invitation and come down to Weald Lodge to-morrow night. I gather you don't want to travel down with a master criminal who might at any moment take your watch and chain."

"I wish you would look at this matter more seriously, Frank," said John Minute earnestly. "I want to get to the truth, and any truth which exonerates you will be very welcome to me."

Frank nodded.

"I will give you credit for that," he said. "You may expect me to-morrow. May I ask you as a personal favor that you will not discuss this matter with me in the presence of your admirable secretary? I have a feeling at the back of my mind that he is at the bottom of all this. Remember that he is as likely to know about Rex Holland as I.

"There has been an audit at the bank," Frank went on, "and I am not so stupid that I don't understand what this has meant. There has also been a certain coldness in the attitude of Brandon, and I have intercepted suspicious and meaning glances from the clerks. I shall not be surprised, therefore, if you tell me that my books are not in order. But again I would point out to you that it is just as possible for Jasper, who has access to the bank at all hours of the day and night, to have altered them as it is for me.

"I hasten to add," he said, with a smile, "that I don't accuse Jasper. He is such a machine, and I cannot imagine him capable of so much initiative as systematically to forge checks and falsify ledgers. I merely mention Jasper because I want to emphasize the injustice of putting any man under suspicion unless you have the strongest and most convincing proof of his guilt. To declare my innocence is unnecessary from my point of view, and probably from yours also; but I declare to you, Uncle John, that I know no more about this matter than you."

He stood leaning on the desk and looking down at his uncle; and John Minute, with all his experience of men, and for all his suspicions, felt just a twinge of remorse. It was not to last long, however.

"I shall expect you to-morrow," he said.

Frank nodded, walked out of the room and out of the bank, and twenty-four pairs of speculative eyes followed him.

A few hours later another curious scene was being enacted, this time near the town of East Grinstead. There is a lonely stretch of road across a heath, which is called, for some reason, Ashdown Forest. A car was drawn up on a patch of turf by the side of the heath. Its owner was sitting in a little clearing out of view of the road, sipping a cup of tea which his chauffeur had made. He finished this and watched his servant take the basket.

"Come back to me when you have finished," he said.

The man touched his hat and disappeared with the package, but returned again in a few minutes.

"Sit down, Feltham," said Mr. Rex Holland. "I dare say you think it was rather strange of me to give you that little commission the other day," said Mr. Holland, crossing his legs and leaning back against a tree.

The chauffeur smiled uncomfortably.

"Yes, sir, I did," he said shortly.

"Were you satisfied with what I gave you?" asked the man.

The chauffeur shuffled his feet uneasily.

"Quite satisfied, sir," he said.

"You seem a little distrait, Feltham; I mean a little upset about something. What is it?"

The man coughed in embarrassed confusion.

"Well, sir," he began, "the fact is, I don't like it."

"You don't like what? The five hundred pounds I gave you?"

"No, sir. It is not that, but it was a queer thing to ask me to do—pretend to be you and send a commissionaire to the bank for your money, and then get away out of London to a quiet little hole like Bilstead."

"So you think it was queer?"

The chauffeur nodded.

"The fact is, sir," he blurted out, "I've seen the papers."

The other nodded thoughtfully.

"I presume you mean the newspapers. And what is there in the newspapers that interests you?"

Mr. Holland took a gold case from his pocket, opened it languidly, and selected a cigarette. He was closing it when he caught the chauffeur's eye and tossed a cigarette to him.

"Thank you, sir," said the man.

"What was it you didn't like?" asked Mr. Holland again, passing a match.

"Well, sir, I've been in all sorts of queer places," said Feltham doggedly, as he puffed away at the cigarette, "but I've always managed to keep clear of anything—funny. Do you see what I mean?"

"By funny I presume you don't mean comic," said Mr. Rex Holland cheerfully. "You mean dishonest, I suppose?"

"That's right, sir, and there's no doubt that I have been in a swindle, and it's worrying me—that bank-forgery case. Why, I read my own description in the paper!"

Beads of perspiration stood upon the little man's forehead, and there was a pathetic droop to his mouth.

"That is a distinction which falls to few of us," said his employer suavely. "You ought to feel highly honored. And what are you going to do about it, Feltham?"

The man looked to left and right as though seeking some friend in need who would step forth with ready-made advice.

"The only thing I can do, sir," he said, "is to give myself up."

"And give me up, too," said the other, with a little laugh. "Oh, no, my dear Feltham. Listen; I will tell you something. A few weeks ago I had a very promising valet chauffeur just like you. He was an admirable man, and he was also a foreigner. I believe he was a Swede. He came to me under exactly the same circumstances as you arrived, and he received exactly the same instructions as you have received, which unfortunately he did not carry out to the letter. I caught him pilfering from me—a few trinkets of no great value—and, instead of the foolish fellow repenting, he blurted out the one fact which I did not wish him to know, and incidentally which I did not wish anybody in the world to know.

"He knew who I was. He had seen me in the West End and had discovered my identity. He even sought an interview with some one to whom it would have been inconvenient to have made known my—character. I promised to find him another job, but he had already decided upon changing and had cut out an advertisement from a newspaper. I parted friendly with him, wished him luck, and he went off to interview his possible employer, smoking one of my cigarettes just as you are smoking—and he threw it away, I have no doubt, just as you have thrown it away when it began to taste a little bitter."

"Look here!" said the chauffeur, and scrambled to his feet. "If you try any monkey tricks with me—"

Mr. Holland eyed him with interest.

"If you try any monkey tricks with me," said the chauffeur thickly, "I'll—"

He pitched forward on his face and lay still.

Mr. Holland waited long enough to search his pockets, and then, stepping cautiously into the road, donned the chauffeur's cap and goggles and set his car running swiftly southward.

CHAPTER X

A MURDER

Constable Wiseman lived in the bosom of his admiring family in a small cottage on the Bexhill Road. That "my father was a policeman" was the proud boast of two small boys, a boast which entitled them to no small amount of respect, because P. C. Wiseman was not only honored in his own circle but throughout the village in which he dwelt.

He was, in the first place, a town policeman, as distinct from a county policeman, though he wore the badge and uniform of the Sussex constabulary. It was felt that a town policeman had more in common with crime, had a vaster experience, and was in consequence a more helpful adviser than a man whose duties began and ended in the patrolling of country lanes and law-abiding villages where nothing more exciting than an occasional dog fight or a charge of poaching served to fill the hiatus of constabulary life.

Constable Wiseman was looked upon as a shrewd fellow, a man to whom might be brought the delicate problems which occasionally perplexed and confused the bucolic mind. He had settled the vexed question as to whether a policeman could or could not enter a house where a man was beating his wife, and had decided that such a trespass could only be committed if the lady involved should utter piercing cries of "Murder!"

He added significantly that the constable who was called upon must be the constable on duty, and not an ornament of the force who by accident was a resident in their midst.

The problem of the straying chicken and the egg that is laid on alien property, the point of law involved in the question as to when a servant should give notice and the date from which her notice should count—all these matters came within Constable Wiseman's purview, and were solved to the satisfaction of all who brought their little obscurities for solution.

But it was in his own domestic circle that Constable Wiseman—appropriately named, as all agreed—shone with an effulgence that was almost dazzling, and was a source of irritation to the male relatives on his wife's side, one of whom had unfortunately come within the grasp of the law over a matter of a snared rabbit and was in consequence predisposed to anarchy in so far as the abolition of law and order affected the police force.

Constable Wiseman sat at tea one summer evening, and about the spotless white cloth which covered the table was grouped all that Constable Wiseman might legally call his. Tea was a function, and to the younger members of the family meant just tea and bread and butter. To Constable Wiseman it meant luxuries of a varied and costly nature. His taste ranged from rump steak to Yarmouth bloaters, and once he had introduced a foreign delicacy—foreign to the village, which had never known before the reason for their existence—sweetbreads.

The conversation, which was well sustained by Mr. Wiseman, was usually of himself, his wife being content to punctuate his autobiography with such encouraging phrases as, "Dear, dear!" "Well, whatever next!" the children doing no more than ask in a whisper for more food. This they did at regular and frequent intervals, but because of their whispers they were supposed to be unheard.

Constable Wiseman spoke about himself because he knew of nothing more interesting to talk about. His evening conversation usually took the form of a very full résumé of his previous day's experience. He left the impression upon his wife—and glad enough she was to have such an impression—that Eastbourne was a well-conducted town mainly as a result of P. C. Wiseman's ceaseless and tireless efforts.

"I never had a clew yet that I never follered to the bitter end," said the preening constable.

"You remember when Raggett's orchard was robbed—who found the thieves?"

"You did, of course; I'm sure you did," said Mrs. Wiseman, jigging her youngest on her knee, the youngest not having arrived at the age where he recognized the necessity for expressing his desires in whispers.

"Who caught them three-card-trick men after the Lewes races last year?" went on Constable Wiseman passionately. "Who has had more summonses for smoking chimneys than any other man in the force? Some people," he added, as he rose heavily and took down his tunic, which hung on the wall—"some people would ask for promotion; but I'm perfectly satisfied. I'm not one of those ambitious sort. Why, I wouldn't know at all what to do with myself if they made me a sergeant."

"You deserve it, anyway," said Mrs. Wiseman.

"I don't deserve anything I don't want," said Mr. Wiseman loftily. "I've learned a few things, too, but I've never made use of what's come to me officially to get me pushed along. You'll hear something in a day or two," he said mysteriously, "and in high life, too, in a manner of speaking—that is, if you can call old Minute high life, which I very much doubt."

"You don't say so!" said Mrs. Wiseman, appropriately amazed.

Her husband nodded his head.

"There's trouble up there," he said. "From certain information I've received, there has been a big row between young Mr. Merrill and the old man, and the

C. I. D. people have been down about it. What's more," he said, "I could tell a thing or two. I've seen that boy look at the old man as though he'd like to kill him. You wouldn't believe it, would you, but I know, and it didn't happen so long ago either. He was always snubbing him when young Merrill was down here acting as his secretary, and as good as called him a fool in front of my face when I served him with that summons for having his lights up. You'll hear something one of these days."

Constable Wiseman was an excellent prophet, vague as his prophecy was.

He went out of the cottage to his duty in a complacent frame of mind, which was not unusual, for Constable Wiseman was nothing if not satisfied with his fate. His complacency continued until a little after seven o'clock that evening.

It so happened that Constable Wiseman, no less than every other member of the force on duty that night, had much to think about, much that was at once exciting and absorbing. It had been whispered before the evening parade that Sergeant Smith was to leave the force. There was some talk of his being dismissed, but it was clear that he had been given the opportunity of resigning, for he was still doing duty, which would not have been the case had he been forcibly removed.

Sergeant Smith's mien and attitude had confirmed the rumor. Nobody was surprised, since this dour officer had been in trouble before. Twice had he been before the deputy chief constable for neglect of, and being drunk while on, duty. On the earlier occasions he had had remarkable escapes. Some people talked of influence, but it is more likely that the man's record had helped him, for he was a first-class policeman with a nose for crime, absolutely fearless, and had, moreover, assisted in the capture of one or two very desperate criminals who had made their way to the south-coast town.

His last offense, however, was too grave to overlook. His inspector, going the rounds, had missed him, and after a search he was discovered outside a public house. It is no great crime to be found outside a public house, particularly when an officer has a fairly extensive area to cover, and in this respect he was well within the limits of that area. But it must be explained that the reason the sergeant was outside the public house was because he had challenged a fellow carouser to fight, and at the moment he was discovered he was stripped to the waist and setting about his task with rare workmanlike skill.

He was also drunk.

To have retained his services thereafter would have been little less than a crying scandal. There is no doubt, however, that Sergeant Smith had made a desperate attempt to use the influence behind him, and use it to its fullest extent.

He had had one stormy interview with John Minute, and had planned another. Constable Wiseman, patrolling the London Road, his mind filled with the great news, was suddenly confronted with the object of his thoughts. The sergeant rode up to where the constable was standing in a professional attitude at the corner of two roads, and jumped off with the manner of a man who has an object in view.

"Wiseman," he said—and his voice was such as to suggest that he had been drinking again—"where will you be at ten o'clock to-night?"

Constable Wiseman raised his eyes in thought.

"At ten o'clock, Sergeant, I shall be opposite the gates of the cemetery."

The sergeant looked round left and right.

"I am going to see Mr. Minute on a matter of business," he said, "and you needn't mention the fact."

"I keep myself to myself," began Constable Wiseman. "What I see with one eye goes out of the other, in the manner of speaking—"

The sergeant nodded, stepped on to his bicycle again, turned it about, and went at full speed down the gentle incline toward Weald Lodge. He made no secret of his visit, but rode through the wide gates up the gravel drive to the front of the house, rang the bell, and to the servant who answered demanded peremptorily to see Mr. Minute.

John Minute received him in the library, where the previous interviews had taken place. Minute waited until the servant had gone and the door was closed, and then he said:

"Now, Crawley, there's no sense in coming to me; I can do nothing for you."

The sergeant put his helmet on the table, walked to a sideboard where a tray and decanter stood, and poured himself out a stiff dose of whisky without invitation. John Minute watched him without any great resentment. This was not civilized Eastbourne they were in. They were back in the old free-and-easy days of Gwelo, where men did not expect invitations to drink.

Smith—or Crawley, to give him his real name—tossed down half a tumbler of neat whisky and turned, wiping his heavy mustache with the back of his hand.

"So you can't do anything, can't you?" he mimicked. "Well, I'm going to show you that you can, and that you will!"

He put up his hand to check the words on John Minute's lips.

"There's no sense in your putting that rough stuff over me about your being able to send me to jail, because you wouldn't do it. It doesn't suit your book, John Minute, to go into the court and testify against me. Too many things would come out in the witness box, and you well know it—besides, Rhodesia is a long way off!"

"I know a place which isn't so far distant," said the other, looking up from his chair—"a place called Felixstowe, for example. There's another place called Cromer. I've been in consultation with a gentleman you may have heard of, a Mr. Saul Arthur Mann."

"Saul Arthur Mann," repeated the other slowly. "I've never heard of him."

"You would not, but he has heard of you," said John Minute calmly. "The fact is, Crawley, there's a big bad record against you, between your serious crimes in Rhodesia and your blackmail of to-day. I've a few facts about you which will interest you. I know the date you came to this country, which I didn't know before, and I know how you earned your living until you found me. I know of some shares in a non-existent Rhodesian mine which you sold to a feeble-minded gentleman at Cromer, and to a lady, equally feeble-minded, at Felixstowe. I've not only got the shares you sold, with your signature as a director, but I have letters and receipts signed by you. It has cost me a lot of money to get them, but it was well worth it."

Crawley's face was livid. He took a step toward the other, but recoiled, for at the first hint of danger John Minute had pulled the revolver he invariably carried.

"Keep just where you are, Crawley!" he said. "You are close enough now to be unpleasant."

"So you've got my record, have you?" said the other, with an oath. "Tucked away with your marriage lines, I'll bet, and the certificate of birth of the kids you left to starve with their mother."

"Get out of here!" said Minute, with dangerous quiet. "Get away while you're safe!"

There was something in his eye which cowed the half-drunken man who, turning with a laugh, picked up his helmet and walked from the room.

The hour was seven-thirty-five by Constable Wiseman's watch; for, slowly patrolling back, he saw the sergeant come flying out of the gateway on his bicycle and turn down toward the town. Constable Wiseman subsequently explained that he looked at his watch because he had a regular point at which he should meet Sergeant Smith at seven-forty-five and he was wondering whether his superior would return.

The chronology of the next three hours has been so often given in various accounts of the events which marked that evening that I may be excused if I give them in detail.

A car, white with dust, turned into the stable yard of the Star Hotel, Maidstone. The driver, in a dust coat and a chauffeur's cap, descended and handed over the car to a garage keeper with instructions to clean it up and have it filled ready for him the following morning. He gave explicit instructions as to the number of tins of petrol he required to carry always and tipped the garage keeper handsomely in advance.

He was described as a young man with a slight black mustache, and he was wearing his motor goggles when he went into the office of the hotel and ordered a bed and a sitting room. Therefore his face was not seen. When his dinner was served, it was remarked by the waiter that his goggles were still on his face. He gave instructions that the whole of the dinner was to be served at once and put upon the sideboard, and that he did not wish to be disturbed until he rang the bell.

When the bell rang the waiter came to find the room empty. But from the adjoining room he received orders to have breakfast by seven o'clock the following morning.

At seven o'clock the driver of the car paid his bill, his big motor goggles still upon his face, again tipped the garage keeper handsomely, and drove his car from the yard. He turned to the right and appeared to be taking the London Road, but later in the day, as has been established, the car was seen on its way to Paddock Wood, and was later observed at Tonbridge. The driver pulled up at a little tea house half a mile from the town, ordered sandwiches and tea, which were brought to him, and which he consumed in the car.

Late in the afternoon the car was seen at Uckfield, and the theory generally held was that the driver was killing time. At the wayside cottage at which he stopped for tea—it was one of those little places that invite cyclists by an ill-printed board to tarry a while and refresh themselves—he had some conversation with the tenant of the cottage, a widow. She seems to have been the usual loquacious, friendly soul who tells one without reserve her business, her troubles, and a fair sprinkling of the news of the day in the shortest possible time.

"I haven't seen a paper," said Rex Holland politely. "It is a very curious thing that I never thought about newspapers."

"I can get you one," said the woman eagerly. "You ought to read about that case."

"The dead chauffeur?" asked Rex Holland interestedly, for that had been the item of general news which was foremost in the woman's conversation.

"Yes, sir; he was murdered in Ashdown Forest. Many's the time I've driven over there."

"How do you know it was a murder?"

She knew for many reasons. Her brother-in-law was gamekeeper to Lord Ferring, and a colleague of his had been the man who had discovered the body, and it had appeared, as the good lady explained, that this same chauffeur was a man for whom the police had been searching in connection with a bank robbery about which much had appeared in the newspapers of the day previous.

"How very interesting!" said Mr. Holland, and took the paper from her hand.

He read the description line by line. He learned that the police were in possession of important clews, and that they were on the track of the man who had been seen in the company of the chauffeur. Moreover, said a most indiscreet newspaper writer, the police had a photograph showing the chauffeur standing by the side of his car, and reproductions of this photograph, showing the type of machine, were being circulated.

"How very interesting!" said Mr. Rex Holland again, being perfectly content in his mind, for his search of the body had revealed copies of this identical picture, and the car in which he was seated was not the car which had been photographed. From this point, a mile and a half beyond Uckfield, all trace of the car and its occupant was lost.

The writer has been very careful to note the exact times and to confirm those about which there was any doubt. At nine-twenty on the night when Constable Wiseman had patrolled the road before Weald Lodge and had seen Sergeant Smith flying down the road on his bicycle, and on the night of that day when Mr. Rex Holland had been seen at Uckfield, there arrived by the London train, which is due at Eastbourne at nine-twenty, Frank Merrill. The train, as a matter of fact, was three minutes late, and Frank, who had been in the latter part of the train, was one of the last of the passengers to arrive at the barrier.

When he reached the barrier, he discovered that he had no railway ticket, a very ordinary and vexatious experience which travelers before now have endured. He searched in every pocket, including the pocket of the light ulster he wore, but without success. He was vexed, but he laughed because he had a strong sense of humor.

"I could pay for my ticket," he smiled, "but I be hanged if I will! Inspector, you search that overcoat."

The amused inspector complied while Frank again went through all his pockets. At his request he accompanied the inspector to the latter's office, and there deposited on the table the contents of his pockets, his money, letters, and pocketbook.

"You're used to searching people," he said. "See if you can find it. I'll swear I've got it about me somewhere."

The obliging inspector felt, probed, but without success, till suddenly, with a roar of laughter, Frank cried:

"What a stupid ass I am! I've got it in my hat!"

He took off his hat, and there in the lining was a first-class ticket from London to Eastbourne.

It is necessary to lay particular stress upon this incident, which had an important bearing upon subsequent events. He called a taxicab, drove to Weald Lodge, and dismissed the driver in the road. He arrived at Weald Lodge, by the testimony of the driver and by that of Constable Wiseman, whom the car had passed, at about nine-forty.

Mr. John Minute at this time was alone; his suspicious nature would not allow the presence of servants in the house during the interview which he was to have with his nephew. He regarded servants as spies and eavesdroppers, and perhaps there was an excuse for his uncharitable view.

At nine-fifty, ten minutes after Frank had entered the gates of Weald Lodge, a car with gleaming headlights came quickly from the opposite direction and pulled up outside the gates. P. C. Wiseman, who at this moment was less than fifty yards from the gate, saw a man descend and pass quickly into the grounds of the house.

At nine-fifty-two or nine-fifty-three the constable, walking slowly toward the house, came abreast of the wall, and, looking up, saw a light flash for a moment in one of the upper windows. He had hardly seen this when he heard two shots fired in rapid succession, and a cry.

Only for a moment did P. C. Wiseman hesitate. He jumped the low wall, pushed through the shrubs, and made for the side of the house from whence a flood of light fell from the open French windows of the library. He blundered into the room a pace or two, and then stopped, for the sight was one which might well arrest even as unimaginative a man as a county constable.

John Minute lay on the floor on his back, and it did not need a doctor to tell that he was dead. By his side, and almost within reach of his hand, was a revolver of a very heavy army pattern. Mechanically the constable picked up the revolver and turned his stern face to the other occupant of the room.

"This is a bad business, Mr. Merrill," he found his breath to say.

Frank Merrill had been leaning over his uncle as the constable entered, but now stood erect, pale, but perfectly self-possessed.

"I heard the shot and I came in," he said.

"Stay where you are," said the constable, and, stepping quickly out on to the lawn, he blew his whistle long and shrilly, then returned to the room.

"This is a bad business, Mr. Merrill," he repeated.

"It is a very bad business," said the other in a low voice.

"Is this revolver yours?"

Frank shook his head.

"I've never seen it before," he said with emphasis.

The constable thought as quickly as it was humanly possible for him to think. He had no doubt in his mind that this unhappy youth had fired the shots which had ended the life of the man on the floor.

"Stay here," he said again, and again went out to blow his whistle. He walked this time on the lawn by the side of the drive toward the road. He had not taken half a dozen steps when he saw a dark figure of a man creeping stealthily along before him in the shade of the shrubs. In a second the constable was on him, had grasped him and swung him round, flashing his lantern into his prisoner's face. Instantly he released his hold.

"I beg your pardon, Sergeant," he stammered.

"What's the matter?" scowled the other. "What's wrong with you, Constable?"

Sergeant Smith's face was drawn and haggard. The policeman looked at him with open-mouthed astonishment.

"I didn't know it was you," he said.

"What's wrong?" asked the other again, and his voice was cracked and unnatural.

"There's been a murder—old Minute—shot!"

Sergeant Smith staggered back a pace.

"Good God!" he said. "Minute murdered? Then he did it! The young devil did it!"

"Come and have a look," invited Wiseman, recovering his balance. "I've got his nephew."

"No, no! I don't want to see John Minute dead! You go back. I'll bring another constable and a doctor."

He stumbled blindly along the drive into the road, and Constable Wiseman went back to the house. Frank was where he had left him, save that he had seated himself and was gazing steadfastly upon the dead man. He looked up as the policeman entered.

"What have you done?" he asked.

"The sergeant's gone for a doctor and another constable," said Wiseman gravely.

"I'm afraid they will be too late," said Frank. "He is—What's that?"

There was a distant hammering and a faint voice calling for help.

"What's that?" whispered Frank again.

The constable strode through the open doorway to the foot of the stairs and listened. The sound came from the upper story. He ran upstairs, mounting two at a time, and presently located the noise. It came from an end room, and somebody was hammering on the panels. The door was locked, but the key had been left in the lock, and this Constable Wiseman turned, flooding the dark interior with light.

"Come out!" he said, and Jasper Cole staggered out, dazed and shaking.

"Somebody hit me on the head with a sandbag," he said thickly. "I heard the shot. What has happened?"

"Mr. Minute has been killed," said the policeman.

"Killed!" He fell back against the wall, his face working. "Killed!" he repeated. "Not killed!"

The constable nodded. He had found the electric switch and the passageway was illuminated.

Presently the young man mastered his emotion.

"Where is he?" he asked, and Wiseman led the way downstairs.

Jasper Cole walked into the room without a glance at Frank and bent over the dead man. For a long time he looked at him earnestly, then he turned to Frank.

"You did this!" he said. "I heard your voice and the shots! I heard you threaten him!"

Frank said nothing. He merely stared at the other, and in his eyes was a look of infinite scorn.

CHAPTER XI

THE CASE AGAINST FRANK MERRILL

Mr. Saul Arthur Mann stood by the window of his office and moodily watched the traffic passing up and down this busy city street at what was the busiest hour of the day. He stood there such a long time that the girl who had sought his help thought he must have forgotten her.

May was pale, and her pallor was emphasized by the black dress she wore. The terrible happening of a week before had left its impression upon her. For her it had been a week of sleepless nights, a week's anguish of mind unspeakable. Everybody had been most kind, and Jasper was as gentle as a woman. Such was the influence that he exercised over her that she did not feel any sense of resentment against him, even though she knew that he was the principal witness for the crown. He was so sincere, so honest in his sympathy, she told herself.

He was so free from any bitterness against the man who he believed had killed his best friend and his most generous employer that she could not sustain the first feeling of resentment she had felt. Perhaps it was because her great sorrow overshadowed all other emotions; yet she was free to analyze her friendship with the man who was working day and night to send the man who loved her to a felon's doom. She could not understand herself; still less could she understand Jasper.

She looked up again at Mr. Mann as he stood by the window, his hands clasped behind him; and as she did so he turned slowly and came back to where she sat. His usually jocund face was lugubrious and worried.

"I have given more thought to this matter than I've given to any other problem I have tackled," he said. "I believe Mr. Merrill to be falsely accused, and I have one or two points to make to his counsel which, when they are brought forward in court, will prove beyond any doubt whatever that he was innocent. I don't believe that matters are so black against him as you think. The other side will certainly bring forward the forgery and the doctored books to supply a motive for the murder. Inspector Nash is in charge of the case, and he promised to call here at four o'clock."

He looked at his watch.

"It wants three minutes. Have you any suggestion to offer?"

She shook her head.

"I can floor the prosecution," Mr. Mann went on, "but what I cannot do is to find the murderer for certain. It is obviously one of three men. It is either

Sergeant Crawley, alias Smith, about whose antecedents Mr. Minute made an inquiry, or Jasper Cole, the secretary, or—"

He shrugged his shoulders.

It was not necessary to say who was the third suspect.

There came a knock at the door, and the clerk announced Inspector Nash. That stout and stoical officer gave a noncommittal nod to Mr. Mann and a smiling recognition to the girl.

"Well, you know how matters stand, Inspector," said Mr. Mann briskly, "and I thought I'd ask you to come here to-day to straighten a few things out."

"It is rather irregular, Mr. Mann," said the inspector, "but as they've no objection at headquarters, I don't mind telling you, within limits, all that I know; but I don't suppose I can tell you any more than you have found out for yourself."

"Do you really think Mr. Merrill committed this crime?" asked the girl.

The inspector raised his eyebrows and pursed his lips.

"It looks uncommonly like it, miss," he said. "We have evidence that the bank has been robbed, and it is almost certainly proved that Merrill had access to the books and was the only person in the bank who could have faked the figures and transferred the money from one account to another without being found out. There are still one or two doubtful points to be cleared up, but there is the motive, and when you've got the motive you are three parts on your way to finding the criminal. It isn't a straightforward case by any means," he confessed, "and the more I go into it the more puzzled I am. I don't mind telling you this frankly: I have seen Constable Wiseman, who swears that at the moment the shots were fired he saw a light flash in the upper window. We have the statement of Mr. Cole that he was in his room, his employer having requested that he should make himself scarce when the nephew came, and he tells us how somebody opened the door quietly and flashed an electric torch upon him."

"What was Cole doing in the dark?" asked Mann quickly.

"He had a headache and was lying down," said the inspector. "When he saw the light he jumped up and made for it, and was immediately slugged; the door closed upon him and was locked. Between his leaving the bed and reaching the door he heard Mr. Merrill's voice threatening his uncle, and the shots. Immediately afterward he was rendered insensible."

"A curious story," said Saul Arthur Mann dryly. "A very curious story!"

The girl felt an unaccountable and altogether amazing desire to defend Jasper against the innuendo in the other's tone, and it was with difficulty that she restrained herself.

"I don't think it is a good story," said the inspector frankly; "but that is between ourselves. And then, of course," he went on, "we have the remarkable behavior of Sergeant Smith."

"Where is he?" asked Mr. Mann.

The inspector shrugged his shoulders.

"Sergeant Smith has disappeared," he said, "though I dare say we shall find him before long. He is only one; the most puzzling element of all is the fourth man concerned, the man who arrived in the motor car and who was evidently Mr. Rex Holland. We have got a very full description of him."

"I also have a very full description of him," said Mr. Mann quietly; "but I've been unable to identify him with any of the people in my records."

"Anyway, it was his car; there is no doubt about that."

"And he was the murderer," said Mr. Mann. "I've no doubt about that, nor have you."

"I have doubts about everything," replied the inspector diplomatically.

"What was in the car?" asked the little man brightly. He was rapidly recovering his good humor.

"That I am afraid I cannot tell you," smiled the detective.

"Then I'll tell you," said Saul Arthur Mann, and, stepping up to his desk, took a memorandum from a drawer. "There were two motor rugs, two holland coats, one white, one brown. There were two sets of motor goggles. There was a package of revolver cartridges, from which six had been extracted, a leather revolver holster, a small garden trowel, and one or two other little things."

Inspector Nash swore softly under his breath.

"I'm blessed if I know how you found all that out," he said, with a little asperity in his voice. "The car was not touched or searched until we came on the scene, and, beyond myself and Sergeant Mannering of my department, nobody knows what the car contained."

Saul Arthur Mann smiled, and it was a very happy and triumphant smile.

"You see, I know!" he purred. "That is one point in Merrill's favor."

"Yes," agreed the detective, and smiled.

"Why do you smile, Mr. Nash?" asked the little man suspiciously.

"I was thinking of a county policeman who seems to have some extraordinary theories on the subject."

"Oh, you mean Wiseman," said Mann, with a grin. "I've interviewed that gentleman. There is a great detective lost in him, Inspector."

"It is lost, all right," said the detective laconically. "Wiseman is very certain that Merrill committed the crime, and I think you are going to have a difficulty in persuading a jury that he didn't. You see Merrill's story is that he came and saw his uncle, that they had a few minutes' chat together, that his uncle suddenly had an attack of faintness, and that he went out of the room into the dining room to get a glass of water. While Merrill was in the dining room he heard the shots, and came running back, still with the glass in his hand, and saw his uncle lying on the ground. I saw the glass, which was half filled.

"I was also there in time to examine the dining room and see that Mr. Merrill had spilled some of the water when he was taking it from the carafe. All that part of the story is circumstantially sound. What we cannot understand, and what a jury will never understand, is how, in the very short space of time, the murderer could have got into the room and made his escape again."

"The French windows were open," said Mr. Mann. "All the evidence that we have is to this effect, including the evidence of P. C. Wiseman."

"In those circumstances, how comes it that the constable, who, when he heard the shot, made straight for the room, did not meet the murderer escaping? He saw nobody in the grounds—"

"Except Sergeant Smith, or Crawley," interspersed Saul Arthur Mann readily. "I have reason to believe, and, indeed, reason to know, that Sergeant Smith, or Crawley, had a motive for being in the house. I supplied Mr. Minute, who was a client of mine, with certain documents, and those documents were in a safe in his bedroom. What is more likely than that this Crawley, to whom it was vitally necessary that the documents in question should be recovered, should have entered the house in search of those documents? I don't mind telling you that they related to a fraud of which he was the author, and they were in themselves all the proof which the police would require to obtain a conviction against him. He was obviously the man who struck down Mr. Cole, and whose light the constable saw flashing in the upper window."

"In that case he cannot have been the murderer," said the detective quickly, "because the shots were fired while he was still in the room. They were almost simultaneous with the appearance of the flash at the upper window."

"H'm!" said Saul Arthur Mann, for the moment nonplussed.

"The more you go into this matter, the more complicated does it become," said the police officer, with a shake of his head, "and to my mind the clearer is the case against Merrill."

"With this reservation," interrupted the other, "that you have to account for the movements of Mr. Rex Holland, who comes on the scene ten minutes after

Frank Merrill arrives and who leaves his car. He leaves his car for a very excellent reason," he went on. "Sergeant Smith, who runs away to get assistance, meets two men of the Sussex constabulary, hurrying in response to Wiseman's whistle. One of them stands by the car, and the other comes into the house. It was, therefore, impossible for the murderer to make use of the car. Here is another point I would have you explain."

He had hoisted himself on the edge of his desk, and sat, an amusing little figure, his legs swinging a foot from the ground.

"The revolver used was a big Webley, not an easy thing to carry or conceal about your person, and undoubtedly brought to the scene of the crime by the man in the car. You will say that Merrill, who wore an overcoat, might have easily brought it in his pocket; but the absolute proof that that could not have been the case is that on his arrival by train from London, Mr. Merrill lost his ticket and very carefully searched himself, a railway inspector assisting, to discover the bit of pasteboard. He turned out everything he had in his pocket in the inspector's presence, and his overcoat—the only place where he could have concealed such a heavy weapon—was searched by the inspector himself."

The detective nodded.

"It is a very difficult case," he agreed, "and one in which I've no great heart; for, to be absolutely honest, my views are that while it might have been Merrill, the balance of proof is that it was not. That is, of course, my unofficial view, and I shall work pretty hard to secure a conviction."

"I am sure you will," said Mr. Mann heartily.

"Must the case go into the court?" asked the girl anxiously.

"There is no other way for it," replied the officer. "You see, we have arrested him, and unless something turns up the magistrate must commit him for trial on the evidence we have secured."

"Poor Frank!" she said softly.

"It is rough on him, if he is innocent," agreed Nash, "but it is lucky for him if he's guilty. My experience of crime and criminals is that it is generally the obvious man who commits that crime; only once in fifty years is he innocent, whether he is acquitted or whether he is found guilty."

He offered his hand to Mr. Mann.

"I'll be getting along now, sir," he said. "The commissioner asked me to give you all the assistance I possibly could, and I hope I have done so."

"What are you doing in the case of Jasper Cole?" asked Mann quickly.

The detective smiled.

"You ought to know, sir," he said, and was amused at his own little joke.

"Well, young lady," said Mann, turning to the girl, after the detective had gone, "I think you know how matters stand. Nash suspects Cole."

"Jasper!" she said, in shocked surprise.

"Jasper," he repeated.

"But that is impossible! He was locked in his room."

"That doesn't make it impossible. I know of fourteen distinct cases of men who committed crimes and were able to lock themselves in their rooms, leaving the key outside. There was a case of Henry Burton, coiner; there was William Francis Rector, who killed a warder while in prison and locked the cell upon himself from the inside. There was—But there; why should I bother you with instances? That kind of trick is common enough. No," he said, "it is the motive that we have to find. Do you still want me to go with you to-morrow, Miss Nuttall?" he asked.

"I should be very glad if you would," she said earnestly. "Poor, dear uncle! I didn't think I could ever enter the house again."

"I can relieve your mind about that," he said. "The will is not to be read in the house. Mr. Minute's lawyers have arranged for the reading at their offices in Lincoln's Inn Fields. I have the address here somewhere."

He fumbled in his pocket and took out a card.

"Power, Commons & Co.," he read, "194 Lincoln's Inn Fields. I will meet you there at three o'clock."

He rumpled his untidy hair with an embarrassed laugh.

"I seem to have drifted into the position of guardian to you, young lady," he said. "I can't say that it is an unpleasant task, although it is a great responsibility."

"You have been splendid, Mr. Mann," she said warmly, "and I shall never forget all you have done for me. Somehow I feel that Frank will get off; and I hope—I pray that it will not be at Jasper's expense."

He looked at her in surprise and disappointment.

"I thought—" he stopped.

"You thought I was engaged to Frank, and so I am," she said, with heightened color. "But Jasper is—I hardly know how to put it."

"I see," said Mr. Mann, though, if the truth be told, he saw nothing which enlightened him.

Punctually at three o'clock the next afternoon, they walked up the steps of the lawyers' office together. Jasper Cole was already there, and to Mr. Mann's surprise so also was Inspector Nash, who explained his presence in a few words.

"There may be something in the will which will open a new viewpoint," he said.

Mr. Power, the solicitor, an elderly man, inclined to rotundity, was introduced, and, taking his position before the fireplace, opened the proceedings with an expression of regret as to the circumstances which had brought them together.

"The will of my late client," he said, "was not drawn up by me. It is written in Mr. Minute's handwriting, and revokes the only other will, one which was prepared some four years ago and which made provisions rather different to those in the present instrument. This will"—he took a single sheet of paper out of an envelope—"was made last year and was witnessed by Thomas Wellington Crawley"—he adjusted his pince-nez and examined the signature—"late trooper of the Matabeleland mounted police, and by George Warrell, who was Mr. Minute's butler at the time. Warrell died in the Eastbourne hospital in the spring of this year."

There was a deep silence. Saul Arthur Mann's face was eagerly thrust forward, his head turned slightly to one side. Inspector Nash showed an unusual amount of interest. Both men had the same thought—a new will, witnessed by two people, one of whom was dead, and the other a fugitive from justice; what did this will contain?

It was the briefest of documents. To his ward he left the sum of two hundred thousand pounds, "a provision which was also made in the previous will, I might add," said the lawyer, and to this he added all his shares in the Gwelo Deep.

"To his nephew, Francis Merrill, he left twenty thousand pounds."

The lawyer paused and looked round the little circle, and then continued:

"The residue of my property, movable and immovable, all my furniture, leases, shares, cash at bankers, and all interests whatsoever, I bequeath to Jasper Cole, so-called, who is at present my secretary and confidential agent."

The detective and Saul Arthur Mann exchanged glances, and Nash's lips moved.

"How is that for a 'motive'?" he whispered.

CHAPTER XII

THE TRIAL OF FRANK MERRILL

The trial of Frank Merrill on the charge that he "did on the twenty-eighth day of June in the year of our Lord one thousand nine hundred—wilfully and wickedly kill and slay by a pistol shot John Minute" was the sensation of a season which was unusually prolific in murder trials. The trial took place at the Lewes Assizes in a crowded courtroom, and lasted, as we know, for sixteen days, five days of which were given to the examination in chief and the cross-examination of the accountants who had gone into the books of the bank.

The prosecution endeavored to establish the fact that no other person but Frank Merrill could have access to the books, and that therefore no other person could have falsified them or manipulated the transfer of moneys. It cannot be said that the prosecution had wholly succeeded; for when Brandon, the bank manager, was put into the witness box he was compelled to admit that not only Frank, but he himself and Jasper Cole, were in a position to reach the books.

The opening speech for the crown had been a masterly one. But that there were many weak points in the evidence and in the assumptions which the prosecution drew was evident to the merest tyro.

Sir George Murphy Jackson, the attorney general, who prosecuted, attempted to dispose summarily of certain conflictions, and it had to be confessed that his explanations were very plausible.

"The defense will tell us," he said, in that shrill, clarion tone of his which has made to quake the hearts of so many hostile witnesses, "that we have not accounted for the fourth man who drove up in his car ten minutes after Merrill had entered the house, and disappeared, but I am going to tell you my theory of that incident.

"Merrill had an accomplice who is not in custody, and that accomplice is Rex Holland. Merrill had planned and prepared this murder, because from some statement which his uncle had made he believed that not only was his whole future dependent upon destroying his benefactor and silencing forever the one man who knew the extent of his villainy, but he had in his cold, shrewd way accurately foreseen the exact consequence of such a shooting. It was a big criminal's big idea.

"He foresaw this trial," he said impressively; "he foresaw, gentlemen of the jury, his acquittal at your hands. He foresaw a reaction which would not only give him the woman he professes to love, but in consequence place in his hands the disposal of her considerable fortune.

"Why should he shoot John Minute? you may ask; and I reply to that question with another: What would have happened had he not shot his uncle? He would have been a ruined man. The doors of his uncle's house would have been closed to him. The legacy would have been revoked, the marriage for which he had planned so long would have been an unrealized dream.

"He knew the extent of the fortune which was coming to Miss Nuttall. Mr. Minute made two wills, in both of which he left an identical sum to his ward. The first of these, revoked by the second and containing the same provision, was witnessed by the man in the dock! He knew, too, that the Rhodesian gold mine, the shares of which were held by John Minute on the girl's behalf, was likely to prove a very rich proposition, and I suggest that the information coming to him as Mr. Minute's secretary, he deliberately suppressed that information for his own purpose.

"What had he to gain? I ask you to believe that if he is acquitted he will have achieved all that he ever hoped to achieve."

There was a little murmur in the court. Frank Merrill, leaning on the ledge of the dock, looked down at the girl in the body of the court, and their eyes met. He saw the indignation in her face and nodded with a little smile, then turned again to the counsel with that eager, half-quizzical look of interest which the girl had so often seen upon his handsome face.

"Much will be made, in the course of this trial, of the presence of another man, and the defense will endeavor to secure capital out of the fact that the man Crawley, who it was suggested was in the house for an improper purpose, has not been discovered. As to the fourth man, the driver of the motor car, there seems little doubt but that he was an accomplice of Merrill. This mysterious Rex Holland, who has been identified by Mrs. Totney, of Uckfield, spent the whole of the day wandering about Sussex, obviously having one plan in his mind, which was to arrive at Mr. Minute's house at the same time as his confederate.

"You will have the taxi-driver's evidence that when Merrill stepped down, after being driven from the station, he looked left and right, as though he were expecting somebody. The plan to some extent miscarried. The accomplice arrived ten minutes too late. On some pretext or other Merrill probably left the room. I suggest that he did not go into the dining room, but that he went out into the garden and was met by his accomplice, who handed him the weapon with which this crime was committed.

"It may be asked by the defense why the accomplice, who was presumably Rex Holland, did not himself commit the crime. I could offer two or three alternative suggestions, all of which are feasible. The deceased man was shot at close quarters, and was found in such an attitude as to suggest that he was wholly unprepared for the attack. We know that he was in some fear and that he invariably went armed; yet it is fairly certain that he made no attempt to draw his weapon, which he certainly would have done had he been suddenly confronted by an armed stranger.

"I do not pretend that I am explaining the strange relationship between Merrill and this mysterious forger. Merrill is the only man who has seen him and has given a vague and somewhat confused description of him. 'He was a man with a short, close-clipped beard' is Merrill's description. The woman who served him with tea near Uckfield describes him as a 'youngish man with a dark mustache, but otherwise clean shaven.'

"There is no reason, of course, why he should not have removed his beard, but as against that suggestion we will call evidence to prove that the man seen driving with the murdered chauffeur was invariably a man with a mustache and no beard, so that the balance of probability is on the side of the supposition that Merrill is not telling the truth. An unknown client with a large deposit at his bank would not be likely constantly to alter his appearance. If he were a criminal, as we know him to be, there would be another reason why he should not excite suspicion in this way."

His address covered the greater part of a day—but he returned to the scene in the garden, to the supposed meeting of the two men, and to the murder.

Saul Arthur Mann, sitting with Frank's solicitor, scratched his nose and grinned.

"I have never heard a more ingenious piece of reconstruction," he said; "though, of course, the whole thing is palpably absurd."

As a theory it was no doubt excellent; but men are not sentenced to death on theories, however ingenious they may be. Probably nobody in the court so completely admired the ingenuity as the man most affected. At the lunch interval on the day on which this theory was put forward he met his solicitor and Saul Arthur Mann in the bare room in which such interviews are permitted.

"It was really fascinating to hear him," said Frank, as he sipped the cup of tea which they had brought him. "I almost began to believe that I had committed the murder! But isn't it rather alarming? Will the jury take the same view?" he asked, a little troubled.

The solicitor shook his head.

"Unsupported theories of that sort do not go well with juries, and, of course, the whole story is so flimsy and so improbable that it will go for no more than a piece of clever reasoning."

"Did anybody see you at the railway station?"

Frank shook his head.

"I suppose hundreds of people saw me, but would hardly remember me."

"Was there any one on the train who knew you?"

"No," said Frank, after a moment's thought. "There were six people in my carriage until we got to Lewes, but I think I told you that, and you have not succeeded in tracing any of them."

"It is most difficult to get into touch with those people," said the lawyer. "Think of the scores of people one travels with, without ever remembering what they looked like or how they were dressed. If you had been a woman, traveling with women, every one of your five fellow passengers would have remembered you and would have recalled your hat."

Frank laughed.

"There are certain disadvantages in being a man," he said. "How do you think the case is going?"

"They have offered no evidence yet. I think you will agree, Mr. Mann," he said respectfully, for Saul Arthur Mann was a power in legal circles.

"None at all," the little fellow agreed.

Frank recalled the first day he had seen him, with his hat perched on the back of his head and his shabby, genteel exterior.

"Oh, by Jove!" he said. "I suppose they will be trying to fasten the death of that man upon me that we saw in Gray Square."

Saul Arthur Mann nodded.

"They have not put that in the indictment," he said, "nor the case of the chauffeur. You see, your conviction will rest entirely upon this present charge, and both the other matters are subsidiary."

Frank walked thoughtfully up and down the room, his hands behind his back.

"I wonder who Rex Holland is," he said, half to himself.

"You still have your theory?" asked the lawyer, eying him keenly.

Frank nodded.

"And you still would rather not put it into words?"

"Much rather not," said Frank gravely.

He returned to the court and glanced round for the girl, but she was not there. The rest of the afternoon's proceedings, taken up as they were with the preliminaries of the case, bored him.

It was on the twelfth day of the trial that Jasper Cole stepped on to the witness stand. He was dressed in black and was paler than usual, but he took the oath in a firm voice and answered the questions which were put to him without hesitation.

The story of Frank's quarrel with his uncle, of the forged checks, and of his own experience on the night of the crime filled the greater part of the forenoon, and it was in the afternoon when Bryan Bennett, one of the most brilliant barristers of his time, stood up to cross-examine.

"Had you any suspicion that your employer was being robbed?"

"I had a suspicion," replied Jasper.

"Did you communicate your suspicion to your employer?"

Jasper hesitated.

"No," he replied at last.

"Why do you hesitate?" asked Bennett sharply.

"Because, although I did not directly communicate my suspicions, I hinted to Mr. Minute that he should have an independent audit."

"So you thought the books were wrong?"

"I did."

"In these circumstances," asked Bennett slowly, "do you not think it was very unwise of you to touch those books yourself?"

"When did I touch them?" asked Jasper quickly.

"I suggest that on a certain night you came to the bank and remained in the bank by yourself, examining the ledgers on behalf of your employer, and that during that time you handled at least three books in which these falsifications were made."

"That is quite correct," said Jasper, after a moment's thought; "but my suspicions were general and did not apply to any particular group of books."

"But did you not think it was dangerous?"

Again the hesitation.

"It may have been foolish, and if I had known how matters were developing I should certainly not have touched them."

"You do admit that there were several periods of time from seven in the evening until nine and from nine-thirty until eleven-fifteen when you were absolutely alone in the bank?"

"That is true," said Jasper.

"And during those periods you could, had you wished and had you been a forger, for example, or had you any reason for falsifying the entries, have made those falsifications?"

"I admit there was time," said Jasper.

"Would you describe yourself as a friend of Frank Merrill's?"

"Not a close friend," replied Jasper.

"Did you like him?"

"I cannot say that I was fond of him," was the reply.

"He was a rival of yours?"

"In what respect?"

Counsel shrugged his shoulders.

"He was very fond of Miss Nuttall."

"Yes."

"And she was fond of him?"

"Yes."

"Did you not aspire to pay your addresses to Miss Nuttall?"

Jasper Cole looked down to the girl, and May averted her eyes. Her cheeks were burning and she had a wild desire to flee from the court.

"If you mean did I love Miss Nuttall," said Jasper Cole, in his quiet, even tone, "I reply that I did."

"You even secured the active support of Mr. Minute?"

"I never urged the matter with Mr. Minute," said Jasper.

"So that if he moved on your behalf he did so without your knowledge?"

"Without my pre-knowledge," corrected the witness. "He told me afterward that he had spoken to Miss Nuttall, and I was considerably embarrassed."

"I understand you were a man of curious habits, Mr. Cole."

"We are all people of curious habits," smiled the witness.

"But you in particular. You were an Orientalist, I believe?"

"I have studied Oriental languages and customs," said Jasper shortly.

"Have you ever extended your study to the realm of hypnotism?"

"I have," replied the witness.

"Have you ever made experiments?"

"On animals, yes."

"On human beings?"

"No, I have never made experiments on human beings."

"Have you also made a study of narcotics?"

The lawyer leaned forward over the table and looked at the witness between half-closed eyes.

"I have made experiments with narcotic herbs and plants," said Jasper, after a moment's hesitation. "I think you should know that the career which was planned for me was that of a doctor, and I have always been very interested in the effects of narcotics."

"You know of a drug called *cannabis indica*?" asked the counsel, consulting his paper.

"Yes; it is 'Indian hemp.'"

"Is there an infusion of *cannabis indica* to be obtained?"

"I do not think there is," said the other. "I can probably enlighten you because I see now the trend of your examination. I once told Frank Merrill, many years ago, when I was very enthusiastic, that an infusion of *cannabis indica*, combined with tincture of opium and hyocine, produced certain effects."

"It is inclined to sap the will power of a man or a woman who is constantly absorbing this poison in small doses?" suggested the counsel.

"That is so."

The counsel now switched off on a new tack.

"Do you know the East of London?"

"Yes, slightly."

"Do you know Silvers Rents?"

"Yes."

"Do you ever go to Silvers Rents?"

"Yes; I go there very regularly."

The readiness of the reply astonished both Frank and the girl. She had been feeling more and more uncomfortable as the cross-examination continued, and had a feeling that she had in some way betrayed Jasper Cole's confidence. She had listened to the cross-examination which revealed Jasper as a scientist with something approaching amazement. She had known of the laboratory, but had associated the place with those entertaining experiments that an idle dabbler in chemistry might undertake.

For a moment she doubted, and searched her mind for some occasion when he had practiced his medical knowledge. Dimly she realized that there *had* been some such occasion, and then she remembered that it had always been Jasper Cole who had concocted the strange drafts which had so relieved the headache to which, when she was a little younger, she had been something of a martyr. Could he—She struggled hard to dismiss the thought as being unworthy of her; and now, when the object of his visits to Silvers Rents was under examination, she found her curiosity growing.

"Why did you go to Silvers Rents?"

There was no answer.

"I will repeat my question: With what object did you go to Silvers Rents?"

"I decline to answer that question," said the man in the box coolly. "I merely tell you that I went there frequently."

"And you refuse to say why?"

"I refuse to say why," repeated the witness.

The judge on the bench made a little note.

"I put it to you," said counsel, speaking impressively, "that it was in Silvers Rents that you took on another identity."

"That is probably true," said the other, and the girl gasped; he was so cool, so self-possessed, so sure of himself.

"I suggest to you," the counsel went on, "that in those Rents Jasper Cole became Rex Holland."

There was a buzz of excitement, a sudden soft clamor of voices through which the usher's harsh demand for silence cut like a knife.

"Your suggestion is an absurd one," said Jasper, without heat, "and I presume that you are going to produce evidence to support so infamous a statement."

"What evidence I produce," said counsel, with asperity, "is a matter for me to decide."

"It is also a matter for the witness," interposed the soft voice of the judge. "As you have suggested that Holland was a party to the murder, and as you are inferring that Rex Holland is Jasper Cole, it is presumed that you will call evidence to support so serious a charge."

"I am not prepared to call evidence, my lord, and if your lordship thinks the question should not have been put I am willing to withdraw it."

The judge nodded and turned his head to the jury.

"You will consider that question as not having been put, gentlemen," he said. "Doubtless counsel is trying to establish the fact that one person might just as easily have been Rex Holland as another. There is no suggestion that Mr. Cole went to Silvers Rents—which I understand is in a very poor neighborhood—with any illegal intent, or that he was committing any crime or behaving in any way improperly by paying such frequent visits. There may be something in the witness's life associated with that poor house which has no bearing on the case and which he does not desire should be ventilated in this court. It happens to many of us," the judge went on, "that we have associations which it would embarrass us to reveal."

This little incident closed that portion of the cross-examination, and counsel went on to the night of the murder.

"When did you come to the house?" he asked.

"I came to the house soon after dark."

"Had you been in London?"

"Yes; I walked from Bexhill."

"It was dark when you arrived?"

"Yes, nearly dark."

"The servants had all gone out?"

"Yes."

"Was Mr. Minute pleased to see you?"

"Yes; he had expected me earlier in the day."

"Did he tell you that his nephew was coming to see him?"

"I knew that."

"You say he suggested that you should make yourself scarce?"

"Yes."

"And as you had a headache, you went upstairs and lay down on your bed?"

"Yes."

"What were you doing in Bexhill?"

"I came down from town and got into the wrong portion of the train."

A junior leaned over and whispered quickly to his leader.

"I see, I see," said the counsel petulantly. "Your ticket was found at Bexhill. Have you ever seen Mr. Rex Holland?" he asked.

"Never."

"You have never met any person of that name?"

"Never."

In this tame way the cross-examination closed, as cross-examinations have a habit of doing.

By the time the final addresses of counsel had ended, and the judge had finished a masterly summing-up, there was no doubt whatever in the mind of any person in the court as to what the verdict would be. The jury was absent from the box for twenty minutes and returned a verdict of "Not guilty!"

The judge discharged Frank Merrill without comment, and he left the court a free but ruined man.

CHAPTER XIII

THE MAN WHO CAME TO MONTREUX

It was two months after the great trial, on a warm day in October, when Frank Merrill stepped ashore from the big white paddle boat which had carried him across Lake Leman from Lausanne, and, handing his bag to a porter, made his way to the hotel omnibus. He looked at his watch. It pointed to a quarter to four, and May was not due to arrive until half past. He went to his hotel, washed and changed and came down to the vestibule to inquire if the instructions he had telegraphed had been carried out.

May was arriving in company with Saul Arthur Mann, who was taking one of his rare holidays abroad. Frank had only seen the girl once since the day of the trial. He had come to breakfast on the following morning, and very little had been said. He was due to leave that afternoon for the Continent. He had a little money, sufficient for his needs, and Jasper Cole had offered no suggestion that he would dispute the will, in so far as it affected Frank. So he had gone abroad and had idled away two months in France, Spain, and Italy, and had then made his leisurely way back to Switzerland by way of Maggiore.

He had grown a little graver, was a little more set in his movements, but he bore upon his face no mark to indicate the mental agony through which he must have passed in that long-drawn-out and wearisome trial. So thought the girl as she came through the swing doors of the hotel, passed the obsequious hotel servants, and greeted him in the big palm court.

If she saw any change in him he remarked a development in her which was a little short of wonderful. She was at that age when the woman is breaking through the beautiful chrysalis of girlhood. In those two months a remarkable change had come over her, a change which he could not for the moment define, for this phenomenon of development had been denied to his experience.

"Why, May," he said, "you are quite old."

She laughed, and again he noticed the change. The laugh was richer, sweeter, purer than the bubbling treble he had known.

"You are not getting complimentary, are you?" she asked.

She was exquisitely dressed, and had that poise which few Englishwomen achieve. She had the art of wearing clothes, and from the flimsy crest of her toque to the tips of her little feet she was all that the most exacting critic could desire. There are well-dressed women who are no more than mannequins. There are fine ladies who cannot be mistaken for anything but fine ladies, whose dresses are a horror and an abomination and whose expressed tastes are execrable.

May Nuttall was a fine lady, finely appareled.

"When you have finished admiring me, Frank," she said, "tell us what you have been doing. But first of all let us have some tea. You know Mr. Mann?"

The little investigator beaming in the background took Frank's hand and shook it heartily. He was dressed in what he thought was an appropriate costume for a mountainous country. His boots were stout, the woolen stockings which covered his very thin legs were very woolen, and his knickerbocker suit was warranted to stand wear and tear. He had abandoned his top hat for a large golf cap, which was perched rakishly over one eye. Frank looked round apprehensively for Saul Arthur's alpenstock, and was relieved when he failed to discover one.

The girl threw off her fur wrap and unbuttoned her gloves as the waiter placed the big silver tray on the table before her.

"I'm afraid I have not much to tell," said Frank in answer to her question. "I've just been loafing around. What is your news?"

"What is my news?" she asked. "I don't think I have any, except that everything is going very smoothly in England, and, oh, Frank, I am so immensely rich!"

He smiled.

"The appropriate thing would be to say that I am immensely poor," he said, "but as a matter of fact I am not. I went down to Aix and won quite a lot of money."

"Won it?" she said.

He nodded with an amused little smile.

"You wouldn't have thought I was a gambler, would you?" he asked solemnly. "I don't think I am, as a matter of fact, but somehow I wanted to occupy my mind."

"I understand," she said quickly.

Another little pause while she poured out the tea, which afforded Saul Arthur Mann an opportunity of firing off fifty facts about Geneva in as many sentences.

"What has happened to Jasper?" asked Frank after a while.

The girl flushed a little.

"Oh, Jasper," she said awkwardly, "I see him, you know. He has become more mysterious than ever, quite like one of those wicked people one reads about in sensational stories. He has a laboratory somewhere in the country, and he does quite a lot of motoring. I've seen him several times at Brighton, for instance."

Frank nodded slowly.

"I should think that he was a good driver," he said.

Saul Arthur Mann looked up and met his eye with a smile which was lost upon the girl.

"He has been kind to me," she said hesitatingly.

"Does he ever speak about—"

She shook her head.

"I don't want to think about that," she said; "please don't let us talk about it."

He knew she was referring to John Minute's death, and changed the conversation.

A few minutes later he had an opportunity of speaking with Mr. Mann.

"What is the news?" he asked.

Saul Arthur Mann looked round.

"I think we are getting near the truth," he said, dropping his voice. "One of my men has had him under observation ever since the day of the trial. There is no doubt that he is really a brilliant chemist."

"Have you a theory?"

"I have several," said Mr. Mann. "I am perfectly satisfied that the unfortunate fellow we saw together on the occasion of our first meeting was Rex Holland's servant. I was as certain that he was poisoned by a very powerful poisoning. When your trial was on the body was exhumed and examined, and the presence of that drug was discovered. It was the same as that employed in the case of the chauffeur. Obviously, Rex Holland is a clever chemist. I wanted to see you about that. He said at the trial that he had discussed such matters with you."

Frank nodded.

"We used to have quite long talks about drugs," he said. "I have recalled many of those conversations since the day of the trial. He even fired me with his enthusiasm, and I used to assist him in his little experiments, and obtained quite a working knowledge of these particular elements. Unfortunately I cannot remember very much, for my enthusiasm soon died, and beyond the fact that he employed hyocine and Indian hemp I have only the dimmest recollection of any of the constituents he employed."

Saul Arthur nodded energetically.

"I shall have more to tell you later, perhaps," he said, "but at present my inquiries are shaping quite nicely. He is going to be a difficult man to catch, because, if all

I believe is true, he is one of the most cold-blooded and calculating men it has ever been my lot to meet—and I have met a few," he added grimly.

When he said men Frank knew that he had meant criminals.

"We are probably doing him a horrible injustice," he smiled. "Poor old Jasper!"

"You are not cut out for police work," snapped Saul Arthur Mann; "you've too many sympathies."

"I don't exactly sympathize," rejoined Frank, "but I just pity him in a way."

Again Mr. Mann looked round cautiously and again lowered his voice, which had risen.

"There is one thing I want to talk to you about. It is rather a delicate matter, Mr. Merrill," he said.

"Fire ahead!"

"It is about Miss Nuttall. She has seen a lot of our friend Jasper, and after every interview she seems to grow more and more reliant upon his help. Once or twice she has been embarrassed when I have spoken about Jasper Cole and has changed the subject."

Frank pursed his lips thoughtfully, and a hard little look came into his eyes, which did not promise well for Jasper.

"So that is it," he said, and shrugged his shoulders. "If she cares for him, it is not my business."

"But it is your business," said the other sharply. "She was fond enough of you to offer to marry you."

Further talk was cut short by the arrival of the girl. Their meeting at Geneva had been to some extent a chance one. She was going through to Chamonix to spend the winter, and Saul Arthur Mann seized the opportunity of taking a short and pleasant holiday. Hearing that Frank was in Switzerland, she had telegraphed him to meet her.

"Are you staying any time in Switzerland?" she asked him as they strolled along the beautiful quay.

"I am going back to London to-night," he replied.

"To-night," she said in surprise.

He nodded.

"But I am staying here for two or three days," she protested.

"I intended also staying for two or three days," he smiled, "but my business will not wait."

Nevertheless, she persuaded him to stay till the morrow.

They were at breakfast when the morning mail was delivered, and Frank noted that she went rapidly through the dozen letters which came to her, and she chose one for first reading. He could not help but see that that bore an English stamp, and his long acquaintance with the curious calligraphy of Jasper Cole left him in no doubt as to who was the correspondent. He saw with what eagerness she read the letter, the little look of disappointment when she turned to an inside sheet and found that it had not been filled, and his mind was made up. He had a post also, which he examined with some evidence of impatience.

"Your mail is not so nice as mine," said the girl with a smile.

"It is not nice at all," he grumbled; "the one thing I wanted, and, to be very truthful, May, the one inducement—"

"To stay over the night," she added, "was—what?"

"I have been trying to buy a house on the lake," he said, "and the infernal agent at Lausanne promised to write telling me whether my terms had been agreed to by his client."

He looked down at the table and frowned. Saul Arthur Mann had a great and extensive knowledge of human nature. He had remarked the disappointment on Frank's face, having identified also the correspondent whose letter claimed priority of attention. He knew that Frank's anger with the house agent was very likely the expression of his anger in quite another direction.

"Can I send the letter on?" suggested the girl.

"That won't help me," said Frank, with a little grimace. "I wanted to settle the business this week."

"I have it," she said. "I will open the letter and telegraph to you in Paris whether the terms are accepted or not."

Frank laughed.

"It hardly seems worth that," he said, "but I should take it as awfully kind of you if you would, May."

Saul Arthur Mann believed in his mind that Frank did not care tuppence whether the agent accepted the terms or not, but that he had taken this as a Heaven-sent opportunity for veiling his annoyance.

"You have had quite a large mail, Miss Nuttall," he said.

"I've only opened one, though. It is from Jasper," she said hurriedly.

Again both men noticed the faint flush, the strange, unusual light which came to her eyes.

"And where does Jasper write from?" asked Frank, steadying his voice.

"He writes from England, but he was going on the Continent to Holland the day he wrote," she said. "It is funny to think that he is here."

"In Switzerland?" asked Frank in surprise.

"Don't be silly," she laughed. "No, I mean on the mainland—I mean there is no sea between us."

She went crimson.

"It sounds thrilling," said Frank dryly.

She flashed round at him.

"You mustn't be horrid about Jasper," she said quickly; "he never speaks about you unkindly."

"I don't see why he should," said Frank; "but let's get off a subject which is—"

"Which is—what?" she challenged

"Which is controversial," said Frank diplomatically.

She came down to the station to see him off. As he looked out of the window, waving his farewells, he thought he had never seen a more lovely being or one more desirable.

It was in the afternoon of that day which saw Frank Merrill speeding toward the Swiss frontier and Paris that Mr. Rex Holland strode into the Palace Hotel at Montreux and seated himself at a table in the restaurant. The hour was late and the room was almost deserted. Giovanni, the head waiter, recognized him and came hurriedly across the room.

"Ah, m'sieur," he said, "you are back from England. I didn't expect you till the winter sports had started. Is Paris very dull?"

"I didn't come through Paris," said the other shortly; "there are many roads leading to Switzerland."

"But few pleasant roads, m'sieur. I have come to Montreux by all manner of ways—from Paris, through Pontarlier, through Ostend, Brussels, through the Hook of Holland and Amsterdam, but Paris is the only way for the man who is flying to this beautiful land."

The man at the table said nothing, scanning the menu carefully. He looked tired as one who had taken a very long journey.

"It may interest you to know," he said, after he had given his order and as Giovanni was turning away, "that I came by the longest route. Tell me, Giovanni, have you a man called Merrill staying at the hotel?"

"No, m'sieur," said the other. "Is he a friend of yours?"

Mr. Rex Holland smiled.

"In a sense he is a friend, in a sense he is not," he said flippantly, and offered no further enlightenment, although Giovanni waited with a deferential cock of his head.

Later, when he had finished his modest dinner, he strolled into the one long street of the town, returning to the writing room of the hotel with a number of papers which included the visitors' list, a publication printed in English, and which, as it related the comings and goings of visitors, not only to Lausanne, Montreux, and Teritet, but also to Evian and Geneva, enjoyed a fair circulation. He sat at the table, and, drawing a sheet of paper from the rack, wrote, addressed an envelope to Frank Merrill, esquire, Hotel de France, Geneva, slipped it into the hotel pillar box, and went to bed.

"There's a letter here for Frank," said the girl. "I wonder if it is from his agent."

She examined the envelope, which bore the Montreux postmark.

"I should imagine it is," said Saul Arthur Mann.

"Well, I am going to open it, anyway," said the girl. "Poor Frank! He will be in a state of suspense."

She tore open the envelope, and took out a letter. Mr. Mann saw her face go white, and the letter trembled in her hand. Without a word she passed it to him, and he read:

"Dear Frank Merrill," said the letter. "Give me another month's grace and then you may tell the whole story. Yours, Rex Holland."

Saul Arthur Mann stared at the letter with open mouth.

"What does it mean?" asked the girl in a whisper.

"It means that Merrill is shielding somebody," said the other. "It means—"

Suddenly his face lit up with excitement.

"The writing!" he gasped.

Her eyes followed his, and for a moment she did not understand; then, with a lightning sweep of her arm, she snatched the letter from his hand and crumpled it in a ball.

"The writing!" said Mr. Mann again. "I've seen it before. It is—Jasper Cole's!"

She looked at him steadily, though her face was white, and the hand which grasped the crumpled paper was shaking.

"I think you are mistaken, Mr. Mann," she said quietly.

CHAPTER XIV

THE MAN WHO LOOKED LIKE FRANK

Saul Arthur Mann came back to England full of his news, and found Frank at the little Jermyn Street hotel where he had installed himself, and Frank listened without interruption to the story of the letter.

"Of course," the little fellow went on, "I went straight over to Montreux. The note heading was not on the paper, but I had no difficulty, by comparing the qualities of papers used at the various hotels, in discovering that it was written from the Palace. The head waiter knew this Rex Holland, who had been a frequent visitor, had always tipped very liberally, and lived in something like style. He could not describe his patron, except that he was a young man with a very languid manner who had arrived the previous morning from Holland and had immediately inquired for Frank Merrill."

"From Holland! Are you sure it was the morning? I have a particular reason for asking," asked Frank quickly.

"No, it was not in the morning, now you mention it. It was in the evening. He left again the following morning by the northern train."

"How did he find my address?" asked Frank.

"Obviously from the visitors' list. The waiter on duty in the writing room remembered having seen him consulting the newspaper. Now, my boy, you have to be perfectly candid with me. What do you know about Rex Holland?"

Frank opened his case, took out a cigarette, and lit it before he replied.

"I know what everybody knows about him," he said, with a hint of bitterness in his voice, "and something which nobody knows but me."

"But, my dear fellow," said Saul Arthur Mann, laying his hand on the other's shoulder, "surely you realize how important it is for you that you should tell me all you know."

Frank shook his head.

"The time is not come," he said, and he would make no further statement.

But on another matter he was emphatic.

"By heaven, Mann, I am not going to stand by and see May ruin her life. There's something sinister in this influence which Jasper is exercising over her. You have seen it for yourself."

Saul Arthur nodded.

"I can't understand what it is," he confessed. "Of course Jasper is not a bad-looking fellow. He has perfect manners and is a charming companion. You don't think—"

"That he is winning on his merits?" Frank shook his head. "No, indeed, I do not. It is difficult for me to discuss my private affairs, and you know how reluctant I am to do so, but you are also aware of what I think of May. I was hoping that we should go back to the place where we left off, and, although she is kindness itself, this girl who is more to me than anything or anybody in the world, and who was prepared to marry me, and would have married me but for Jasper's machinations, was almost cold."

He was walking up and down the room, and now halted in his stride and spread out his arms despairingly.

"What am I to do? I cannot lose her. I cannot!"

There was a fierceness in his tone which revealed the depth of his feeling, and Saul Arthur Mann understood.

"I think it is too soon to say you have lost her, Frank," he said.

He had conceived a genuine liking for Frank Merrill, and the period of tribulation through which the young man had passed had heightened the respect in which he held him.

"We shall see light in dark places before we go much farther," he said. "There is something behind this crime, Frank, which I don't understand, but which I am certain is no mystery to you. I am sure that you are shielding somebody, for what reason I am not in a position to tell, but I will get to the bottom of it."

No event in the interesting life of this little man, who had spent his years in the accumulation of facts, had so distressed and piqued him as the murder of John Minute. The case had ended where the trial had left it.

Crawley, who might have offered a new aspect to the tragedy, had disappeared as completely as though the earth had swallowed him. The most strenuous efforts which the official police had made, added to the investigations which Saul Arthur Mann had conducted independently, had failed to trace the fugitive ex-sergeant of police. Obviously, he was not to be confounded with Rex Holland. He was a distinct personality working possibly in collusion, but there the association ended.

It had occurred to the investigator that possibly Crawley had accompanied Rex Holland in his flight, but the most careful inquiries which he had pursued at Montreux were fruitless in this respect as in all others.

To add to his bewilderment, investigations nearer at home were constantly bringing him across the track of Frank Merrill. It was as though fate had conspired to show the boy in the blackest light. Frank had been acting as secretary to his uncle, and then Jasper Cole had suddenly appeared upon the scene from nowhere in particular. The suggestion had been made somewhat vaguely that he had come from "abroad," and it was certain that he arrived as a result of long negotiations which John Minute himself had conducted. They were negotiations which involved months of correspondence, no letter of which either from one or the other had Frank seen.

While the trial was pending, the little man collected quite a volume of information, both from Frank and the girl, but nothing had been quite as inexplicable as this intrusion of Jasper Cole upon the scene, or the extraordinary mystery which John Minute had made of his engagement.

He had written and posted all the letters to Jasper himself, and had apparently received the replies, which he had burned, at some other address of which Frank was ignorant.

Jasper had come, and then one day there had been a quarrel, not between the two young men, but between Frank and his uncle. It was a singularly bitter quarrel, and again Frank refused to discuss the cause. He left the impression upon Saul Arthur's mind that he had to some extent been responsible. And here was another fact which puzzled "The Man Who Knew." Sergeant Smith, as he was then, had been to some extent responsible. It was Frank who had introduced the sergeant to Eastbourne and brought him to his uncle. But this was only one aspect of the mystery. There were others as obscure.

Saul Arthur Mann went back to his bureau, and for the twentieth time gathered the considerable dossiers he had accumulated relating to the case and to the characters, and went through them systematically and carefully.

He left his office near midnight, but at nine o'clock the next morning was on his way to Eastbourne. Constable Wiseman was, by good fortune, enjoying a day's holiday, and was at work in his kitchen garden when Mr. Mann's car pulled up before the cottage. Wiseman received his visitor importantly, for, though the constable's prestige was regarded in official circles as having diminished as a result of the trial, it was felt by the villagers that their policeman, if he had not solved the mystery of John Minute's death, had at least gone a long way to its solution.

In the spotless room which was half kitchen and half sitting room, with its red-tiled floor covered by bright matting, Mrs. Wiseman produced a well-dusted Windsor chair, which she placed at Saul Arthur Mann's disposal before she politely vanished. In a very few words the investigator stated his errand, and Constable Wiseman listened in noncommittal silence. When his visitor had finished, he shook his head.

"The only thing about the sergeant I know," he said, "I have already told the chief constable who sat in that very chair," he explained. "He was always a bit of a mystery—the sergeant, I mean. When he was 'tanked,' if I may use the expression, he would tell you stories by the hour, but when he was sober you couldn't get a word out of him. His daughter only lived with him for about a fortnight."

"His daughter!" said Mr. Mann quickly.

"He had a daughter, as I've already notified my superiors," said Constable Wiseman gravely. "Rather a pretty girl. I never saw much of her, but she was in Eastbourne off and on for about a fortnight after the sergeant came. Funny thing, I happen to know the day he arrived, because the wheel of his fly came off on my beat, and I noticed the circumstances according to law and reported the same. I don't even know if she was living with him. He had a cottage down at Birlham Gap, and that is where I saw her. Yes, she was a pretty girl," he said reminiscently; "one of the slim and slender kind, very dark and with a complexion like milk. But they never found her," he said.

Again Mr. Mann interrupted.

"You mean the police?"

Constable Wiseman shook his head.

"Oh, no," he said; "they've been looking for her for years; long before Mr. Minute was killed."

"Who are 'they'?"

"Well, several people," said the constable slowly. "I happen to know that Mr. Cole wanted to find out where she was. But then he didn't start searching until weeks after she disappeared. It is very rum," mused Constable Wiseman, "the way Mr. Cole went about it. He didn't come straight to us and ask our assistance, but he had a lot of private detectives nosing round Eastbourne; one of 'em happened to be a cousin of my wife's. So we got to know about it. Cole spent a lot of money trying to trace her, and so did Mr. Minute."

Saul Arthur Mann saw a faint gleam of daylight.

"Mr. Minute, too?" he asked. "Was he working with Mr. Cole?"

"So far as I can find out, they were both working independent of the other— Mr. Cole and Mr. Minute," explained Mr. Wiseman. "It is what I call a mystery within a mystery, and it has never been properly cleared up. I thought something was coming out about it at the trial, but you know what a mess the lawyers made of it."

It was Constable Wiseman's firm conviction that Frank Merrill had escaped through the incompetence of the crown authorities, and there were moments in his domestic circle when he was bitter and even insubordinate on the subject.

"You still think Mr. Merrill was guilty?" asked Saul Arthur Mann as he took his leave of the other.

"I am as sure of it as I am that I am standing here," said the constable, not without a certain pride in the consistency of his view. "Didn't I go into the room? Wasn't he there with the deceased? Wasn't his revolver found? Hadn't there been some jiggery-pokery with his books in London?"

Saul Arthur Mann smiled.

"There are some of us who think differently, Constable," he said, shaking hands with the implacable officer of the law.

He brought back to London a few new facts to be added to his record of Sergeant Crawley, alias Smith, and on these he went painstakingly to work.

As has been already explained, Saul Arthur Mann had a particularly useful relationship with Scotland Yard, and fortunately, about that time, he was on the most excellent terms with official police headquarters, for he had been able to assist them in running to earth one of the most powerful blackmailing gangs that had ever operated in Europe. His files had been drawn upon to such good purpose that the police had secured convictions against the seventeen members of the gang who were in England.

He sought an interview with the chief commissioner, and that same night, accompanied by a small army of detectives, he made a systematic search of Silvers Rents. The house into which Jasper Cole had been seen to enter was again raided, and again without result. The house was empty save for one room, a big room which was simply furnished with a truckle-bed, a table, a chair, a lamp, and a strip of carpet. There were four rooms—two upstairs, which were never used, and two on the ground floor.

At the end of a passage was a kitchen, which also was empty, save for a length of bamboo ladder. From the kitchen a bolted door led on to a tiny square of yard which was separated by three walls from yards of similar dimensions to left and right and to the back of the premises. At the back of Silvers Rents was Royston Court, which was another cul-de-sac, running parallel with Silvers Rents.

Mr. Mann returned to the house, and again searched the upstairs rooms, looking particularly for a trapdoor, for the bamboo ladder suggested some such exit. This time, however, he completely failed. Jasper Cole, he found, had made only one visit to the house since John Minute's death.

It is a curious fact, as showing the localizing of interest, that Silvers Rents knew nothing of what had occurred almost at its doors, and, though it had at its finger tips all the gossip of the docks and the Thames Iron Works, it was profoundly ignorant of what was common property in Royston Court. It is even more remarkable that Saul Arthur Mann, with his squadron of detectives, should have confined their investigations to Silvers Rents.

The investigator was baffled and disappointed, but by the oddest of chances he was to pick up yet another thread of the Minute mystery, a thread which, however, was to lead him into an ever-deeper maze than that which he had already and so unsuccessfully attempted to penetrate.

Three days after his search of Silvers Rents, business took Mr. Mann to Camden Town. To be exact, he had gone at the request of the police to Holloway Jail to see a prisoner who had turned state's evidence on a matter in which the police and Mr. Mann were equally interested. Very foolishly he had dismissed his taxi, and when he emerged from the doors there was no conveyance in sight. He decided, rather than take the trams which would have carried him to King's Cross, to walk, and, since he hated main roads, he had taken a short cut, which, as he knew, would lead him into the Hampstead Road.

Thus he found himself in Flowerton Road, a thoroughfare of respectable detached houses occupied by the superior industrial type. He was striding along, swinging his umbrella and humming, as was his wont, an unmusical rendering of a popular tune, when his attention was attracted to a sight which took his breath away and brought him to a halt.

It was half past five, and dull, but his eyesight was excellent, and it was impossible for him to make a mistake. The houses of Flowerton Road stand back and are separated from the sidewalk by diminutive gardens. The front doors are approached by six or seven steps, and it was on the top of one of these flights in front of an open door that the scene was enacted which brought Mr. Mann to a standstill.

The characters were a young man and a girl. The girl was extremely pretty and very pale. The man was the exact double of Frank Merrill. He was dressed in a rough tweed suit, and wore a soft felt hat with a fairly wide brim. But it was not the appearance of this remarkable apparition which startled the investigator. It was the attitude of the two people. The girl was evidently pleading with her companion. Saul Arthur Mann was too far away to hear what she said, but he saw the young man shake himself loose from the girl. She again grasped his arm and raised her face imploringly.

Mr. Mann gasped, for he saw the young man's hand come up and strike her back into the house. Then he caught hold of the door and banged it savagely, walked down the stairs, and, turning, hurried away.

The investigator stood as though he were rooted to the spot, and before he could recover himself the fellow had turned the corner of the road and was out of sight. Saul Arthur Mann took off his hat and wiped his forehead. All his initiative was for the moment paralyzed. He walked slowly up to the gate and hesitated. What excuse could he have for calling? If this were Frank, assuredly his own views were all wrong, and the mystery was a greater mystery still.

His energies began to reawaken. He took a note of the number of the house, and hurried off after the young man. When he turned the corner his quarry had vanished. He hurried to the next corner, but without overtaking the object of his pursuit. Fortunately, at this moment, he found an empty taxicab and hailed it.

"Grimm's Hotel, Jermyn Street," he directed.

At least he could satisfy his mind upon one point.

CHAPTER XV

A LETTER IN THE GRATE

Grimm's Hotel is in reality a block of flats, with a restaurant attached. The restaurant is little more than a kitchen from whence meals are served to residents in their rooms. Frank's suite was on the third floor, and Mr. Mann, paying his cabman, hurried into the hall, stepped into the automatic lift, pressed the button, and was deposited at Frank's door. He knocked with a sickening sense of apprehension that there would be no answer. To his delight and amazement, he heard Frank's firm step in the tiny hall of his flat, and the door was opened. Frank was in the act of dressing for dinner.

"Come in, S. A. M.," he said cheerily, "and tell me all the news."

He led the way back to his room and resumed the delicate task of tying his dress bow.

"How long have you been here?" asked Mr. Mann.

Frank looked at him inquiringly.

"How long have I been here?" he repeated. "I cannot tell you the exact time, but I have been here since a short while after lunch."

Mr. Mann was bewildered and still unconvinced.

"What clothes did you take off?"

It was Frank's turn to look amazed and bewildered.

"Clothes?" he repeated. "What are you driving at, my dear chap?"

"What suit were you wearing to-day?" persisted Saul Arthur Mann.

Frank disappeared into his dressing room and came out with a tumbled bundle which he dropped on a chair. It was the blue suit which he usually affected.

"Now what is the joke?"

"It is no joke," said the other. "I could have sworn that I saw you less than half an hour ago in Camden Town."

"I won't pretend that I don't know where Camden Town is," smiled Frank, "but I have not visited that interesting locality for many years."

Saul Arthur Mann was silent. It was obvious to him that whoever was the occupant of 69 Flowerton Road, it was not Frank Merrill. Frank listened to the narrative with interest.

"You were probably mistaken; the light played you a trick, I expect," he said.

But Mr. Mann was emphatic.

"I could have taken an oath in a court that it was you," he said.

Frank stared out of the window.

"How very curious!" he mused. "I suppose I cannot very well prosecute a man for looking like me—poor girl!"

"Of whom are you thinking?" asked the other.

"I was thinking of the unfortunate woman," answered Frank. "What brutes there are in the world!"

"You gave me a terrible fright," admitted his friend.

Frank's laugh was loud and hearty.

"I suppose you saw me figuring in a court, charged with common assault," he said.

"I saw more than that," said the other gravely, "and I see more than that now. Suppose you have a double, and suppose that double is working in collusion with your enemies."

Frank shook his head wearily.

"My dear friend," he said, with a little smile, "I am tired of supposing things. Come and dine with me."

But Mr. Mann had another engagement. Moreover, he wanted to think things out.

Thinking things out was a process which brought little reward in this instance, and he went to bed that night a vexed and puzzled man. He always had his breakfast in bed at ten o'clock in the morning, for he had reached the age of habits and had fixed ten o'clock, since it gave his clerks time to bring down his personal mail from the office to his private residence.

It was a profitable mail, it was an exciting mail, and it contained an element of rich promise, for it included a letter from Constable Wiseman:

> DEAR SIR: Re our previous conversation, I have just come across one of the photographs of the young lady—Sergeant Smith's daughter. It was given to the private detective who was searching for her. It was given to my wife by her cousin, and I send it to you hoping it may be of some use.
>
> Yours respectfully,
>
> PETER JOHN WISEMAN.

The photograph was wrapped in a piece of tissue paper, and Saul Arthur Mann opened it eagerly. He looked at the oblong card and gasped, for the girl who was depicted there was the girl he had seen on the steps of 69 Flowerton Road.

A telephone message prepared Frank for the news, and an hour later the two men were together in the office of the bureau.

"I am going along to that house to see the girl," said Saul Arthur Mann. "Will you come?"

"With all the pleasure in life," said Frank. "Curiously enough, I am as eager to find her as you. I remember her very well, and one of the quarrels I had with my uncle was due to her. She had come up to the house on behalf of her father, and I thought uncle treated her rather brutally."

"Point number one cleared up," thought Saul Arthur Mann.

"Then she disappeared," Frank went on, "and Jasper came on the scene. There was some association between this girl and Jasper, which I have never been able to fathom. All I know is that he took a tremendous interest in her and tried to find her, and, so far as I remember, he never succeeded."

Mr. Mann's car was at the door, and in a few minutes they were deposited before the prim exterior of Number 69.

The door was opened by a girl servant, who stared from Saul Arthur Mann to his companion.

"There is a lady living here," said Mr. Mann.

He produced the photograph.

"This is the lady?"

The girl nodded, still staring at Frank.

"I want to see her."

"She's gone," said the girl.

"You are looking at me very intently," said Frank. "Have you ever seen me before?"

"Yes, sir," said the girl; "you used to come here, or a gentleman very much like you. You are Mr. Merrill."

"That is my name," smiled Frank, "but I do not think I have ever been here before."

"Where has the lady gone?" asked Saul Arthur.

"She went last night. Took all her boxes and went off in a cab."

"Is anybody living in the house?"

"No, sir," said the girl.

"How long have you been in service here?"

"About a week, sir," replied the girl.

"We are friends of hers," said Saul Arthur shamelessly, "and we have been asked to call to see if everything is all right."

The girl hesitated, but Saul Arthur Mann, with that air of authority which he so readily assumed, swept past her and began an inspection of the house.

It was plainly furnished, but the furniture was good.

"Apparently the spurious Mr. Merrill had plenty of money," said Saul Arthur Mann.

There were no photographs or papers visible until they came to the bedroom, where, in the grate, was a torn sheet of paper bearing a few lines of fine writing, which Mr. Mann immediately annexed. Before they left, Frank again asked the girl:

"Was the gentleman who lived here really like me?"

"Yes, sir," said the little slavey.

"Have a good look at me," said Frank humorously, and the girl stared again.

"Something like you," she admitted.

"Did he talk like me?"

"I never heard him talk, sir," said the girl.

"Tell me," said Saul Arthur Mann, "was he kind to his wife?"

A faint grin appeared on the face of the little servant.

"They was always rowing," she admitted. "A bullying fellow he was, and she was frightened of him. Are you the police?" she asked with sudden interest.

Frank shook his head.

"No, we are not the police."

He gave the girl half a crown, and walked down the steps ahead of his companion.

"It is rather awkward if I have a double who bullies his wife and lives in Camden Town," he said as the car hummed back to the city office.

Saul Arthur Mann was silent during the journey, and only answered in monosyllables.

Again in the privacy of his office, he took the torn letter and carefully pieced it together on his desk. It bore no address, and there were no affectionate preliminaries:

> You must get out of London. Saul Arthur Mann saw you both to-day. Go to the old place and await instructions.

There was no signature, but across the table the two men looked at one another, for the writing was the writing of Jasper Cole.

CHAPTER XVI

THE COMING OF SERGEANT SMITH

Jasper Cole at that moment was trudging through the snow to the little châlet which May Nuttall had taken on the slope of the mountain overlooking Chamonix. The sleigh which had brought him up from the station was at the foot of the rise. May saw him from the veranda, and coo-ooed a welcome. He stamped the snow from his boots and ran up the steps of the veranda to meet her.

"This is a very pleasant surprise," she said, giving him both her hands and looking at him approvingly. He had lost much of his pallor, and his face was tanned and healthy, though a little fine drawn.

"It was rather a mad thing to do, wasn't it?" he confessed ruefully.

"You are such a confirmed bachelor, Jasper, that I believe you hate doing anything outside your regular routine. Why did you come all the way from Holland to the Haute Savoie?"

He had followed her into the warm and cozy sitting room, and was warming his chilled fingers by the big log fire which burned on the hearth.

"Can you ask? I came to see you."

"And how are all the experiments going?"

She turned him to another topic in some hurry.

"There have been no experiments since last month; at least not the kind of experiments you mean. The one in which I have been engaged has been very successful."

"And what was that?" she asked curiously.

"I will tell you one of these days," he said.

He was staying at the Hôtel des Alpes, and hoped to be a week in Chamonix. They chatted about the weather, the early snow which had covered the valley in a mantle of white, about the tantalizing behavior of Mont Blanc, which had not been visible since May had arrived, of the early avalanches, which awakened her with their thunder on the night of her arrival, of the pleasant road to Argentières, of the villages by the Col de Balme, which are buried in snow, of the sparkling, ethereal green of the great glacier—of everything save that which was nearest to their thoughts and to their hearts.

Jasper broke the ice when he referred to Frank's visit to Geneva.

"How did you know?" she asked, suddenly grave.

"Somebody told me," he said casually.

"Jasper, were you ever at Montreux?" she asked, looking him straight in the eye.

"I have been to Montreux, or rather to Caux," he said. "That is the village on the mountain above, and one has to go through Montreux to reach it. Why did you ask?"

A sudden chill had fallen upon her, which she did not shake off that day or the next.

They made the usual excursions together, climbed up the wooded slopes of the Butte, and on the third morning after his arrival stood together in the clear dawn and watched the first pink rays of the sun striking the humped summit of Mont Blanc.

"Isn't it glorious?" she whispered.

He nodded.

The serene beauty of it all, the purity, the majestic aloofness of mountains at once depressed and exalted her, brought her nearer to the sublimity of ancient truths, cleansed her of petty fears. She turned to him unexpectedly and asked:

"Jasper, who killed John Minute?"

He made no reply. His wistful eyes were fixed hungrily upon the glories of light and shade, of space, of inaccessibility, of purity, of coloring, of all that dawn upon Mont Blanc comprehended. When he spoke his voice was lowered to almost a whisper.

"I know that the man who killed John Minute is alive and free," he said.

"Who was he?"

"If you do not know now, you may never know," he said.

There was a silence which lasted for fully five minutes, and the crimson light upon the mountain top had paled to lemon yellow.

Then she asked again:

"Are you directly or indirectly guilty?"

He shook his head.

"Neither directly nor indirectly," he said shortly, and the next minute she was in his arms.

There had been no word of love between them, no tender passage, no letter which the world could not read. It was a love-making which had begun where other love-makings end—in conquest and in surrender. In this strange way, beyond all understanding, May Nuttall became engaged, and announced the fact in the briefest of letters to her friends.

A fortnight later the girl arrived in England, and was met at Charing Cross by Saul Arthur Mann. She was radiantly happy and bubbling over with good spirits, a picture of health and beauty.

All this Mr. Mann observed with a sinking heart. He had a duty to perform, and that duty was not a pleasant one. He knew it was useless to reason with the girl. He could offer her no more than half-formed theories and suspicions, but at least he had one trump card. He debated in his mind whether he should play this, for here, too, his information was of the scantiest description. He carried his account of the girl to Frank Merrill.

"My dear Frank, she is simply infatuated," said the little man in despair. "Oh, if that infernal record of mine was only completed I could convince her in a second! There is no single investigation I have ever undertaken which has been so disappointing."

"Can nothing be done?" asked Frank, "I cannot believe that it will happen. Marry Jasper! Great Cæsar! After all—"

His voice was hoarse. The hand he raised in protest shook.

Saul Arthur Mann scratched his chin reflectively.

"Suppose you saw her," he suggested, and added a little grimly: "I will see Mr. Cole at the same time."

Frank hesitated.

"I can understand your reluctance," the little man went on, "but there is too much at stake to allow your finer feelings to stop you. This matter has got to be prevented at all costs. We are fighting for time. In a month, possibly less, we may have the whole of the facts in our hands."

"Have you found out anything about the girl in Camden Town?" asked Frank.

"She has disappeared completely," replied the other. "Every clew we have had has led nowhere."

Frank dressed himself with unusual care that afternoon, and, having previously telephoned and secured the girl's permission to call, he presented himself to the minute. She was, as usual, cordiality itself.

"I was rather hurt at your not calling before, Frank," she said. "You have come to congratulate me?"

She looked at him straight in the eyes as she said this.

"You can hardly expect that, May," he said gently, "knowing how much you are to me and how greatly I wanted you. Honestly, I cannot understand it, and I can only suppose that you, whom I love better than anything in the world—and you mean more to me than any other being—share the suspicion which surrounds me like a poison cloud."

"Yet if I shared that suspicion," she said calmly, "would I let you see me? No, Frank, I was a child when—you know. It was only a few months ago, but I believe—indeed I know—it would have been the greatest mistake I could possibly have made. I should have been a very unhappy woman, for I have loved Jasper all along."

She said this evenly, without any display of emotion or embarrassment. Frank, narrating the interview to Saul Arthur Mann, described the speech as almost mechanical.

"I hope you are going to take it nicely," she went on, "that we are going to be such good friends as we always were, and that even the memory of your poor uncle's death and the ghastly trial which followed and the part that Jasper played will not spoil our friendship."

"But don't you see what it means to me?" he burst forth, and for a second they looked at one another, and Frank divined her thoughts and winced.

"I know what you are thinking," he said huskily; "you are thinking of all the beastly things that were said at the trial, that if I had gained you I should have gained all that I tried to gain."

She went red.

"It was horrid of me, wasn't it?" she confessed. "And yet that idea came to me. One cannot control one's thoughts, Frank, and you must be content to know that I believe in your innocence. There are some thoughts which flourish in one's mind like weeds, and which refuse to be uprooted. Don't blame me if I recalled the lawyer's words; it was an involuntary, hateful thought."

He inclined his head.

"There is another thought which is not involuntary," she went on, "and it is because I want to retain our friendship and I want everything to go on as usual that I am asking you one question. Your twenty-fourth birthday has come and gone; you told me that your uncle's design was to keep you unmarried until that day. You are still unmarried, and your twenty-fourth birthday has passed. What has happened?"

"Many things have happened," he replied quietly. "My uncle is dead. I am a rich man apart from the accident of his legacy. I could meet you on level terms."

"I knew nothing of this," she said quickly.

He shrugged his shoulders.

"Didn't Jasper tell you?" he asked.

"No—Jasper told me nothing."

Frank drew a long breath.

"Then I can only say that until the mystery of my uncle's death is solved you cannot know," he said. "I can only repeat what I have already told you."

She offered her hand.

"I believe you, Frank," she said, "and I was wrong even to doubt you in the smallest degree."

He took her hand and held it.

"May," he said, "what is this strange fascination that Jasper has over you?"

For the second time in that interview she flushed and pulled her hand back.

"There is nothing unusual in the fascination which Jasper exercises," she smiled, quickly recovering, almost against her will, from the little twinge of anger she felt. "It is the influence which every woman has felt and which you one day will feel."

He laughed bitterly.

"Then nothing will make you change your mind?" he said.

"Nothing in the world," she answered emphatically.

For a moment she was sorry for him, as he stood, both hands resting on a chair, his eyes on the ground, a picture of despair, and she crossed to him and slipped her arm through his.

"Don't take it so badly, Frank," she said softly. "I am a capricious, foolish girl, I know, and I am really not worth a moment's suffering."

He shook himself together, gathered up his hat, his stick, and his overcoat and offered his hand.

"Good-by," he said, "and good luck!"

In the meantime another interview of a widely different character was taking place in the little house which Jasper Cole occupied on the Portsmouth Road. Jasper and Saul Arthur Mann had met before, but this was the first visit that the investigator had paid to the home of John Minute's heir.

Jasper was waiting at the door to greet the little man when he arrived, and had offered him a quiet but warm welcome and led the way to the beautiful study which was half laboratory, which he had built for himself since John Minute's death.

"I am coming straight to the point without any beating about the bush, Mr. Cole," said the little man, depositing his bag on the side of his chair and opening it with a jerk. "I will tell you frankly that I am acting on Mr. Merrill's behalf and that I am also acting, as I believe, in the interests of justice."

"Your motives, at any rate, are admirable," said Jasper, pushing back the papers which littered his big library table, and seating himself on the edge.

"You are probably aware that you are to some extent under suspicion, Mr. Cole."

"Under your suspicion or the suspicion of the authorities?" asked the other coolly.

"Under mine," said Saul Arthur Mann emphatically. "I cannot speak for the authorities."

"In what direction does this suspicion run?"

He thrust his hands deep in his trousers pockets, and eyed the other keenly.

"My first suspicion is that you are well aware as to who murdered John Minute."

Jasper Cole nodded.

"I am perfectly aware that he was murdered by your friend, Mr. Merrill," he said.

"I suggest," said Saul Arthur Mann calmly, "that you know the murderer, and you know the murderer was *not* Frank Merrill."

Jasper made no reply, and a faint smile flickered for a second at the corner of his mouth, but he gave no other sign of his inward feelings.

"And the other point you wish to raise?" he asked.

"The other is a more delicate subject, since it involves a lady," said the little man. "You are about to be married to Miss Nuttall."

Jasper Cole nodded.

"You have obtained an extraordinary influence over the lady in this past few months."

"I hope so," said the other cheerfully.

"It is an influence which might have been brought about by normal methods, but it is also one," Saul Arthur leaned over and tapped the table emphatically with each word, "which might be secured by a very clever chemist who had found a way of sapping the will of his victim."

"By the administration of drugs?" asked Jasper.

"By the administration of drugs," repeated Saul Arthur Mann.

Jasper Cole smiled.

"I should like to know the drug," he said. "One would make a fortune, to say nothing of benefiting humanity to an extraordinary degree by its employment.

For example, I might give you a dose and you would tell me all that you know; I am told that your knowledge is fairly extensive," he bantered. "Surely you, Mr. Mann, with your remarkable collection of information on all subjects under the sun, do not suggest that such a drug exists?"

"On the contrary," said "The Man Who Knew" in triumph, "it is known and is employed. It was known as long ago as the days of the Borgias. It was employed in France in the days of Louis XVI. It has been, to some extent, rediscovered and used in lunatic asylums to quiet dangerous patients."

He saw the interest deepen in the other's eyes.

"I have never heard of that," said Jasper slowly; "the only drug that is employed for that purpose is, as far as I know, bromide of potassium."

Mr. Mann produced a slip of paper, and read off a list of names, mostly of mental institutions in the United States of America and in Germany.

"Oh, that drug!" said Jasper Cole contemptuously. "I know the use to which that is put. There was an article on the subject in the *British Medical Journal* three months ago. It is a modified kind of 'twilight sleep'—hyocine and morphia. I'm afraid, Mr. Mann," he went on, "you have come on a fruitless errand, and, speaking as a humble student of science, I may suggest without offense that your theories are wholly fantastic."

"Then I will put another suggestion to you, Mr. Cole," said the little man without resentment, "and to me this constitutes the chief reason why you should not marry the lady whose confidence I enjoy and who, I feel sure, will be influenced by my advice."

"And what is that?" asked Jasper.

"It affects your own character, and it is in consequence a very embarrassing matter for me to discuss," said the little man.

Again the other favored him with that inscrutable smile of his.

"My moral character, I presume, is now being assailed," he said flippantly. "Please go on; you promise to be interesting."

"You were in Holland a short time ago. Does Miss Nuttall know this?"

Jasper nodded.

"She is well aware of the fact."

"You were in Holland with a lady," accused Mr. Mann slowly. "Is Miss Nuttall well aware of this fact, too?"

Jasper slipped from the table and stood upright. Through his narrow lids he looked down upon his accuser.

"Is that all you know?" he asked softly.

"Not all, but one of the things I know," retorted the other. "You were seen in her company. She was staying in the same hotel with you as 'Mrs. Cole.'"

Jasper nodded.

"You will excuse me if I decline to discuss the matter," he said.

"Suppose I ask Miss Nuttall to discuss it?" challenged the little man.

"You are the master of your own actions," said Jasper Cole quickly, "and I dare say, if you regard it as expedient, you will tell her, but I can promise you that whether you tell her or not I shall marry Miss Nuttall."

With this he ushered his visitor to the door, and hardly waited for the car to drive off before he had shut that door behind him.

Late that night the two friends forgathered and exchanged their experiences.

"I am sure there is something very wrong indeed," said Frank emphatically. "She was not herself. She spoke mechanically, almost as though she were reciting a lesson. You had the feeling that she was connected by wires with somebody who was dictating her every word and action. It is damnable, Mann. What can we do?"

"We must prevent the marriage," said the little man quietly, "and employ every means that opportunity suggests to that purpose. Make no mistake," he said emphatically; "Cole will stop at nothing. His attitude was one big bluff. He knows that I have beaten him. It was only by luck that I found out about the woman in Holland. I got my agent to examine the hotel register, and there it was, without any attempt at disguise: 'Mr. and Mrs. Cole, of London.'"

"The thing to do is to see May at once," said Frank, "and put all the facts before her, though I hate the idea; it seems like sneaking."

"Sneaking!" exploded Saul Arthur Mann. "What nonsense you talk! You are too full of scruples, my friend, for this work. I will see her to-morrow."

"I will go with you," said Frank, after a moment's thought. "I have no wish to escape my responsibility in the matter. She will probably hate me for my interference, but I have reached beyond the point where I care—so long as she can be saved."

It was agreed that they should meet one another at the office in the morning and make their way together.

"Remember this," said Mann, seriously, before they parted, "that if Cole finds the game is up he will stop at nothing."

"Do you think we ought to take precautions?" asked Frank.

"Honestly I do," confessed the other, "I don't think we can get the men from the Yard, but there is a very excellent agency which sometimes works for me, and they can provide a guard for the girl."

"I wish you would get in touch with them," said Frank earnestly. "I am worried sick over this business. She ought never to be left out of their sight. I will see if I can have a talk to her maid, so that we may know whenever she is going out. There ought to be a man on a motor cycle always waiting about the Savoy to follow her wherever she goes."

They parted at the entrance of the bureau, Saul Arthur Mann returning to telephone the necessary instructions. How necessary they were was proved that very night.

At nine o'clock May was sitting down to a solitary dinner when a telegram was delivered to her. It was from the chief of the little mission in which she had been interested, and ran:

> Very urgent. Have something of the greatest importance to tell you.

It was signed with the name of the matron of the mission, and, leaving her dinner untouched, May only delayed long enough to change her dress before she was speeding in a taxi eastward.

She arrived at the "hall," which was the headquarters of the mission, to find it in darkness. A man who was evidently a new helper was waiting in the doorway and addressed her.

"You are Miss Nuttall, aren't you? I thought so. The matron has gone down to Silvers Rents, and she asked me to go along with you."

The girl dismissed the taxi, and in company with her guide threaded the narrow tangle of streets between the mission and Silvers Rents. She was halfway along one of the ill-lighted thoroughfares when she noticed that drawn up by the side of the road was a big, handsome motor car, and she wondered what had brought this evidence of luxurious living to the mean streets of Canning Town. She was not left in doubt very long, for as she came up to the lights and was shielding her eyes from their glare her arms were tightly grasped, a shawl was thrown over her head, and she was lifted and thrust into the car's interior. A hand gripped her throat.

"You scream and I will kill you!" hissed a voice in her ear.

At that moment the car started, and the girl, with a scream which was strangled in her throat, fell swooning back on the seat.

May recovered consciousness to find the car still rushing forward in the dark and the hand of her captor still resting at her throat.

"You be a sensible girl," said a muffled voice, "and do as you're told and no harm will come to you."

It was too dark to see his face, and it was evident that even if there were light the face was so well concealed that she could not recognize the speaker. Then she remembered that this man, who had acted as her guide, had been careful to keep in the shadow of whatever light there was while he was conducting her, as he said, to the matron.

"Where are you taking me?" she asked.

"You'll know in time," was the noncommittal answer.

It was a wild night; rain splashed against the windows of the car, and she could hear the wind howling above the noise of the engines. They were evidently going into the country, for now and again, by the light of the headlamps, she glimpsed hedges and trees which flashed past. Her captor suddenly let down one of the windows and leaned out, giving some instructions to the driver. What they were she guessed, for the lights were suddenly switched off and the car ran in darkness.

The girl was in a panic for all her bold showing. She knew that this desperate man was fearless of consequence, and that, if her death would achieve his ends and the ends of his partners, her life was in imminent peril. What were those ends, she wondered. Were these the same men who had done to death John Minute?

"Who are you?" she asked.

There was a little, chuckling laugh.

"You'll know soon enough."

The words were hardly out of his mouth when there was a terrific crash. The car stopped suddenly and canted over, and the girl was jerked forward to her knees. Every pane of glass in the car was smashed, and it was clear, from the angle at which it lay, that irremediable damage had been done. The man scrambled up, kicked open the door, and jumped out.

"Level-crossing gate, sir," said the voice of the chauffeur. "I've broken my wrist."

With the disappearance of her captor, the girl had felt for the fastening of the opposite door, and had turned it. To her delight it opened smoothly, and had evidently been unaffected by the jam. She stepped out to the road, trembling in every limb.

She felt, rather than saw, the level-crossing gate, and knew that at one side was a swing gate for passengers. She reached this when her abductor discovered her flight.

"Come back!" he cried hoarsely.

She heard a roar and saw a flashing of lights and fled across the line just as an express train came flying northward. It missed her by inches, and the force of the wind threw her to the ground. She scrambled up, stumbled across the remaining rails, and, reaching the gate opposite, fled down the dark road She had gained just that much time which the train took in passing. She ran blindly along the dark road, slipping and stumbling in the mud, and she heard her pursuer squelching through the mud in the rear.

The wind flew her hair awry, the rain beat down upon her face, but she stumbled on. Suddenly she slipped and fell, and as she struggled to her feet the heavy hand of her pursuer fell upon her shoulder, and she screamed aloud.

"None of that," said the voice, and his hand covered her mouth.

At that moment a bright light enveloped the two, a light so intensely, dazzlingly white, so unexpected that it hit the girl almost like a blow. It came from somewhere not two yards away, and the man released his hold upon the girl and stared at the light.

"Hello!" said a voice from the darkness. "What's the game?"

She was behind the man, and could not see his face. All that she knew was that here was help, unexpected, Heaven sent, and she strove to recover her breath and her speech.

"It's all right," growled the man. "She's a lunatic and I'm taking her to the asylum."

Suddenly the light was pushed forward to the man's face, and a heavy hand was laid upon his shoulder.

"You are, are you?" said the other. "Well, I am going to take you to a lunatic asylum, Sergeant Smith or Crawley or whatever your name is. You know me; my name's Wiseman."

For a moment the man stood as though petrified, and then, with a sudden jerk, he wrenched his hand free and sprang at the policeman with a wild yell of rage, and in a second both men were rolling over in the darkness. Constable Wiseman was no child, but he had lost his initial advantage, and by the time he got to his feet and had found his electric torch Crawley had vanished.

CHAPTER XVII

THE MAN CALLED "MERRILL"

"If Wiseman did not think you were a murderer, I should regard him as an intelligent being," said Saul Arthur Mann.

"Have they found Crawley?" asked Frank.

"No, he got away. The chauffeur and the car were hired from a West End garage, with this story of a lunatic who had to be removed to an asylum, and apparently Crawley, or Smith, was the man who hired them. He even paid a little extra for the damage which the alleged lunatic might do the car. The chauffeur says that he had some doubt, and had intended to inform the police after he had arrived at his destination. As a matter of fact, they were just outside Eastbourne when the accident occurred." "The Man Who Knew" paused.

"Where did he say he was taking her?" he asked Frank.

"He was told to drive into Eastbourne, where more detailed instructions would be given to him. The police have confirmed his story, and he has been released.

"I have just come from May," said Frank. "She looks none the worse for her exciting adventure. I hope you have arranged to have her guarded?"

Saul Arthur Mann nodded.

"It will be the last adventure of that kind our friend will attempt," he said.

"Still, this enlightens us a little. We know that Mr. Rex Holland has an accomplice, and that accomplice is Sergeant Smith, so we may presume that they were both in the murder. Constable Wiseman has been suitably rewarded, as he well deserves," said Frank heartily.

"You bear no malice," smiled Saul Arthur Mann.

Frank laughed, and shook his head.

"How can one?" he asked simply.

May had another visitor. Jasper Cole came hurriedly to London at the first intimation of the outrage, but was reassured by the girl's appearance.

"It was awfully thrilling," she said, "but really I am not greatly distressed; in fact, I think I look less tired than you."

He nodded.

"That is very possible. I did not go to bed until very late this morning," he said. "I was so engrossed in my research work that I did not realize it was morning until they brought me my tea."

"You haven't been in bed all night?" she said, shocked, and shook her head reprovingly. "That is one of your habits of life which will have to be changed," she warned him.

Jasper Cole did not dismiss her unpleasant experience as lightly as she.

"I wonder what the object of it all was," he said, "and why they took you back to Eastbourne? I think we shall find that the headquarters of this infernal combination is somewhere in Sussex."

"Mr. Mann doesn't think so," she said, "but believes that the car was to be met by another at Eastbourne and I was to be transferred. He says that the idea of taking me there was to throw the police off the scent."

She shivered.

"It wasn't a nice experience," she confessed.

The interview took place in the afternoon, and was some two hours after Frank had interviewed the girl; Saul Arthur Mann had gone to Eastbourne to bring her back. Jasper had arranged to spend the night in town, and had booked two stalls at the Hippodrome. She had told Saul Arthur Mann this, in accordance with her promise to keep him informed as to her movements, and she was, therefore, surprised when, half an hour later, the little investigator presented himself.

She met him in the presence of her fiancé, and it was clear to Jasper what Saul Arthur Mann's intentions were.

"I don't want to make myself a nuisance," he said, "but before we go any further, Miss Nuttall, there are certain matters on which you ought to be informed. I have every reason to believe that I know who was responsible for the outrage of last night, and I do not intend risking a repetition."

"Who do you think was responsible?" asked the girl quietly.

"I honestly believe that the author is in this room," was the startling response.

"You mean me?" asked Jasper Cole angrily.

"I mean you, Mr. Cole. I believe that you are the man who planned the coup and that you are its sole author," said the other.

The girl stared at him in astonishment.

"You surely do not mean what you say."

"I mean that Mr. Cole has every reason for wishing to marry you," he said. "What that reason is I do not know completely, but I shall discover. I am satisfied," he went on slowly, "that Mr. Cole is already married."

She looked from one to the other.

"Already married?" repeated Jasper.

"If he is not already married," said Saul Arthur Mann bluntly, "then I have been indiscreet. The only thing I can tell you is that your fiancé has been traveling on the Continent with a lady who describes herself as Mrs. Cole."

Jasper said nothing for a moment, but looked at the other oddly and thoughtfully.

"I understand, Mr. Mann," he said at length, "that you collect facts as other people collect postage stamps?"

Saul Arthur Mann bristled.

"You may carry this off, sir," he began, "if you can—"

"Let me speak," said Jasper Cole, raising his voice. "I want to ask you this: Have you a complete record of John Minute's life?"

"I know it so well," said Saul Arthur Mann emphatically, "that I could repeat his history word for word."

"Will you sit down, May?" said Jasper, taking the girl's hand in his and gently forcing her to a chair. "We are going to put Mr. Mann's memory to the test."

"Do you seriously mean that you want me to repeat that history?" asked the other suspiciously.

"I mean just that," said Jasper, and drew up a chair for his unpleasant visitor.

The record of John Minute's life came trippingly from Mann's tongue. He knew to an extraordinary extent the details of that strange and wild career.

"In 1892," said the investigator, continuing his narrative, "he was married at St. Bride's church, Port Elizabeth, to Agnes Gertrude Cole."

"Cole," murmured Jasper.

The little man looked at him with open mouth.

"Cole! Good Lord—you are—"

"I am his son," said Jasper quietly. "I am one of his two children. Your information is that there was one. As a matter of fact, there were two. My mother left my father with one of the greatest scoundrels that has ever lived. He took her to Australia, where my sister was born six months after she had left John Minute. There her friend deserted her, and she worked for seven years as a kitchen maid, in Melbourne, in order to save up enough money to bring us to Cape Town. My mother opened a tea shop off Aderley Street, and earned enough to educate me and my sister. It was there she met Crawley, and Crawley promised to use his influence with my father to bring about a reconciliation for her children's sake. I do not know what was the result of his attempt, but I gather it was unsuccessful, and things went on very much as they were before.

"Then one day, when I was still at the South African College, my mother went home, taking my sister with her. I have reason to believe that Crawley was responsible for her sailing and that he met them on landing. All that I knew was that from that day my mother disappeared. She had left me a sum of money to continue my studies, but after eight months had passed, and no word had come from her, I decided to go on to England. I have since learned what had happened. My mother had been seized with a stroke and had been conveyed to the workhouse infirmary by Crawley, who had left her there and had taken my sister, who apparently he passed off as his own daughter.

"I did not know this at the time, but being well aware of my father's identity I wrote to him, asking him for help to discover my mother. He answered, telling me that my mother was dead, that Crawley had told him so, and that there was no trace of Marguerite, my sister. We exchanged a good many letters, and then my father asked me to come and act as his secretary and assist him in his search for Marguerite. What he did not know was that Crawley's alleged daughter, whom he had not seen, was the girl for whom he was seeking. I fell into the new life, and found John Minute—I can scarcely call him 'father'—much more bearable than I expected—and then one day I found my mother."

"You found your mother?" said Saul Arthur Mann, a light dawning upon him.

"Your persistent search of the little house in Silvers Rents produced nothing," he smiled. "Had you taken the bamboo ladder and crossed the yard at the back of the house into another yard, then through the door, you would have come to Number 16 Royston Court, and you would have been considerably surprised to find an interior much more luxurious than you would have expected in that quarter. In Royston Court they spoke of Number 16 as 'the house with the nurses' because there were always three nurses on duty, and nobody ever saw the inside of the house but themselves. There you would have found my mother, bedridden, and, indeed, so ill that the doctors who saw her would not allow her to be moved from the house.

"I furnished this hovel piece by piece, generally at night, because I did not want to excite the curiosity of the people in the court, nor did I wish this matter to reach the ears of John Minute. I felt that while I retained his friendship and his confidence there was at least a chance of his reconciliation with my mother, and that, before all things, she desired. It was not to be," he said sadly. "John Minute was struck down at the moment my plans seemed as though they were going to result in complete success. Strangely enough, with his death, my mother made an extraordinary recovery, and I was able to move her to the Continent. She had always wanted to see Holland, France, and at this moment"—he turned to the girl with a smile—"she is in the châlet which you occupied during your holiday."

Mr. Mann was dumfounded. All his pet theories had gone by the board.

"But what of your sister?" he asked at last.

A black look gathered in Jasper Cole's face.

"My sister's whereabouts are known to me now," he said shortly. "For some time she lived in Camden Town, at Number 69 Flowerton Road. At the present moment she is nearer and is watched night and day, almost as carefully as Mr. Mann's agents are watching you." He smiled again at the girl.

"Watching me?" she said, startled.

Saul Arthur Mann went red.

"It was my idea," he said stiffly.

"And a very excellent one," agreed Jasper, "but unfortunately you appointed your guards too late."

Mr. Mann went back to his office, his brain in a whirl, yet such was his habit that he did not allow himself to speculate upon the new and amazing situation until he had carefully jotted down every new fact he had collected.

It was astounding that he had overlooked the connection between Jasper Cole and John Minute's wife. His labors did not cease until eleven o'clock, and he was preparing to go home when the commissionaire who acted as caretaker came to tell him that a lady wished to see him.

"A lady? At this hour of the night?" said Mr. Mann, perturbed. "Tell her to come in the morning."

"I have told her that, sir, but she insists upon seeing you to-night."

"What is her name?"

"Mrs. Merrill," said the commissionaire.

Saul Arthur Mann collapsed into his chair.

"Show her up," he said feebly.

He had no difficulty in recognizing the girl, who came timidly into the room, as the original of the photograph which had been sent to him by Constable Wiseman. She was plainly dressed and wore no ornament, and she was undeniably pretty, but there was about her a furtiveness and a nervous indecision which spoke of her apprehension.

"Sit down," said Mr. Mann kindly. "What do you want me to do for you?"

"I am Mrs. Merrill," she said timidly.

"So the commissionaire said," replied the little man. "You are nervous about something?"

"Oh, I am so frightened!" said the girl, with a shudder. "If he knows I have been here he'll—"

"You have nothing to be frightened about Just sit here for one moment."

He went into the next room, which had a branch telephone connection, and called up May. She was out, and he left an urgent message that she was to come, bringing Jasper with her, as soon as she returned. When he got back to his office, he found the girl as he had left her, sitting on the edge of a big armchair, plucking nervously at her handkerchief.

"I have heard about you," she said. "He mentioned you once—before we went to that Sussex cottage with Mr. Crawley. They were going to bring another lady, and I was to look after her, but he—"

"Who is 'he'?" asked Mr. Mann.

"My husband," said the girl.

"How long have you been married?" demanded the little man.

"I ran away with him a long time ago," she said. "It has been an awful life; it was Mr. Crawley's idea. He told me that if I married Mr. Merrill he would take me to see my mother and Jasper. But he was so cruel—"

She shuddered again.

"We've been living in furnished houses all over the country, and I have been alone most of the time, and he would not let me go out by myself or do anything."

She spoke in a subdued, monotonous tone that betrayed the nearness of a bad, nervous breakdown.

"What does your husband call himself?"

"Why, Frank Merrill," said the girl in astonishment; "that's his name. Mr. Crawley always told me his name was Merrill. Isn't it?"

Mr. Mann shook his head.

"My poor girl," he said sympathetically, "I am afraid you have been grossly deceived. The man you married as Merrill is an impostor."

"An impostor?" she faltered.

Mr. Mann nodded.

"He has taken a good man's name, and I am afraid has committed abominable crimes in that man's name," said the investigator gently. "I hope we shall be able to rid you and the world of a great villain."

Still she stared uncomprehendingly.

"He has always been a liar," she said slowly. "He lied naturally and acted things so well that you believed him. He told me things which I know aren't true. He told me my brother was dead, but I saw his name in the paper the other day, and that is why I came to you. Do you know Jasper?"

She was as naïve and as unsophisticated as a schoolgirl, and it made the little man's heart ache to hear the plaintive monotony of tone and see the trembling lip.

"I promise you that you will meet your brother," he said.

"I have run away from Frank," she said suddenly. "Isn't that a wicked thing to do? I could not stand it. He struck me again yesterday, and he pretends to be a gentleman. My mother used to say that no gentleman ever treats a woman badly, but Frank does."

"Nobody shall treat you badly any more," said Mr. Mann.

"I hate him!" she went on with sudden vehemence. "He sneers and says he's going to get another wife, and—oh!"

He saw her hands go up to her face, and saw her staring eyes turn to the door in affright.

Frank Merrill stood in the doorway, and looked at her without recognition.

"I am sorry," he said. "You have a visitor?"

"Come in," said Mr. Mann. "I am awfully glad you called."

The girl had risen to her feet, and was shrinking back to the wall.

"Do you know this lady?"

Frank looked at her keenly.

"Why, yes, that's Sergeant Smith's daughter," he said, and he smiled. "Where on earth have you been?"

"Don't touch me!" she breathed, and put her hands before her, warding him off.

He looked at her in astonishment, and from her to Mann. Then he looked back at the girl, his brow wrinkled in perplexity.

"This girl," said Mr. Mann, "thinks she is your wife."

"My wife?" said Frank, and looked again at her.

"Is this a bad joke or something—do you say that I am your husband?" he asked.

She did not speak, but nodded slowly.

He sat down in a chair and whistled.

"This rather complicates matters," he said blankly, "but perhaps you can explain?"

"I only know what the girl has told me," said Mr. Mann, shaking his head. "I am afraid there is a terrible mistake here."

Frank turned to the girl.

"But did your husband look like me?"

She nodded.

"And did he call himself Frank Merrill?"

Again she nodded.

"Where is he now?"

She nodded, this time at him.

"But, great heavens," said Frank, with a gesture of despair, "you do not suggest that I am the man?"

"You are the man," said the girl.

Again Frank looked appealingly at his friend, and Saul Arthur Mann saw dismay and laughter in his eyes.

"I don't know what I can do," he said. "Perhaps if you left me alone with her for a minute—"

"Don't! Don't!" she breathed. "Don't leave me alone with him. Stay here."

"And where have you come from now?" asked Frank.

"From the house where you took me. You struck me yesterday," she went on inconsequently.

Frank laughed.

"I am not only married, but I am a wife beater apparently," he said desperately. "Now what can I do? I think the best thing that can be done is for this lady to tell us where she lives and I will take her back and confront her husband."

"I won't go with you!" cried the girl. "I won't! I won't! You said you'd look after me, Mr. Mann. You promised."

The little investigator saw that she was distraught to a point where a collapse was imminent.

"This gentleman will look after you also," he said encouragingly. "He is as anxious to save you from your husband as anybody."

"I will not go," she cried, "If that man touches me," and she pointed to Frank, "I'll scream."

Again came the tap at the door, and Frank looked round.

"More visitors?" he asked.

"It is all right," said Saul Arthur Mann. "There's a lady and a gentleman to see me, isn't there?" he asked the commissionaire. "Show them in."

May came first, saw the little tableau, and stopped, knowing instinctively all that it portended. Jasper followed her.

The girl, who had been watching Frank, shifted her eyes for a moment to the visitors, and at sight of Jasper flung across the room. In an instant her brother's arms were around her, and she was sobbing on his breast.

"Am I entitled to ask what all this means?" asked Frank quietly. "I am sure you will overlook my natural irritation, but I have suffered so much and I have been the victim of so many surprises that I do not feel inclined to accept all the shocks which fate sends me in a spirit of joyful resignation. Perhaps you will be good enough to elucidate this new mystery. Is everybody mad—or am I the sole sufferer?"

"There is no mystery about it," said Jasper, still holding the girl. "I think you know this lady?"

"I have never met her before in my life," said Frank, "but she persists in regarding me as her husband for some reason. Is this a new scheme of yours, Jasper?"

"I think you know this lady," said Jasper Cole again.

Frank shrugged his shoulders.

"You are almost monotonous. I repeat that I have never seen her before."

"Then I will explain to you," said Jasper.

He put the girl gently from him for a moment, and turned and whispered something to May. Together they passed out of the room.

"You were confidential secretary to John Minute for some time, Merrill, and in that capacity you made several discoveries. The most remarkable discovery was made when Sergeant Smith came to blackmail my father. Oh, don't pretend you didn't know that John Minute was my father!" he said in answer to the look of amazement on Frank Merrill's face.

"Smith took you into his confidence, and you married his alleged daughter. John Minute discovered this fact, not that he was aware that it was his own daughter, or that he thought that your association with my sister was any more than an intrigue beneath the dignity of his nephew. You did not think the time was ripe to spring a son-in-law upon him, and so you waited until you had seen his will. In that will he made no mention of a daughter, because the child had been born after his wife had left him, and he refused to recognize his paternity.

"Later, in some doubt as to whether he was doing an injustice to what might have been his own child, he endeavored to find her. Had you known of those investigations, you could have helped considerably, but as it happened you did not. You married her because you thought you would get a share of John Minute's millions, and when you found your plan had miscarried you planned an act of bigamy in order to secure a portion of Mr. Minute's fortune, which you knew would be considerable."

He turned to Saul Arthur Mann.

"You think I have not been very energetic in pursuing my inquiries as to who killed John Minute? There is the explanation of my tolerance."

He pointed his finger at Frank.

"This man is the husband of my sister. To ruin him would have meant involving her in that ruin. For a time I thought they were happily married. It was only recently that I have discovered the truth."

Frank shook his head.

"I don't know whether to laugh or cry," he said. "I have certainly not heard—"

"You will hear more," said Jasper Cole. "I will tell you how the murder was committed and who was the mysterious Rex Holland.

"Your father was a forger. That is known. You also have been forging signatures since you were a boy. You were Rex Holland. You came to Eastbourne on the night of the murder, and by an ingenious device you secured evidence in your favor in advance. Pretending to have lost your ticket, you allowed station officials to search you and to testify that you had no weapon. You were dropped at the gate of my father's house, and, as soon as the cab driver had disappeared, you made your way to where you had hidden your car in a field at a short distance from the house.

"You had arrived there earlier in the evening, and had made your way across the metals to Polegate Junction, where you joined the train. As you had taken the precaution to have your return ticket clipped in London, your trick was not discovered. You had regained your car, and drove up to the house ten minutes after you had been seen to disappear through the gateway. From your car you had taken the revolver, and with that revolver you murdered my father. In order to shield yourself you threw suspicion on me and made friends with one of the shrewdest men," he inclined his head toward the speechless Mr. Mann, "and through him conveyed those suspicions to authoritative quarters. It was you who, having said farewell to Miss Nuttall in Geneva, reappeared the same evening at Montreux and wrote a note forging my handwriting. It was you who left a torn sheet of paper in the room at Number 69 Flowerton Road, also in your writing.

"You have never moved a step but that I have followed you. My agents have been with you day and night ever since the day of the murder. I have waited my time, and that has come now."

Frank heaved a long sigh, and took up his hat.

"To-morrow morning I shall have a story to tell," he said.

"You are an excellent actor," said Jasper, "and an excellent liar, but you have never deceived me."

He flung open the door.

"There is your road. You have twenty thousand pounds which my father left you. You have some fifty-five thousand pounds which you buried on the night of the murder—you remember the gardener's trowel in the car?" he said, turning to Mann.

"I give you twenty-four hours to leave England. We cannot try you for the murder of John Minute; you can still be tried for the murder of your unfortunate servants."

Frank Merrill made no movement toward the door. He walked over to the other end of the room, and stood with his back to them. Then he turned.

"Sometimes," he said, "I feel that it isn't worth while going on. It has been rather a strain—all this."

Jasper Cole sprang toward him and caught him as he fell. They laid him down, and Saul Arthur Mann called urgently on the telephone for a doctor, but Frank Merrill was dead.

"I knew," said Constable Wiseman, when the story came to him.

THE END

The Angel of Terror

Chapter I

The hush of the court, which had been broken when the foreman of the jury returned their verdict, was intensified as the Judge, with a quick glance over his pince-nez at the tall prisoner, marshalled his papers with the precision and method which old men display in tense moments such as these. He gathered them together, white paper and blue and buff and stacked them in a neat heap on a tiny ledge to the left of his desk. Then he took his pen and wrote a few words on a printed paper before him.

Another breathless pause and he groped beneath the desk and brought out a small square of black silk and carefully laid it over his white wig. Then he spoke:

"James Meredith, you have been convicted after a long and patient trial of the awful crime of wilful murder. With the verdict of the jury I am in complete agreement. There is little doubt, after hearing the evidence of the unfortunate lady to whom you were engaged, and whose evidence you attempted in the most brutal manner to refute, that, instigated by your jealousy, you shot Ferdinand Bulford. The evidence of Miss Briggerland that you had threatened this poor young man, and that you left her presence in a temper, is unshaken. By a terrible coincidence, Mr. Bulford was in the street outside your fiancée's door when you left, and maddened by your insane jealousy, you shot him dead.

"To suggest, as you have through your counsel, that you called at Miss Briggerland's that night to break off your engagement and that the interview was a mild one and unattended by recriminations is to suggest that this lady has deliberately committed perjury in order to swear away your life, and when to that disgraceful charge you produce a motive, namely that by your death or imprisonment Miss Briggerland, who is your cousin, would benefit to a considerable extent, you merely add to your infamy. Nobody who saw the young girl in the box, a pathetic, and if I may say, a beautiful figure, could accept for one moment your fantastic explanation.

"Who killed Ferdinand Bulford? A man without an enemy in the world. That tragedy cannot be explained away. It now only remains for me to pass the sentence which the law imposes. The jury's recommendation to mercy will be forwarded to the proper quarter...."

He then proceeded to pass sentence of death, and the tall man in the dock listened without a muscle of his face moving.

So ended the great Berkeley Street Murder Trial, and when a few days later it was announced that the sentence of death had been commuted to one of penal servitude for life, there were newspapers and people who hinted at mistaken leniency and suggested that James Meredith would have been hanged if he were a poor man instead of being, as he was, the master of vast wealth.

"That's that," said Jack Glover between his teeth, as he came out of court with the eminent King's Counsel who had defended his friend and client, "the little lady wins."

His companion looked sideways at him and smiled.

"Honestly, Glover, do you believe that poor girl could do so dastardly a thing as lie about the man she loves?"

"She loves!" repeated Jack Glover witheringly.

"I think you are prejudiced," said the counsel, shaking his head. "Personally, I believe that Meredith is a lunatic; I am satisfied that all he told us about the interview he had with the girl was born of a diseased imagination. I was terribly impressed when I saw Jean Briggerland in the box. She—by Jove, there is the lady!"

They had reached the entrance of the Court. A big car was standing by the kerb and one of the attendants was holding open the door for a girl dressed in black. They had a glimpse of a pale, sad face of extraordinary beauty, and then she disappeared behind the drawn blinds.

The counsel drew a long sigh.

"Mad!" he said huskily. "He must be mad! If ever I saw a pure soul in a woman's face, it is in hers!"

"You've been in the sun, Sir John—you're getting sentimental," said Jack Glover brutally, and the eminent lawyer choked indignantly.

Jack Glover had a trick of saying rude things to his friends, even when those friends were twenty years his senior, and by every rule of professional etiquette entitled to respectful treatment.

"Really!" said the outraged Sir John. "There are times, Glover, when you are insufferable!"

But by this time Jack Glover was swinging along the Old Bailey, his hands in his pockets, his silk hat on the back of his head.

He found the grey-haired senior member of the firm of Rennett, Glover and Simpson (there had been no Simpson in the firm for ten years) on the point of going home.

Mr. Rennett sat down at the sight of his junior.

"I heard the news by 'phone," he said. "Ellbery says there is no ground for appeal, but I think the recommendation to mercy will save his life—besides it is a *crime passionelle*, and they don't hang for homicidal jealousy. I suppose it was the girl's evidence that turned the trick?"

Jack nodded.

"And she looked like an angel just out of the refrigerator," he said despairingly. "Ellbery did his poor best to shake her, but the old fool is half in love with her— I left him raving about her pure soul and her other celestial etceteras."

Mr. Rennett stroked his iron grey beard.

"She's won," he said, but the other turned on him with a snarl.

"Not yet!" he said almost harshly. "She hasn't won till Jimmy Meredith is dead or——"

"Or——?" repeated his partner significantly. "That 'or' won't come off, Jack. He'll get a life sentence as sure as 'eggs is eggs.' I'd go a long way to help Jimmy; I'd risk my practice and my name."

Jack Glover looked at his partner in astonishment.

"You old sportsman!" he said admiringly. "I didn't know you were so fond of Jimmy?"

Mr. Rennett got up and began pulling on his gloves. He seemed a little uncomfortable at the sensation he had created.

"His father was my first client," he said apologetically. "One of the best fellows that ever lived. He married late in life, that was why he was such a crank over the question of marriage. You might say that old Meredith founded our firm. Your father and Simpson and I were nearly at our last gasp when Meredith gave us his business. That was our turning point. Your father—God rest him—was never tired of talking about it. I wonder he never told you."

"I think he did," said Jack thoughtfully. "And you really would go a long way— Rennett—I mean, to help Jim Meredith?"

"All the way," said old Rennett shortly.

Jack Glover began whistling a long lugubrious tune.

"I'm seeing the old boy to-morrow," he said. "By the way, Rennett, did you see that a fellow had been released from prison to a nursing home for a minor operation the other day? There was a question asked in Parliament about it. Is it usual?"

"It can be arranged," said Rennett. "Why?"

"Do you think in a few months' time we could get Jim Meredith into a nursing home for—say an appendix operation?"

"Has he appendicitis?" asked the other in surprise.

"He can fake it," said Jack calmly. "It's the easiest thing in the world to fake."

Rennett looked at the other under his heavy eyebrows.

"You're thinking of the 'or'?" he challenged, and Jack nodded.

"It can be done—if he's alive," said Rennett after a pause.

"He'll be alive," prophesied his partner, "now the only thing is—where shall I find the girl?"

Chapter II

Lydia Beale gathered up the scraps of paper that littered her table, rolled them into a ball and tossed them into the fire.

There was a knock at the door, and she half turned in her chair to meet with a smile her stout landlady who came in carrying a tray on which stood a large cup of tea and two thick and wholesome slices of bread and jam.

"Finished, Miss Beale?" asked the landlady anxiously.

"For the day, yes," said the girl with a nod, and stood up stretching herself stiffly.

She was slender, a head taller than the dumpy Mrs. Morgan. The dark violet eyes and the delicate spiritual face she owed to her Celtic ancestors, the grace of her movements, no less than the perfect hands that rested on the drawing board, spoke eloquently of breed.

"I'd like to see it, miss, if I may," said Mrs. Morgan, wiping her hands on her apron in anticipation.

Lydia pulled open a drawer of the table and took out a large sheet of Windsor board. She had completed her pencil sketch and Mrs. Morgan gasped appreciatively. It was a picture of a masked man holding a villainous crowd at bay at the point of a pistol.

"That's wonderful, miss," she said in awe. "I suppose those sort of things happen too?"

The girl laughed as she put the drawing away.

"They happen in stories which I illustrate, Mrs. Morgan," she said dryly. "The real brigands of life come in the shape of lawyers' clerks with writs and summonses. It's a relief from those mad fashion plates I draw, anyway. Do you know, Mrs. Morgan, that the sight of a dressmaker's shop window makes me positively ill!"

Mrs. Morgan shook her head sympathetically and Lydia changed the subject.

"Has anybody been this afternoon?" she asked.

"Only the young man from Spadd & Newton," replied the stout woman with a sigh. "I told 'im you was out, but I'm a bad liar."

The girl groaned.

"I wonder if I shall ever get to the end of those debts," she said in despair. "I've enough writs in the drawer to paper the house, Mrs. Morgan."

Three years ago Lydia Beale's father had died and she had lost the best friend and companion that any girl ever had. She knew he was in debt, but had no idea how extensively he was involved. A creditor had seen her the day after the funeral and had made some uncouth reference to the convenience of a death which had automatically cancelled George Beale's obligations. It needed only that to spur the girl to an action which was as foolish as it was generous. She had written to all the people to whom her father owed money and had assumed full responsibility for debts amounting to hundreds of pounds.

It was the Celt in her that drove her to shoulder the burden which she was ill-equipped to carry, but she had never regretted her impetuous act.

There were a few creditors who, realising what had happened, did not bother her, and there were others....

She earned a fairly good salary on the staff of the *Daily Megaphone*, which made a feature of fashion, but she would have had to have been the recipient of a cabinet minister's emoluments to have met the demands which flowed in upon her a month after she had accepted her father's obligations.

"Are you going out to-night, miss?" asked the woman.

Lydia roused herself from her unpleasant thoughts.

"Yes. I'm making some drawings of the dresses in Curfew's new play. I'll be home somewhere around twelve."

Mrs. Morgan was half-way across the room when she turned back.

"One of these days you'll get out of all your troubles, miss, you see if you don't! I'll bet you'll marry a rich young gentleman."

Lydia, sitting on the edge of the table, laughed.

"You'd lose your money, Mrs. Morgan," she said, "rich young gentlemen only marry poor working girls in the kind of stories I illustrate. If I marry it will probably be a very poor young gentleman who will become an incurable invalid and want nursing. And I shall hate him so much that I can't be happy with him, and pity him so much that I can't run away from him."

Mrs. Morgan sniffed her disagreement.

"There are things that happen——" she began.

"Not to me—not miracles, anyway," said Lydia, still smiling, "and I don't know that I want to get married. I've got to pay all these bills first, and by the time they are settled I'll be a grey-haired old lady in a mob cap."

Lydia had finished her tea and was standing somewhat scantily attired in the middle of her bedroom, preparing for her theatre engagement, when Mrs. Morgan returned.

"I forgot to tell you, miss," she said, "there was a gentleman and a lady called."

"A gentleman and a lady? Who were they?"

"I don't know, Miss Beale. I was lying down at the time, and the girl answered the door. I gave her strict orders to say that you were out."

"Did they leave any name?"

"No, miss. They just asked if Miss Beale lived here, and could they see her."

"H'm!" said Lydia with a frown. "I wonder what we owe them!"

She dismissed the matter from her mind, and thought no more of it until she stopped on her way to the theatre to learn from the office by telephone the number of drawings required.

The chief sub-editor answered her.

"And, by the way," he added, "there was an inquiry for you at the office to-day—I found a note of it on my desk when I came in to-night. Some old friends of yours who want to see you. Brand told them you were going to do a show at the Erving Theatre to-night, so you'll probably see them."

"Who are they?" she asked, puzzled.

She had few friends, old or new.

"I haven't the foggiest idea," was the reply.

At the theatre she saw nobody she knew, though she looked round interestedly, nor was she approached in any of the *entr'actes*.

In the row ahead of her, and a little to her right, were two people who regarded her curiously as she entered. The man was about fifty, very dark and bald—the skin of his head was almost copper-coloured, though he was obviously a European, for the eyes which beamed benevolently upon her through powerful spectacles were blue, but so light a blue that by contrast with the mahogany skin of his clean-shaven face, they seemed almost white.

The girl who sat with him was fair, and to Lydia's artistic eye, singularly lovely. Her hair was a mop of fine gold. The colour was natural, Lydia was too sophisticated to make any mistake about that. Her features were regular and flawless. The young artist thought she had never seen so perfect a "cupid" mouth in her life. There was something so freshly, fragrantly innocent about the girl that Lydia's heart went out to her, and she could hardly keep her eyes on the stage. The unknown seemed to take almost as much interest in her, for twice Lydia surprised her backward scrutiny. She found herself wondering who she was. The girl was beautifully dressed, and about her neck was a platinum chain that must have hung to her waist—a chain which was broken every few inches by a big emerald.

It required something of an effort of concentration to bring her mind back to the stage and her work. With a book on her knee she sketched the somewhat bizarre costumes which had aroused a mild public interest in the play, and for the moment forgot her entrancing companion.

She came through the vestibule at the end of the performance, and drew her worn cloak more closely about her slender shoulders, for the night was raw, and a sou'westerly wind blew the big wet snowflakes under the protecting glass awning into the lobby itself. The favoured playgoers minced daintily through the slush to their waiting cars, then taxis came into the procession of waiting vehicles, there was a banging of cab doors, a babble of orders to the scurrying attendants, until something like order was evolved from the chaos.

"Cab, miss?"

Lydia shook her head. An omnibus would take her to Fleet Street, but two had passed, packed with passengers, and she was beginning to despair, when a particularly handsome taxi pulled up at the kerb.

The driver leant over the shining apron which partially protected him from the weather, and shouted:

"Is Miss Beale there?"

The girl started in surprise, taking a step toward the cab.

"I am Miss Beale," she said.

"Your editor has sent me for you," said the man briskly.

The editor of the *Megaphone* had been guilty of many eccentric acts. He had expressed views on her drawing which she shivered to recall. He had aroused her in the middle of the night to sketch dresses at a fancy dress ball, but never before had he done anything so human as to send a taxi for her. Nevertheless, she would not look at the gift cab too closely, and she stepped into the warm interior.

The windows were veiled with the snow and the sleet which had been falling all the time she had been in the theatre. She saw blurred lights flash past, and realised that the taxi was going at a good pace. She rubbed the windows and tried to look out after a while. Then she endeavoured to lower one, but without success. Suddenly she jumped up and tapped furiously at the window to attract the driver's attention. There was no mistaking the fact that they were crossing a bridge and it was not necessary to cross a bridge to reach Fleet Street.

If the driver heard he took no notice. The speed of the car increased. She tapped at the window again furiously. She was not afraid, but she was angry. Presently fear came. It was when she tried to open the door, and found that it was fastened from the outside, that she struck a match to discover that the windows had been screwed tight—the edge of the hole where the screw had gone in was rawly new, and the screw's head was bright and shining.

She had no umbrella—she never carried one to the theatre—and nothing more substantial in the shape of a weapon than a fountain pen. She could smash the windows with her foot. She sat back in the seat, and discovered that it was not so easy an operation as she had thought. She hesitated even to make the attempt; and then the panic sense left her, and she was her own calm self again. She was not being abducted. These things did not happen in the twentieth century, except in sensational books. She frowned. She had said almost the same thing to somebody that day—to Mrs. Morgan, who had hinted at a romantic marriage. Of course, nothing was wrong. The driver had called her by name. Probably the editor wanted to see her at his home, he lived somewhere in South London, she remembered. That would explain everything. And yet her instinct told her that something unusual was happening, that some unpleasant experience was imminent.

She tried to put the thought out of her mind, but it was too vivid, too insistent.

Again she tried the door, and then, conscious of a faint reflected glow on the cloth-lined roof of the cab, she looked backward through the peep-hole. She saw two great motor-car lamps within a few yards of the cab. A car was following, she glimpsed the outline of it as they ran past a street standard.

They were in one of the roads of the outer suburbs. Looking through the window over the driver's shoulder she saw trees on one side of the road, and a long grey fence. It was while she was so looking that the car behind shot suddenly past and ahead, and she saw its tail lights moving away with a pang of hopelessness. Then, before she realised what had happened, the big car ahead slowed and swung sideways, blocking the road, and the cab came to a jerky stop that flung her against the window. She saw two figures in the dim light of the taxi's head lamps, heard somebody speak, and the door was jerked open.

"Will you step out, Miss Beale," said a pleasant voice, and though her legs seemed queerly weak, she obliged. The second man was standing by the side of the driver. He wore a long raincoat, the collar of which was turned up to the tip of his nose.

"You may go back to your friends and tell them that Miss Beale is in good hands," he was saying. "You may also burn a candle or two before your favourite saint, in thanksgiving that you are alive."

"I don't know what you're talking about," said the driver sulkily. "I'm taking this young lady to her office."

"Since when has the *Daily Megaphone* been published in the ghastly suburbs?" asked the other politely.

He saw the girl, and raised his hat.

"Come along, Miss Beale," he said. "I promise you a more comfortable ride—even if I cannot guarantee that the end will be less startling."

Chapter III

The man who had opened the door was a short, stoutly built person of middle age. He took the girl's arm gently, and without questioning she accompanied him to the car ahead, the man in the raincoat following. No word was spoken, and Lydia was too bewildered to ask questions until the car was on its way. Then the younger man chuckled.

"Clever, Rennett!" he said. "I tell you, those people are super-humanly brilliant!"

"I'm not a great admirer of villainy," said the other gruffly, and the younger man, who was sitting opposite the girl, laughed.

"You must take a detached interest, my dear chap. Personally, I admire them. I admit they gave me a fright when I realised that Miss Beale had not called the cab, but that it had been carefully planted for her, but still I can admire them."

"What does it mean?" asked the puzzled girl. "I'm so confused—where are we going now? To the office?"

"I fear you will not get to the office to-night," said the young man calmly, "and it is impossible to explain to you just why you were abducted."

"Abducted?" said the girl incredulously. "Do you mean to say that man——"

"He was carrying you into the country," said the other calmly. "He would probably have travelled all night and have left you stranded in some un-get-at-able place. I don't think he meant any harm—they never take unnecessary risks, and all they wanted was to spirit you away for the night. How they came to know that we had chosen you baffles me," he said. "Can you advance any theory, Rennett?"

"Chosen me?" repeated the startled girl. "Really, I feel I'm entitled to some explanation, and if you don't mind, I would like you to take me back to my office. I have a job to keep," she added grimly.

"Six pounds ten a week, and a few guineas extra for your illustrations," said the man in the raincoat. "Believe me, Miss Beale, you'll never pay off your debts on that salary, not if you live to be a hundred."

She could only gasp.

"You seem to know a great deal about my private affairs," she said, when she had recovered her breath.

"A great deal more than you can imagine."

She guessed he was smiling in the darkness, and his voice was so gentle and apologetic that she could not take offence.

"In the past twelve months you have had thirty-nine judgments recorded against you, and in the previous year, twenty-seven. You are living on exactly thirty shillings a week, and all the rest is going to your father's creditors."

"You're very impertinent!" she said hotly and, as she felt, foolishly.

"I'm very pertinent, really. By the way, my name is Glover—John Glover, of the firm of Rennett, Glover and Simpson. The gentleman at your side is Mr. Charles Rennett, my senior partner. We are a firm of solicitors, but how long we shall remain a firm," he added pointedly, "depends rather upon you."

"Upon me?" said the girl in genuine astonishment. "Well, I can't say that I have so much love for lawyers———"

"That I can well understand," murmured Mr. Glover.

"But I certainly do not wish to dissolve your partnership," she went on.

"It is rather more serious than that," said Mr. Rennett, who was sitting by her side. "The fact is, Miss Beale, we are acting in a perfectly illegal manner, and we are going to reveal to you the particulars of an act we contemplate, which, if you pass on the information to the police, will result in our professional ruin. So you see this adventure is infinitely more important to us than at present it is to you. And here we are!" he said, interrupting the girl's question.

The car turned into a narrow drive, and proceeded some distance through an avenue of trees before it pulled up at the pillared porch of a big house.

Rennett helped her to alight and ushered her through the door, which opened almost as they stopped, into a large panelled hall.

"This is the way, let me show you," said the younger man.

He opened a door and she found herself in a big drawing-room, exquisitely furnished and lit by two silver electroliers suspended from the carved roof.

To her relief an elderly woman rose to greet her.

"This is my wife, Miss Beale," said Rennett. "I need hardly explain that this is also my home."

"So you found the young lady," said the elderly lady, smiling her welcome, "and what does Miss Beale think of your proposition?"

The young man Glover came in at that moment, and divested of his long raincoat and hat, he proved to be of a type that the Universities turn out by the hundred. He was good-looking too, Lydia noticed with feminine inconsequence, and there was something in his eyes that inspired trust. He nodded with a smile to Mrs. Rennett, then turned to the girl.

"Now Miss Beale, I don't know whether I ought to explain or whether my learned and distinguished friend prefers to save me the trouble."

"Not me," said the elder man hastily. "My dear," he turned to his wife, "I think we'll leave Jack Glover to talk to this young lady."

"Doesn't she know?" asked Mrs. Rennett in surprise, and Lydia laughed, although she was feeling far from amused.

The possible loss of her employment, the disquieting adventure of the evening, and now this further mystery all combined to set her nerves on edge.

Glover waited until the door closed on his partner and his wife and seemed inclined to wait a little longer, for he stood with his back to the fire, biting his lips and looking down thoughtfully at the carpet.

"I don't just know how to begin, Miss Beale," he said. "And having seen you, my conscience is beginning to work overtime. But I might as well start at the beginning. I suppose you have heard of the Bulford murder?"

The girl stared at him.

"The Bulford murder?" she said incredulously, and he nodded.

"Why, of course, everybody has heard of that."

"Then happily it is unnecessary to explain all the circumstances," said Jack Glover, with a little grimace of distaste.

"I only know," interrupted the girl, "that Mr. Bulford was killed by a Mr. Meredith, who was jealous of him, and that Mr. Meredith, when he went into the witness-box, behaved disgracefully to his fiancée."

"Exactly," nodded Glover with a twinkle in his eye. "In other words, he repudiated the suggestion that he was jealous, swore that he had already told Miss Briggerland that he could not marry her, and he did not even know that Bulford was paying attention to the lady."

"He did that to save his life," said Lydia quietly. "Miss Briggerland swore in the witness-box that no such interview had occurred."

Glover nodded.

"What you do not know, Miss Beale," he said gravely, "is that Jean Briggerland was Meredith's cousin, and unless certain things happen, she will inherit the greater part of six hundred thousand pounds from Meredith's estate. Meredith, I might explain, is one of my best friends, and the fact that he is now serving out a life sentence does not make him any less a friend. I am as sure, as I am sure of your sitting there, that he no more killed Bulford than I did. I believe the whole thing was a plot to secure his death or imprisonment. My partner thinks the same. The truth is that Meredith was engaged to this girl; he discovered certain things about her and her father which are not greatly to their credit. He was never really in love with her, beautiful as she is, and he was trapped into the proposal. When he found out how things were shaping and heard some of the queer stories which were told about Briggerland and his daughter, he broke off the engagement and went that night to tell her so."

The girl had listened in some bewilderment to this recital.

"I don't exactly see what all this is to do with me," she said, and again Jack Glover nodded.

"I can quite understand," he said, "but I will tell you yet another part of the story which is not public property. Meredith's father was an eccentric man who believed in early marriages, and it was a condition of his will that if Meredith was not married by his thirtieth birthday, the money should go to his sister, her heirs and successors. His sister was Mrs. Briggerland, who is now dead. Her heirs are her husband and Jean Briggerland."

There was a silence. The girl stared thoughtfully into the fire.

"How old is Mr. Meredith?"

"He is thirty next Monday," said Glover quietly, "and it is necessary that he should be married before next Monday."

"In prison?" she asked.

He shook his head.

"If such things are allowed that could have been arranged, but for some reason the Home Secretary refuses to exercise his discretion in this matter, and has resolutely refused to allow such a marriage to take place. He objects on the ground of public policy, and I dare say from his point of view he is right. Meredith has a twenty-years sentence to serve."

"Then how——" began Lydia.

"Let me tell this story more or less understandably," said Glover with that little smile of his. "Believe me, Miss Beale, I'm not so keen upon the scheme as I was.

If by chance," he spoke deliberately, "we could get James Meredith into this house to-morrow morning, would you marry him?"

"Me?" she gasped. "Marry a man I've not seen—a murderer?"

"Not a murderer," he said gently.

"But it is preposterous, impossible!" she protested. "Why me?"

He was silent for a moment.

"When this scheme was mooted we looked round for some one to whom such a marriage would be of advantage," he said, speaking slowly. "It was Rennett's idea that we should search the County Court records of London to discover if there was a girl who was in urgent need of money. There is no surer way of unearthing financial skeletons than by searching County Court records. We found four, only one of whom was eligible and that was you. Don't interrupt me for a moment, please," he said, raising his hand warningly as she was about to speak. "We have made thorough inquiries about you, too thorough in fact, because the Briggerlands have smelt a rat, and have been on our trail for a week. We know that you are not engaged to be married, we know that you have a fairly heavy burden of debts, and we know, too, that you are unencumbered by relations or friends. What we offer you, Miss Beale, and believe me I feel rather a cad in being the medium through which the offer is made, is five thousand pounds a year for the rest of your life, a sum of twenty thousand pounds down, and the assurance that you will not be troubled by your husband from the moment you are married."

Lydia listened like one in a dream. It did not seem real. She would wake up presently and find Mrs. Morgan with a cup of tea in her hand and a plate of her indigestible cakes. Such things did not happen, she told herself, and yet here was a young man, standing with his back to the fire, explaining in the most commonplace conversational tone, an offer which belonged strictly to the realm of romance, and not too convincing romance at that.

"You've rather taken my breath away," she said after a while. "All this wants thinking about, and if Mr. Meredith is in prison——"

"Mr. Meredith is not in prison," said Glover quietly. "He was released two days ago to go to a nursing home for a slight operation. He escaped from the nursing home last night and at this particular moment is in this house."

She could only stare at him open-mouthed, and he went on.

"The Briggerlands know he has escaped; they probably thought he was here, because we have had a police visitation this afternoon, and the interior of the house and grounds have been searched. They know, of course, that Mr. Rennett and I were his legal advisers, and we expected them to come. How he escaped their observation is neither here nor there. Now, Miss Beale, what do you say?"

"I don't know what to say," she said, shaking her head helplessly. "I know I'm dreaming, and if I had the moral courage to pinch myself hard, I should wake up. Somehow I don't want to wake, it is so fascinatingly impossible."

He smiled.

"Can I see Mr. Meredith?"

"Not till to-morrow. I might say that we've made every arrangement for your wedding, the licence has been secured and at eight o'clock to-morrow morning—marriages before eight or after three are not legal in this country, by the way—a clergyman will attend and the ceremony will be performed."

There was a long silence.

Lydia sat on the edge of her chair, her elbows on her knees, her face in her hands.

Glover looked down at her seriously, pityingly, cursing himself that he was the exponent of his own grotesque scheme. Presently she looked up.

"I think I will," she said a little wearily. "And you were wrong about the number of judgment summonses, there were seventy-five in two years—and I'm so tired of lawyers."

"Thank you," said Jack Glover politely.

Chapter IV

All night long she had sat in the little bedroom to which Mrs. Rennett had led her, thinking and thinking and thinking. She could not sleep, although she had tried hard, and most of the night she spent pacing up and down from window to door turning over the amazing situation in which she found herself. She had never thought of marriage seriously, and really a marriage such as this presented no terrors and might, had the prelude been a little less exciting, been accepted by her with relief. The prospect of being a wife in name only, even the thought that her husband would be, for the next twenty years, behind prison walls, neither distressed nor horrified her. Somehow she accepted Glover's statement that Meredith was innocent, without reservation.

She wondered what Mrs. Morgan would say and what explanation she would give at the office. She was not particularly in love with her work, and it would be no wrench for her to drop it and give herself up to the serious study of art. Five thousand pounds a year! She could live in Italy, study under the best masters, have a car of her own—the possibilities seemed illimitable—and the disadvantages?

She shrugged her shoulders as she answered the question for the twentieth time. What disadvantages were there? She could not marry, but then she did not want to marry. She was not the kind to fall in love, she told herself, she was too independent, too sophisticated, and understood men and their weaknesses only too well.

"The Lord designed me for an old maid," she said to herself.

At seven o'clock in the morning—a grey, cheerless morning it was, thought Lydia, looking out of the window—Mrs. Rennett came in with some tea.

"I'm afraid you haven't slept, my dear," she said with a glance at the bed. "It's very trying for you."

She laid her hand upon the girl's arm and squeezed it gently.

"And it's very trying for all of us," she said with a whimsical smile. "I expect we shall all get into fearful trouble."

That had occurred to the girl too, remembering the gloomy picture which Glover had painted in the car.

"Won't this be very serious for you, if the authorities find that you have connived at the escape?" she asked.

"Escape, my dear?" Mrs. Rennett's face became a mask. "I have not heard anything of an escape. All that we know is that poor Mr. Meredith, anticipating that the Home Office would allow him to get married, had made arrangements for the marriage at this house. How Mr. Meredith comes here is quite a matter outside our knowledge," said the diplomatic lady, and Lydia laughed in spite of herself.

She spent half an hour making herself presentable for the forthcoming ordeal.

As a church clock struck eight, there came another tap on the door. It was Mrs. Rennett again.

"They are waiting," she said. Her face was a little pale and her lips trembled.

Lydia, however, was calmness itself, as she walked into the drawing-room ahead of her hostess.

There were four men. Glover and Rennett she knew. A third man wearing a clerical collar she guessed was the officiating priest, and all her attention was concentrated upon the fourth. He was a gaunt, unshaven man, his hair cut short, his face and figure wasted, so that the clothes he wore hung on him. Her first feeling was one of revulsion. Her second was an impulse of pity. James Meredith, for she guessed it was he, appeared wretchedly ill. He swung round as she came in, and looked at her intently, then, walking quickly towards her, he held out his thin hand.

"Miss Beale, isn't it?" he said. "I'm sorry to meet you under such unpleasant circumstances. Glover has explained everything, has he not?"

She nodded.

His deep-set eyes had a magnetic quality that fascinated her.

"You understand the terms? Glover has told you just why this marriage must take place?" he said, lowering his voice. "Believe me, I am deeply grateful to you for falling in with my wishes."

Without preliminary he walked over to where the parson stood.

"We will begin now," he said simply.

The ceremony seemed so unreal to the girl that she did not realise what it portended, not even when a ring (a loosely-fitting ring, for Jack Glover had made the wildest guess at the size) was slipped over her finger. She knelt to receive the solemn benediction and then got slowly to her feet and looked at her husband strangely.

"I think I'm going to faint," she said.

It was Jack Glover who caught her and carried her to the sofa. She woke with a confused idea that somebody was trying to hypnotise her, and she opened her eyes to look upon the sombre face of James Meredith.

"Better?" he asked anxiously. "I'm afraid you've had a trying time, and no sleep you said, Mrs. Rennett?"

Mrs. Rennett shook her head.

"Well, you'll sleep to-night better than I shall," he smiled, and then he turned to Rennett, a grave and anxious man, who stood nervously stroking his little beard, watching the bridegroom. "Mr. Rennett," he said, "I must tell you in the presence of witnesses, that I have escaped from a nursing home to which I had been sent by the clemency of the Secretary of State. When I informed you that I had received permission to come to your house this morning to get married, I told you that which was not true."

"I'm sorry to hear that," said Rennett politely. "And, of course, it is my duty to hand you over to the police, Mr. Meredith." It was all part of the game. The girl watched the play, knowing that this scene was carefully rehearsed, in order to absolve Rennett and his partner from complicity in the escape.

Rennett had hardly spoken when there was a loud rat-tat at the front door, and Jack Glover hastened into the hall to answer. But it was not the policeman he had expected. It was a girl in a big sable coat, muffled up to her eyes. She pushed past Jack, crossed the hall, and walked straight into the drawing-room.

Lydia, standing shakily by Mrs. Rennett's side, saw the visitor come in, and then, as she unfastened her coat, recognised her with a gasp. It was the beautiful girl she had seen in the stalls of the theatre the night before!

"And what can we do for you?" It was Glover's voice again, bland and bantering.

"I want Meredith," said the girl shortly, and Glover chuckled.

"You have wanted Meredith for a long time, Miss Briggerland," he said, "and you're likely to want. You have arrived just a little too late."

The girl's eyes fell upon the parson.

"Too late," she said slowly, "then he is married?"

She bit her red lips and nodded, then she looked at Lydia, and the blue eyes were expressionless.

Meredith had disappeared. Lydia looked round for him in her distress, but he had gone. She wondered if he had gone out to the police, to make his surrender, and she was still wondering when there came the sound of a shot.

It was from the outside of the house, and at the sound Glover ran through the doorway, crossed the hall and flew into the open. It was still snowing, and there was no sign of any human being. He raced along a path which ran parallel with the house, turned the corner and dived into a shrubbery. Here the snow had not laid, and he followed the garden path that twisted and turned through the thick laurel bushes and ended at a roughly-built tool house. As he came in sight of the shed he stopped.

A man lay on the ground, his arm extended, his head in a pool of blood, his grey hand clutching a revolver.

Jack uttered an exclamation of horror and ran to the side of the fallen man.

It was James Meredith, and he was dead.

Chapter V

Jack Glover heard footsteps coming down the path, and turned to meet a man who had "detective" written largely all over him. Jack turned and looked down again at the body as the man came up.

"Who is this?" asked the officer sharply.

"It is James Meredith," said Jack simply.

"Dead?" said the officer, startled. "He has committed suicide!"

Jack did not reply, and watched the inspector as he made his brief, quick examination of the body. A bullet had entered just below the left temple, and there was a mark of powder near the face.

"A very bad business, Mr. Glover," said the police officer seriously. "Can you account for this man being here?"

"He came to get married," said Jack listlessly. "I dare say that startles you, but it is the fact. He was married less than ten minutes ago. If you will come up to the house I will explain his presence here."

The detective hesitated, but just then another of his comrades came on the scene, and Jack led the way back to the house through a back door into Rennett's study.

The lawyer was waiting for them, and he was alone.

"If I'm not very much mistaken, you're Inspector Colhead, of Scotland Yard," said Glover.

"That is my name," nodded the officer. "Between ourselves, Mr. Glover, I don't think I should make any statement which you are not prepared to verify publicly."

Jack noted the significance of the warning with a little smile, and proceeded to tell the story of the wedding.

"I can only tell you," he said in answer to a further inquiry, "that Mr. Meredith came into this house at a quarter to eight this morning, and surrendered himself to my partner. At eight o'clock exactly, as you are well aware, Mr. Rennett telephoned to Scotland Yard to say that Mr. Meredith was here. During the period of his waiting he was married."

"Did a parson happen to be staying here, sir?" asked the police officer sarcastically.

"He happened to be staying here," said Jack calmly, "because I had arranged for him to be here. I knew that if it was humanly possible, Mr. Meredith would come to this house, and that his desire was to be married, for reasons which my partner will explain."

"Did you help him to escape? That is asking you a leading question," smiled the detective.

Jack shook his head.

"I can answer you with perfect truth that I did not, any more than the Home Secretary helped him when he gave him permission to go to a nursing home."

Soon after the detective returned to the shed, and Jack and his partner were left alone.

"Well?" said Rennett, in a shaking voice, "what happened?"

"He's dead," said Jack quietly.

"Suicide?"

Jack looked at him oddly.

"Did Bulford commit suicide?" he asked.

"Where is the angel?"

"I left her in the drawing-room with Mrs. Rennett and Miss Beale."

"Mrs. Meredith," corrected Jack quietly.

"This complicates matters," said Rennett, "but I think we can get out of our share of the trouble, though it is going to look a little black."

They found the three women in the drawing-room. Lydia, looking very white, came to meet them.

"What happened?" she asked, and then she guessed from his face. "He's not dead?" she gasped.

Jack nodded. All the time his eyes were on the other girl. Her beautiful lips were drooped a little. There was a look of pain and sorrow in her eyes that caught his breath.

"Did he shoot himself?" she asked in a low voice.

Jack regarded her coldly.

"The only thing that I am certain about," and Lydia winced at the cruelty in his voice, "is that you did not shoot him, Miss Briggerland."

"How dare you!" flamed Jean Briggerland. The quick flush that came to her cheek was the only other evidence of emotion she betrayed.

"I dare say a lot," said Jack curtly. "You asked me if it is a case of suicide, and I tell you that it is not—it is a case of murder. James Meredith was found with a revolver clutched in his right hand. He was shot through the left temple, and if you'll explain to me how any man, holding a pistol in a normal way, can perform that feat, I will accept your theory of suicide."

There was a dead silence.

"Besides," Jack went on, with a little shrug, "poor Jimmy had no pistol."

Jean Briggerland had dropped her eyes, and stood there with downcast head and compressed lips. Presently she looked up.

"I know how you feel, Mr. Glover," she said gently. "I can well understand, believing such dreadful things about me as you do, that you must hate me."

Her mouth quivered and her voice grew husky with sorrow.

"I loved James Meredith," she said, "and he loved me."

"He loved you well enough to marry somebody else," said Jack Glover, and Lydia was shocked.

"Mr. Glover," she said reproachfully, "do you think it is right to say these things, with poor Mr. Meredith lying dead?"

He turned slowly toward her, and she saw in his humorous eyes a hardness that she had not seen before.

"Miss Briggerland has told us that I hate her," he said in an even voice, "and she spoke nothing but the truth. I hate her perhaps beyond understanding—Mrs. Meredith." He emphasised the words, and the girl winced. "And one day, if the Circumstantialists spare me———"

"The Circumstantialists," said Jean Briggerland slowly. "I don't quite understand you."

Jack Glover laughed, and it was not a pleasant laugh.

"Perhaps you will," he said shortly. "As to your loving poor Jim—well, you know best. I am trying to be polite to you, Miss Briggerland, and not to gloat over the fact that you arrived too late to stop this wedding! And shall I tell you why you arrived too late?" His eyes were laughing again. "It was because I had arranged with the vicar of St. Peter's to be here at nine o'clock this morning, well knowing that you and your little army of spies would discover the hour of the wedding, and would take care to be here before. And then I secretly sent for an old Oxford friend of mine to be here at eight—he was here last night."

Still she stood regarding him without visible evidence of the anger which Lydia thought would have been justified.

"I had no desire to stop the wedding," said the girl, in a low, soft voice. "If Jim preferred to be married in this way to somebody who does not know him, I can only accept his choice." She turned to the girl and held out her hand. "I am very sorry that this tragedy has come to you, Mrs. Meredith," she said. "May I wish you a greater happiness than any you have found?"

Lydia was touched by the sincerity, hurt a little by Glover's uncouthness, and could only warmly grip the little hand that was held out to her.

"I'm sorry too," she said a little unsteadily. "For you more than for—anything else."

The girl lowered her eyes and again her lips quivered, and then without a word she walked out of the room, pulling her sable wrap about her throat.

It was noon before Rennett's car deposited Lydia Meredith at the door of her lodging.

She found Mrs. Morgan in a great state of anxiety, and the stout little woman almost shed tears of joy at the sight of her.

"Oh, miss, you've no idea how worried I've been," she babbled, "and they've been round here from your newspaper office asking where you are. I thought you had been run over or something, and the *Daily Megaphone* have sent to all the hospitals———"

"I have been run over," said Lydia wearily. "My poor mind has been under the wheels of a dozen motor-buses, and my soul has been in a hundred collisions."

Mrs. Morgan gaped at her. She had no sense of metaphor.

"It's all right, Mrs. Morgan," laughed her lodger over her shoulder as she went up the stairs. "I haven't really you know, only I've had a worrying time—and by the way, my name is Meredith."

Mrs. Morgan collapsed on to a hall chair.

"Meredith, miss?" she said incredulously. "Why I knew your father———"

"I've been married, that's all," said Lydia grimly. "You told me yesterday that I should be married romantically, but even in the wildest flights of your imagination, Mrs. Morgan, you could never have supposed that I should be married in such a violent, desperate way. I'm going to bed." She paused on the landing and looked down at the dumbfounded woman. "If anybody calls for me, I am not at home. Oh, yes, you can tell the *Megaphone* that I came home very late and that I've gone to bed, and I'll call to-morrow to explain."

"But, miss," stammered the woman, "your husband———"

"My husband is dead," said the girl calmly. She felt a brute, but somehow she could not raise any note of sorrow. "And if that lawyer man comes, will you please tell him that I shall have twenty thousand pounds in the morning," and with that last staggering statement, she went to her room, leaving her landlady speechless.

Chapter VI

The police search of the house and grounds at Dulwich Grange, Mr. Rennett's residence, occupied the whole of the morning, and neither Rennett's nor Jack's assistance was invited or offered.

Before luncheon Inspector Colhead came to the study.

"We've had a good look round your place, Mr. Rennett," he said, "and I think we know where the deceased hid himself."

"Indeed!" said Mr. Rennett.

"That hut of yours in the garden is used, I suppose, for a tool house. There are no tools there now, and one of my men discovered that you can pull up the whole of the floor, it works on a hinge and is balanced with counter-weights."

Mr. Rennett nodded.

"I believe it was used as a wine cellar by a former tenant of the house," he said coolly. "We have no cellars at the Grange, you know. I do not drink wine, and I've never had occasion to use it."

"That's where he was hidden. We found a blanket, and pillows, down there, and, as you say, it has obviously been a wine cellar, because there is a ventilating shaft leading up into the bushes. We should never have found the trap, but one of my men felt one of the corners of the floor give under his feet."

The two men said nothing.

"Another thing," the detective went on slowly, "is that I'm inclined to agree that Meredith did not commit suicide. We found footmarks, quite fresh, leading round to the back of the hut."

"A big foot or a little foot?" asked Jack quickly.

"It is rather a big foot," said the detective, "and it has rubber heels. We traced it to a gate at the back of your premises, and the gate has been opened recently—probably by Mr. Meredith when he came to the house. It's a queer case, Mr. Rennett."

"What is the pistol?"

"That's new too," said Colhead. "Belgian make and impossible to trace, I should imagine. You can't keep track of these Belgian weapons. You can buy them in any shop in any town in Ostend or Brussels, and I don't think it is the practice for the sellers to keep any record of the numbers."

"In fact," said Jack quietly, "it is the same kind of pistol that killed Bulford."

Colhead raised his eyebrows.

"So it was, but wasn't it established that that was Mr. Meredith's own weapon?"

Jack shook his head.

"The only thing that was established was that he had seen the body and he picked up the pistol which was lying near the dead man. The shot was fired as he opened the door of Mr. Briggerland's house. Then he saw the figure on the pavement and picked up the pistol. He was in that position when Miss Briggerland, who testified against him, came out of the house and saw him."

The detective nodded.

"I had nothing to do with the case," he said, "but I remember seeing the weapon, and it was identical with this. I'll talk to the chief and let you know what he says about the whole affair. You'll have to give evidence at the inquest of course."

When he had gone the two men looked at one another.

"Well, Rennett, do you think we're going to get into hot water, or are we going to perjure our way to safety?"

"There's no need for perjury, not serious perjury," said the other carefully. "By the way, Jack, where was Briggerland the night Bulford was murdered?"

"When Miss Jean Briggerland had recovered from her horror, she went upstairs and aroused her father, who, despite the early hour, was in bed and asleep. When the police came, or rather, when the detective in charge of the case arrived, which must have been some time after the policeman on point duty put in an appearance, Mr. Briggerland was discovered in a picturesque dressing gown and, I presume, no less picturesque pyjamas."

"Horrified, too, I suppose," said Rennett dryly.

Jack was silent for a long time. Then: "Rennett," he said, "do you know I am more rattled about this girl than I am about any consequences to ourselves."

"Which girl are you talking about?"

"About Mrs. Meredith. Whilst poor Meredith was alive she was in no particular danger. But do you realise that what were advantages from our point of view, namely, the fact that she had no relations in the world, are to-day a source of considerable peril to this unfortunate lady?"

"I had forgotten that," said Rennett thoughtfully. "What makes matters a little more complicated, is the will which Meredith made this morning before he was married."

Jack whistled.

"Did he make a will?" he said in surprise.

His partner nodded.

"You remember he was here with me for half an hour. Well, he insisted upon writing out a will and my wife and Bolton, the butler, witnessed it."

"And he has left his money——?"

"To his wife absolutely," replied the other. "The poor old chap was so frantically keen on keeping the money out of the Briggerland exchequer, that he was prepared to entrust the whole of his money to a girl he had not seen."

Jack was serious now.

"And the Briggerlands are her heirs? Do you realise that, Rennett—there's going to be hell!"

Mr. Rennett nodded.

"I thought that too," he said quietly.

Jack sank down in a seat, his face screwed up into a hideous frown, and the elder man did not interrupt his thoughts. Suddenly Jack's face cleared and he smiled.

"Jaggs!" he said softly.

"Jaggs?" repeated his puzzled partner.

"Jaggs," said Jack, nodding, "he's the fellow. We've got to meet strategy with strategy, Rennett, and Jaggs is the boy to do it."

Mr. Rennett looked at him helplessly.

"Could Jaggs get us out of our trouble too?" he asked sarcastically.

"He could even do that," replied Jack.

"Then bring him along, for I have an idea he'll have the time of his life."

Chapter VII

Miss Jean Briggerland reached her home in Berkeley Street soon after nine o'clock. She did not ring, but let herself in with a key and went straight to the dining-room, where her father sat eating his breakfast, with a newspaper propped up before him.

He was the dark-skinned man whom Lydia had seen at the theatre, and he looked up over his gold-rimmed spectacles as the girl came in.

"You have been out very early," he said.

She did not reply, but slowly divesting herself of her sable coat she threw it on to a chair, took off the toque that graced her shapely head, and flung it after the coat. Then she drew out a chair, and sat down at the table, her chin on her palms, her blue eyes fixed upon her parent.

Nature had so favoured her that her face needed no artificial embellishment—the skin was clear and fine of texture, and the cold morning had brought only a faint pink to the beautiful face.

"Well, my dear," Mr. Briggerland looked up and beamed through his glasses, "so poor Meredith has committed suicide?"

She did not speak, keeping her eyes fixed on him.

"Very sad, very sad," Mr. Briggerland shook his head.

"How did it happen?" she asked quietly.

Mr. Briggerland shrugged his shoulders.

"I suppose at the sight of you he bolted back to his hiding place where—er—had been located by—er—interested persons during the night, then seeing me by the shed—he committed the rash and fatal act. Somehow I thought he would run back to his dug-out."

"And you were prepared for him?" she said.

He smiled.

"A clear case of suicide, my dear," he said.

"Shot through the left temple, and the pistol was found in his right hand," said the girl.

Mr. Briggerland started.

"Damn it," he said. "Who noticed that?"

"That good-looking young lawyer, Glover."

"Did the police notice?"

"I suppose they did when Glover called their attention to the fact," said the girl.

Mr. Briggerland took off his glasses and wiped them.

"It was done in such a hurry—I had to get back through the garden gate to join the police. When I got there, I found they'd been attracted by the shot and had entered the house. Still, nobody would know I was in the garden, and anyway my association with the capture of an escaped convict would not get into the newspapers."

"But a case of suicide would," said the girl. "Though I don't suppose the police will give away the person who informed them that James Meredith would be at Dulwich Grange."

Mr. Briggerland sat back in his chair, his thick lips pursed, and he was not a beautiful sight.

"One can't remember everything," he grumbled.

He rose from his chair, went to the door, and locked it. Then he crossed to a bureau, pulled open a drawer and took out a small revolver. He threw out the cylinder, glanced along the barrel and the chambers to make sure it was not loaded, then clicked it back in position, and standing before a glass, he endeavoured, the pistol in his right hand, to bring the muzzle to bear on his left temple. He found this impossible, and signified his annoyance with a grunt. Then he tried the pistol with his thumb on the trigger and his hand clasping the back of the butt. Here he was more successful.

"That's it," he said with satisfaction. "It could have been done that way."

She did not shudder at the dreadful sight, but watched him with the keenest interest, her chin still in the palm of her hand. He might have been explaining a new way of serving a tennis ball, for all the emotion he evoked.

Mr. Briggerland came back to the table, toyed with a piece of toast and buttered it leisurely.

"Everybody is going to Cannes this year," he said, "but I think I shall stick to Monte Carlo. There is a quiet about Monte Carlo which is very restful, especially if one can get a villa on the hill away from the railway. I told Morden yesterday to take the new car across and meet us at Boulogne. He says that the new body is exquisite. There is a microphonic attachment for telephoning to the driver, the electrical heating apparatus is splendid and——"

"Meredith was married."

If she had thrown a bomb at him she could not have produced a more tremendous sensation. He gaped at her, and pushed himself back from the table.

"Married?" His voice was a squeak.

She nodded.

"It's a lie," he roared. All his suavity dropped away from him, his face was distorted and puckered with anger and grew a shade darker. "Married, you lying little beast! He couldn't have been married! It was only a few minutes after eight, and the parson didn't come till nine. I'll break your neck if you try to scare me! I've told you about that before...."

He raved on, and she listened unmoved.

"He was married at eight o'clock by a man they brought down from Oxford, and who stayed the night in the house," she repeated with great calmness. "There's no sense in lashing yourself into a rage. I've seen the bride, and spoken to the clergyman."

From the bullying, raging madman, he became a whimpering, pitiable thing. His chin trembled, the big hands he laid on the tablecloth shook with a fever.

"What are we going to do?" he wailed. "My God, Jean, what are we going to do?"

She rose and went to the sideboard, poured out a stiff dose of brandy from a decanter and brought it across to him without a word. She was used to these tantrums, and to their inevitable ending. She was neither hurt, surprised, nor disgusted. This pale, ethereal being was the dominant partner of the combination. Nerves she did not possess, fears she did not know. She had acquired the precise sense of a great surgeon in whom pity was a detached emotion, and one which never intruded itself into the operating chamber. She was no more phenomenal than they, save that she did not feel bound by the conventions and laws which govern them as members of an ordered society. It requires no greater nerve to slay than to cure. She had had that matter out with herself, and had settled it to her own satisfaction.

"You will have to put off your trip to Monte Carlo," she said, as he drank the brandy greedily.

"We've lost everything now," he stuttered, "everything."

"This girl has no relations," said the daughter steadily. "Her heirs-at-law are ourselves."

He put down the glass, and looked at her, and became almost immediately his old self.

"My dear," he said admiringly, "you are really wonderful. Of course, it was childish of me. Now what do you suggest?"

"Unlock that door," she said in a low voice, "I want to call the maid."

As he walked to the door, she pressed the footbell, and soon after the faded woman who attended her came into the room.

"Hart," she said, "I want you to find my emerald ring, the small one, the little pearl necklet, and the diamond scarf pin. Pack them carefully in a box with cotton wool."

"Yes, madam," said the woman, and went out.

"Now what are you going to do, Jean?" asked her father.

"I am returning them to Mrs. Meredith," said the girl coolly. "They were presents given to me by her husband, and I feel after this tragic ending of my dream that I can no longer bear the sight of them."

"He didn't give you those things, he gave you the chain. Besides, you are throwing away good money?"

"I know he never gave them to me, and I am not throwing away good money," she said patiently. "Mrs. Meredith will return them, and she will give me an opportunity of throwing a little light upon James Meredith, an opportunity which I very much desire."

Later she went up to her pretty little sitting-room on the first floor, and wrote a letter.

> "Dear Mrs. Meredith.—I am sending you the few trinkets which James gave to me in happier days. They are all that I have of his, and you, as a woman, will realise that whilst the possession of them brings me many unhappy memories, yet they have been a certain comfort to me. I wish I could dispose of memory as easily as I send these to you (for I feel they are really your property) but more do I wish that I could recall and obliterate the occasion which has made Mr. Glover so bitter an enemy of mine.
>
> "Thinking over the past, I see that I was at fault, but I know that you will sympathise with me when the truth is revealed to you. A young girl, unused to the ways of men, perhaps I attached too much importance to Mr. Glover's attentions, and resented them too crudely. In those days I thought it was unpardonable that a man who professed to be poor James's best friend, should make love to his fiancée, though I suppose that such things happen, and are[Pg 61] endured by the modern girl. A man does not readily forgive a woman for making him feel a fool—it is the one unpardonable offence that a girl can commit. Therefore, I do not resent his enmity as much as you might think. Believe me, I feel for you very much in these trying days. Let me say again that I hope your future will be bright."

She blotted the letter, put it in an envelope, and addressed it, and taking down a book from one of the well-stocked shelves, drew her chair to the fire, and began reading.

Mr. Briggerland came in an hour after, looked over her shoulder at the title, and made a sound of disapproval.

"I can't understand your liking for that kind of book," he said.

The book was one of the two volumes of "Chronicles of Crime," and she looked up with a smile.

"Can't you? It's very easily explained. It is the most encouraging work in my collection. Sit down for a minute."

"A record of vulgar criminals," he growled. "Their infernal last dying speeches, their processions to Tyburn—phaugh!"

She smiled again, and looked down at the book. The wide margins were covered with pencilled notes in her writing.

"They're a splendid mental exercise," she said. "In every case I have written down how the criminal might have escaped arrest, but they were all so vulgar, and so stupid. Really the police of the time deserve no credit for catching them. It is the same with modern criminals...."

She went to the shelf, and took down two large scrap-books, carried them across to the fire, and opened one on her knees.

"Vulgar and stupid, every one of them," she repeated, as she turned the leaves rapidly.

"The clever ones get caught at times," said Briggerland gloomily.

"Never," she said, and closed the book with a snap. "In England, in France, in America, and in almost every civilised country, there are murderers walking about to-day, respected by their fellow citizens. Murderers, of whose crimes the police are ignorant. Look at these." She opened the book again. "Here is the case of Rell, who poisons a troublesome creditor with weed-killer. Everybody in the town knew he bought the weed-killer; everybody knew that he was in debt to this man. What chance had he of escaping? Here's Jewelville—he kills his wife, buries her in the cellar, and then calls attention to himself by running away. Here's Morden, who kills his sister-in-law for the sake of her insurance money, and who also buys the poison in broad daylight, and is found with a bottle in his pocket. Such people deserve hanging."

"I wish to heaven you wouldn't talk about hanging," said Briggerland tremulously, "you're inhuman, Jean, by God—"

"I'm an angel," she smiled, "and I have press cuttings to prove it! The *Daily Recorder* had half a column on my appearance in the box at Jim's trial."

He looked over toward the writing-table, saw the letter, and picked it up.

"So you've written to the lady. Are you sending her the jewels?"

She nodded.

He looked at her quickly.

"You haven't been up to any funny business with them, have you?" he asked suspiciously, and she smiled.

"My dear parent," drawled Jean Briggerland, "after my lecture on the stupidity of the average criminal, do you imagine I should do anything so *gauche*?"

Chapter VIII

"And now, Mrs. Meredith," said Jack Glover, "what are you going to do?"

He had spent the greater part of the morning with the new heiress, and Lydia had listened, speechless, as he recited a long and meaningless list of securities, of estates, of ground rents, balances and the like, which she had inherited.

"What am I going to do?" she said, shaking her head, hopelessly. "I don't know. I haven't the slightest idea, Mr. Glover. It is so bewildering. Do I understand that all this property is mine?"

"Not yet," said Jack with a smile, "but it is so much yours that on the strength of the will we are willing to advance you money to almost any extent. The will has to be proved, and probate must be taken, but when these legal formalities are settled, and we have paid the very heavy death duties, you will be entitled to dispose of your fortune as you wish. As a matter of fact," he added, "you could do that now. At any rate, you cannot live here in Brinksome Street, and I have taken the liberty of hiring a furnished flat on your behalf. One of our clients has gone away to the Continent and left the flat for me to dispose of. The rent is very low, about twenty guineas a week."

"Twenty guineas a week!" gasped the horrified girl, "why, I can't——"

And then she realised that she "could."

Twenty guineas a week was as nothing to her. This fact more than anything else, brought her to an understanding of her fortune.

"I suppose I had better move," she said dubiously. "Mrs. Morgan is giving up this house, and she asked me whether I had any plans. I think she'd be willing to come as my housekeeper."

"Excellent," nodded Jack. "You'll want a maid as well and, of course, you will have to put up Jaggs for the nights."

"Jaggs?" she said in astonishment.

"Jaggs," repeated Jack solemnly. "You see, Miss—I beg your pardon, Mrs. Meredith, I'm rather concerned about you, and I want you to have somebody on hand I can rely on, sleeping in your flat at night. I dare say you think I am an old woman," he said as he saw her smile, "and that my fears are groundless, but you will agree that your own experience of last week will support the theory that anything may happen in London."

"But really, Mr. Glover, you don't mean that I am in any serious danger—from whom?"

"From a lot of people," he said diplomatically.

"From poor Miss Briggerland?" she challenged, and his eyes narrowed.

"Poor Miss Briggerland," he said softly. "She certainly is poorer than she expected to be."

"Nonsense," scoffed the girl. She was irritated, which was unusual in her. "My dear Mr. Glover, why do you pursue your vendetta against her? Do you think it is playing the game, honestly now? Isn't it a case of wounded vanity on your part?"

He stared at her in astonishment.

"Wounded vanity? Do you mean pique?"

She nodded.

"Why should I be piqued?" he asked slowly.

"You know best," replied Lydia, and then a light dawned on him.

"Have I been making love to Miss Briggerland by any chance?" he asked.

"You know best," she repeated.

"Good Lord!" and then he began to laugh, and she thought he would never stop.

"I suppose I made love to her, and she was angry because I dared to commit such an act of treachery to her fiancé! Yes, that was it. I made love to her behind poor Jim's back, and she 'ticked me off,' and that's why I'm so annoyed with her?"

"You have a very good memory," said Lydia, with a scornful little smile.

"My memory isn't as good as Miss Briggerland's power of invention," said Jack. "Doesn't it strike you, Mrs. Meredith, that if I had made love to that young lady, I should not be seen here to-day?"

"What do you mean?" she asked.

"I mean," said Jack Glover soberly, "that it would not have been Bulford, but I, who would have been lured from his club by a telephone message, and told to wait outside the door in Berkeley Street. It would have been I, who would have been shot dead by Miss Briggerland's father from the drawing-room window."

The girl looked at him in amazement.

"What a preposterous charge to make!" she said at last indignantly. "Do you suggest that this girl has connived at a murder?"

"I not only suggest that she connived at it, but I stake my life that she planned it," said Jack carefully.

"But the pistol was found near Mr. Bulford's body," said Lydia almost triumphantly, as she conceived this unanswerable argument.

Jack nodded.

"From Bulford's body to the drawing-room window was exactly nine feet. It was possible to pitch the pistol so that it fell near him. Bulford was waiting there by the instructions of Jean Briggerland. We have traced the telephone call that came through to him from the club—it came from the Briggerlands' house in Berkeley Street, and the attendant at the club was sure it was a woman's voice. We didn't find that out till after the trial. Poor Meredith was in the hall when the shot was fired. The signal was given when he turned the handle to let himself out. He heard the shot, rushed down the steps and saw the body. Whether he picked up the pistol or not, I do not know. Jean Briggerland swears he had it in his hand, but, of course, Jean Briggerland is a hopeless liar!"

"You can't know what you're saying," said Lydia in a low voice. "It is a dreadful charge to make, dreadful, against a girl whose very face refutes such an accusation."

"Her face is her fortune," snapped Jack, and then penitently, "I'm sorry I'm rude, but somehow the very mention of Jean Briggerland arouses all that is worst in me. Now, you will accept Jaggs, won't you?"

"Who is he?" she asked.

"He is an old army pensioner. A weird bird, as shrewd as the dickens, in spite of his age a pretty powerful old fellow."

"Oh, he's old," she said with some relief.

"He's old, and in some ways, incapacitated. He hasn't the use of his right arm, and he's a bit groggy in one of his ankles as the result of a Boer bullet."

She laughed in spite of herself.

"He doesn't sound a very attractive kind of guardian. He's a perfectly clean old bird, though I confess he doesn't look it, and he won't bother you or your servants. You can give him a room where he can sit, and you can give him a bit of bread and cheese, and a glass of beer, and he'll not bother you."

Lydia was amused now. It was absurd that Jack Glover should imagine she needed a guardian at all, but if he insisted, as he did, it would be better to have somebody as harmless as the unattractive Jaggs.

"What time will he come?"

"At about ten o'clock every night, and he'll leave you at about seven in the morning. Unless you wish, you need never see him," said Jack.

"How did you come to know him?" she asked curiously.

"I know everybody," said the boastful young man, "you mustn't forget that I am a lawyer and have to meet very queer people."

He gathered up his papers and put them into his little bag.

"And now what are your plans for to-day?" he demanded.

She resented the self-imposed guardianship which he had undertaken, yet she could not forget what she owed him.

By some extraordinary means he had kept her out of the Meredith case and she had not been called as a witness at the inquest. Incidentally, in as mysterious a way he had managed to whitewash his partner and himself, although the Law Society were holding an inquiry of their own (this the girl did not know) it seemed likely that he would escape the consequence of an act which was a flagrant breach of the law.

"I am going to Mrs. Cole-Mortimer's to tea," she said.

"Mrs. Cole-Mortimer?" he said quickly. "How do you come to know that lady?"

"Really, Mr. Glover, you are almost impertinent," she smiled in spite of her annoyance. "She came to call on me two or three days after that dreadful morning. She knew Mr. Meredith and was an old friend of the family's."

"As a matter of fact," said Jack icily, "she did not know Meredith, except to say 'how-do-you-do' to him, and she was certainly not a friend of the family. She is, however, a friend of Jean Briggerland."

"Jean Briggerland!" said the exasperated girl. "Can't you forget her? You are like the man in Dickens's books—she's your King Charles's head! Really, for a respectable and a responsible lawyer, you're simply eaten up with prejudices. Of course, she was a friend of Mr. Meredith's. Why, she brought me a photograph of him taken when he was at Eton."

"Supplied by Jean Briggerland," said the unperturbed Jack calmly, "and if she'd brought you a pair of socks he wore when he was a baby I suppose you would have accepted those too."

"Now you are being really abominable," said the girl, "and I've got a lot to do."

He paused at the door.

"Don't forget you can move into Cavendish Mansions to-morrow. I'll send the key round, and the day you move in, Jaggs will turn up for duty, bright and smiling. He doesn't talk a great deal——"

"I don't suppose you ever give the poor man a chance," she said cuttingly.

Chapter IX

Mrs. Cole-Mortimer was a representative of a numerous class of women who live so close to the border-line which separates good society from society which is not quite as good, that the members of either set thought she was in the other. She had a small house where she gave big parties, and nobody quite knew how this widow of an Indian colonel made both ends meet. It was the fact that her menage was an expensive one to maintain; she had a car, she entertained in London in the season, and disappeared from the metropolis when it was the correct thing to disappear, a season of exile which comes between the Goodwood Race Meeting in the south and the Doncaster Race Meeting in the north.

Lydia had been surprised to receive a visit from this elegant lady, and had readily accepted the story of her friendship with James Meredith. Mrs. Cole-Mortimer's invitation she had welcomed. She needed some distraction, something which would smooth out the ravelled threads of life which were now even more tangled than she had ever expected they could be.

Mr. Rennett had handed to her a thousand pounds the day after the wedding, and when she had recovered from the shock of possessing such a large sum, she hired a taxicab and indulged herself in a wild orgy of shopping.

The relief she experienced when he informed her he was taking charge of her affairs and settling the debts which had worried her for three years was so great that she felt as though a heavy weight had been lifted from her heart.

It was in one of her new frocks that Lydia, feeling more confident than usual, made her call. She had expected to find a crowd at the house in Hyde Park Crescent, and she was surprised when she was ushered into the drawing-room to find only four people present.

Mrs. Cole-Mortimer was a chirpy, pale little woman of forty-something. It would be ungallant to say how much that "something" represented. She came toward Lydia with outstretched hands.

"My dear," she said with extravagant pleasure, "I am glad you were able to come. You know Miss Briggerland and Mr. Briggerland?"

Lydia looked up at the tall figure of the man she had seen in the stalls the night before her wedding and recognised him instantly.

"Mr. Marcus Stepney, I don't think you have met."

Lydia bowed to a smart looking man of thirty, immaculately attired. He was very handsome, she thought, in a dark way, but he was just a little too "new" to please her. She did not like fashion-plate men, and although the most captious of critics could not have found fault with his correct attire, he gave her the impression of being over-dressed.

Lydia had not expected to meet Miss Briggerland and her father, although she had a dim recollection that Mrs. Cole-Mortimer had mentioned her name. Then in a flash she recalled the suspicions of Jack Glover, which she had covered with ridicule. The association made her feel a little uncomfortable, and Jean Briggerland, whose intuition was a little short of uncanny, must have read the doubt in her face.

"Mrs. Meredith expected to see us, didn't she, Margaret?" she said, addressing the twittering hostess. "Surely you told her we were great friends?"

"Of course I did, my dear. Knowing your dear cousin and his dear father, it was not remarkable that I should know the whole of the family," and she smiled wisely from one to the other.

Of course! How absurd she was, thought Lydia. She had almost forgotten, and probably Jack Glover had forgotten too, that the Briggerlands and the Merediths were related.

She found herself talking in a corner of the room with the girl, and fell to studying her face anew. A closer inspection merely consolidated her earlier judgment. She smiled inwardly as she remembered Jack Glover's ridiculous warning. It was like killing a butterfly with a steam hammer, to loose so much vengeance against this frail piece of china.

"And how do you feel now that you're very rich?" asked Jean kindly.

"I haven't realised it yet," smiled Lydia.

Jean nodded.

"I suppose you have yet to settle with the lawyers. Who are they? Oh yes, of course Mr. Glover was poor Jim's solicitor." She sighed. "I dislike lawyers," she said with a shiver, "they are so heavily paternal! They feel that they and they only are qualified to direct your life and your actions. I suppose it is second nature with them. Then, of course, they make an awful lot of money out of commissions and fees, though I'm sure Jack Glover wouldn't worry about that. He's really a nice boy," she said earnestly, "and I don't think you could have a better friend."

Lydia glowed at the generosity of this girl whom the man had so maligned.

"He has been very good to me," she said, "although, of course, he is a little fussy."

Jean's lips twitched with amusement.

"Has he warned you against me?" she asked solemnly. "Has he told you what a terrible ogre I am?" And then without waiting for a reply: "I sometimes think poor Jack is just a little—well, I wouldn't say mad, but a little queer. His dislikes are so violent. He positively loathes Margaret, though why I have never been able to understand."

"He doesn't hate me," laughed Lydia, and Jean looked at her strangely.

"No, I suppose not," she said. "I can't imagine anybody hating you, Lydia. May I call you by your Christian name?"

"I wish you would," said Lydia warmly.

"I can't imagine anybody hating you," repeated the girl thoughtfully. "And, of course, Jack wouldn't hate you because you're his client—a very rich and attractive client too, my dear." She tapped the girl's cheek and Lydia, for some reason, felt foolish.

But as though unconscious of the embarrassment she had caused, Jean went on.

"I don't really blame him, either. I've a shrewd suspicion that all these warnings against me and against other possible enemies will furnish a very excellent excuse for seeing you every day and acting as your personal bodyguard!"

Lydia shook her head.

"That part of it he has relegated already," she said, giving smile for smile. "He has appointed Mr. Jaggs as my bodyguard."

"Mr. Jaggs?" The tone was even, the note of inquiry was not strained.

"He's an old gentleman in whom Mr. Glover is interested, an old army pensioner. Beyond the fact that he hasn't the use of his right arm, and limps with his left leg, and that he likes beer and cheese, he seems an admirable watch dog," said Lydia humorously.

"Jaggs?" repeated the girl. "I wonder where I've heard that name before. Is he a detective?"

"No, I don't think so. But Mr. Glover thinks I ought to have some sort of man sleeping in my new flat and Jaggs was duly engaged."

Soon after this Mr. Marcus Stepney came over and Lydia found him rather uninteresting. Less boring was Briggerland, for he had a fund of stories and experiences to relate, and he had, too, one of those soft soothing voices that are so rare in men.

It was dark when she came out with Mr. and Miss Briggerland, and she felt that the afternoon had not been unprofitably spent.

For she had a clearer conception of the girl's character, and was getting Jack Glover's interest into better perspective. The mercenary part of it made her just a little sick. There was something so mysterious, so ugly in his outlook on life, and there might not be a little self-interest in his care for her.

She stood on the step of the house talking to the girl, whilst Mr. Briggerland lit a cigarette with a patent lighter. Hyde Park Crescent was deserted save for a man who stood near the railings which protected the area of Mrs. Cole-Mortimer's house. He was apparently tying his shoe laces.

They went down on the sidewalk, and Mr. Briggerland looked for his car.

"I'd like to take you home. My chauffeur promised to be here at four o'clock. These men are most untrustworthy."

From the other end of the Crescent appeared the lights of a car. At first Lydia thought it might be Mr. Briggerland's, and she was going to make her excuses for she wanted to go home alone. The car was coming too, at a tremendous pace. She watched it as it came furiously toward her, and she did not notice that Mr. Briggerland and his daughter had left her standing alone on the sidewalk and had withdrawn a few paces.

Suddenly the car made a swerve, mounted the sidewalk and dashed upon her. It seemed that nothing could save her, and she stood fascinated with horror, waiting for death.

Then an arm gripped her waist, a powerful arm that lifted her from her feet and flung her back against the railings, as the car flashed past, the mud-guard missing her by an inch. The machine pulled up with a jerk, and the white-faced girl saw Briggerland and Jean running toward her.

"I should never have forgiven myself if anything had happened. I think my chauffeur must be drunk," said Briggerland in an agitated voice.

She had no words. She could only nod, and then she remembered her preserver, and she turned to meet the solemn eyes of a bent old man, whose pointed, white beard and bristling white eyebrows gave him a hawk-like appearance. His right hand was thrust into his pocket. He was touching his battered hat with the other.

"Beg pardon, miss," he said raucously, "name of Jaggs! And I have reported for dooty!"

Chapter X

Jack Glover listened gravely to the story which the girl told. He had called at her lodgings on the following morning to secure her signature to some documents, and breathlessly and a little shamefacedly, she told him what had happened.

"Of course it was an accident," she insisted, "in fact, Mr. and Miss Briggerland were almost knocked down by the car. But you don't know how thankful I am your Mr. Jaggs was on the spot."

"Where is he now?" asked Jack.

"I don't know," replied the girl. "He just limped away without another word and I did not see him again, though I thought I caught a glimpse of him as I came into this house last night. How did he come to be on the spot?" she asked curiously.

"That is easily explained," replied Jack. "I told the old boy not to let you out of his sight from sundown to sun up."

"Then you think I'm safe during the day?" she rallied him.

He nodded.

"I don't know whether to laugh at you or to be very angry," she said, shaking her head reprovingly. "Of course it was an accident!"

"I disagree with you," said Jack. "Did you catch a glimpse of the chauffeur?"

"No," she said in surprise. "I didn't think of looking at him."

He nodded.

"If you had, you would probably have seen an old friend, namely, the gentleman who carried you off from the Erving Theatre," he said quietly.

It was difficult for Lydia to analyse her own feelings. She knew that Jack Glover was wrong, monstrously wrong. She was perfectly confident that his fantastic theory had no foundation, and yet she could not get away from his sincerity. Remembering Jean's description of him as "a little queer" she tried to fit that description into her knowledge of him, only to admit to herself that he had been exceptionally normal as far as she was concerned. The suggestion that his object was mercenary, and that he looked upon her as a profitable match for himself, she dismissed without consideration.

"Anyway, I like your Mr. Jaggs," she said.

"Better than you like me, I gather from your tone," smiled Jack. "He's not a bad old boy."

"He is a very strong old boy," she said. "He lifted me as though I were a feather—I don't know now how I escaped. The steering gear went wrong," she explained unnecessarily.

"Dear me," said Jack politely, "and it went right again in time to enable the chauffeur to keep clear of Briggerland and his angel daughter!"

She gave a gesture of despair.

"You're hopeless," she said. "These things happened in the dark ages; men and women do not assassinate one another in the twentieth century."

"Who told you that?" he demanded. "Human nature hasn't changed for two thousand years. The instinct to kill is as strong as ever, or wars would be impossible. If any man or woman could commit one cold-blooded murder, there is no reason why he or she should not commit a hundred. In England, America, and France fifty cold-blooded murders are detected every year. Twice that number are undetected. It does not make the crime more impossible because the criminal is good looking."

"You're hopeless," she said again, and Jack made no further attempt to convince her.

On the Thursday of that week she exchanged her lodgings for a handsome flat in Cavendish Place, and Mrs. Morgan had promised to join her a week later, when she had settled up her own business affairs.

Lydia was fortunate enough to get two maids from one of the agencies, one of whom was to sleep on the premises. The flat was not illimitable, and she regretted that she had promised to place a room at the disposal of the aged Mr. Jaggs. If he was awake all night as she presumed he would be, and slept in the day, he might have been accommodated in the kitchen, and she hinted as much to Jack. To her surprise the lawyer had turned down that idea.

"You don't want your servants to know that you have a watchman."

"What do you imagine they will think he is?" she asked scornfully. "How can I have an old gentleman in the flat without explaining why he is there?"

"Your explanation could be that he did the boots."

"It wouldn't take him all night to do the boots. Of course, I'm too grateful to him to want him to do anything."

Mr. Jaggs reported again for duty that night. He came at half-past nine, a shabby-looking old man, and Lydia, who had not yet got used to her new magnificence, came out into the hall to meet him.

He was certainly not a prepossessing object, and Lydia discovered that, in addition to his other misfortunes, he had a slight squint.

"I hadn't an opportunity of thanking you the other day, Mr. Jaggs," she said. "I think you saved my life."

"That's all right, miss," he said, in his hoarse voice. "Dooty is dooty!"

She thought he was looking past her, till she realised that his curious slanting line of vision was part of his infirmity.

"I'll show you to your room," she said hastily.

She led the way down the corridor, opened the door of a small room which had been prepared for him, and switched on the light.

"Too much light for me, miss," said the old man, shaking his head. "I like to sit in the dark and listen, that's what I like, to sit in the dark and listen."

"But you can't sit in the dark, you'll want to read, won't you?"

"Can't read, miss," said Jaggs cheerfully. "Can't write, either. I don't know that I'm any worse off."

Reluctantly she switched out the light.

"But you won't be able to see your food."

"I can feel for that, miss," he said with a hoarse chuckle. "Don't you worry about me. I'll just sit here and have a big think."

If she was uncomfortable before, she was really embarrassed now. The very sight of the door behind which old Jaggs sat having his "big think" was an irritation to her. She could not sleep for a long time that night for thinking of him sitting in the darkness, and "listening" as he put it, and had firmly resolved on ending a condition of affairs which was particularly distasteful to her, when she fell asleep.

She woke when the maid brought her tea, to learn that Jaggs had gone.

The maid, too, had her views on the "old gentleman." She hadn't slept all night for the thought of him, she said, though probably this was an exaggeration.

The arrangement must end, thought Lydia, and she called at Jack Glover's office that afternoon to tell him so. Jack listened without comment until she had finished.

"I'm sorry he is worrying you, but you'll get used to him in time, and I should be obliged if you kept him for a month. You would relieve me of a lot of anxiety."

At first she was determined to have her way, but he was so persistent, so pleading, that eventually she surrendered.

Lucy, the new maid, however, was not so easily convinced.

"I don't like it, miss," she said, "he's just like an old tramp, and I'm sure we shall be murdered in our beds."

"How cheerful you are, Lucy," laughed Lydia. "Of course, there is no danger from Mr. Jaggs, and he really was very useful to me."

The girl grumbled and assented a little sulkily, and Lydia had a feeling that she was going to lose a good servant. In this she was not mistaken.

Old Jaggs called at half-past nine that night, and was admitted by the maid, who stalked in front of him and opened his door.

"There's your room," she snapped, "and I'd rather have your room than your company."

"Would you, miss?" wheezed Jaggs, and Lydia, attracted by the sound of voices, came to the door and listened with some amusement.

"Lord, bless me life, it ain't a bad room, either. Put the light out, my dear, I don't like light. I like 'em dark, like them little cells in Holloway prison, where you were took two years ago for robbing your missus."

Lydia's smile left her face. She heard the girl gasp.

"You old liar!" she hissed.

"Lucy Jones you call yourself—you used to be Mary Welch in them days," chuckled old Jaggs.

"I'm not going to be insulted," almost screamed Lucy, though there was a note of fear in her strident voice. "I'm going to leave to-night."

"No you ain't, my dear," said old Jaggs complacently. "You're going to sleep here to-night, and you're going to leave in the morning. If you try to get out of that door before I let you, you'll be pinched."

"They've got nothing against me," the girl was betrayed into saying.

"False characters, my dear. Pretending to come from the agency, when you didn't. That's another crime. Lord bless your heart, I've got enough against you to put you in jail for a year."

Lydia came forward.

"What is this you're saying about my maid?"

"Good evening, ma'am."

The old man knuckled his forehead.

"I'm just having an argument with your young lady."

"Do you say she is a thief?"

"Of course she is, miss," said Jaggs scornfully. "You ask her!"

But Lucy had gone into her room, slammed the door and locked it.

The next morning when Lydia woke, the flat was empty, save for herself. But she had hardly finished dressing when there came a knock at the door, and a trim, fresh-looking country girl, with an expansive smile and a look of good cheer that warmed Lydia's heart, appeared.

"You're the lady that wants a maid, ma'am, aren't you?"

"Yes," said Lydia in surprise. "But who sent you?"

"I was telegraphed for yesterday, ma'am, from the country."

"Come in," said Lydia helplessly.

"Isn't it right?" asked the girl a little disappointedly. "They sent me my fare. I came up by the first train."

"It is quite all right," said Lydia, "only I'm wondering who is running this flat, me or Mr. Jaggs?"

Chapter XI

Jean Briggerland had spent a very busy afternoon. There had been a string of callers at the handsome house in Berkeley Street.

Mr. Briggerland was of a philanthropic bent, and had instituted a club in the East End of London which was intended to raise the moral tone of Limehouse, Wapping, Poplar and the adjacent districts. It was started without ostentation with a man named Faire as general manager. Mr. Faire had had in his lifetime several hectic contests with the police, in which he had been invariably the loser. And it was in his role as a reformed character that he undertook the management of this social uplift club.

Well-meaning police officials had warned Mr. Briggerland that Faire had a bad character. Mr. Briggerland listened, was grateful for the warning, but explained that Faire had come under the influence of the new uplift movement, and from henceforward he would be an exemplary citizen. Later, the police had occasion to extend their warning to its founder. The club was being used by known criminal characters; men who had already been in jail and were qualifying for a return visit.

Again Mr. Briggerland pointed to the object of the institution which was to bring bad men into the society of good men and women, and to arouse in them a desire for better things. He quoted a famous text with great effect. But still the police were unconvinced.

It was the practice of Miss Jean Briggerland to receive selected members of the club and to entertain them at tea in Berkeley Street. Her friends thought it was very "sweet" and very "daring," and wondered whether she wasn't afraid of catching some kind of disease peculiar to the East End of London. But Jean did not worry about such things. On this afternoon, after the last of her callers had gone, she went down to the little morning-room where such entertainments occurred and found two men, who rose awkwardly as she entered.

The gentle influence of the club had not made them look anything but what they were. "Jail-bird" was written all over them.

"I'm very glad you men have come," said Jean sweetly. "Mr. Hoggins——"

"That's me, miss," said one, with a grin.

"And Mr. Talmot."

The second man showed his teeth.

"I'm always glad to see members of the club," said Jean busy with the teapot, "especially men who have had so bad a time as you have. You have only just come out of prison, haven't you, Mr. Hoggins?" she asked innocently.

Hoggins went red and coughed.

"Yes, miss," he said huskily and added inconsequently, "I didn't do it!"

"I'm sure you were innocent," she said with a smile of sympathy, "and really if you were guilty I don't think you men are so much to blame. Look what a bad time you have! What disadvantages you suffer, whilst here in the West End people are wasting money that really ought to go to your wives and children."

"That's right," said Mr. Hoggins.

"There's a girl I know who is tremendously rich," Jean prattled on. "She lives at 84, Cavendish Mansions, just on the top floor, and, of course, she's very foolish to sleep with her windows open, especially as people could get down from the roof—there is a fire escape there. She always has a lot of jewellery—keeps it under her pillow I think, and there is generally a few hundred pounds scattered about the bedroom. Now that is what I call putting temptation in the way of the weak."

She lifted her blue eyes, saw the glitter in the man's eyes and went on.

"I've told her lots of times that there is danger, but she only laughs. There is an old man who sleeps in the house—quite a feeble old man who has only the use of one arm. Of course, if she cried out, I suppose he would come to her rescue, but then a real burglar wouldn't let her cry out, would he?" she asked.

The two men looked at one another.

"No," breathed one.

"Especially as they could get clean away if they were clever," said Jean, "and it isn't likely that they would leave her in a condition to betray them, is it?"

Mr. Hoggins cleared his throat.

"It's not very likely, miss," he said.

Jean shrugged her shoulders.

"Women do these things, and then they blame the poor man to whom a thousand pounds would be a fortune because he comes and takes it. Personally, I should not like to live at 84, Cavendish Mansions."

"84, Cavendish Mansions," murmured Mr. Hoggins absent-mindedly.

His last sentence had been one of ten years' penal servitude. His next sentence would be for life. Nobody knew this better than Jean Briggerland as she went on to talk of the club and of the wonderful work which it was doing.

She dismissed her visitors and went back to her sitting-room. As she turned to go up the stairway her maid intercepted her.

"Mary is in your room, miss," she said in a low voice.

Jean frowned but made no reply.

The woman who stood awkwardly in the centre of the room awaiting the girl, greeted her with an apologetic smile.

"I'm sorry, miss," she said, "but I lost my job this morning. That old man spotted me. He's a split—a detective."

Jean Briggerland regarded her with an unmoved face save that her beautiful mouth took on the pathetic little droop which had excited the pity of a judge and an army of lawyers.

"When did this happen?" she asked.

"Last night, miss. He came and I got a bit cheeky to him, and he turned on me, the old devil, and told me my real name and that I'd got the job by forging recommendations."

Jean sat down slowly in the padded Venetian chair before her writing table.

"Jaggs?" she asked.

"Yes, miss."

"And why didn't you come here at once?"

"I thought I might be followed, miss."

The girl bit her lip and nodded.

"You did quite right," she said, and then after a moment's reflection, "We shall be in Paris next week. You had better go by the night train and wait for us at the flat."

She gave the maid some money and after she had gone, sat for an hour before the fire looking into its red depths.

She rose at last a little stiffly, pulled the heavy silken curtain across the windows and switched on the light, and there was a smile on her face that was very beautiful to see. For in that hour came an inspiration.

She sought her father in his study and told him her plan, and he blanched and shivered with the very horror of it.

Chapter XII

Mr. Briggerland, it seemed, had some other object in life than the regeneration of the criminal classes. He was a sociologist—a loose title which covers a great deal of inquisitive investigation into other people's affairs. Moreover, he had published a book on the subject. His name was on the title page and the book had been reviewed to his credit; though in truth he did no more than suggest the title, the work in question having been carried out by a writer on the subject who, for a consideration, had allowed Mr. Briggerland to adopt the child of his brain.

On a morning when pale yellow sunlight brightened his dining-room, Mr. Briggerland put down his newspaper and looked across the table at his daughter. He had a club in the East End of London and his manager had telephoned that morning sending a somewhat unhappy report.

"Do you remember that man Talmot, my dear?" he asked.

She nodded, and looked up quickly.

"Yes, what about him?"

"He's in hospital," said Mr. Briggerland. "I fear that he and Hoggins were engaged in some nefarious plan and that in making an attempt to enter—as, of course, they had no right to enter—a block of flats in Cavendish Place, poor Talmot slipped and fell from the fourth floor window-sill, breaking his leg. Hoggins had to carry him to hospital."

The girl reached for bacon from the hot plate.

"He should have broken his neck," she said calmly. "I suppose now the police are making tender inquiries?"

"No, no," Mr. Briggerland hastened to assure her. "Nobody knows anything about it, not even the—er—fortunate occupant of the flat they were evidently trying to burgle. I only learnt of it because the manager of the club, who gets information of this character, thought I would be interested."

"Anyway I'm glad they didn't succeed," said Jean after a while. "The possibility of their trying rather worried me. The Hoggins type is such a bungler that it was almost certain they would fail."

It was a curious fact that whilst her father made the most guarded references to all their exploits and clothed them with garments of euphemism, his daughter never attempted any such disguise. The psychologist would find in Mr.

Briggerland's reticence the embryo of a once dominant rectitude, no trace of which remained in his daughter's moral equipment.

"I have been trying to place this man Jaggs," she went on with a little puzzled frown, "and he completely baffles me. He arrives every night in a taxicab, sometimes from St. Pancras, sometimes from Euston, sometimes from London Bridge Station."

"Do you think he is a detective?"

"I don't know," she said thoughtfully. "If he is, he has been imported from the provinces. He is not a Scotland Yard man. He may, of course, be an old police pensioner, and I have been trying to trace him from that source."

"It should not be difficult to find out all about him," said Mr. Briggerland easily. "A man with his afflictions should be pretty well-known."

He looked at his watch.

"My appointment at Norwood is at eleven o'clock," he said. He made a little grimace of disgust.

"Would you rather I went?" asked the girl.

Mr. Briggerland would much rather that she had undertaken the disagreeable experience which lay before him, but he dare not confess as much.

"You, my dear? Of course not! I would not allow you to have such an experience. No, no, I don't mind it a bit."

Nevertheless, he tossed down two long glasses of brandy before he left.

His car set him down before the iron gates of a squat and ugly stucco building, surrounded by high walls, and the uniformed attendant, having examined his credentials, admitted him. He had to wait a little while before a second attendant arrived to conduct him to the medical superintendent, an elderly man who did not seem overwhelmed with joy at the honour Mr. Briggerland was paying him.

"I'm sorry I shan't be able to show you round, Mr. Briggerland," he said. "I have an engagement in town, but my assistant, Dr. Carew, will conduct you over the asylum and give you all the information you require. This, of course, as you know, is a private institution. I should have thought you would have got more material for your book in one of the big public asylums. The people who are sent to Norwood, you know, are not the mild cases, and you will see some rather terrible sights. You are prepared for that?"

Mr. Briggerland nodded. He was prepared to the extent of two full noggins of brandy. Moreover, he was well aware that Norwood was the asylum to which the more dangerous of lunatics were transferred.

Dr. Carew proved to be a young and enthusiastic alienist whose heart and soul was in his work.

"I suppose you are prepared to see jumpy things," he said with a smile, as he conducted Mr. Briggerland along a stone-vaulted corridor.

He opened a steel gate, the bars of which were encased with thick layers of rubber, crossed a grassy plot (there were no stone-flagged paths at Norwood) and entered one of the three buildings which constituted the asylum proper.

It was a harrowing, heart-breaking, and to some extent, a disappointing experience for Mr. Briggerland. True, his heart did not break, because it was made of infrangible material, and his disappointment was counter-balanced by a certain vague relief.

At the end of two hours' inspection they were standing out on the big playing fields, watching the less violent of the patients wandering aimlessly about. Except one, they were unattended by keepers, but in the case of this one man, two stalwart uniformed men walked on either side of him.

"Who is he?" asked Briggerland.

"That is rather a sad case," said the alienist cheerfully. He had pointed out many "sad cases" in the same bright manner. "He's a doctor and a genuine homicide. Luckily they detected him before he did any mischief or he would have been in Broadmoor."

"Aren't you ever afraid of these men escaping?" asked Mr. Briggerland.

"You asked that before," said the doctor in surprise. "No. You see, an insane asylum is not like a prison; to make a good get-away from prison you have to have outside assistance. Nobody wants to help a lunatic escape, otherwise it would be easier than getting out of prison, because we have no patrols in the grounds, the wards can be opened from the outside without a key and the night patrol who visits the wards every half-hour has no time for any other observation. Would you like to talk to Dr. Thun?"

Mr. Briggerland hesitated only for a second.

"Yes," he said huskily.

There was nothing in the appearance of the patient to suggest that he was in any way dangerous. A fair, bearded man, with pale blue eyes, he held out his hand impulsively to the visitor, and after a momentary hesitation, Mr. Briggerland took it and found his hand in a grip like a vice. The two attendants exchanged glances with the asylum doctor and strolled off.

"I think you can talk to him without fear," said the doctor in a low voice, not so low, however, that the patient did not hear it, for he laughed.

"Without fear, favour or prejudice, eh? Yes, that was how they swore the officers at my court martial."

"The doctor was the general who was responsible for the losses at Caperetto," explained Dr. Carew. "That was where the Italians lost so heavily."

Thun nodded.

"Of course, I was perfectly innocent," he explained to Briggerland seriously, and taking the visitor's arm he strolled across the field, the doctor and the two attendants following at a distance. Mr. Briggerland breathed a little more quickly as he felt the strength of the patient's biceps.

"My conviction," said Dr. Thun seriously, "was due to the fact that women were sitting on the court martial, which is, of course, against all regulations."

"Certainly," murmured Mr. Briggerland.

"Keeping me here," Thun went on, "is part of the plot of the Italian government. Naturally, they do not wish me to get at my enemies, who I have every reason to believe are in London."

Mr. Briggerland drew a long breath.

"They are in London," he said a little hoarsely. "I happen to know where they are."

"Really?" said the other easily, and then a cloud passed over his face and he shook his head.

"They are safe from my vengeance," he said a little sadly. "As long as they keep me in this place pretending that I am mad, there is no possible chance for me."

The visitor looked round and saw that the three men who were following were out of ear shot.

"Suppose I came to-morrow night," he said, lowering his voice, "and helped you to get away? What is your ward?"

"No. 6," said the other in the same tone. His eyes were blazing.

"Do you think you will remember?" asked Briggerland.

Thun nodded.

"You will come to-morrow night—No. 6, the first cubicle on the left," he whispered, "you will not fail me? If I thought you'd fail me——" His eyes lit up again.

"I shall not fail you," said Mr. Briggerland hastily. "When the clock strikes twelve you may expect me."

"You must be Marshal Foch," murmured Thun, and then with all a madman's cunning, changed the conversation as the doctor and attendants, who had noticed his excitement, drew nearer. "Believe me, Mr. Briggerland," he went on airily, "the strategy of the Allies was at fault until I took up the command of the army...."

Ten minutes later Mr. Briggerland was in his car driving homeward, a little breathless, more than a little terrified at the unpleasant task he had set himself; jubilant, too, at his amazing success.

Jean had said he might have to visit a dozen asylums before he found his opportunity and the right man, and he had succeeded at the first attempt. Yet—he shuddered at the picture he conjured—that climb over the high wall (he had already located the ward, for he had followed the General and the attendants and had seen him safely put away), the midnight association with a madman....

He burst in upon Jean with his news.

"At the first attempt, my dear, what do you think of that?" His dark face glowed with almost childish pride, and she looked at him with a half-smile.

"I thought you would," she said quietly. "That's the rough work done, at any rate."

"The rough work!" he said indignantly.

She nodded.

"Half the difficulty is going to be to cover up your visit to the asylum, because this man is certain to mention your name, and it will not all be dismissed as the imagination of a madman. Now I think I will make my promised call upon Mrs. Meredith."

Chapter XIII

There was one thing which rather puzzled and almost piqued Lydia Meredith, and that was the failure of Jean Briggerland's prophecy to materialise. Jean had said half jestingly that Jack Glover would be a frequent visitor at the flat; in point of fact, he did not come at all. Even when she visited the offices of Rennett, Glover and Simpson, it was Mr. Rennett who attended to her, and Jack was invisible. Mr. Rennett sometimes explained that he was at the courts, for Jack did all the court work, sometimes that he had gone home.

She caught a glimpse of him once as she was driving past the Law Courts in the Strand. He was standing on the pavement talking to a be-wigged counsel, so possibly Mr. Rennett had not stated more than the truth when he said that the young man's time was mostly occupied by the processes of litigation.

She was curious enough to look through the telephone directory to discover where he lived. There were about fifty Glovers, and ten of these were John Glovers, and she was enough of a woman to call up six of the most likely only to discover that her Mr. Glover was not amongst them. She did not know till later that his full name was Bertram John Glover, or she might have found his address without difficulty.

Mrs. Morgan had now arrived, to Lydia's infinite relief, and had taken control of the household affairs. The new maid was as perfect as a new maid could be, and but for the nightly intrusion of the taciturn Jaggs, to whom, for some reason, Mrs. Morgan took a liking, the current of her domestic life ran smoothly.

She was already becoming accustomed to the possession of wealth. The habit of being rich is one of the easiest acquired, and she found herself negotiating for a little house in Curzon Street and a more pretentious establishment in Somerset, with a sangfroid which astonished and frightened her.

The purchase and arrival of her first car, and the engagement of her chauffeur had been a thrilling experience. It was incredible, too, that her new bankers should, without hesitation, deliver to her enormous sums of money at the mere affixing of her signature to an oblong slip of paper.

She had even got over the panic feeling which came to her on her first few visits to the bank. On these earlier occasions she had felt rather like an inexpert forger, who was endeavouring to get money by false pretence, and it was both a relief and a wonder to her when the nonchalant cashier thrust thick wads of banknotes under the grille, without so much as sending for a policeman.

"It's a lovely flat," said Jean Briggerland, looking round the pink drawing-room approvingly, "but of course, my dear, this is one that was already furnished for you. I'm dying to see what you will make of your own home when you get one."

She had telephoned that morning to Lydia saying that she was paying a call, asking if it was convenient, and the two girls were alone.

"It *is* a nice flat, and I shall be sorry to leave it," agreed Lydia. "It is so extraordinarily quiet. I sleep like a top. There is no noise to disturb one, except that there was rather an unpleasant happening the other morning."

"What was that?" asked Jean, stirring her tea.

"I don't know really what happened," said Lydia. "I heard an awful groaning very early in the morning and I got up and looked out of the window. There were two men in the courtyard. One, I think, had hurt himself very badly. I never discovered what happened."

"They must have been workmen, I should think," said Jean, "or else they were drunk. Personally, I have never liked taking furnished flats," she went on. "One always breaks things, and there's such a big bill to pay at the end. And then I always lose the keys. One usually has two or three. You should be very careful about that, my dear, they make an enormous charge for lost keys," she prattled on.

"I think the house agent gave me three," said Lydia. She walked to her little secretaire, opened it and pulled out a drawer.

"Yes, three," she said, "there is one here, one I carry, and Mrs. Morgan has one."

"Have you seen Jack Glover lately?"

Jean never pursued an enquiry too far, by so much as one syllable.

"No, I haven't seen him," smiled Lydia, "You weren't a good prophet."

"I expect he is busy," said the girl carelessly. "I think I could like Jack awfully— if he hadn't such a passion for ordering people about. How careless of me!" She had tipped over her teacup and its contents were running across the little tea table. She pulled out her handkerchief quickly and tried to stop the flow.

"Oh, please, please don't spoil your beautiful handkerchief," said Lydia, rising hurriedly, "I will get a duster."

She ran out of the room and was back almost immediately, to find Jean standing with her back to the secretaire examining the ruins of her late handkerchief with a smile.

"Let me put your handkerchief in water or it will be stained," said Lydia, putting out her hand.

"I would rather do it myself," laughed Jean Briggerland, and pushed the handkerchief into her bag.

There were many reasons why Lydia should not handle that flimsy piece of cambric and lace, the most important of which was the key which Jean had taken from the secretaire in Lydia's absence, and had rolled inside the tea-stained handkerchief.

A few days later Mr. Bertram John Glover interviewed a high official at Scotland Yard, and the interview was not a particularly satisfactory one to the lawyer. It might have been worse, had not the police commissioner been a friend of Jack's partner.

The official listened patiently whilst the lawyer, with professional skill, marshalled all his facts, attaching to them the suspicions which had matured to convictions.

"I have sat in this chair for twenty-five years," said the head of the C.I.D., "and I have heard stories which beat the best and the worst of detective stories hollow. I have listened to cranks, amateur detectives, crooks, parsons and expert fictionists, but never in my experience have I ever heard anything quite so improbable as your theory. It happens that I have met Briggerland and I've met his daughter too, and a more beautiful girl I don't think it has been my pleasure to meet."

Jack groaned.

"Aren't you feeling well?" asked the chief unpleasantly.

"I'm all right, sir," said Jack, "only I'm so tired of hearing about Jean Briggerland's beauty. It doesn't seem a very good argument to oppose to the facts—"

"Facts!" said the other scornfully. "What facts have you given us?"

"The fact of the Briggerlands' history," said Jack desperately. "Briggerland was broke when he married Miss Meredith under the impression that he would get a fortune with his wife. He has lived by his wits all his life, and until this girl was about fifteen, they were existing in a state of poverty. They lived in a tiny house in Ealing, the rent of which was always in arrears, and then Briggerland became acquainted with a rich Australian of middle age who was crazy about his daughter. The rich Australian died suddenly."

"From an overdose of veronal," said the chief. "It was established at the inquest—I got all the documents out after I received your letter—that he was in the habit of taking veronal. You suggest he was murdered. If he was, for what? He left the girl about six thousand pounds."

"Briggerland thought she was going to get it all," said Jack.

"That is conjecture," interrupted the chief. "Go on."

"Briggerland moved up west," Jack went on, "and when the girl was seventeen she made the acquaintance of a man named Gunnesbury, who went just as mad about her. Gunnesbury was a midland merchant with a wife and family. He was so infatuated with her that he collected all the loose money he could lay his hands on—some twenty-five thousand pounds—and bolted to the continent. The girl was supposed to have gone on ahead, and he was to join her at Calais. He never reached Calais. The theory was that he jumped overboard. His body was found and brought in to Dover, but there was none of the money in his possession that he had drawn from the Midland Bank."

"That is a theory, too," said the chief, shaking his head. "The identity of the girl was never established. It was known that she was a friend of Gunnesbury's, but there was proof that she was in London on the night of his death. It was a clear case of suicide."

"A year later," Jack went on, "she forced a meeting with Meredith, her cousin. His father had just died—Jim had come back from Central Africa to put things in order. He was not a woman's man, and was a grave, retiring sort of fellow, who had no other interest in life than his shooting. The story of Meredith you know."

"And is that all?" asked the chief politely.

"All the facts I can gather. There must be other cases which are beyond the power of the investigator to unearth."

"And what do you expect me to do?"

Jack smiled.

"I don't expect you to do anything," he said frankly. "You are not exactly supporting my views with enthusiasm."

The chief rose, a signal that the interview was at an end.

"I'd like to help you if you had any real need for help," he said. "But when you come to me and tell me that Miss Briggerland, a girl whose innocence shows in her face, is a heartless criminal and murderess, and a conspirator—why, Mr. Glover, what do you expect me to say?"

"I expect you to give adequate protection to Mrs. Meredith," said Jack sharply. "I expect you, sir, to remember that I've warned you that Mrs. Meredith may die one of those accidental deaths in which Mr. and Miss Briggerland specialise. I'm going to put my warning in black and white, and if anything happens to Lydia Meredith, there is going to be serious trouble on the Thames Embankment."

The chief touched a bell, and a constable came in.

"Show Mr. Glover the way out," he said stiffly.

Jack had calmed down considerably by the time he reached the Thames Embankment, and was inclined to be annoyed with himself for losing his temper.

He stopped a newsboy, took a paper from his hand, and, hailing a cab, drove to his office.

There was little in the early edition save the sporting news, but on the front page a paragraph arrested his eye.

"DANGEROUS LUNATIC AT LARGE."

"The Medical Superintendent at Norwood Asylum reports that Dr. Algernon John Thun, an inmate of the asylum, escaped last night, and is believed to be at large in the neighbourhood. Search parties have been organised, but no trace of the man has been found. He is known to have homicidal tendencies, a fact which renders his immediate recapture a very urgent necessity."

There followed a description of the wanted man. Jack turned to another part of the paper, and dismissed the paragraph from his mind.

His partner, however, was to bring the matter up at lunch. Norwood Asylum was near Dulwich, and Mr. Rennett was pardonably concerned.

"The womenfolk at my house are scared to death," he said at lunch. "They won't go out at night, and they keep all the doors locked. How did your interview with the commissioner go on?"

"We parted the worst of friends," said Jack, "and, Rennett, the next man who talks to me about Jean Briggerland's beautiful face is going to be killed dead through it, even though I have to take a leaf from her book and employ the grisly Jaggs to do it."

Chapter XIV

That night the "grisly Jaggs" was later than usual. Lydia heard him shuffling along the passage, and presently the door of his room closed with a click. She was sitting at the piano, and had stopped playing at the sound of his knock, and when Mrs. Morgan came in to announce his arrival, she closed the piano and swung round on the music stool, a look of determination on her delicate face.

"He's come, miss."

"And for the last time," said Lydia ominously. "Mrs. Morgan, I can't stand that weird old gentleman any longer. He has got on my nerves so that I could scream when I think of him."

"He's not a bad old gentleman," excused Mrs. Morgan.

"I'm not so worried about his moral character, and I dare say that it is perfectly blameless," said Lydia determinedly, "but I have written a note to Mr. Glover to tell him that I really must dispense with his services."

"What's he here for, miss?" asked Mrs. Morgan.

Her curiosity had been aroused, but this was the first time she had given it expression.

"He's here because——" Lydia hesitated, "well, because Mr. Glover thinks I ought to have a man in the house to look after me."

"Why, miss?" asked the startled woman.

"You'd better ask Mr. Glover that question," said Lydia grimly.

She was beginning to chafe under the sense of restraint. She was being "schoolmarmed" she thought. No girl likes the ostentatious protection of the big brother or the head mistress. The soul of the schoolgirl yearns to break from the "crocodile" in which she is marched to church and to school, and this sensation of being marshalled and ordered about, and of living her life according to a third person's programme, and that third person a man, irked her horribly.

Old Jaggs was the outward and visible sign of Jack Glover's unwarranted authority, and slowly there was creeping into her mind a suspicion that Jean Briggerland might not have been mistaken when she spoke of Jack's penchant for "ordering people about."

Life was growing bigger for her. She had broken down the barriers which had confined her to a narrow promenade between office and home. The hours which she had had to devote to work were now entirely free, and she could sketch or paint whenever the fancy took her—which was not very often, though she promised herself a period of hard work when once she was settled down.

Toward the good-looking young lawyer her point of view had shifted. She hardly knew herself how she regarded him. He irritated, and yet in some indefinable way, pleased her. His sincerity—? She did not doubt his sincerity. She admitted to herself that she wished he would call a little more frequently than he did. He might have persuaded her that Jaggs was a necessary evil, but he hadn't even taken the trouble to come. Therefore—but this she did not admit—Jaggs must go.

"I don't think the old gentleman's quite right in his head, you know, sometimes," said Mrs. Morgan.

"Why ever not, Mrs. Morgan?" asked the girl in surprise.

"I often hear him sniggering to himself as I go past his door. I suppose he stays in his room all night, miss?"

"He doesn't," said the girl emphatically, "and that's why he's going. I heard him in the passage at two o'clock this morning; I'm getting into such a state of nerves that the slightest sound awakens me. He had his boots off and was creeping about in his stockings, and when I went out and switched the light on he bolted back to his room. I can't have that sort of thing going on, and I won't! it's altogether too creepy!"

Mrs. Morgan agreed.

Lydia had not been out in the evening for several days, she remembered, as she began to undress for the night. The weather had been unpleasant, and to stay in the warm, comfortable flat was no great hardship. Even if she had gone out, Jaggs would have accompanied her, she thought ironically.

And then she had a little twinge of conscience, remembering that Jaggs's presence on a memorable afternoon had saved her from destruction.

She wondered for the twentieth time what was old Jaggs's history, and where Jack had found him. Once she had been tempted to ask Jaggs himself, but the old man had fenced with the question, and had talked vaguely of having worked in the country, and she was as wise as she had been before.

But she must get rid of old Jaggs, she thought, as she switched off the light and kicked out the innumerable water-bottles, with which Mrs. Morgan, in mistaken kindness, had encumbered the bed ... old Jaggs must go ... he was a nuisance....

She woke with a start from a dreamless sleep. The clock in the hall was striking three. She realised this subconsciously. Her eyes were fixed on the window, which was open at the bottom. Mrs. Morgan had pulled it down at the top, but now it was wide open, and her heart began to thump, thump, rapidly. Jaggs! He was her first thought. She would never have believed that she could have thought of that old man with such a warm glow of thankfulness. There was nothing to be seen. The storm of the early night had passed over, and a faint light came into the room from the waning moon. And then she saw the curtains move, and opened her mouth to scream, but fear had paralysed her voice, and she lay staring at the hangings, incapable of movement or sound. As she watched the curtain she saw it move again, and a shape appeared faintly against the gloomy background.

The spell was broken. She swung herself out of the opposite side of the bed, and raced to the door, but the man was before her. Before she could scream, a big hand gripped her throat and flung her back against the rail of the bed.

Horrified she stared into the cruel face that leered down at her, and felt the grip tighten. And then as she looked into the face she saw a sudden grimace, and sensed the terror in his eyes. The hand relaxed; he bubbled something thickly and fell sideways against the bed. And now she saw. A man had come through the doorway, a tall man, with a fair beard and eyes that danced with insane joy.

He came slowly toward her, wiping on his cuff the long-handled knife that had sent her assailant to the floor.

He was mad. She knew it instinctively, and remembered in a hazy, confused way, a paragraph she had read about an escaped lunatic. She tried to dash past him to the open door, but he caught her in the crook of his left arm, and pressed her to him, towering head and shoulders over her.

"You have no right to sit on a court martial, madam," he said with uncanny politeness, and at that moment the light in the room was switched on and Jaggs appeared in the doorway, his bearded lips parted in an ugly grin, a long-barrelled pistol in his left hand.

"Drop your knife," he said, "or I'll drop you."

The mad doctor turned his head slowly and frowned at the intruder.

"Good morning, General," he said calmly. "You came in time," and he threw the knife on to the ground. "We will try her according to regulations!"

Chapter XV

A TRAGIC AFFAIR IN THE WEST END.

Mad Doctor Wounds a Burglar in a Society Woman's Bedroom.

"There was an extraordinary and tragic sequel to the escape of Dr. Thun from Norwood Asylum, particulars of which appeared in our early edition of yesterday. This morning at four o'clock, in answer to a telephone call, Detective-Sergeant Miller, accompanied by another officer, went to 84, Cavendish Mansions, a flat occupied by Mrs. Meredith, and there found and took into custody Dr. Algernon Thun, who had escaped from Norwood Asylum. In the room was also found a man named Hoggins, a person well known to the police. It appears that Hoggins had effected an entrance into Mrs. Meredith's flat, descending from the roof by means of a rope, making his way into the premises through the window of Mrs. Meredith's bedroom. Whilst there he was detected by Mrs. Meredith, who would undoubtedly have been murdered had not Dr. Thun, who, in some mysterious manner, had gained admission to the flat, intervened. In the struggle that followed the doctor, who is suffering from the delusion of persecution, severely wounded the man, who is not expected to live. He then turned his attention to the lady. Happily an old man who works at the flat, who was sleeping on the premises at the time, was roused by the sound of the struggle, and succeeded in releasing the lady from the maniacal grasp of the intruder. The wounded burglar was removed to hospital and the lunatic was taken to the police station and was afterwards sent under a strong guard to the asylum from whence he had escaped. He made a rambling statement to the police to the effect that General Foch had assisted his escape and had directed him to the home of his persecutors."

Jean Briggerland put down the paper and laughed.

"It is nothing to snigger about," growled Briggerland savagely.

"If I didn't laugh I should do something more emotional," said the girl coolly. "To think that that fool should go back and make the attempt single-handed. I never imagined that."

"Faire tells me that he's not expected to live," said Mr. Briggerland. He rubbed his bald head irritably. "I wonder if that lunatic is going to talk?"

"What does it matter if he does?" said the girl impatiently.

"You said the other day——" he began.

"The other day it mattered, my dear father. To-day nothing matters very much. I think we have got well out of it. I ignored all the lessons which my textbook teaches when I entrusted work to other hands. Jaggs," she said softly.

"Eh?" said the father.

"I'm repeating a well-beloved name," she smiled and rose, folding her serviette. "I am going for a long run in the country. Would you like to come? Mordon is very enthusiastic about the new car, the bill for which, by the way, came in this morning. Have we any money?"

"A few thousands," said her father, rubbing his chin. "Jean, we shall have to sell something unless things brighten."

Jean's lips twitched, but she said nothing.

On her way to the open road she called at Cavendish Mansions, and was neither surprised nor discomfited to discover that Jack Glover was there.

"My dear," she said, warmly clasping both the girl's hands in hers, "I was so shocked when I read the news! How terrible it must have been for you."

Lydia was looking pale, and there were dark shadows under her eyes, but she treated the matter cheerfully.

"I've just been trying to explain to Mr. Glover what happened. Unfortunately, the wonderful Jaggs is not here. He knows more about it than I, for I collapsed in the most feminine way."

"How did he get in—I mean this madman?" asked the girl.

"Through the door."

It was Jack who answered.

"It is the last way in the world a lunatic would enter a flat, isn't it? He came in with a key, and he was brought here by somebody who struck a match to make sure it was the right number."

"He might have struck the match himself," said Jean, "but you're so clever that you would not say a thing like that unless you had proof."

"We found two matches in the hall outside," said Jack, "and when Dr. Thun was searched no matches were found on him, and I have since learnt that, like most homicidal lunatics, he had a horror of fire in any form. The doctor to whom I have been talking is absolutely sure that he would not have struck the match himself. Oh, by the way, Miss Briggerland, your father met this unfortunate man. I understand he paid a visit to the asylum a few days ago?"

"Yes, he did," she answered without hesitation. "He was talking about him this morning. You see, father has been making a tour of the asylums. He is writing a book about such things. Father was horrified when he heard the man had escaped, because the doctor told him that he was a particularly dangerous lunatic. But who would have imagined he would have turned up here?"

Her big, sad eyes were fixed on Jack as she shook her head in wonder.

"If one had read that in a book one would never have believed it, would one?"

"And the man Hoggins," said Jack, who did not share her wonder. "He was by way of being an acquaintance of yours, a member of your father's club, wasn't he?"

She knit her brows.

"I don't remember the name, but if he is a very bad character," she said with a little smile, "I should say distinctly that he was a member of father's club! Poor daddy, I don't think he will ever regenerate the East End."

"I don't think he will," agreed Jack heartily. "The question is, whether the East End will ever regenerate him."

A slow smile dawned on her face.

"How unkind!" she said, mockery in her eyes now. "I wonder why you dislike him so. He is so very harmless, really. My dear," she turned to the girl with a gesture of helplessness. "I am afraid that even in this affair Mr. Glover is seeing my sinister influence!"

"You're the most un-sinister person I have ever met, Jean," laughed Lydia, "and Mr. Glover doesn't really think all these horrid things."

"Doesn't he?" said Jean softly, and Jack saw that she was shaking with laughter.

There was a certain deadly humour in the situation which tickled him too, and he grinned.

"I wish to heaven you'd get married and settle down, Miss Briggerland," he said incautiously.

It was her chance. She shook her head, the lips drooped, the eyes again grew moist with the pain she could call to them at will.

"I wish I could," she said in a tone a little above a whisper, "but, Jack, I could never marry you, never!"

She left Jack Glover bereft of speech, totally incapable of arousing so much as a moan.

Lydia, returning from escorting her visitor to the door, saw his embarrassment and checked his impulsive explanation a little coldly.

"I—I believed you when you said it wasn't true, Mr. Glover," she said, and there was a reproach in her tone for which she hated herself afterwards.

Chapter XVI

Lydia had promised to go to the theatre that night with Mrs. Cole-Mortimer, and she was glad of the excuse to leave her tragic home.

Mrs. Cole-Mortimer, who was not lavish in the matter of entertainments that cost money, had a box, and although Lydia had seen the piece before (it was in fact the very play she had attended to sketch dresses on the night of her adventure) it was a relief to sit in silence, which her hostess, with singular discretion, did not attempt to disturb.

It was during the last act that Mrs. Cole-Mortimer gave her an invitation which she accepted joyfully.

"I've got a house at Cap Martin," said Mrs. Cole-Mortimer. "It is only a tiny place, but I think you would rather like it. I hate going to the Riviera alone, so if you care to come as my guest, I shall be most happy to chaperon you. They are bringing my yacht down to Monaco, so we ought to have a really good time."

Lydia accepted the yacht and the house as she had accepted the invitation—without question. That the yacht had been chartered that morning and the house hired by telegram on the previous day, she could not be expected to guess. For all she knew, Mrs. Cole-Mortimer might be a very wealthy woman, and in her wildest dreams she did not imagine that Jean Briggerland had provided the money for both.

It had not been a delicate negotiation, because Mrs. Cole-Mortimer had the skin of a pachyderm.

Years later Lydia discovered that the woman lived on borrowed money, money which never could and never would be repaid, and which the borrower had no intention of refunding.

A hint dropped by Jean that there was somebody on the Riviera whom she desired to meet, without her father's knowledge, accompanied by the plain statement that she would pay all expenses, was quite sufficient for Mrs. Cole-Mortimer, and she had fallen in with her patron's views as readily as she had agreed to pose as a friend of Meredith's. To do her justice, she had the faculty of believing in her own invention, and she was quite satisfied that James Meredith had been a great personal friend of hers, just as she would believe that the house on the Riviera and the little steam-yacht had been procured out of her own purse.

It was harder for her, however, to explain the great system which she was going to work in Monte Carlo and which was to make everybody's fortune.

Lydia, who was no gambler and only mildly interested in games of chance, displayed so little evidence of interest in the scheme that Mrs. Cole-Mortimer groaned her despair, not knowing that she was expected to do no more than stir the soil for the crop which Jean Briggerland would plant and reap.

They went on to supper at one of the clubs, and Lydia thought with amusement of poor old Jaggs, who apparently took his job very seriously indeed.

Again her angle of vision had shifted, and her respect for the old man had overcome any annoyance his uncouth presence brought to her.

As she alighted at the door of the club she looked round, half expecting to see him. The club entrance was up a side street off Leicester Square, an ill-lit thoroughfare which favoured Mr. Jaggs's retiring methods, but there was no sign of him, and she did not wait in the drizzling night to make any closer inspection.

Mrs. Cole-Mortimer had not disguised the possibility of Jean Briggerland being at the club, and they found her with a gay party of young people, sitting in one of the recesses. Jean made a place for the girl by her side and introduced her to half a dozen people whose names Lydia did not catch, and never afterwards remembered.

Mr. Marcus Stepney, however, that sleek, dark man, who bowed over her hand and seemed as though he were going to kiss it, she had met before, and her second impression of him was even less favourable than the first.

"Do you dance?" asked Jean.

A jazz band was playing an infectious two-step. At the girl's nod Jean beckoned one of her party, a tall, handsome boy who throughout the subsequent dance babbled into Lydia's ear an incessant pæan in praise of Jean Briggerland.

Lydia was amused.

"Of course she is very beautiful," she said in answer to the interminable repetition of his question. "I think she's lovely."

"That's what I say," said the young man, whom she discovered was Lord Stoker. "The most amazingly beautiful creature on the earth, I think."

"Of course you're awfully good-looking, too," he blundered, and Lydia laughed aloud.

"But she's got enemies," said the young man viciously, "and if ever I meet that infernal cad, Glover, he'll be sorry."

The smile left Lydia's face.

"Mr. Glover is a friend of mine," she said a little quickly.

"Sorry," he mumbled, "but——"

"Does Miss Briggerland say he is so very bad?"

"Of course not. She never says a word against him really." His lordship hastened to exonerate his idol. "She just says she doesn't know how long she's going to stand his persecutions. It breaks one's heart to see how sad this—your friend makes her."

Lydia was a very thoughtful girl for the rest of the evening; she was beginning in a hazy way to see things which she had not seen before. Of course Jean never said anything against Jack Glover. And yet she had succeeded in arousing this youth to fury against the lawyer, and Lydia realised, with a sense of amazement, that Jean had also made her feel bad about Jack. And yet she had said nothing but sweet things.

When she got back to the flat that night she found that Mr. Jaggs had not been there all the evening. He came in a few minutes after her, wrapped up in an old army coat, and from his appearance she gathered that he had been standing out in the rain and sleet the whole of the evening.

"Why, Jaggs," she said impulsively, "wherever have you been?"

"Just dodging round, miss," he grunted. "Having a look at the little ducks in the pond."

"You've been outside the theatre, and you've been waiting outside Niro's Club," she said accusingly.

"Don't know it, miss," he said. "One theayter is as much like another one to me."

"You must take your things off and let Mrs. Morgan dry your clothes," she insisted, but he would not hear of this, compromising only with stripping his sodden great coat.

He disappeared into his dark room, there to ruminate upon such matters as appeared of interest to him. A bed had been placed for him, but only once had he slept on it.

After the flat grew still and the last click of the switch told that the last light had been extinguished, he opened the door softly, and, carrying a chair in his hand, he placed this gently with its back to the front door, and there he sat and dozed throughout the night. When Lydia woke the next morning he was gone as usual.

Chapter XVII

Lydia had plenty to occupy her days. The house in Curzon Street had been bought and she had been a round of furnishers, paper-hangers and fitters of all variety.

The trip to the Riviera came at the right moment. She could leave Mrs. Morgan in charge and come back to her new home, which was to be ready in two months.

Amongst other things, the problem of the watchful Mr. Jaggs would be settled automatically.

She spoke to him that night when he came.

"By the way, Mr. Jaggs, I am going to the South of France next week."

"A pretty place by all accounts," volunteered Mr. Jaggs.

"A lovely place—by all accounts," repeated Lydia with a smile. "And you're going to have a holiday, Mr. Jaggs. By the way, what am I to pay you?"

"The gentleman pays me, miss," said Mr. Jaggs with a sniff. "The lawyer gentleman."

"Well, he must continue paying you whilst I am away," said the girl. "I am very grateful to you and I want to give you a little present before I go. Is there anything you would like, Mr. Jaggs?"

Mr. Jaggs rubbed his beard, scratched his head and thought he would like a pipe.

"Though bless you, miss, I don't want any present."

"You shall have the best pipe I can buy," said the girl. "It seems very inadequate."

"I'd rather have a briar, miss," said old Jaggs mistakenly.

He was on duty until the morning she left, and although she rose early he had gone. She was disappointed, for she had not given him the handsome case of pipes she had bought, and she wanted to thank him. She felt she had acted rather meanly towards him. She owed her life to him twice.

"Didn't you see him go?" she asked Mrs. Morgan.

"No, miss," the stout housekeeper shook her head. "I was up at six and he'd gone then, but he'd left his chair in the passage—I've got an idea that's where he slept, miss, if he slept at all."

"Poor old man," said the girl gently. "I haven't been very kind to him, have I? And I do owe him such a lot."

"Maybe he'll turn up again," said Mrs. Morgan hopefully. She had the mother feeling for the old, which is one of the beauties of her class, and she regretted Lydia's absence probably as much because it would entail the disappearance of old Jaggs as for the loss of her mistress. But old Jaggs did not turn up. Lydia hoped to see him at the station, hovering on the outskirts of the crowd in his furtive way, but she was disappointed.

She left by the eleven o'clock train, joining Mrs. Cole-Mortimer on the station. That lady had arranged to spend a day in Paris, and the girl was not sorry, after a somewhat bad crossing of the English Channel, that she had not to continue her journey through the night.

The South of France was to be a revelation to her. She had no conception of the extraordinary change of climate and vegetation that could be experienced in one country.

She passed from a drizzly, bedraggled Paris into a land of sunshine and gentle breezes; from the bare sullen lands of the Champagne, into a country where flowers grew by the side of the railway, and that in February; to a semi-tropic land, fragrant with flowers, to white beaches by a blue, lazy sea and a sky over all unflecked by clouds.

It took her breath away, the beauty of it; and the sense and genial warmth of it. The trees laden with lemons, the wisteria on the walls, the white dust on the road, and the glory of the golden mimosa that scented the air with its rare and lovely perfume.

They left the train at Nice and drove along the Grande Corniche. Mrs. Cole-Mortimer had a call to make in Monte Carlo and the girl sat back in the car and drank in the beauty of this delicious spot, whilst her hostess interviewed the house agent.

Surely the place must be kept under glass. It looked so fresh and clean and free from stain.

The Casino disappointed her—it was a place of plaster and stucco, and did not seem built for permanent use.

They drove back part of the way they had come, on to the peninsula of Cap Martin and she had a glimpse of beautiful villas between the pines and queer little roads that led into mysterious dells. Presently the car drew up before a good looking house (even Mrs. Cole-Mortimer was surprised into an expression of her satisfaction at the sight of it).

Lydia, who thought that this was Mrs. Cole-Mortimer's own demesne, was delighted.

"You are lucky to have a beautiful home like this, Mrs. Cole-Mortimer," she said, "it must be heavenly living here."

The habit of wealth had not been so well acquired that she could realise that she also could have a beautiful house if she wished—she thought of that later. Nor did she expect to find Jean Briggerland there, and Mr. Briggerland too, sitting on a big cane chair on the veranda overlooking the sea and smoking a cigar of peace.

Mrs. Cole-Mortimer had been very careful to avoid all mention of Jean on the journey.

"Didn't I tell you they would be here?" she said in careless amazement. "Why, of course, dear Jean left two days before we did. It makes such a nice little party. Do you play bridge?"

Lydia did not play bridge, but was willing to be taught.

She spent the remaining hour of daylight exploring the grounds which led down to the road which fringed the sea.

She could look across at the lights already beginning to twinkle at Monte Carlo, to the white yachts lying off Monaco, and farther along the coast to a little cluster of lights that stood for Beaulieu.

"It is glorious," she said, drawing a long breath.

Mrs. Cole-Mortimer, who had accompanied her in her stroll, purred the purr of the pleased patron whose protégée has been thankful for favours received.

Dinner was a gay meal, for Jean was in her brightest mood. She had a keen sense of fun and her sly little sallies, sometimes aimed at her father, sometimes at Lydia's expense, but more often directed at people in the social world, whose names were household words, kept Lydia in a constant gurgle of laughter.

Mrs. Cole-Mortimer alone was nervous and ill at ease. She had learnt unpleasant news and was not sure whether she should tell the company or keep her secret to herself. In such dilemma, weak people take the most sensational course, and presently she dropped her bombshell.

"Celeste says that the gardener's little boy has malignant smallpox," she almost wailed.

Jean was telling a funny story to the girl who sat by her, and did not pause for so much as a second in her narrative. The effect on Mr. Briggerland was, however, wholly satisfactory to Mrs. Cole-Mortimer. He pushed back his chair and blinked at his "hostess."

"Smallpox?" he said in horror, "here—in Cap Martin? Good God, did you hear that, Jean?"

"Did I hear what?" she asked lazily, "about the gardener's little boy? Oh, yes. There has been quite an epidemic on the Italian Riviera, in fact they closed the frontier last week."

"But—but here!" spluttered Briggerland.

Lydia could only look at him in open-eyed amazement. The big man's terror was pitiably apparent. The copper skin had turned a dirty grey, his lower lip was trembling like a frightened child's.

"Why not here?" said Jean coolly, "there is nothing to be scared about. Have you been vaccinated recently?" she turned to the girl, and Lydia shook her head.

"Not since I was a baby—and then I believe the operation was not a success."

"Anyway, the child is isolated in the cottage and they are taking him to Nice to-night," said Jean. "Poor little fellow! Even his own mother has deserted him. Are you going to the Casino?" she asked.

"I don't know," replied Lydia. "I'm very tired but I should love to go."

"Take her, father—and you go, Margaret. By the time you return the infection will be removed."

"Won't you come too?" asked Lydia.

"No, I'll stay at home to-night. I turned my ankle to-day and it is rather stiff. Father!"

This time her voice was sharp, menacing almost, thought Lydia, and Mr. Briggerland made an heroic attempt to recover his self-possession.

"Cer—certainly, my dear—I shall be delighted—er—delighted."

He saw her alone whilst Lydia was changing in her lovely big dressing-room, overlooking the sea.

"Why didn't you tell me there was smallpox in Cap Martin?" he demanded fretfully.

"Because I didn't know till Margaret relieved her mind at our expense," said his daughter coolly. "I had to say something. Besides, I'd heard one of the maids say that somebody's mother had deserted him—I fitted it in. What a funk you are, father!"

"I hate the very thought of disease," he growled. "Why aren't you coming with us—there is nothing the matter with your ankle?"

"Because I prefer to stay at home."

He looked at her suspiciously.

"Jean," he said in a milder voice, "hadn't we better let up on the girl for a bit—until that lunatic doctor affair has blown over?"

She reached out and took a gold case from his waistcoat pocket, extracted a cigarette and replaced the case before she spoke.

"We can't afford to 'let up' as you call it, for a single hour. Do you realise that any day her lawyer may persuade her to make a will leaving her money to a—a home for cats, or something equally untouchable? If there was no Jack Glover we could afford to wait months. And I'm less troubled about him than I am about the man Jaggs. Father, you will be glad to learn that I am almost afraid of that freakish old man."

"Neither of them are here—" he began.

"Exactly," said Jean, "neither are here—Lydia had a telegram from him just before dinner asking if he could come to see her next week."

At this moment Lydia returned and Jean Briggerland eyed her critically.

"My dear, you look lovely," she said and kissed her.

Mr. Briggerland's nose wrinkled, as it always did when his daughter shocked him.

Chapter XVIII

Jean Briggerland waited until she heard the sound of the departing car sink to a faint hum, then she went up to her room, opened the bureau and took out a long and tightly fitting dust-coat that she wore when she was motoring. She had seen a large bottle of peroxide in Mrs. Cole-Mortimer's room. It probably contributed to the dazzling glories of Mrs. Cole-Mortimer's hair, but it was also a powerful germicide. She soaked a big silk handkerchief in a basin of water, to which she added a generous quantity of the drug, and squeezing the handkerchief nearly dry, she knotted it loosely about her neck. A rubber bathing cap she pulled down over her head, and smiled at her queer reflection in the glass. Then she found a pair of kid gloves and drew them on.

She turned out the light and went softly down the carpeted stairs. The servants were at their dinner, and she opened the front door and crossed the lawn into a belt of trees, beyond which she knew, for she had been in the house two days, was the gardener's cottage.

A dim light burnt in one of the two rooms and the window was uncurtained. She saw the bed and its tiny occupant, but nobody else was in the room. The maid had said that the mother had deserted the little sufferer, but this was not quite true. The doctor had ordered the mother into isolation, and had sent a nurse from the infection hospital to take her place. That lady, at the moment, was waiting at the end of the avenue for the ambulance to arrive.

Jean opened the door and stepped in, pulling up the saturated handkerchief until it covered nose and mouth. The place was deserted, and, without a moment's hesitation, she lifted the child, wrapped a blanket about it and crossed the lawn again. She went quietly up the stairs straight to Lydia's room. There was enough light from the dressing-room to see the bed, and unwrapping the blanket she pulled back the covers and laid him gently in the bed. The child was unconscious. The hideous marks of the disease had developed with remarkable rapidity and he made no sound.

She sat down in a chair, waiting. Her almost inhuman calm was not ruffled by so much as a second's apprehension. She had provided for every contingency and was ready with a complete explanation, whatever happened.

Half an hour passed, and then rising, she wrapped the child in the blanket and carried him back to the cottage. She heard the purr of the motor and footsteps as she flitted back through the trees.

First she went to Lydia's room and straightened the bed, spraying the room with the faint perfume which she found on the dressing table; then she went back again into the garden, stripped off the dust coat, cap and handkerchief, rolling them into a bundle, which she thrust through the bars of an open window which she knew ventilated a cellar. Last of all she stripped her gloves and sent them after the bundle.

She heard the voices of the nurse and attendant as they carried the child to the ambulance.

"Poor little kid," she murmured, "I hope he gets better."

And, strangely enough, she meant it.

It had been a thrilling evening for Lydia, and she returned to the house at Cap Martin very tired, but very happy. She was seeing a new world, a world the like of which had never been revealed to her, and though she could have slept, and her head did nod in the car, she roused herself to talk it all over again with the sympathetic Jean.

Mrs. Cole-Mortimer retired early. Mr. Briggerland had gone up to bed the moment he returned, and Lydia would have been glad to have ended her conversation; since her head reeled with weariness, but Jean was very talkative, until——

"My dear, if I don't go to bed I shall sleep on the table," smiled Lydia, rising and suppressing a yawn.

"I'm so sorry," said the penitent Jean.

She accompanied the girl upstairs, her arm about her waist, and left her at the door of her dressing-room.

A maid had laid out her night things on a big settee (a little to Lydia's surprise) and she undressed quickly.

She opened the door of her bedroom, her hand was on a switch, when she was conscious of a faint and not unpleasant odour. It was a clean, pungent smell. "Disinfectant," said her brain mechanically. She turned on the light, wondering where it came from. And then as she crossed the room she came in sight of her bed and stopped, for it was saturated with water—water that dropped from the hanging coverlet, and made little pools on the floor. From the head of the bed to the foot there was not one dry place. Whosoever had done the work was thorough. Blankets, sheets, pillows were soddened, and from the soaked mass came a faint acrid aroma which she recognised, even before she saw on the floor an empty bottle labelled "Peroxide of Hydrogen."

She could only stand and stare. It was too late to arouse the household, and she remembered that there was a very comfortable settee in the dressing-room with a rug and a pillow, and she went back.

A few minutes later she was fast asleep. Not so Miss Briggerland, who was sitting up in bed, a cigarette between her lips, a heavy volume on her knees, reading:

"Such malignant cases are almost without exception rapidly fatal, sometimes so early that no sign of the characteristic symptoms appear at all," she read and, dropping the book on the floor, extinguished her cigarette on an alabaster tray, and settled herself to sleep. She was dozing when she remembered that she had forgotten to say her prayers.

"Oh, damn!" said Jean, getting out reluctantly to kneel on the cold floor by the side of the bed.

Chapter XIX

Her maid woke Jean Briggerland at eight o'clock the next morning.

"Oh, miss," she said, as she drew up the table for the chocolate, "have you heard about Mrs. Meredith?"

Jean blinked open her eyes, slipped into her dressing jacket and sat up with a yawn.

"Have I heard about Mrs. Meredith? Many times," she said.

"But what somebody did last night, miss?"

Jean was wide awake now.

"What has happened to Mrs. Meredith?" she asked.

"Why, miss, somebody played a practical joke on her. Her bed's sopping."

"Sopping?" frowned the girl.

"Yes, miss," the woman nodded. "They must have poured buckets of water over it, and used up all Mrs. Cole-Mortimer's peroxide, what she uses for keeping her hands nice."

Jean swung out of her bed and sat looking down at her tiny white feet.

"Where did Mrs. Meredith sleep? Why didn't she wake us up?"

"She slept in the dressing-room, miss. I don't suppose the young lady liked making a fuss."

"Who did it?"

"I don't know who did it. It's a silly kind of practical joke, and I know none of the maids would have dared, not the French ones."

Jean put her feet into her slippers, exchanged her jacket for a gown, and went on a tour of inspection.

Lydia was dressing in her room, and the sound of her fresh, young voice, as she carolled out of sheer love of life, came to the girl before she turned into the room.

One glance at the bed was sufficient. It was still wet, and the empty peroxide bottle told its own story.

Jean glanced at it thoughtfully as she crossed into the dressing-room.

"Whatever happened last night, Lydia?"

Lydia turned at the voice.

"Oh, the bed you mean," she made a little face. "Heaven knows. It occurred to me this morning that some person, out of mistaken kindness, had started to disinfect the room—it was only this morning that I recalled the little boy who was ill—and had overdone it."

"They've certainly overdone it," said Jean grimly. "I wonder what poor Mrs. Cole-Mortimer will say. You haven't the slightest idea———"

"Not the slightest idea," said Lydia, answering the unspoken question.

"I'll see Mrs. Cole-Mortimer and get her to change your bed—there's another room you could have," suggested Jean.

She went back to her own apartment, bathed and dressed leisurely.

She found her father in the garden reading the *Nicoise*, under the shade of a bush, for the sun was not warm, but at that hour, blinding.

"I've changed my plans," she said without preliminary.

He looked up over his glasses.

"I didn't know you had any," he said with heavy humour.

"I intended going back to London and taking you with me," she said unexpectedly.

"Back to London?" he said incredulously. "I thought you were staying on for a month."

"I probably shall now," she said, pulling up a basket-chair and sitting by his side. "Give me a cigarette."

"You're smoking a lot lately," he said as he handed his case to her.

"I know I am."

"Have your nerves gone wrong?"

She looked at him out of the corner of her eye and her lips curled.

"It wouldn't be remarkable if I inherited a little of your yellow streak," she said coolly, and he growled something under his breath. "No, my nerves are all right, but a cigarette helps me to think."

"A yellow streak, have I?" Mr. Briggerland was annoyed. "And I've been out since five o'clock this morning——" he stopped.

"Doing—what?" she asked curiously.

"Never mind," he said with a lofty gesture.

Thus they sat, busy with their own thoughts, for a quarter of an hour.

"Jean."

"Yes," she said without turning her head.

"Don't you think we'd better give this up and get back to London? Lord Stoker is pretty keen on you."

"I'm not pretty keen on him," she said decidedly. "He has his regimental pay and £500 a year, two estates, mortgaged, no brains and a title—what is the use of his title to me? As much use as a coat of paint! Beside which, I am essentially democratic."

He chuckled, and there was another silence.

"Do you think the lawyer is keen on the girl?"

"Jack Glover?"

Mr. Briggerland nodded.

"I imagine he is," said Jean thoughtfully. "I like Jack—he's clever. He has all the moral qualities which one admires so much in the abstract. I could love Jack myself."

"Could he love you?" bantered her father.

"He couldn't," she said shortly. "Jack would be a happy man if he saw me stand in Jim Meredith's place in the Old Bailey. No, I have no illusion about Jack's affections."

"He's after Lydia's money I suppose," said Mr. Briggerland, stroking his bald head.

"Don't be a fool," was the calm reply. "That kind of man doesn't worry about a girl's money. I wish Lydia was dead," she added without malice. "It would make things so easy and smooth."

Her father swallowed something.

"You shock me sometimes, Jean," he said, a statement which amused her.

"You're such a half-and-half man," she said with a note of contempt in her voice. "You were quite willing to benefit by Jim Meredith's death; you killed him as cold-bloodedly as you killed poor little Bulford, and yet you must whine and snivel whenever your deeds are put into plain language. What does it matter if Lydia dies now or in fifty years time?" she asked. "It would be different if she were immortal. You people attach so much importance to human life—the ancients, and the Japanese amongst the modern, are the only people who have the matter in true perspective. It is no more cruel to kill a human being than it is to cut the throat of a pig to provide you with bacon. There's hardly a dish at your table which doesn't represent wilful murder, and yet you never think of it, but because the man animal can talk and dresses himself or herself in queer animal and vegetable fabrics, and decorates the body with bits of metal and pieces of glittering quartz, you give its life a value which you deny to the cattle within your gates! Killing is a matter of expediency. Permissible if you call it war, terrible if you call it murder. To me it is just killing. If you are caught in the act of killing they kill you, and people say it is right to do so. The sacredness of human life is a slogan invented by cowards who fear death—as you do."

"Don't you, Jean?" he asked in a hushed voice.

"I fear life without money," she said quietly. "I fear long days of work for a callous, leering employer, and strap-hanging in a crowded tube on my way home to one miserable room and the cold mutton of yesterday. I fear getting up and making my own bed and washing my own handkerchiefs and blouses, and renovating last year's hats to make them look like this year's. I fear a poor husband and a procession of children, and doing the housework with an incompetent maid, or maybe without any at all. Those are the things I fear, Mr. Briggerland."

She dusted the ash from her dress and got up.

"I haven't forgotten the life we lived at Ealing," she said significantly.

She looked across the bay to Monte Carlo glittering in the morning sunlight, to the green-capped head of Cap-d'Ail, to Beaulieu, a jewel set in greystone and shook her head.

"'It is written'," she quoted sombrely and left him in the midst of the question he was asking. She strolled back to the house and joined Lydia who was looking radiantly beautiful in a new dress of silver grey charmeuse.

Chapter XX

"Have you solved the mystery of the submerged bed?" smiled Jean.

Lydia laughed.

"I'm not probing too deeply into the matter," she said. "Poor Mrs. Cole-Mortimer was terribly upset."

"She would be," said Jean. "It was her own eiderdown!"

This was the first hint Lydia had received that the house was rented furnished.

They drove into Nice that morning, and Lydia, remembering Jack Glover's remarks, looked closely at the chauffeur, and was startled to see a resemblance between him and the man who had driven the taxicab on the night she had been carried off from the theatre. It is true that the taxi-driver had a moustache and that this man was clean-shaven, and moreover, had tiny side whiskers, but there was a resemblance.

"Have you had your driver long?" she asked as they were running through Monte Carlo, along the sea road.

"Mordon? Yes, we have had him six or seven years," said Jean carelessly. "He drives us when we are on the continent, you know. He speaks French perfectly and is an excellent driver. Father has tried to persuade him to come to England, but he hates London—he was telling me the other day that he hadn't been there for ten years."

That disposed of the resemblance, thought Lydia, and yet—she could remember his voice, she thought, and when they alighted on the Promenade des Anglaise she spoke to him. He replied in French, and it is impossible to detect points of resemblance in a voice that speaks one language and the same voice when it speaks another.

The promenade was crowded with saunterers. A band was playing by the jetty and although the wind was colder than it had been at Cap Martin the sun was warm enough to necessitate the opening of a parasol.

It was a race week, and the two girls lunched at the Negrito. They were in the midst of their meal when a man came toward them and Lydia recognised Mr. Marcus Stepney. This dark, suave man was no favourite of hers, though why she could not have explained. His manners were always perfect and, towards her, deferential.

As usual, he was dressed with the precision of a fashion-plate. Mr. Marcus Stepney was a man, a considerable portion of whose time was taken up every morning by the choice of cravats and socks and shirts. Though Lydia did not know this, his smartness, plus a certain dexterity with cards, was his stock in trade. No breath of scandal had touched him, he moved in a good set and was always at the right place at the proper season.

When Aix was full he was certain to be found at the Palace, in the Deauville week you would find him at the Casino punting mildly at the baccarat table. And after the rooms were closed, and even the Sports Club at Monte Carlo had shut its doors, there was always a little game to be had in the hotels and in Marcus Stepney's private sitting-room.

And it cannot be denied that Mr. Stepney was lucky. He won sufficient at these out-of-hour games to support him nobly through the trials and vicissitudes which the public tables inflict upon their votaries.

"Going to the races," he said, "how very fortunate! Will you come along with me? I can give you three good winners."

"I have no money to gamble," said Jean, "I am a poor woman. Lydia, who is rolling in wealth, can afford to take your tips, Marcus."

Marcus looked at Lydia with a speculative eye.

"If you haven't any money with you, don't worry. I have plenty and you can pay me afterwards. I could make you a million francs to-day."

"Thank you," said Jean coolly, "but Mrs. Meredith does not bet so heavily."

Her tone was a clear intimation to the man of wits that he was impinging upon somebody else's preserves and he grinned amiably.

Nevertheless, it was a profitable afternoon for Lydia. She came back to Cap Martin twenty thousand francs richer than she had been when she started off.

"Lydia's had a lot of luck she tells me," said Mr. Briggerland.

"Yes. She won about five hundred pounds," said his daughter. "Marcus was laying ground bait. She did not know what horses he had backed until after the race was run, when he invariably appeared with a few *mille* notes and Lydia's pleasure was pathetic. Of course she didn't win anything. The twenty thousand francs was a sprat—he's coming to-night to see how the whales are blowing!"

Mr. Marcus Stepney arrived punctually, and, to Mr. Briggerland's disgust, was dressed for dinner, a fact which necessitated the older man's hurried retreat and reappearance in conventional evening wear.

Marcus Stepney's behaviour at dinner was faultless. He devoted himself in the main to Mrs. Cole-Mortimer and Jean, who apparently never looked at him and yet observed his every movement, knew that he was merely waiting his opportunity.

It came when the dinner was over and the party adjourned to the big stoep facing the sea. The night was chilly and Mr. Stepney found wraps and furs for the ladies, and so manoeuvred the arrangement of the chairs that Lydia and he were detached from the remainder of the party, not by any great distance, but sufficient, as the experienced Marcus knew, to remove a murmured conversation from the sharpest eavesdropper.

Jean, who was carrying on a three-cornered conversation with her father and Mrs. Cole-Mortimer, did not stir, until she saw, by the light of a shaded lamp in the roof, the dark head of Mr. Marcus Stepney droop more confidently towards his companion. Then she rose and strolled across.

Marcus did not curse her because he did not express his inmost thoughts aloud.

He gave her his chair and pulled another forward.

"Does Miss Briggerland know?" asked Lydia.

"No," said Mr. Stepney pleasantly.

"May I tell her?"

"Of course."

"Mr. Stepney has been telling me about a wonderful racing coup to be made to-morrow. Isn't it rather thrilling, Jean? He says it will be quite possible for me to make five million francs without any risk at all."

"Except the risk of a million, I suppose," smiled Jean. "Well, are you going to do it?" Lydia shook her head.

"I haven't a million francs in France, for one thing," she said, "and I wouldn't risk it if I had."

And Jean smiled again at the discomfiture which Mr. Marcus Stepney strove manfully to hide.

Later she took his arm and led him into the garden.

"Marcus," she said when they were out of range of the house, "I think you are several kinds of a fool."

"Why?" asked the other, who was not in the best humour.

"It was so crude," she said scornfully, "so cheap and confidence-trickish. A miserable million francs—twenty thousand pounds. Apart from the fact that your name would be mud in London if it were known that you had robbed a girl——"

"There's no question of robbery," he said hotly, "I tell you Valdau is a certainty for the Prix."

"It would not be a certainty if her money were on," said Jean dryly. "It would finish an artistic second and you would be full of apologies, and poor Lydia would be a million francs to the bad. No, Marcus, that is cheap."

"I'm nearly broke," he said shortly.

He made no disguise of his profession, nor of his nefarious plan.

Between the two there was a queer kind of camaraderie. Though he may not have been privy to the more tremendous of her crimes, yet he seemed to accept her as one of those who lived on the frontiers of illegality.

"I was thinking about you, as you sat there telling her the story," said Jean thoughtfully. "Marcus, why don't you marry her?"

He stopped in his stride and looked down at the girl.

"Marry her, Jean; are you mad? She wouldn't marry me."

"Why not?" she asked. "Of course she'd marry you, you silly fool, if you went the right way about it."

He was silent.

"She is worth six hundred thousand pounds, and I happen to know that she has nearly two hundred thousand pounds in cash on deposit at the bank," said Jean.

"Why do you want me to marry her?" he asked significantly. "Is there a rake-off for you?"

"A big rake-off," she said. "The two hundred thousand on deposit should be easily get-at-able, Marcus, and she'd even give you more——"

"Why?" he asked.

"To agree to a separation," she said coolly. "I know you. No woman could live very long with you and preserve her reason."

He chuckled.

"And I'm to hand it all over to you?"

"Oh no," she corrected. "I'm not greedy. It is my experience that the greedy people get into bad trouble. The man or woman who 'wants it all' usually gets the dressing-case the 'all' was kept in. No, I'd like to take a half."

He sat down on a garden seat and she followed his example.

"What is there to be?" he asked. "An agreement between you and me? Something signed and sealed and delivered, eh?"

Her sad eyes caught his and held them.

"I trust you, Marcus," she said softly. "If I help you in this—and I will if you will do all that I tell you to do—I will trust you to give me my share."

Mr. Marcus Stepney fingered his collar a little importantly.

"I've never let a pal down in my life," he said with a cough. "I'm as straight as they make 'em, to people who play the game with me."

"And you are wise, so far as I am concerned," said the gentle Jean. "For if you double-crossed me, I should hand the police the name and address of your other wife who is still living."

His jaw dropped.

"Wha—what?" he stammered.

"Let us join the ladies," mocked Jean, as she rose and put her arm in his.

It pleased her immensely to feel this big man trembling.

Chapter XXI

It seemed to Lydia that she had been abroad for years, though in reality she had been three days in Cap Martin, when Mr. Marcus Stepney became a regular caller.

Even the most objectionable people improve on acquaintance, and give the lie to first impressions.

Mr. Stepney never bored her. He had an inexhaustible store of anecdotes and reminiscences, none of which was in the slightest degree offensive. He was something of a sportsman, too, and he called by arrangement the next morning, after his introduction to the Cap Martin household, and conducting her to a sheltered cove, containing two bathing huts, he introduced her to the exhilarating Mediterranean.

Sea bathing is not permitted in Monte Carlo until May, and the water was much colder than Lydia had expected. They swam out to a floating platform when Mr. Briggerland and Jean put in an appearance. Jean had come straight from the house in her bathing-gown, over which she wore a light wrap. Lydia watched her with amazement, for the girl was an expert swimmer. She could dive from almost any height and could remain under water an alarming time.

"I never thought you had so much energy and strength in your little body," said Lydia, as Jean, with a shriek of enjoyment, drew herself on the raft and wiped the water from her eyes.

"There's a man up there looking at us through glasses," said Briggerland suddenly. "I saw the flash of the sun on them."

He pointed to the rising ground beyond the seashore, but they could see nothing.

Presently there was a glitter of light amongst the green, and Lydia pointed.

"I thought that sort of thing was never done except in comic newspapers," she said, but Jean did not smile. Her eyes were focused on the point where the unseen observer lay or sat, and she shaded her eyes.

"Some visitor from Monte Carlo, I expect. People at Cap Martin are much too respectable to do anything so vulgar."

Mr. Briggerland, at a glance from his daughter, slipped into the water, and with strong heavy strokes, made his way to the shore.

"Father is going to investigate," said Jean, "and the water really is the warmest place," and with that she fell sideways into the blue sea like a seal, dived down into its depths, and presently Lydia saw her walking along the white floor of the ocean, her little hands keeping up an almost imperceptible motion. Presently she shot up again, shook her head and looked round, only to dive again.

In the meantime, though Lydia, who was fascinated by the manœuvre of the girl, did not notice the fact, Mr. Briggerland had reached the shore, pulled on a pair of rubber shoes, and with his mackintosh buttoned over his bathing dress, had begun to climb through the underbrush towards the spot where the glasses had glistened. When Lydia looked up he had disappeared.

"Where is your father?" she asked the girl.

"He went into the bushes." Mr. Stepney volunteered the information. "I suppose he's looking for the Paul Pry."

Mr. Stepney had been unusually glum and silent, for he was piqued by the tactless appearance of the Briggerlands.

"Come into the water, Marcus," said Jean peremptorily, as she put her foot against the edge of the raft, and pushed herself backward, "I want to see Mrs. Meredith dive."

"Me?" said Lydia in surprise. "Good heavens, no! After watching you I don't intend making an exhibition of myself."

"I want to show you the proper way to dive," said Jean. "Stand up on the edge of the raft."

Lydia obeyed.

"Straight up," said Jean. "Now put both your arms out wide. Now———"

There was a sharp crack from the shore; something whistled past Lydia's head, struck an upright post, splintering the edge, and with a whine went ricochetting into the sea.

Lydia's face went white.

"What—what was that?" she gasped. She had hardly spoken before there was another shot. This time the bullet must have gone very high, and immediately afterwards came a yell of pain from the shore.

Jean did not wait. She struck out for the beach, swimming furiously. It was not the shot, but the cry which had alarmed her, and without waiting to put on coat or sandals, she ran up the little road where her father had gone, following the path through the undergrowth. Presently she came to a grassy plot, in the centre of which two tall pines grew side by side, and lying against one of the trees was the huddled figure of Briggerland. She turned him over. He was breathing heavily and was unconscious. An ugly wound gaped at the back of his head, and his mackintosh and bathing dress were smothered with blood.

She looked round quickly for his assailant, but there was nobody in sight, and nothing to indicate the presence of a third person but two shining brass cartridges which lay on the grass.

Chapter XXII

Lydia Meredith only remembered swooning twice in her life, and both these occasions had happened within a few weeks.

She never felt quite so unprepared to carry on as she did when, with an effort she threw herself into the water at Marcus Stepney's side and swam slowly toward the shore.

She dare not let her mind dwell upon the narrowness of her escape. Whoever had fired that shot had done so deliberately, and with the intention of killing her. She had felt the wind of the bullet in her face.

"What do you suppose it was?" asked Marcus Stepney as he assisted her up the beach. "Do you think it was soldiers practising?"

She shook her head.

"Oh," said Mr. Stepney thoughtfully, and then: "If you don't mind, I'll run up and see what has happened."

He wrapped himself in the dressing gown he had brought with him, and followed Jean's trail, coming up with her as Mr. Briggerland opened his eyes and stared round.

"Help me to hold him, Marcus," said Jean.

"Wait a moment," said Mr. Stepney, feeling in his pocket and producing a silk handkerchief, "bandage him with that."

She shook her head.

"He's lost all the blood he's going to lose," she said quietly, "and I don't think there's a fracture. I felt the skull very carefully with my finger."

Mr. Stepney shivered.

"Hullo," said Briggerland drowsily, "Gee, he gave me a whack!"

"Who did it?" asked the girl.

Mr. Briggerland shook his head and winced with the pain of it.

"I don't know," he moaned. "Help me up, Stepney."

With the man's assistance he rose unsteadily to his feet.

"What happened?" asked Stepney.

"Don't ask him any questions now," said the girl sharply. "Help him back to the house."

A doctor was summoned and stitched the wound. He gave an encouraging report, and was not too inquisitive as to how the injury had occurred. Foreign visitors get extraordinary things in the regions of Monte Carlo, and medical men lose nothing by their discretion.

It was not until that afternoon, propped up with pillows in a chair, the centre of a sympathetic audience, that Mr. Briggerland told his story.

"I had a feeling that something was wrong," he said, "and I went up to investigate. I heard a shot fired, almost within a few yards of me, and dashing through the bushes, I saw the fellow taking aim for the second time, and seized him. You remember the second shot went high."

"What sort of a man was he?" asked Stepney.

"He was an Italian, I should think," answered Mr. Briggerland. "At any rate, he caught me an awful whack with the back of his rifle, and I knew no more until Jean found me."

"Do you think he was firing at me?" asked Lydia in horror.

"I am certain of it," said Briggerland. "I realised it the moment I saw the fellow."

"How am I to thank you?" said the girl impulsively. "Really, it was wonderful of you to tackle an armed man with your bare hands."

Mr. Briggerland closed his eyes and sighed.

"It was nothing," he said modestly.

Before dinner he and his daughter were left alone for the first time since the accident.

"What happened?" she asked.

"It was going to be a little surprise for you," he said. "A little scheme of my own, my dear; you're always calling me a funk, and I wanted to prove——"

"What happened?" she asked tersely.

"Well, I went out yesterday morning and fixed it all. I bought the rifle, an old English rifle, at Amiens from a peasant. I thought it might come in handy, especially as the man threw in a packet of ammunition. Yesterday morning, lying awake before daybreak, I thought it out. I went up to the hill—the land belongs to an empty house, by the way—and I located the spot, put the rifle where I could find it easily, and fixed a pair of glass goggles on to one of the bushes, where the sun would catch it. The whole scheme was not without its merit as a piece of strategy, my dear," he said complacently.

"And then———?" she said.

"I thought we'd go bathing yesterday, but we didn't, but to-day—it was a long time before anybody spotted the glasses, but once I had the excuse for going ashore and investigating, the rest was easy."

She nodded.

"So that was why you asked me to keep her on the raft, and make her stand up?"

He nodded.

"Well———?" she demanded.

"I went up to the spot, got the rifle and took aim. I've always been a pretty good shot———"

"You didn't advertise it to-day," she said sardonically. "Then I suppose somebody hit you on the head?"

He nodded and made a grimace, but any movement of his injured cranium was excessively painful.

"Who was it?" she asked.

He shrugged his shoulders.

"Don't ask fool questions," he said petulantly. "I know nothing. I didn't even feel the blow. I just remember taking aim, and then everything went dark."

"And how would you have explained it all, supposing you had succeeded?"

"That was easy," he said. "I should have said that I went in search of the man we had seen, I heard a shot and rushed forward and found nothing but the rifle."

She was silent, pinching her lips absently.

"And you took the risk of some peasant or visitor seeing you—took the risk of bringing the police to the spot and turning what might have easily been a case of accidental death into an obvious case of wilful murder. I think you called yourself a strategist," she asked politely.

"I did my best," he growled.

"Well, don't do it again, father," she said. "Your foolhardiness appals me, and heaven knows, I never expected that I should be in a position to call you foolhardy."

And with this she left him to bask in the hero-worship which the approaching Mrs. Cole-Mortimer would lavish upon him.

The "accident" kept them at home that night, and Lydia was not sorry. A settee is not a very comfortable sleeping place, and she was ready for a real bed that night. Mr. Stepney found her yawning surreptitiously, and went home early in disgust.

The night was warmer than the morning had been. The *Föhn* wind was blowing and she found her room with its radiator a little oppressive. She opened the long French windows, and stepped out on to the balcony. The last quarter of the moon was high in the sky, and though the light was faint, it gave shadows to trees and an eerie illumination to the lawn.

She leant her arms on the rail and looked across the sea to the lights of Monte Carlo glistening in the purple night. Her eyes wandered idly to the grounds and she started. She could have sworn she had seen a figure moving in the shadow of the tree, nor was she mistaken.

Presently it left the tree belt, and stepped cautiously across the lawn, halting now and again to look around. She thought at first that it was Marcus Stepney who had returned, but something about the walk of the man seemed familiar. Presently he stopped directly under the balcony and looked up and she uttered an exclamation, as the faint light revealed the iron-grey hair and the grisly eyebrows of the intruder.

"All right, miss," he said in a hoarse whisper, "it's only old Jaggs."

"What are you doing?" she answered in the same tone.

"Just lookin' round," he said, "just lookin' round," and limped again into the darkness.

Chapter XXIII

So old Jaggs was in Monte Carlo! Whatever was he doing, and how was he getting on with these people who spoke nothing but French, she wondered! She had something to think about before she went to sleep.

She opened her eyes singularly awake as the dawn was coming up over the grey sea. She looked at her watch; it was a quarter to six. Why she had wakened so thoroughly she could not tell, but remembered with a little shiver another occasion she had wakened, this time before the dawn, to face death in a most terrifying shape.

She got up out of bed, put on a heavy coat and opened the wire doors that led to the balcony. The morning was colder than she imagined, and she was glad to retreat to the neighbourhood of the warm radiator.

The fresh clean hours of the dawn, when the mind is clear, and there is neither sound nor movement to distract the thoughts, are favourable to sane thinking.

Lydia reviewed the past few weeks in her life, and realised, for the first time, the miracle which had happened. It was like a legend of old—the slave had been lifted from the king's anteroom—the struggling artist was now a rich woman. She twiddled the gold ring on her hand absent-mindedly—and she was married ... and a widow! She had an uncomfortable feeling that, in spite of her riches, she had not yet found her niche. She was an odd quantity, as yet. The Cole-Mortimers and the Briggerlands did not belong to her ideal world, and she could find no place where she fitted.

She tried, in this state of mind so favourable to the consideration of such a problem, to analyse Jack Glover's antagonism toward Jean Briggerland and her father.

It seemed unnatural that a healthy young man should maintain so bitter a feud with a girl whose beauty was almost of a transcendant quality and all because she had rejected him.

Jack Glover was a public school boy, a man with a keen sense of honour. She could not imagine him being guilty of a mean action. And such men did not pursue vendettas without good reason. If they were rejected by a woman, they accepted their *congé* with a good grace, and it was almost unthinkable that Jack should have no other reason for his hatred. Yet she could not bring herself even to consider the possibility that the reason was the one he had advanced. She came again to the dead end of conjecture. She could believe in Jack's judgment up to a point—beyond that she could not go.

She had her bath, dressed, and was in the garden when the eastern horizon was golden with the light of the rising sun. Nobody was about, the most energetic of the servants had not yet risen, and she strolled through the avenue to the main road. As she stood there looking up and down a man came out from the trees that fringed the road and began walking rapidly in the direction of Monte Carlo.

"Mr. Jaggs!" she called.

He took no notice, but seemed to increase his limping pace, and after a moment's hesitation, she went flying down the road after him. He turned at the sound of her footsteps and in his furtive way drew into the shadow of a bush. He looked more than usually grimy; on his hands were an odd pair of gloves and a soft slouch hat that had seen better days, covered his head.

"Good-morning, miss," he wheezed.

"Why were you running away, Mr. Jaggs?" she asked, a little out of breath.

"Not runnin' away, miss," he said, glancing at her sharply from under his heavy white eyebrows. "Just havin' a look round!"

"Do you spend all your nights looking round?" she smiled at him.

"Yes, miss."

At that moment a cyclist gendarme came into view. He slowed down as he approached the two and dismounted.

"Good morning, madame," he said politely, and then looking at the man, "is this man in your employ? I have seen him coming out of your house every morning?"

"Oh, yes," said Lydia hastily, "he's my——"

She was at a loss to describe him, but old Jaggs saved her the trouble.

"I'm madame's courier," he said, and to Lydia's amazement he spoke in perfect French, "I am also the watchman of the house."

"Yes, yes," said Lydia, after she had recovered from her surprise. "M'sieur is the watchman, also."

"*Bien*, madame," said the gendarme. "Forgive my asking, but we have so many strangers here."

They watched the gendarme out of sight. Then old Jaggs chuckled.

"Pretty good French, miss, wasn't it?" he said, and without another word, turned and limped in the trail of the police.

She looked after him in bewilderment. So he spent every night in the grounds, or somewhere about the house? The knowledge gave her a queer sense of comfort and safety.

When she went back to the villa she found the servants were up. Jean did not put in an appearance until breakfast, and Lydia had an opportunity of talking to the French housekeeper whom Mrs. Cole-Mortimer had engaged when she took the villa. From her she learnt a bit of news, which she passed on to Jean almost as soon as she put in an appearance.

"The gardener's little boy is going to get well, Jean."

Jean nodded.

"I know," she said. "I telephoned to the hospital yesterday."

It was so unlike her conception of the girl, that Lydia stared.

"The mother is in isolation," Lydia went on, "and Madame Souviet says that the poor woman has no money and no friends. I thought of going down to the hospital to-day to see if I could do anything for her."

"You'd better not, my dear," warned Mrs. Cole-Mortimer nervously. "Let us be thankful we've got the little brat out of the neighbourhood without our catching the disease. One doesn't want to seek trouble. Keep away from the hospital."

"Rubbish!" said Jean briskly. "If Lydia wants to go, there is no reason why she shouldn't. The isolation people are never allowed to come into contact with visitors, so there is really no danger."

"I agree with Mrs. Cole-Mortimer," grumbled Briggerland. "It is very foolish to ask for trouble. You take my advice, my dear, and keep away."

"I had a talk with a gendarme this morning," said Lydia to change the subject. "When he stopped and got off his bicycle I thought he was going to speak about the shooting. I suppose it was reported to the police?"

"Er—yes," said Mr. Briggerland, not looking up from his plate, "of course. Have you been into Monte Carlo?"

Lydia shook her head.

"No, I couldn't sleep, and I was taking a walk along the road when he passed." She said nothing about Mr. Jaggs. "The police at Monaco are very sociable."

Mr. Briggerland sniffed.

"Very," he said.

"Have they any theories?" she asked. In her innocence she was persisting in a subject which was wholly distasteful to Mr. Briggerland. "About the shooting I mean?"

"Yes, they have theories, but my dear, I should advise you not to discuss the matter with the police. The fact is," invented Mr. Briggerland, "I told them that you were unaware of the fact that you had been shot at, and if you discussed it with the police, you would make me look rather foolish."

When Lydia and Mrs. Cole-Mortimer had gone, Jean seized an opportunity which the absence of the maid offered.

"I hope you are beginning to see how perfectly insane your scheme was," she said. "You have to support your act with a whole series of bungling lies. Possibly Marcus, like a fool, has mentioned it in Monte Carlo, and we shall have the detectives out here asking why you have not reported the matter."

"If I were as clever as you———" he growled.

"You're not," said Jean, rolling her serviette. "You're the most un-clever man I know."

Chapter XXIV

Lydia went up to her bedroom to put away her clothes and found the maid making the bed.

"Oh, madame," said the girl, "I forgot to speak to you about a matter—I hope madame will not be angry."

"I'm hardly likely to be angry on a morning like this," said Lydia.

"It is because of this matter," said the girl. She groped in her pocket and brought out a small shining object, and Lydia took it from her hand.

"This matter" was a tiny silver cross, so small that a five-franc piece would have covered it easily. It was brightly polished and apparently had seen service.

"When we took your bed, after the atrocious and mysterious happening," said the maid rapidly, "this was found in the sheets. It was not thought that it could possibly be madame's, because it was so poor, until this morning when it was suggested that it might be a souvenir that madame values."

"You found it in the sheets?" asked Lydia in surprise.

"Yes, madame."

"It doesn't belong to me," said Lydia. "Perhaps it belongs to Madame Cole-Mortimer. I will show it to her."

Mrs. Cole-Mortimer was a devout Catholic and it might easily be some cherished keep-sake of hers.

The girl carried the cross to the window; an "X" had been scrawled by some sharp-pointed instrument at the junction of the bars. There was no other mark to identify the trinket.

She put the cross in her bag, and when she saw Mrs. Cole-Mortimer again she forgot to ask her about it.

The car drove her into Nice alone. Jean did not feel inclined to make the journey and Lydia rather enjoyed the solitude.

The isolation hospital was at the top of the hill and she found some difficulty in obtaining admission at this hour. The arrival of the chief medical officer, however, saved her from making the journey in vain. The report he gave about the child was very satisfactory; the mother was in the isolation ward.

"Can she be seen?"

"Yes, madame," said the urbane Frenchman in charge. "You understand, you will not be able to get near her? It will be rather like interviewing a prisoner, for she will be behind one set of bars and you behind another."

Lydia was taken to a room which was, she imagined, very much like a room in which prisoners interviewed their distressed relations. There were not exactly bars, but two large mesh nets of steel separated the visitor from the patient under observation. After a time a nun brought in the gardener's wife, a tall, gaunt woman, who was a native of Marseilles, and spoke the confusing patois of that city with great rapidity. It was some time before Lydia could accustom her ear to the queer dialect.

Her boy was getting well, she said, but she herself was in terrible trouble. She had no money for the extra food she required. Her husband who was away in Paris when the child had been taken, had not troubled to write to her. It was terrible being in a place amongst other fever cases, and she was certain that her days were numbered....

Lydia pushed a five-hundred franc note through the grating to the nun, to settle her material needs.

"And, oh, madame," wailed the gardener's wife, "my poor little boy has lost the gift of the Reverend Mother of San Surplice! His own cross which has been blessed by his holiness the Pope! It is because I left his cross in his little shirt that he is getting better, but now it is lost and I am sure these thieving doctors have taken it."

"A cross?" said Lydia. "What sort of a cross?"

"It was a silver cross, madame; the value in money was nothing—it was priceless. Little Xavier——"

"Xavier?" repeated Lydia, remembering the "X" on the trinket that had been found in her bed. "Wait a moment, madame." She opened her bag and took out the tiny silver symbol, and at the sight of it the woman burst into a volley of joyful thanks.

"It is the same, the same, madame! It has a small 'X' which the Reverend Mother scratched with her own blessed scissors!"

Lydia pushed the cross through the net and the nun handed it to the woman.

"It is the same, it is the same!" she cried. "Oh, thank you, madame! Now my heart is glad...."

Lydia came out of the hospital and walked through the gardens by the doctor's side. But she was not listening to what he was saying—her mind was fully occupied with the mystery of the silver cross.

It was little Xavier's ... it had been tucked inside his bed when he lay, as his mother thought, dying ... and it had been found in her bed! Then little Xavier had been in her bed! Her foot was on the step of the car when it came to her—the meaning of that drenched couch and the empty bottle of peroxide.

Xavier had been put there, and somebody who knew that the bed was infected had so soaked it with water that she could not sleep in it. But who? Old Jaggs!

She got into the car slowly, and went back to Cap Martin along the Grande Corniche.

Who had put the child there? He could not have walked from the cottage; that was impossible.

She was half-way home when she noticed a parcel lying on the floor of the car, and she let down the front window and spoke to the chauffeur. It was not Mordon, but a man whom she had hired with the car.

"It came from the hospital, madame," he said. "The porter asked me if I came from Villa Casa. It was something sent to the hospital to be disinfected. There was a charge of seven francs for the service, madame, and this I paid."

She nodded.

She picked up the parcel—it was addressed to "Mademoiselle Jean Briggerland" and bore the label of the hospital.

Lydia sat back in the car with her eyes closed, tired of turning over this problem, yet determined to get to the bottom of the mystery.

Jean was out when she got back and she carried the parcel to her own room. She was trying to keep out of her mind the very possibility that such a hideous crime could have been conceived as that which all the evidence indicated had been attempted. Very resolutely she refused to believe that such a thing could have happened. There must be some explanation for the presence of the cross in her bed. Possibly it had been found after the wet sheets had been taken to the servants' part of the house.

She rang the bell, and the maid who had given her the trinket came.

"Tell me," said Lydia, "where was this cross found?"

"In your bed, mademoiselle."

"But where? Was it before the clothing was removed from this room or after?"

"It was before, madame," said the maid. "When the sheets were turned back we found it lying exactly in the middle of the bed."

Lydia's heart sank.

"Thank you, that will do," she said. "I have found the owner of the cross and have restored it."

Should she tell Jean? Her first impulse was to take the girl into her confidence, and reveal the state of her mind. Her second thought was to seek out old Jaggs, but where could he be found? He evidently lived somewhere in Monte Carlo, but his name was hardly likely to be in the visitors' list. She was still undecided when Marcus Stepney called to take her to lunch at the Café de Paris.

The whole thing was so amazingly improbable. It belonged to a world of unreality, but then, she told herself, she also was living in an unreal world, and had been so for weeks.

Chapter XXV

Mr. Stepney had become more bearable. A week ago she would have shrunk from taking luncheon with him, but now such a prospect had no terrors. His views of things and people were more generous than she had expected. She had anticipated his attitude would be a little cynical, but to her surprise he oozed loving-kindness. Had she known Mr. Marcus Stepney as well as Jean knew him, she would have realised that he adapted his mental attitude to his audience. He was a man whose stock-in-trade was a knowledge of human nature, and the ability to please. He would no more have attempted to shock or frighten her, than a first-class salesman would shock or annoy a possible customer.

He had goods to sell, and it was his business to see that they satisfied the buyer. In this case the goods were represented by sixty-nine inches of good-looking, well-dressed man, and it was rather important that he should present the best face of the article to the purchaser. It was almost as important that the sale should be a quick one. Mr. Stepney lived from week to week. What might happen next year seldom interested him, therefore his courting must be rapid.

He told the story of his life at lunch, a story liable to move a tender-hearted woman to at least a sympathetic interest. The story of his life varied also with the audience. In this case, it was designed for one whom he knew had had a hard struggle, whose father had been heavily in debt, and who had tasted some of the bitterness of defeat. Jean had given him a very precise story of the girl's career, and Mr. Marcus Stepney adapted it for his own purpose.

"Why, your life has almost run parallel with mine," said Lydia.

"I hope it may continue," said Mr. Stepney not without a touch of sadness in his voice. "I am a very lonely man—I have no friends except the acquaintances one can pick up at night clubs, and the places where the smart people go in the season, and there is an artificiality about society friends which rather depresses me."

"I feel that, too," said the sympathetic Lydia.

"If I could only settle down!" he said, shaking his head. "A little house in the country, a few horses, a few cows, a woman who understood me...."

A false move this.

"And a few pet chickens to follow you about?" she laughed. "No, it doesn't sound quite like you, Mr. Stepney."

He lowered his eyes.

"I am sorry you think that," he said. "All the world thinks that I'm a gadabout, an idler, with no interest in existence, except the pleasure I can extract."

"And a jolly good existence, too," said Lydia briskly. She had detected a note of sentiment creeping into the conversation, and had slain it with the most effective weapon in woman's armoury.

"And now tell me all about the great Moorish Pretender who is staying at your hotel—I caught a glimpse of him on the promenade—and there was a lot about him in the paper."

Mr. Stepney sighed and related all that he knew of the redoubtable Muley Hafiz on the way to the rooms. Muley Hafiz was being lionised in France just then, to the annoyance of the Spanish authorities, who had put a price on his head.

Lydia showed much more interest in the Moorish Pretender than she did in the pretender who walked by her side.

He was not in the best of tempers when he brought her back to the Villa Casa, and Jean, who entertained him whilst Lydia was changing, saw that his first advances had not met with a very encouraging result.

"There will be no wedding bells, Jean," he said.

"You take a rebuff very easily," said the girl, but he shook his head.

"My dear Jean, I know women as well as I know the back of my hand, and I tell you that there's nothing doing with this girl. I'm not a fool."

She looked at him earnestly.

"No, you're not a fool," she said at last. "You're hardly likely to make a mistake about that sort of thing. I'm afraid you'll have to do something more romantic."

"What do you mean?" he asked.

"You'll have to run away with her; and like the knights of old carry off the lady of your choice."

"The knights of old didn't have to go before a judge and jury and serve seven years at Dartmoor for their sins," he said unpleasantly.

She was sitting on a low chair overlooking the sea, whittling a twig with a silver-handled knife she had taken from her bag—a favourite occupation of hers in moments of cogitation.

"All the ladies of old didn't go to the police," she said. "Some of them were quite happy with their powerful lords, especially delicate-minded ladies who shrank from advertising their misfortune to the readers of the Sunday press. I think most women like to be wooed in the cave-man fashion, Marcus."

"Is that the kind of treatment you'd like, Jean?"

There was a new note in his voice. Had she looked at him she would have seen a strange light in his eyes.

"I'm merely advancing a theory," she said, "a theory which has been supported throughout the ages."

"I'd let her go and her money, too," he said. He was speaking quickly, almost incoherently. "There's only one woman in the world for me, Jean, and I've told you that before. I'd give my life and soul for her."

He bent over, and caught her arm in his big hand.

"You believe in the cave-man method, do you?" he breathed. "It is the kind of treatment you'd like, eh, Jean?"

She did not attempt to release her arm.

"Keep your hand to yourself, Marcus, please," she said quietly.

"You'd like it, wouldn't you, Jean? My God, I'd sacrifice my soul for you, you little devil!"

"Be sensible," she said. It was not her words or her firm tone that made him draw back. Twice and deliberately she drew the edge of her little knife across the back of his hand, and he leapt away with a howl of pain.

"You—you beast," he stammered, and she looked at him with her sly smile.

"There must have been cave women, too, Marcus," she said coolly, as she rose. "They had their methods—give me your handkerchief, I want to wipe this knife."

His face was grey now. He was looking at her like a man bereft of his senses.

He did not move when she took his handkerchief from his pocket, wiped the knife, closed and slipped it into her bag, before she replaced the handkerchief tidily. And all the time he stood there with his hand streaming with blood, incapable of movement. It was not until she had disappeared round the corner of the house that he pulled out the handkerchief and wrapped it about his hand.

"A devil," he whimpered, almost in tears, "a devil!"

Chapter XXVI

Jean Briggerland discovered a new arrival on her return to the house.

Jack Glover had come unexpectedly from London, so Lydia told her, and Jack himself met her with extraordinary geniality.

"You lucky people to be in this paradise!" he said. "It is raining like the dickens in London, and miserable beyond description. And you're looking brown and beautiful, Miss Briggerland."

"The spirit of the warm south has got into your blood, Mr. Glover," she said sarcastically. "A course at the Riviera would make you almost human."

"And what would make you human?" asked Jack blandly.

"I hope you people aren't going to quarrel as soon as you meet," said Lydia.

Jean was struck by the change in the girl. There was a colour in her cheeks, and a new and a more joyous note in her voice, which was unmistakable to so keen a student as Jean Briggerland.

"I never quarrel with Jack," she said. She assumed a proprietorial air toward Jack Glover, which unaccountably annoyed Lydia. "He invents the quarrels and carries them out himself. How long are you staying?"

"Two days," said Jack, "then I'm due back in town."

"Have you brought your Mr. Jaggs with you?" asked Jean innocently.

"Isn't he here?" asked Jack in surprise. "I sent him along a week ago."

"Here?" repeated Jean slowly. "Oh, he's here, is he? Of course." She nodded. Certain things were clear to her now; the unknown drencher of beds, the stranger who had appeared from nowhere and had left her father senseless, were no longer mysteries.

"Oh, Jean," it was Lydia who spoke. "I'm awfully remiss, I didn't give you the parcel I brought back from the hospital."

"From the hospital?" said Jean. "What parcel was that?"

"Something you had sent to be sterilized. I'll get it."

She came back in a minute or two with the parcel which she had found in the car.

"Oh yes," said Jean carelessly, "I remember. It is a rug that I lent to the gardener's wife when her little boy was taken ill."

She handed the packet to the maid.

"Take it to my room," she said.

She waited just long enough to find an excuse for leaving the party, and went upstairs. The parcel was on her bed. She tore off the wrapping—inside, starched white and clean, was the dust coat she had worn the night she had carried Xavier from the cottage to Lydia's bed. The rubber cap was there, discoloured from the effects of the disinfectant, and the gloves and the silk handkerchief, neatly washed and pressed. She looked at them thoughtfully.

She put the articles away in a drawer, went down the servants' stairs and through a heavy open door into the cellar. Light was admitted by two barred windows, through one of which she had thrust her bundle that night, and she could see every corner of the cellar, which was empty—as she had expected. The clothing she had thrown down had been gathered by some mysterious agent, who had forwarded it to the hospital in her name.

She came slowly up the stairs, fastened the open door behind her, and walked out into the garden to think.

"Jaggs!" she said aloud, and her voice was as soft as silk. "I think, Mr. Jaggs, you ought to be in heaven."

Chapter XXVII

"Who were the haughty individuals interviewing Jean in the saloon?" asked Jack Glover, as Lydia's car panted and groaned on the stiff ascent to La Turbie.

Lydia was concerned, and he had already noted her seriousness.

"Poor Jean is rather worried," she said. "It appears that she had a love affair with a man three or four years ago, and recently he has been bombarding her with threatening letters."

"Poor soul," said Jack dryly, "but I should imagine she could have dealt with that matter without calling in the police. I suppose they were detectives. Has she had a letter recently?"

"She had one this morning—posted in Monte Carlo last night."

"By the way, Jean went into Monte Carlo last night, didn't she?" asked Jack.

She looked at him reproachfully.

"We all went into Monte Carlo," she said severely. "Now, please don't be horrid, Mr. Glover, you aren't suggesting that Jean wrote this awful letter to herself, are you?"

"Was it an awful letter?" asked Jack.

"A terrible letter, threatening to kill her. Do you know that Mr. Briggerland thinks that the person who nearly killed me was really shooting at Jean."

"You don't say," said Jack politely. "I haven't heard about people shooting at you—but it sounds rather alarming."

She told him the story, and he offered no comment.

"Go on with your thrilling story of Jean's mortal enemy. Who is he?"

"She doesn't know his name," said Lydia. "She met him in Egypt—an elderly man who positively dogged her footsteps wherever she went, and made himself a nuisance."

"Doesn't know his name, eh?" said Jack with a sniff. "Well, that's convenient."

"I think you're almost spiteful," said Lydia hotly. "Poor girl, she was so distressed this morning; I have never seen her so upset."

"And are the police going to keep guard and follow her wherever she goes? And is that impossible person, Mr. Marcus Stepney, also in the vendetta? I saw him wandering about this morning like a wounded hero, with his arm in a sling."

"He hurt his hand gathering wild flowers for me on the—"

But Jack's outburst of laughter checked her, and she glared at him.

"I think you're boorish," she snapped angrily. "I'm sorry I came out with you."

"And I'm sorry I've been such a fool," apologised the penitent Jack, "but the vision of the immaculate Mr. Stepney gathering wild flowers in a top hat and a morning suit certainly did appeal to me as being comical!"

"He doesn't wear a top hat or a morning suit in Monte Carlo," she said, furious at his banter. "Let us talk about somebody else than my friends."

"I haven't started to talk about your friends yet," he said. "And please don't try to tell your chauffeur to turn round—the road is too narrow, and he'd have the car over the cliff before you knew where you were, if he were stupid enough to try. I'm sorry, deeply sorry, Mrs. Meredith, but I think that Jean was right when she said that the southern air had got into my blood. I'm a little hysterical—yes, put it down to that. It runs in the family," he babbled on. "I have an aunt who faints at the sight of strawberries, and an uncle who swoons whenever a cat walks into the room."

"I hope you don't visit him very much," she said coldly.

"Two points to you," said Jack, "but I must warn Jaggs, in case he is mistaken for the elderly Lothario. Obviously Jean is preparing the way for an unpleasant end to poor old Jaggs."

"Why do you think these things about Jean?" she asked, as they were running into La Turbie.

"Because I have a criminal mind," he replied promptly. "I have the same type of mind as Jean Briggerland's, wedded to a wholesome respect for the law, and a healthy sense of right and wrong. Some people couldn't be happy if they owned a cent that had been earned dishonestly; other people are happy so long as they have the money—so long as it is real money. I belong to the former category. Jean—well, I don't know what would make Jean happy."

"And what would make you happy—Jean?" she asked.

He did not answer this question until they were sitting on the stoep of the National, where a light luncheon was awaiting them.

"Jean?" he said, as though the question had just been asked. "No, I don't want Jean. She is wonderful, really, Mrs. Meredith, wonderful! I find myself thinking about her at odd moments, and the more I think the more I am amazed. Lucretia Borgia was a child in arms compared with Jean—poor old Lucretia has been maligned, anyway. There was a woman in the sixteenth century rather like her, and another girl in the early days of New England, who used to denounce witches for the pleasure of seeing them burn, but I can't think of an exact parallel, because Jean gets no pleasure out of hurting people any more than you will get out of cutting that cantaloup. It has just got to be cut, and the fact that you are finally destroying the life of the melon doesn't worry you."

"Have cantaloups life?" She paused, knife in hand, eyeing the fruit with a frown. "No, I don't think I want it. So Jean is a murderess at heart?"

She asked the question in solemn mockery, but Jack was not smiling.

"Oh yes—in intention, at any rate. I don't know whether she has ever killed anybody, but she has certainly planned murders."

Lydia sighed and sat back in her chair patiently.

"Do you still suggest that she harbours designs against my young life?"

"I not only suggest it, but I state positively that there have been four attempts on your life in the past fortnight," he said calmly.

"Let us have this out," she said recklessly. "Number one?"

"The nearly-a-fatal accident in Berkeley Street," said Jack.

"Will you explain by what miracle the car arrived at the psychological moment?" she asked.

"That's easy," he said with a smile. "Old man Briggerland lit his cigar standing on the steps of the house. That light was a brilliant one, Jaggs tells me. It was the signal for the car to come on. The next attempt was made with the assistance of a lunatic doctor who was helped to escape by Briggerland, and brought to your house by him. In some way he got hold of a key—probably Jean manœuvred it. Did she ever talk to you about keys?"

"No," said the girl, "she——" She stopped suddenly, remembering that Jean had discussed keys with her.

"Are you sure she didn't?" asked Jack, watching her.

"I think she may have done," said the girl defiantly; "what was the third attempt?"

"The third attempt," said Jack slowly, "was to infect your bed with a malignant fever."

"Jean did it?" said the girl incredulously. "Oh no, that would be impossible."

"The child was in your bed. Jaggs saw it and threw two buckets of water over the bed, so that you should not sleep in it."

She was silent.

"And I suppose the next attempt was the shooting?"

He nodded.

"Now do you believe?" he asked.

She shook her head.

"No, I don't believe," she said quietly. "I think you have worked up a very strong case against poor Jean, and I am sure you think you're justified."

"You are quite right there," he said.

He lifted a pair of field glasses which he had put on the table, and surveyed the road from the sea. "Mrs. Meredith, I want you to do something and tell Jean Briggerland when you have done it."

"What is that?" she asked.

"I want you to make a will. I don't care where you leave your property, so long as it is not to somebody you love."

She shivered.

"I don't like making wills. It's so gruesome."

"It will be more gruesome for you if you don't," he said significantly. "The Briggerlands are your heirs at law."

She looked at him quickly.

"So that is what you are aiming at? You think that all these plots are designed to put me out of the way so that they can enjoy my money?"

He nodded, and she looked at him wonderingly.

"If you weren't a hard-headed lawyer, I should think you were a writer of romantic fiction," she said. "But if it will please you I will make a will. I haven't the slightest idea who I could leave the money to. I've got rather a lot of money, haven't I?"

"You have exactly £160,000 in hard cash. I want to talk to you about that," said Jack. "It is lying at your bankers in your current account. It represents property which has been sold or was in process of being sold when you inherited the money, and anybody who can get your signature and can satisfy the bankers that they are bona fide payees, can draw every cent you have of ready money. I might say in passing that we are prepared for that contingency, and any large cheque will be referred to me or to my partner."

He raised his field glasses for a second time and looked steadily down along the hill road up which they had come.

"Are you expecting anybody?" she asked.

"I'm expecting Jean," he said grimly.

"But we left her———"

"The fact that we left her talking to the police doesn't mean that she will not be coming up here, to watch us. Jean doesn't like me, you know, and she will be scared to death of this *tête-à-tête*."

The conversation had been arrested by the arrival of the soup and now there was a further interruption whilst the table was being cleared. When the *maître d'hôtel* had gone the girl asked:

"What am I to do with the money? Reinvest it?"

"Exactly," said Jack, "but the most important thing is to make your will."

He looked along the deserted veranda. They were the only guests present who had come early. From the veranda two curtained doors led into the *salon* of the hotel and it struck him that one of these had not been ajar when he looked at it before, and it was the door opposite to the table where they were sitting.

He noted this idly without attaching any great importance to the fact.

"Suppose somebody were to present a cheque to the bank in my name?" she asked. "What would happen?"

"If it were for a large sum? The manager would call us up and one of us would probably go round to your bank. It is only a block from our office. If Rennett or I said it was all right the cheque would be honoured. You may be sure that I should make very drastic inquiries as to the origin of the signature."

And then she saw him stiffen and his eyes go to the door. He waited a second, then rising noiselessly, crossed the wooden floor of the veranda quickly and pushed open the door, to find himself face to face with the smiling Jean Briggerland.

Chapter XXVIII

"However did you get here?" asked Lydia in surprise.

"I went into Nice," said the girl carelessly. "The detectives were going there and I gave them a lift."

"I see," said Jack, "so you came into Turbie by the back road? I wondered why I hadn't seen your car."

"You expected me, did you?" she smiled, as she sat down at the table and selected a peach from its cotton-wool bed. "I only arrived a second ago, in fact I was opening the door when you almost knocked my head off. What a violent man you are, Jack! I shall have to put you into my story."

Glover had recovered his self-possession by now.

"So you are adding to your other crimes by turning novelist, are you?" he said good-humouredly. "What is the book, Miss Briggerland?"

"It is going to be called 'Suspected,'" she said coolly. "And it will be the Story of a Hurt Soul."

"Oh, I see, a humorous story," said Jack, wilfully dense. "I didn't know you were going to write a biography."

"But do tell me about this, it is very thrilling, Jean," said Lydia, "and it is the first I've heard of it."

Jean was skinning the peach and was smiling as at an amusing thought.

"I've been two years making up my mind to write it," she said, "and I'm going to dedicate it to Jack. I started work on it three or four days ago. Look at my wrist!" She held out her beautiful hand for the girl's inspection.

"It is a very pretty wrist," laughed Lydia, "but why did you want me to see it?"

"If you had a professional eye," said the girl, resuming her occupation, "you would have noticed the swelling, the result of writers' cramp."

"The yarn about your elderly admirer ought to provide a good chapter," said Jack, "and isn't there a phrase 'A Chapter of Accidents'—*that* ought to go in?"

She did not raise her eyes.

"Don't discourage me," she said a little sadly. "I have to make money somehow."

How much had she heard? Jack was wondering all the time, and he groaned inwardly when he saw how little effect his warning had upon the girl he was striving to protect. Women are natural actresses, but Lydia was not acting now. She was genuinely fond of Jean and he could see that she had accepted his warnings as the ravings of a diseased imagination. He confirmed this view when after a morning of sight-seeing and the exploration of the spot where, two thousand years before, the Emperor Augustine had erected his lofty "trophy," they returned to the villa. There are some omissions which are marked, and when Lydia allowed him to depart without pressing him to stay to dinner he realised that he had lost the trick.

"When are you going back to London?" she asked.

"To-morrow morning," said Jack. "I don't think I shall come here again before I go."

She did not reply immediately. She was a little penitent at her lack of hospitality, but Jack had annoyed her and the more convincing he had become, the greater had been the irritation he had caused. One question he had to ask but he hesitated.

"About that will——" he began, but her look of weariness stopped him.

It was a very annoyed young man that drove back to the Hôtel de Paris. He had hardly gone before Lydia regretted her brusqueness. She liked Jack Glover more than she was prepared to admit, and though he had only been in Cap Martin for two days she felt a little sense of desolation at his going. Very resolutely she refused even to consider his extraordinary views about Jean. And yet——

Jean left her alone and watched her strolling aimlessly about the garden, guessing the little storm which had developed in her breast. Lydia went to bed early that night, another significant sign Jean noted, and was not sorry, because she wanted to have her father to herself.

Mr. Briggerland listened moodily whilst Jean related all that she had learnt, for she had been in the *salon* at the National for a good quarter of an hour before Jack had discovered her.

"I thought he would want her to make a will," she said, "and, of course, although she has rejected the idea now, it will grow on her. I think we have the best part of a week."

"I suppose you have everything cut and dried as usual," growled Mr. Briggerland. "What is your plan?"

"I have three," said Jean thoughtfully, "and two are particularly appealing to me because they do not involve the employment of any third person."

"Had you one which brought in somebody else?" asked Briggerland in surprise. "I thought a clever girl like you——"

"Don't waste your sarcasm on me," said Jean quietly. "The third person whom I considered was Marcus Stepney," and she told him the gist of her conversation with the gambler. Mr. Briggerland was not impressed.

"A thief like Marcus will get out of paying," he said, "and if he can stall you long enough to get the money you may whistle for your share. Besides, a fellow like that isn't really afraid of a charge of bigamy."

Jean, curled up in a big arm-chair, looked up under her eyelashes at her father and laughed.

"I had no intention of letting Marcus marry Lydia," she said coolly, "but I had to dangle something in front of his eyes, because he may serve me in quite another way."

"How did he get those two slashes on his hand?" asked Mr. Briggerland suddenly.

"Ask him," she said. "Marcus is getting a little troublesome. I thought he had learnt his lesson and had realised that I am not built for matrimony, especially for a hectic attachment to a man who gains his livelihood by cheating at cards."

"Now, now, my dear," said her father.

"Please don't be shocked," she mocked him. "You know as well as I do how Marcus lives."

"The boy is very fond of you."

"The boy is between thirty and thirty-six," she said tersely. "And he's not the kind of boy that I am particularly fond of. He is useful and may be more useful yet."

She rose, stretched her arms and yawned.

"I'm going up to my room to work on my story. You are watching for Mr. Jaggs?"

"Work on what?" he said.

"The story I am writing and which I think will create a sensation," she said calmly.

"What's this?" asked Briggerland suspiciously. "A story? I didn't know you were writing that kind of stuff."

"There are lots of important things that you know nothing about, parent," she said and left him a little dazed.

For once Jean was not deceiving him. A writing table had been put in her room and a thick pad of paper awaited her attention. She got into her kimono and with a little sigh sat down at the table and began to write. It was half-past two when she gathered up the sheets and read them over with a smile which was half contempt. She was on the point of getting into bed when she remembered that her father was keeping watch below. She put on her slippers and went downstairs and tapped gently at the door of the darkened dining-room.

Almost immediately it was opened.

"What did you want to tap for?" he grumbled. "You gave me a start."

"I preferred tapping to being shot," she answered. "Have you heard anything or seen anybody?"

The French windows of the dining-room were open, her father was wearing his coat and on his arm she saw by the reflected starlight from outside he carried a shot-gun.

"Nothing," he said. "The old man hasn't come to-night."

She nodded.

"Somehow I didn't think he would," she said.

"I don't see how I can shoot him without making a fuss."

"Don't be silly," said Jean lightly. "Aren't the police well aware that an elderly gentleman has threatened my life, and would it be remarkable if seeing an ancient man prowl about this house you shot him on sight?"

She bit her lips thoughtfully.

"Yes, I think you can go to bed," she said. "He will not be here to-night. To-morrow night, yes."

She went up to her room, said her prayers and went to bed and was asleep immediately.

Lydia had forgotten about Jean's story until she saw her writing industriously at a small table which had been placed on the lawn. It was February, but the wind and the sun were warm and Lydia thought she had never seen a more beautiful picture than the girl presented sitting there in a garden spangled with gay flowers, heavy with the scent of February roses, a dainty figure of a girl, almost ethereal in her loveliness.

"Am I interrupting you?"

"Not a bit," said Jean, putting down her pen and rubbing her wrist. "Isn't it annoying. I've got to quite an exciting part, and my wrist is giving me hell."

She used the word so naturally that Lydia forgot to be shocked.

"Can I do anything for you?"

Jean shook her head.

"I don't exactly see what you can do," she said, "unless you could—but, no, I would not ask you to do that!"

"What is it?" asked Lydia.

Jean puckered her brows in thought.

"I suppose you could do it," she said, "but I'd hate to ask you. You see, dear, I've got a chapter to finish and it really ought to go off to London to-day. I am very keen on getting an opinion from a literary friend of mine—but, no, I won't ask you."

"What is it?" smiled Lydia. "I'm sure you're not going to ask the impossible."

"The thought occurred to me that perhaps you might write as I dictated. It would only be two or three pages," said the girl apologetically. "I'm so full of the story at this moment that it would be a shame if I allowed the divine fire of inspiration—that's the term, isn't it—to go out."

"Of course I'll do it," said Lydia. "I can't write shorthand, but that doesn't matter, does it?"

"No, longhand will be quick enough for me. My thoughts aren't so fast," said the girl.

"What is it all about?"

"It is about a girl," said Jean, "who has stolen a lot of money——"

"How thrilling!" smiled Lydia.

"And she's got away to America. She is living a very full and joyous life, but the thought of her sin is haunting her and she decides to disappear and let people think she has drowned herself. She is really going into a convent. I've got to the point where she is saying farewell to her friend. Do you feel capable of being harrowed?"

"I never felt fitter for the job in my life," said Lydia, and sitting down in the chair the girl had vacated, she took up the pencil which the other had left.

Jean strolled up and down the lawn in an agony of mental composition and presently she came back and began slowly to dictate.

Word by word Lydia wrote down the thrilling story of the girl's remorse, and presently came to the moment when the heroine was inditing a letter to her friend.

"Take a fresh page," said Jean, as Lydia paused half-way down one sheet. "I shall want to write something in there myself when my hand gets better. Now begin:

"MY DEAR FRIEND."

Lydia wrote down the words and slowly the girl dictated.

> "I do not know how I can write you this letter. I intended to tell you when I saw you the other day how miserable I was. Your suspicion hurt me less than your ignorance of the one vital event in my life which has now made living a

burden. My money has brought no joy to me. I have met a man I love, but with whom I know a union is impossible. We are determined to die together—farewell—"

"You said she was going away," interrupted Lydia.

"I know," Jean nodded. "Only she wants to give the impression———"

"I see, I see," said Lydia. "Go on."

"Forgive me for the act I am committing, which you may think is the act of a coward, and try to think as well of me as you possibly can. Your friend———"

"I don't know whether to make her sign her name or put her initials," said Jean, pursing her lips.

"What is her name?"

"Laura Martin. Just put the initials L.M."

"They're mine also," smiled Lydia. "What else?"

"I don't think I'll do any more," said Jean. "I'm not a good dictator, am I? Though you're a wonderful amanuensis."

She collected the papers tidily, put them in a little portfolio and tucked them under her arm.

"Let us gamble the afternoon away," said Jean. "I want distraction."

"But your story? Haven't you to send it off?"

"I'm going to wrestle with it in secret, even if it breaks my wrist," said Jean brightly.

She took the portfolio up to her room, locked the door and sorted over the pages. The page which held the farewell letter she put carefully aside. The remainder, including all that part of the story she had written on the previous night, she made into a bundle, and when Lydia had gone off with Marcus Stepney to swim, she carried the paper to a remote corner of the grounds and burnt it sheet by sheet. Again she examined the "letter," folded it and locked it in a drawer.

Lydia, returning from her swim, was met by Jean half-way up the hill.

"By the way, my dear, I wish you would give me Jack Glover's London address," she said as they went into the house. "Write it here. Here is a pencil." She pulled out an envelope from a stationery rack and Lydia, in all innocence, wrote as she requested.

The envelope Jean carried upstairs, put into it the letter signed "L. M.," and sealed it down. Lydia Meredith was nearer to death at that moment than she had been on the afternoon when Mordon the chauffeur brought his big Fiat on to the pavement of Berkeley Street.

Chapter XXIX

It was in the evening of the next day that Lydia received a wire from Jack Glover. It was addressed from London and announced his arrival.

"Doesn't it make you feel nice, Lydia," said Jean, when she saw the telegram, "to have a man in London looking after your interests—a sort of guardian angel—and another guardian angel prowling round your demesne at Cap Martin?"

"You mean Jaggs? Have you seen him?"

"No, I have not seen him," said the girl softly. "I should rather like to see him. Do you know where he is staying at Monte Carlo?"

Lydia shook her head.

"I hope I shall see him before I go," said Jean. "He must be a very interesting old gentleman."

It was Mr. Briggerland who first caught a glimpse of Lydia's watchman. Mr. Briggerland had spent the greater part of the day sleeping. He was unusually wakeful at one o'clock in the morning, and sat on the veranda in a fur-lined overcoat, his gun lay across his knees. He had seen many mysterious shapes flitting across the lawn, only to discover on investigation that they were no more than the shadows which the moving tree-tops cast.

At two o'clock he saw a shape emerge from the tree belt and move stealthily in the shadow of the bushes toward the house. He did not fire because there was a chance that it might have been one of the detectives who had promised to keep an eye upon the Villa Casa in view of the murderous threats which Jean had received.

Noiselessly he rose and stepped in his rubber shoes to the darker end of the stoep. It was old Jaggs. There was no mistaking him. A bent man who limped cautiously across the lawn and was making for the back of the house. Mr. Briggerland cocked his gun and took aim....

Both girls heard the shot, and Lydia, springing out of bed, ran on to the balcony.

"It's all right, Mrs. Meredith," said Briggerland's voice. "It was a burglar, I think."

"You haven't hurt him?" she cried, remembering old Jaggs's nocturnal habits.

"If I have, he's got away," said Briggerland. "He must have seen me and dropped."

Jean flew downstairs in her dressing-gown and joined her father on the lawn.

"Did you get him?" she asked in a low voice.

"I could have sworn I shot him," said her father in the same tone, "but the old devil must have dropped."

He heard the quick catch of her breath and turned apprehensively.

"Now, don't make a fuss about it, Jean, I couldn't help it."

"You couldn't help it!" she almost snarled. "You had him under your gun and you let him go. Do you think he'll ever come again, you fool?"

"Now look here, I'm not going to——" began Mr. Briggerland, but she snatched the gun from his hand, looked swiftly at the lock and ran across the lawn toward the trees.

Somebody was hiding. She sensed that and all her nerves were alert. Presently she saw a crouching figure and lifted the gun, but before she could fire it was wrested from her hand.

She opened her lips to cry out for help, but a hand closed over her mouth, and swung her round so that her back was toward her assailant, and then in a flash his arm came round her neck, the flex of the elbow against her throat.

"Say one of them prayers of yours," said a voice in her ear, and the arm tightened.

She struggled furiously, but the man held her as though she were a child.

"You're going to die," whispered the voice. "How do you like the sensation?"

The arm tightened on her neck. She was suffocating, dying she thought, and her heart was filled with a wild, mad longing for life and a terror undreamt of. She could faintly hear her father's voice calling her and then consciousness departed.

When Jean came to herself she was in Lydia Meredith's arms. She opened her eyes and saw the pathetic face of her father looming from the background. Her hand went up to her throat.

"Hallo, people—how did I get here?" she asked as she struggled into a sitting position.

"I came in search of you and found you lying on the ground," quavered Mr. Briggerland.

"Did you see the man?" she asked.

"No. What happened to you, darling?"

"Nothing," she said with that composure which she could command. "I must have fainted. It was rather ridiculous of me, wasn't it?" she smiled.

She got unsteadily to her feet and again she felt her throat. Lydia noticed the action.

"Did he hurt you?" she asked anxiously. "It couldn't have been Jaggs."

"Oh no," smiled Jean, "it couldn't have been Jaggs. I think I'll go to bed."

She did not expect to sleep. For the first time in her extraordinary life fear had come to her, and she had shivered on the very edge of the abyss. She felt the shudder she could not repress and shook herself impatiently. Then she extinguished the light and went to the window and looked out. Somewhere there in the darkness she knew her enemy was hidden, and again that sense of apprehension swept over her.

"I'm losing my nerve," she murmured.

It was extraordinary to Lydia Meredith that the girl showed no sign of her night's adventure when she came in to breakfast on the following morning. She looked bright. Her eyes were clear and her delicate irony as pointed as though she had slept the clock round.

Lydia did not swim that day, and Mr. Stepney had his journey out to Cap Martin in vain. Nor was she inclined to go back with him to Monte Carlo to the Casino in the afternoon, and Mr. Stepney began to realise that he was wasting valuable time.

Jean found her scribbling in the garden and Lydia made no secret of the task she was undertaking.

"Making your will? What a grisly idea?" she said as she put down the cup of tea she had carried out to the girl.

"Isn't it," said Lydia with a grimace. "It is the most worrying business, too, Jean. There is nobody I want to leave money to except you and Mr. Glover."

"For heaven's sake don't leave me any or Jack will think I am conspiring to bring about your untimely end," said Jean. "Why make a will at all?"

There was no need for her to ask that, but she was curious to discover what reply the girl would make, and to her surprise Lydia fenced with the question.

"It is done in all the best circles," she said good-humouredly. "And, Jean, I'm not interested in a single public institution! I don't know by title the name of any home for dogs, and I shouldn't be at all anxious to leave my money to one even if I did."

"Then you'd better leave it to Jack Glover," said the girl, "or to the Lifeboat Institution."

Lydia threw down her pencil in disgust.

"Fancy making one's will on a beautiful day like this, and giving instructions as to where one should be buried. Brrr! Jean," she asked suddenly, "was it Mr. Jaggs you saw in the wood?"

Jean shook her head.

"I saw nobody," she said. "I went in to look for the burglar; the excitement must have been too much for me, and I fainted."

But Lydia was not satisfied.

"I can't understand Mr. Jaggs myself," she said, but Jean interrupted her with a cry.

Lydia looked up and saw her eyes shining and her lips parting in a smile.

"Of course," she said softly. "He used to sleep at your flat, didn't he?"

"Yes, why?" asked the girl in surprise.

"What a fool I am, what a perfect fool!" said Jean, startled out of her accustomed self-possession.

"I don't quite know where your folly comes in, but perhaps you will tell me," but Jean was laughing softly.

"Go on and make your will," she said mockingly. "And when you've finished we'll go into the rooms and chase the lucky numbers. Poor dear Mrs. Cole-Mortimer is feeling a little neglected, too, we ought to do something for her."

The day and night passed without any untoward event. In the evening Jean had an interview with her French chauffeur, and afterwards disappeared into her room. Lydia tapping at her door to bid her good night received no answer.

Day was breaking when old Jaggs came out from the trees in his furtive way and glancing up and down the road made his halting way toward Monte Carlo. The only objects in sight was a donkey laden with market produce led by a bare-legged boy who was going in the same direction as he.

A little more than a mile along the road he turned sharply to the right and began climbing a steep and narrow bridle path which joined the mountain road, half-way up to La Turbie. The boy with the donkey turned off to the main road and continued the steep climb toward the Grande Corniche. There were many houses built on the edge of the road and practically on the edge of precipices, for the windows facing the sea often looked sheer down for two hundred feet. At first these dwellings appeared in clusters, then as the road climbed higher, they occurred at rare intervals.

The boy leading the donkey kept his eye upon the valley below, and from time to time caught a glimpse of the old man who had now left the bridle path, and was picking his way up the rough hill-side. He was making for a dilapidated house which stood at one of the hairpin bends of the road, and the donkey-boy, shading his eyes from the glare of the rising sun, saw him disappear into what must have been the cellar of the house, since the door through which he went was a good twenty feet beneath the level of the road. The donkey-boy continued his climb, tugging at his burdened beast, and presently he came up to the house.

Smoke was rising from one of the chimneys, and he halted at the door, tied the rope he held to a rickety gate post, and knocked gently.

A bright-faced peasant woman came to the open door and shook her head at the sight of the wares with which the donkey was laden.

"We want none of your truck, my boy," she said. "I have my own garden. You are not a Monogasque."

"No, signora," replied the boy, flashing his teeth with a smile. "I am from San Remo, but I have come to live in Monte Carlo to sell vegetables for my uncle, and he told me I should find a lodging here."

She looked at him dubiously.

"I have one room which you could have, boy," she said, "though I do not like Italians. You must pay me a franc a night, and your donkey can go into the shed of my brother-in-law up the hill."

She led the way down a flight of ancient stairs and showed him a tiny room overlooking the valley.

"I have one other man who lives here," she said. "An old one, who sleeps all day and goes out all night. But he is a very respectable man," she added in defence of her client.

"Where does he sleep?" asked the boy.

"There!" The woman pointed to a room on the opposite side of the narrow landing. "He has just come in, I can hear him." She listened.

"Will madame get me change for this?" The boy produced a fifty-franc note, and the woman's eyebrows rose.

"Such wealth!" she said good-naturedly. "I did not think that a little boy like you could have such money."

She bustled upstairs to her own room, leaving the boy alone. He waited until her heavy footsteps sounded overhead, and then gently he tried the door of the other lodger. Mr. Jaggs had not yet bolted the door, and the spy pushed it open and looked. What he saw satisfied him, for he pulled the door tight again, and as the footfall of old Jaggs came nearer the door, the donkey-boy flew upstairs with extraordinary rapidity.

"I will come later, madame," he said, when he had received the change. "I must take my donkey into Monte Carlo."

She watched the boy and his beast go down the road, and went back to the task of preparing her lodger's breakfast.

To Monte Carlo the cabbage seller did not go. Instead, he turned back the way he had come, and a hundred yards from the gate of Villa Casa, Mordon, the chauffeur, appeared, and took the rope from his hand.

"Did you find what you wanted, mademoiselle?" he asked.

Jean nodded. She got into the house through the servants' entrance and up to her room without observation. She pulled off the black wig and applied herself to removing the stains from her face. It had been a good morning's work.

"You must keep Mrs. Meredith fully occupied to-day." She waylaid her father on the stairs to give him these instructions.

For her it was a busy morning. First she went to the Hôtel de Paris, and on the pretext of writing a letter in the lounge, secured two or three sheets of the hotel paper and an envelope. Next she hired a typewriter and carried it with her back to the house. She was working for an hour before she had the letter finished. The signature took her some time. She had to ransack Lydia's writing case before she found a letter from Jack Glover—Lydia's signature was easy in comparison.

This, and a cheque drawn from the back of Lydia Meredith's cheque-book, completed her equipment.

That afternoon Mordon, the chauffeur, motored into Nice, and by nine o'clock that night an aeroplane deposited him in Paris. He was in London the following morning, a bearer of an urgent letter to Mr. Rennett, the lawyer, which, however, he did not present in person.

Mordon knew a French girl in London, and she it was who carried the letter to Charles Rennett—a letter that made him scratch his head many times before he took a sheet of paper, and addressing the manager of Lydia's bank, wrote:

"This cheque is in order. Please honour."

Chapter XXX

"Desperate diseases," said Jean Briggerland, "call for desperate remedies."

Mr. Briggerland looked up from his book.

"What was that tale you were telling Lydia this morning," he asked, "about Glover's gambling? He was only here a day, wasn't he?"

"He was here long enough to lose a lot of money," said Jean. "Of course he didn't gamble, so he did not lose. It was just a little seed-sowing on my part—one never knows how useful the right word may be in the right season."

"Did you tell Lydia that he was losing heavily?" he asked quickly.

"Am I a fool? Of course not! I merely said that youth would be served, and if you have the gambling instinct in you, why, it didn't matter what position you held in society or what your responsibilities were, you must indulge your passion."

Mr. Briggerland stroked his chin. There were times when Jean's schemes got very far beyond him, and he hated the mental exercise of catching up. The only thing he knew was that every post from London bore urgent demands for money, and that the future held possibilities which he did not care to contemplate. He was in the unfortunate position of having numerous pensioners to support, men and women who had served him in various ways and whose approval, but what was more important, whose loyalty, depended largely upon the regularity of their payments.

"I shall gamble or do something desperate," he said with a frown. "Unless you can bring off a coup that will produce twenty thousand pounds of ready money we are going to get into all kinds of trouble, Jean."

"Do you think I don't know that?" she asked contemptuously. "It is because of this urgent need of money that I have taken a step which I hate."

He listened in amazement whilst she told him what she had done to relieve her pressing needs.

"We are getting deeper and deeper into Mordon's hands," he said, shaking his head. "That is what scares me at times."

"You needn't worry about Mordon," she smiled. Her smile was a little hard. "Mordon and I are going to be married."

She was examining the toe of her shoe attentively as she spoke, and Mr. Briggerland leapt to his feet.

"What!" he squeaked. "Marry a chauffeur? A fellow I picked out of the gutter? You're mad! The fellow is a rascal who has earned the guillotine time and time again."

"Who hasn't?" she asked, looking up.

"It is incredible! It's madness!" he said. "I had no idea——" he stopped for want of breath.

Mordon was becoming troublesome. She had known that better than her father.

"It was after the 'accident' that didn't happen that he began to get a little tiresome," she said. "You say we are getting deeper and deeper into his hands? Well, he hinted as much, and I did not like it. When he began to get a little loving I accepted that way out as an easy alternative to a very unpleasant exposure. Whether he would have betrayed us I don't know; probably he would."

Mr. Briggerland's face was dark.

"When is this interesting event to take place?"

"My marriage? In two months, I think. When is Easter? That class of person always wants to be married at Easter. I asked him to keep our secret and not to mention it to you, and I should not have spoken now if you had not referred to the obligation we were under."

"In two months?" Mr. Briggerland nodded. "Let me know when you want this to end, Jean," he said.

"It will end almost immediately. Please do not trouble," said Jean, "and there is one other thing, father. If you see Mr. Jaggs in the garden to-night, I beg of you do not attempt to shoot him. He is a very useful man."

Her father sank back in his chair.

"You're beyond me," he said, helplessly.

Mordon occupied two rooms above the garage, which was conveniently situated for Jean's purpose. He arrived late the next night, and a light in his window, which was visible from the girl's room, told her all she wanted to know.

Mr. Mordon was a good-looking man by certain standards. His hair was dark and glossily brushed. His normal pallor of countenance gave him the interesting appearance which men of his kind did not greatly dislike, and he had a figure which was admired in a dozen servants' halls, and a manner which passed amongst housemaids for "gentlemanly," and amongst gentlemen as "superior." He heard the foot of the girl on the stairs, and opened the door.

"You have brought it?" she said, without a preliminary word.

She had thrown a dark cloak over her evening dress, and the man's eyes feasted on her.

"Yes, I have brought it—Jean," he said.

She put her finger to her lips.

"Be careful, François," she cautioned in a low voice.

Although the man spoke English as well as he spoke French, it was in the latter language that the conversation was carried on. He went to a grip which lay on the bed, opened it and took out five thick packages of thousand-franc notes.

"There are a thousand in each, mademoiselle. Five million francs. I changed part of the money in Paris, and part in London."

"The woman—there is no danger from her?"

"Oh no, mademoiselle," he smiled complacently. "She is not likely to betray me, and she does not know my name or where I am living. She is a girl I met at a dance at the Swiss Waiters' Club," he explained. "She is not a good character. I think the French police wish to find her, but she is very clever."

"What did you tell her?" asked Jean.

"That I was working a coup with Vaud and Montheron. These are two notorious men in Paris whom she knew. I gave her five thousand francs for her work."

"There was no trouble?"

"None whatever, mademoiselle. I watched her, and saw she carried the letter to the bank. As soon as the money was changed I left Croydon by air for Paris, and came on from Paris to Marseilles by aeroplane."

"You did well, François," she said, and patted his hand.

He would have seized hers, but she drew back.

"You have promised, François," she said with dignity, "and a French gentleman keeps his word."

François bowed.

He was not a French gentleman, but he was anxious that this girl should think he was, and to that end had told her stories of his birth which had apparently impressed her.

"Now will you do something more for me?"

"I will do anything in the world, Jean," he cried passionately, and again a restraining hand fell on his shoulder.

"Then sit down and write; your French is so much better than mine."

"What shall I write?" he asked. She had never called upon him for proof of his scholarship, and he was childishly eager to reveal to the woman he loved attainments of which he had no knowledge.

"Write, 'Dear Mademoiselle'." He obeyed.

> *"'have returned from London, and have confessed to Madame Meredith that I have forged her name and have drawn £100,000 from her bank———'"*

"Why do I write this, Jean?" he asked in surprise.

"I will tell you one day—go on. François," she continued her dictation.

> *"'And now I have learnt that Madame Meredith loves me. There is only one end to this—that which you see———'"*

"Do you intend passing suspicion to somebody else?" he asked, evidently fogged, "but why should I say———?"

She stopped his mouth with her hand.

"How wonderful you are, Jean," he said, admiringly, as he blotted the paper and handed it to her. "So that if this matter is traced to you———" She looked into his eyes and smiled.

"There will be trouble for somebody," she said, softly, as she put the paper in her pocket.

Suddenly, before she could realise what was happening he had her in his arms, his lips pressed against hers.

"Jean, Jean!" he muttered. "You adorable woman!"

Gently she pressed him back and she was still smiling, though her eyes were like granite.

"Gently, François," she said, "you must have patience!"

She slipped through the door and closed it behind her, and even in her then state of mind she did not slam it, nor did she hurry down the stairs, but went out, taking her time, and was back in the house without her absence having been noticed. Her face, reflected in her long mirror, was serene in its repose, but within her a devil was alive, hungry for destruction. No man had roused the love of Jean Briggerland, but at least one had succeeded in bringing to life a consuming hate which, for the time being, absorbed her.

From the moment she drew her wet handkerchief across her red lips and flung the dainty thing as though it were contaminated through the open window, François Mordon was a dead man.

Chapter XXXI

A letter from Jack Glover arrived the next morning. He had had an easy journey, was glad to have had the opportunity of seeing Lydia, and hoped she would think over the will. Lydia was not thinking of wills, but of an excuse to get back to London. Of a sudden the loveliness of Monte Carlo had palled upon her, and she had almost forgotten the circumstances which had made the change of scene and climate so welcome.

"Go back to London, my dear?" said Mrs. Cole-Mortimer, shocked. "What a—a rash notion! Why it is *freezing* in town and foggy and ... and I really can't let you go back!"

Mrs. Cole-Mortimer was agitated at the very thought. Her own good time on the Riviera depended upon Lydia staying. Jean had made that point very clear. She, herself, she explained to her discomforted hostess, was ready to go back at once, and the prolongation of Mrs. Cole-Mortimer's stay depended upon Lydia's plans. A startling switch of cause and effect, for Mrs. Cole-Mortimer had understood that Jean's will controlled the plans of the party.

Lydia might have insisted, had she really known the reason for her sudden longing for the grimy metropolis. But she could not even convince herself that the charms of Monte Carlo were contingent upon the presence there of a man who had aroused her furious indignation and with whom she had spent most of the time quarrelling. She mentioned her unrest to Jean, and Jean as usual seemed to understand.

"The Riviera is rather like Turkish Delight—very sweet, but unsatisfying," she said. "Stay another week and then if you feel that way we'll all go home together."

"This means breaking up your holiday," said Lydia in self-reproach.

"Not a bit," denied the girl, "perhaps I shall feel as you do in a week's time."

A week! Jean thought that much might happen in a week. In truth events began to move quickly from that night, but in a way she had not anticipated.

Mr. Briggerland, who had been reading the newspaper through the conversation, looked up.

"They are making a great fuss of this Moor in Nice," he said, "but if I remember rightly, Nice invariably has some weird lion to adore."

"Muley Hafiz," said Lydia. "Yes, I saw him the day I went to lunch with Mr. Stepney, a fine-looking man."

"I'm not greatly interested in natives," said Jean carelessly. "What is he, a negro?"

"Oh, no, he's fairer than—" Lydia was about to say "your father," but thought it discreet to find another comparison. "He's fairer than most of the people in the south of France," she said, "but then all very highly-bred Moors are, aren't they?"

Jean shook her head.

"Ethnology means nothing to me," she said humorously. "I've got my idea of Moors from Shakespeare, and I thought they were mostly black. What is he then? I haven't read the papers."

"He is the Pretender to the Moorish throne," said Lydia, "and there has been a lot of trouble in the French Senate about him. France supports his claims, and the Spaniards have offered a reward for his body, dead or alive, and that has brought about a strained relationship between Spain and France."

Jean regarded her with an amused smile.

"Fancy taking an interest in international politics. I suppose that is due to your working on a newspaper, Lydia."

Jean discovered that she was to take a greater interest in Muley Hafiz than she could have thought was possible. She had to go into Monte Carlo to do some shopping. Mentone was nearer, but she preferred the drive into the principality.

The Rooms had no great call for her, and whilst Mordon went to a garage to have a faulty cylinder examined, she strolled on to the terrace of the Casino, down the broad steps towards the sea. The bathing huts were closed at this season, but the little road down to the beach is secluded and had been a favourite walk of hers in earlier visits.

Near the huts she passed a group of dark-looking men in long white jellabs, and wondered which of these was the famous Muley. One she noticed with a particularly negro type of face, wore on his flowing robe the scarlet ribbon of the Legion of Honour. Somehow or other he did not seem interesting enough to be Muley, she thought as she went on to a strip of beach.

A man was standing on the sea shore, a tall, commanding man, gazing out it seemed across the sunlit ocean as though he were in search of something. He could not have heard her footfall because she was walking on the sand, and yet he must have realised her presence, for he turned, and she almost stopped at the sight of his face. He might have been a European; his complexion was fair, though his eyebrows and eyes were jet black, as also was the tiny beard and moustache he wore. Beneath the conventional jellab he wore a dark green jacket, and she had a glimpse of glittering decorations before he pulled over his cloak so that they were hidden. But it was his eyes which held her. They were large and as black as night, and they were set in a face of such strength and dignity that Jean knew instinctively that she was looking upon the Moorish Pretender.

They stood for a second staring at one another, and then the Moor stepped aside.

"Pardon," he said in French, "I am afraid I startled you."

Jean was breathing a little quicker. She could not remember in her life any man who had created so immediate and favourable an impression. She forgot her contempt for native people, forgot his race, his religion (and religion was a big thing to Jean), forgot everything except that behind those eyes she recognised something which was kin to her.

"You are English, of course," he said in that language.

"Scottish," smiled Jean.

"It is almost the same, isn't it?" He spoke without any trace of an accent, without an error of grammar, and his voice was the voice of a college man.

He had left the way open for her to pass on, but she lingered.

"You are Muley Hafiz, aren't you?" she asked, and he turned his head. "I've read a great deal about you," she added, though in truth she had read nothing.

He laughed, showing two rows of perfect white teeth. It was only by contrast with their whiteness that she noticed the golden brown of his complexion.

"I am of international interest," he said lightly and glanced round toward his attendants.

She thought he was going and would have moved on, but he stopped her.

"You are the first English speaking person I have talked to since I've been in France," he said, "except the American Ambassador." He smiled as at a pleasant recollection.

"You talk almost like an Englishman yourself."

"I was at Oxford," he said. "My brother was at Harvard. My father, the brother of the late Sultan, was a very progressive man and believed in the Western education for his children. Won't you sit down?" he asked, pointing to the sand.

She hesitated a second, and then sank to the ground, and crossing his legs he sat by her side.

"I was in France for four years," he carried on, evidently anxious to hold her in conversation, "so I speak both languages fairly well. Do you speak Arabic?" He asked the question solemnly, but his eyes were bright with laughter.

"Not very well," she answered gravely. "Are you staying very long?" It was a conventional question and she was unprepared for the reply.

"I leave to-night," he said, "though very few people know it. You have surprised a State secret," he smiled again.

And then he began to talk of Morocco and its history, and with extraordinary ease he traced the story of the families which had ruled that troubled State.

He touched lightly on his own share in the rebellion which had almost brought about a European war.

"My uncle seized the throne, you know," he said, taking up a handful of sand and tossing it up in the air. "He defeated my father and killed him, and then we caught his two sons."

"What happened to them?" asked Jean curiously.

"Oh, we killed them," he said carelessly. "I had them hanged in front of my tent. You're shocked?"

She shook her head.

"Do you believe in killing your enemies?"

She nodded.

"Why not? It is the only logical thing to do."

"My brother joined forces with the present Sultan, and if I ever catch him I shall hang him too," he smiled.

"And if he catches you?" she asked.

"Why, he'll hang me," he laughed. "That is the rule of the game."

"How strange!" she said, half to herself.

"Do you think so? I suppose from the European standpoint——"

"No, no," she stopped him. "I wasn't thinking of that. You are logical and you do the logical thing. That is how I would treat my enemies."

"If you had any," he suggested.

She nodded.

"If I had any," she repeated with a hard little smile. "Will you tell me this—do I call you Mr. Muley or Lord Muley?"

"You may call me Wazeer, if you're so hard up for a title," he said, and the little idiom sounded queer from him.

"Well, Wazeer, will you tell me: Suppose somebody who had something that you wanted very badly and they wouldn't give it to you, and you had the power to destroy them, what would you do?"

"I should certainly destroy them," said Muley Hafiz. "It is unnecessary to ask. 'The common rule, the simple plan'" he quoted.

Her eyes were fixed on his face, and she was frowning, though this she did not know.

"I am glad I met you this afternoon," she said. "It must be wonderful living in that atmosphere, the atmosphere of might and power, where men and women aren't governed by the finicking rules which vitiate the Western world."

He laughed.

"Then you are tired of your Western civilisation," he said as he rose and helped her to her feet (his hands were long and delicate, and she grew breathless at the touch of them). "You must come along to my little city in the hills where the law is the sword of Muley Hafiz."

She looked at him for a moment.

"I almost wish I could," she said and held out her hand.

He took it in the European fashion and bowed over it. She seemed so tiny a thing by the side of him, her head did not reach his shoulder.

"Good-bye," she said hurriedly and turning, walked back the way she had come, and he stood watching her until she was out of sight.

Chapter XXXII

"Jean!"

She looked round to meet the scowling gaze of Marcus Stepney.

"I must say you're the limit," he said violently. "There are lots of things I imagine you'd do, but to stand there in broad daylight talking to a nigger——"

"If I stand in broad daylight and talk to a card-sharper, Marcus, I think I'm just low enough to do almost anything."

"A damned Moorish nigger," he spluttered, and her eyes narrowed.

"Walk up the road with me, and if you possibly can, keep your voice down to the level which gentlemen usually employ when talking to women," she said.

She was in better condition than he, and he was a little out of breath by the time they reached the Café de Paris, which was crowded at that hour with the afternoon tea people.

He found a quiet corner, and by this time his anger, and a little of his courage, had evaporated.

"I've only your interest at heart, Jean," he said almost pleadingly, "but you don't want people in our set to know you've been hobnobbing with this infernal Moor."

"When you say 'our set,' to which set are you referring?" she asked unpleasantly. "Because if it is the set I believe you mean, they can't think too badly of me for my liking. It would be a degradation to me to be admired by your set, Marcus."

"Oh, come now," he began feebly.

"I thought I had made it clear to you and I hoped you would carry the marks to your dying day"—there was malice in her voice, and he winced—"that I do not allow you to dominate my life or to censor my actions. The 'nigger' you referred to was more of a gentleman than you can ever be, Marcus, because he has breed, which the Lord didn't give to you."

The waiter brought the tea at that moment, and the conversation passed to unimportant topics till he had gone.

"I'm rather rattled," he apologised. "I lost six thousand louis last night."

"Then you have six thousand reasons why you should keep on good terms with me," said Jean smiling cheerfully.

"That cave man stuff?" he asked, and shook his head. "She'd raise Cain."

Jean was laughing inside herself, but she did not show her merriment.

"You can but try," she said. "I've already told you how it can be done."

"I'll try to-morrow," he said after a thought. "By heavens, I'll try to-morrow!"

It was on the tip of her tongue to say "Not to-morrow," but she checked herself.

Mordon came round with the car to pick her up soon after. Mordon! Her little chin jerked up with a gesture of annoyance, which she seldom permitted herself. And yet she felt unusually cheered. Her meeting with the Moor was a milestone in her life from which memory she could draw both encouragement and comfort.

"You met Muley?" said Lydia. "How thrilling! What is he like, Jean? Was he a blackamoor?"

"No, he wasn't a blackamoor," said the girl quietly. "He was an unusually intelligent man."

"H'm," grunted her father. "How did you come to meet him, my dear?"

"I picked him up on the beach," said Jean coolly, "as any flapper would pick up any nut."

Mr. Briggerland choked.

"I hate to hear you talking like that, Jean. Who introduced him?"

"I told you," she said complacently. "I introduced myself. I talked to him on the beach and he talked to me, and we sat down and played with the sand and discussed one another's lives."

"But how enterprising of you, Jean," said the admiring Lydia.

Mr. Briggerland was going to say something, but thought better of it.

There was a concert at the theatre that night and the whole party went. They had a box, and the interval had come before Lydia saw somebody ushered into a box on the other side of the house with such evidence of deference that she would have known who he was even if she had not seen the scarlet fez and the white robe.

"It is your Muley," she whispered.

Jean looked round.

Muley Hafiz was looking across at her; his eyes immediately sought the girl's, and he bowed slightly.

"What the devil is he bowing at?" grumbled Mr. Briggerland. "You didn't take any notice of him, did you, Jean?"

"I bowed to him," said his daughter, not troubling to look round. "Don't be silly, father; anyway, if he weren't nice, it would be quite the right thing to do. I'm the most distinguished woman in the house because I know Muley Hafiz, and he has bowed to me! Don't you realise the social value of a lion's recognition?"

Lydia could not see him distinctly. She had an impression of a white face, two large black spaces where his eyes were and a black beard. He sat all the time in the shadow of a curtain.

Jean looked round to see if Marcus Stepney was present, hoping that he had witnessed the exchange of courtesies, but Marcus at that moment was watching little bundles of twelve thousand franc notes raked across to the croupier's end of the table—which is the business end of Monte Carlo.

Jean was the last to leave the car when it set them down at the Villa Casa. Mordon called her respectfully.

"Excuse me, mademoiselle," he said, "I wish you would come to the garage and see the new tyres that have arrived. I don't like them."

It was a code which she had agreed he should use when he wanted her.

"Very good, Mordon, I will come to the garage later," she said carelessly.

"What does Mordon want you for?" asked her father, with a frown.

"You heard him. He doesn't approve of some new tyres that have been bought for the car," she said coolly. "And don't ask me questions. I've got a headache and I'm dying for a cup of chocolate."

"If that fellow gives you any trouble he'll be sorry," said Briggerland. "And let me tell you this, Jean, that marriage idea of yours——"

She only looked at him, but he knew the look and wilted.

"I don't want to interfere with your private affairs," he mumbled, "but the very thought of it gets me crazy."

The garage was a brick building erected by the side of the carriage drive, built much nearer the house than is usually the case.

Jean waited a reasonable time before she slipped away. Mordon was waiting for her before the open doors of the garage. The place was in darkness; she did not see him standing in the entrance until she was within a few paces of the man.

"Come up to my room," he said briskly.

"What do you want?" she asked.

"I want to speak to you and this is not the place."

"This is the only place where I am prepared to speak to you at the moment, François," she said reproachfully. "Don't you realise that my father is within hearing, and at any moment Madame Meredith may come out? How would I explain my presence in your room?"

He did not answer for the moment, then:

"Jean, I am worried," he said, in a troubled voice. "I cannot understand your plans—they are too clever for me, and I have known men and women of great attainment. The great Bersac———"

"The great Bersac is dead," she said coldly. "He was a man of such great attainments that he came to the knife. Besides, it is not necessary that you should understand my plans, François."

She knew quite well what was troubling him, but she waited.

"I cannot understand the letter which I wrote for you," said Mordon. "The letter in which I say Madame Meredith loved me. I have thought this matter out, Jean, and it seems to me that I am compromised."

She laughed softly.

"Poor François," she said mockingly. "With whom could you be compromised but with your future wife? If I desire you to write that letter, what else matters?"

Again he was silent.

"I cannot speak here," he said almost roughly. "You must come to my room."

She hesitated. There was something in his voice she did not like.

"Very well," she said, and followed him up the steep stairs.

Chapter XXXIII

"Now explain." His words were a command, his tone peremptory.

Jean, who knew men, and read them without error, realised that this was not a moment to temporise.

"I will explain to you, François, but I do not like the way you speak," she said. "It is not you I wish to compromise, but Madame Meredith."

"In this letter I wrote for you I said I was going away. I confessed to you that I had forged a cheque for five million francs. That is a very serious document, mademoiselle, to be in the possession of anybody but myself." He looked at her straight in the eyes and she met his gaze unflinchingly.

"The thing will be made very clear to you to-morrow, François," she said softly, "and really there is no reason to worry. I wish to end this unhappy state of affairs."

"With me?" he asked quickly.

"No, with Madame Meredith," she answered. "I, too, am tired of waiting for marriage and I intend asking my father's permission for the wedding to take place next week. Indeed, François," she lowered her eyes modestly, "I have already written to the British Consul at Nice, asking him to arrange for the ceremony to be performed."

The sallow face of the chauffeur flushed a dull red.

"Do you mean that?" he said eagerly. "Jean, you are not deceiving me?"

She shook her head.

"No, François," she said in that low plaintive voice of hers, "I could not deceive you in a matter so important to myself."

He stood watching her, his breast heaving, his burning eyes devouring her, then:

"You will give me back that letter I wrote, Jean?" he said.

"I will give it to you to-morrow."

"To-night," he said, and took both her hands in his. "I am sure I am right. It is too dangerous a letter to be in existence, Jean, dangerous for you and for me—you will let me have it to-night?"

She hesitated.

"It is in my room," she said, an unnecessary statement, and, in the circumstances, a dangerous one, for his eyes dropped to the bag that hung at her wrist.

"It is there," he said. "Jean darling, do as I ask," he pleaded. "You know, every time I think of that letter I go cold. I was a madman when I wrote it."

"I have not got it here," she said steadily. She tried to draw back, but she was too late. He gripped her wrists and pulled the bag roughly from her hand.

"Forgive me, but I know I am right," he began, and then like a fury she flew at him, wrenched the bag from his hand, and by the very violence of her attack, flung him backward.

He stared at her, and the colour faded from his face leaving it a dead white.

"What is this you are trying to do?" he glowered at her.

"I will see you in the morning, François," she said and turned.

Before she could reach the head of the stairs his arm was round her and he had dragged her back.

"My friend," he said between his teeth, "there is something in this matter which is bad for me."

"Let me go," she breathed and struck at his face.

For a full minute they struggled, and then the door opened and Mr. Briggerland came in, and at the sight of his livid face, Mordon released his hold.

"You swine!" hissed the big man. His fist shot out and Mordon went down with a crash to the ground. For a moment he was stunned, and then with a snarl he turned over on his side and whipped a revolver from his hip pocket. Before he could fire, the girl had gripped the pistol and wrenched it from his hand.

"Get up," said Briggerland sternly. "Now explain to me, my friend, what you mean by this disgraceful attack upon mademoiselle."

The man rose and dusted himself mechanically and there was that in his face which boded no good to Mr. Briggerland.

Before he could speak Jean intervened.

"Father," she said quietly, "you have no right to strike François."

"François," spluttered Briggerland, his dark face purple with rage.

"François," she repeated calmly. "It is right that you should know that François and I will be married next week."

Mr. Briggerland's jaw dropped.

"What?" he almost shrieked.

She nodded.

"We are going to be married next week," she said, "and the little scene you witnessed has nothing whatever to do with you."

The effect of these words on Mordon was magical. The malignant frown which had distorted his face cleared away. He looked from Jean to Briggerland as though it were impossible to believe the evidence of his ears.

"François and I love one another," Jean went on in her even voice. "We have quarrelled to-night on a matter which has nothing to do with anybody save ourselves."

"You're—going—to—marry—him—next—week?" said Mr. Briggerland dully. "By God, you'll do nothing of the sort!"

She raised her hand.

"It is too late for you to interfere, father," she said quietly. "François and I shall go our way and face our own fate. I'm sorry you disapprove, because you have always been a very loving father to me."

That was the first hint Mr. Briggerland had received that there might be some other explanation for her words, and he became calmer.

"Very well," he said, "I can only tell you that I strongly disapprove of the action you have taken and that I shall do nothing whatever to further your reckless scheme. But I must insist upon your coming back to the house now. I cannot have my daughter talked about."

She nodded.

"I will see you to-morrow morning early, François," she said. "Perhaps you will drive me into Nice before breakfast. I have some purchases to make."

He bowed, and reached out his hand for the revolver which she had taken from him.

She looked at the ornate weapon, its silver-plated metal parts, the graceful ivory handle.

"I'm not going to trust you with this to-night," she said with her rare smile. "Good night, François."

He took her hand and kissed it.

"Good night, Jean," he said in a tremulous voice. For a moment their eyes met, and then she turned as though she dared not trust herself and followed her father down the stairs.

They were half-way to the house when she laid her hand on Briggerland's arm.

"Keep this," she said. It was François' revolver. "It is probably loaded and I thought I saw some silver initials inlaid in the ivory handle. If I know François Mordon, they are his."

"What do you want me to do with it?" he said as he slipped the weapon in his pocket.

She laughed.

"On your way to bed, come in to my room," she said. "I've quite a lot to tell you," and she sailed into the drawing-room to interrupt Mrs. Cole-Mortimer, who was teaching a weary Lydia the elements of bezique.

"Where have you been, Jean?" asked Lydia, putting down her cards.

"I have been arranging a novel experience for you, but I'm not so sure that it will be as interesting as it might—it all depends upon the state of your young heart," said Jean, pulling up a chair.

"My young heart is very healthy," laughed Lydia. "What is the interesting experience?"

"Are you in love?" challenged Jean, searching in a big chintz bag where she kept her handiwork for a piece of unfinished sewing. (Jean's domesticity was always a source of wonder to Lydia.)

"In love—good heavens, no."

"So much the better," nodded Jean, "that sounds as though the experience will be fascinating."

She waited until she had threaded the fine needle before she explained.

"If you really are not in love and you sit on the Lovers' Chair, the name of your future husband will come to you. If you're in love, of course, that complicates matters a little."

"But suppose I don't want to know the name of my future husband?"

"Then you're inhuman," said Jean.

"Where is this magical chair?"

"It is on the San Remo road beyond the frontier station. You've been there, haven't you, Margaret?"

"Once," said Mrs. Cole-Mortimer, who had not been east of Cap Martin, but whose rule it was never to admit that she had missed anything worth seeing.

"In a wild, eerie spot," Jean went on, "and miles from any human habitation."

"Are you going to take me?"

Jean shook her head.

"That would ruin the spell," she said solemnly. "No, my dear, if you want that thrill, and, seriously, it is worth while, because the scenery is the most beautiful of any along the coast, you must go alone."

Lydia nodded.

"I'll try it. Is it too far to walk?" she asked.

"Much too far," said Jean. "Mordon will drive you out. He knows the road very well and you ought not to take anybody but an experienced driver. I have a *permis* for the car to pass the frontier; you will probably meet father in San Remo—he is taking a motor-cycle trip, aren't you, daddy?"

Mr. Briggerland drew a long breath and nodded. He was beginning to understand.

Chapter XXXIV

There was lying in Monaco harbour a long white boat with a stumpy mast, which delighted in the name of *Jungle Queen*. It was the property of an impecunious English nobleman who made a respectable income from letting the vessel on hire.

Mrs. Cole-Mortimer had seemed surprised at the reasonable fee demanded for two months' use until she had seen the boat the day after her arrival at Cap Martin.

She had pictured a large and commodious yacht; she found a reasonably sized motor-launch with a whale-deck cabin. The description in the agent's catalogue that the *Jungle Queen* would "sleep four" was probably based on the experience of a party of young roisterers who had once hired the vessel. Supposing that the "four" were reasonably drunk or heavily drugged, it was possible for them to sleep on board the *Jungle Queen*. Normally two persons would have found it difficult, though by lying diagonally across the "cabin" one small-sized man could have slumbered without discomfort.

The *Jungle Queen* had been a disappointment to Jean also. Her busy brain had conceived an excellent way of solving her principal problem, but a glance at the *Jungle Queen* told her that the money she had spent on hiring the launch—and it was little better—was wasted. She herself hated the sea and had so little faith in the utility of the boat, that she had even dismissed the youth who attended to its well-worn engines.

Mr. Marcus Stepney, who was mildly interested in motor-boating, and considerably interested in any form of amusement which he could get at somebody else's expense, had so far been the sole patron of the *Jungle Queen*. It was his practice to take the boat out every morning for a two hours' sail, generally alone, though sometimes he would take somebody whose acquaintance he had made, and who was destined to be a source of profit to him in the future.

Jean's talk of the cave-man method of wooing had made a big impression upon him, emphasised as it had been, and still was, by the two angry red scars across the back of his hand. Things were not going well with him; the supply of rich and trusting youths had suddenly dried up. The little games in his private sitting-room had dwindled to feeble proportions. He was still able to eke out a living, but his success at his private séances had been counter-balanced by heavy losses at the public tables.

It is a known fact that people who live outside the law keep to their own plane. The swindler very rarely commits acts of violence. The burglar who practises card-sharping as a side-line, is virtually unknown.

Mr. Stepney lived on a plausible tongue and a pair of highly dexterous hands. It had never occurred to him to go beyond his own sphere, and indeed violence was as repugnant to him as it was vulgar.

Yet the cave-man suggestion appealed to him. He had a way with women of a certain kind, and if his confidence had been rather shaken by Jean's savagery and Lydia's indifference, he had not altogether abandoned the hope that both girls in their turn might be conquered by the adoption of the right method.

The method for dealing with Jean he had at the back of his mind.

As for Lydia—Jean's suggestion was very attractive. It was after a very heavily unprofitable night spent at the Nice Casino, that he took his courage in both hands and drove to the Villa Casa.

He was an early arrival, but Lydia had already finished her *petite déjeuner* and she was painfully surprised to see him.

"I'm not swimming to-day, Mr. Stepney," she said, "and you don't look as if you were either."

He was dressed in perfectly fitting white duck trousers, white shoes, and a blue nautical coat with brass buttons; a yachtsman's cap was set at an angle on his dark head.

"No, I'm going out to do a little fishing," he said, "and I was wondering whether, in your charity, you would accompany me."

She shook her head.

"I'm sorry—I have another engagement this morning," she said.

"Can't you break it?" he pleaded, "as an especial favour to me? I've made all preparations and I've got a lovely lunch on board—you said you would come fishing with me one day."

"I'd like to," she confessed, "but I really have something very important to do this morning."

She did not tell him that her important duty was to sit on the Lovers' Chair. Somehow her trip seemed just a little silly in the cold clear light of morning.

"I could have you back in time," he begged. "Do come along, Mrs. Meredith! You're going to spoil my day."

"I'm sure Lydia wouldn't be so unkind."

Jean had made her appearance as they were speaking.

"What is the scheme, Lydia?"

"Mr. Stepney wants me to go out in the yacht," said the girl, and Jean smiled.

"I'm glad you call it a 'yacht,'" she said dryly. "You're the second person who has so described it. The first was the agent. Take her to-morrow, Marcus."

There was a glint of amusement in her eyes, and he felt that she knew what was at the back of his mind.

"All right," he said in a tone which suggested that it was anything but all right, and added, "I saw you flying through Nice this morning with that yellow-faced chauffeur of yours, Jean."

"Were you up so early?" she asked carelessly.

"I wasn't dressed, I was looking out of the window—my room faces the Promenade d'Anglaise. I don't like that fellow."

"I shouldn't let him know," said Jean coolly. "He is very sensitive. There are so many fellows that you dislike, too."

"I don't think you ought to allow him so much freedom," Marcus Stepney went on. He was not in an amiable frame of mind, and the knowledge that he was annoying the girl encouraged him. "If you give these French chauffeurs an inch they'll take a kilometre."

"I suppose they would," said Jean thoughtfully. "How is your poor hand, Marcus?"

He growled something under his breath and thrust his hand deep into the pocket of his reefer coat.

"It is quite well," he snapped, and went back to Monaco and his solitary boat trip, flaming.

"One of these days ..." he muttered, as he tuned up the motor. He did not finish his sentence, but sent the nose of the *Jungle Queen* at full speed for the open sea.

Jean's talk with Mordon that morning had not been wholly satisfactory. She had calmed his suspicions to an extent, but he still harped upon the letter, and she had promised to give it to him that evening.

"My dear," she said, "you are too impulsive—too Gallic. I had a terrible scene with father last night. He wants me to break off the engagement; told me what my friends in London would say, and how I should be a social outcast."

"And you—you, Jean?" he asked.

"I told him that such things did not trouble me," she said, and her lips drooped sadly. "I know I cannot be happy with anybody but you, François, and I am willing to face the sneers of London, even the hatred and scorn of my father, for your sake."

He would have seized her hand, though they were in the open road, but she drew away from him.

"Be careful, François," she warned him.

"Remember that you have a very little time to wait."

"I cannot believe my good fortune," he babbled, as he brought the car up the gentle incline into Monte Carlo. He dodged an early morning tram, missing an unsuspecting passenger, who had come round the back of the tram-car, by inches, and set the big Italia up the palm avenue into the town.

"It is incredible, and yet I always thought some great thing would happen to me, and, Jean, I have risked so much for you. I would have killed Madame in London if she had not been dragged out of the way by that old man, and did I not watch for you when the man Meredith———"

"Hush," she said in a low voice. "Let us talk about something else."

"Shall I see your father? I am sorry for what I did last night," he said when they were nearing the villa.

"Father has taken his motor-bicycle and gone for a trip into Italy," she said. "No, I do not think I should speak to him, even if he were here. He may come round in time, François. You can understand that it is terribly distressing; he hoped I would make a great marriage. You must allow for father's disappointment."

He nodded. He did not drive her to the house, but stopped outside the garage.

"Remember, at half-past ten you will take Madame Meredith to the Lovers' Chair—you know the place?"

"I know it very well," he said. "It is a difficult place to turn—I must take her almost into San Remo. Why does she want to go to the Lovers' Chair? I thought only the cheap people went there———"

"You must not tell her that," she said sharply. "Besides, I myself have been there."

"And who did you think of, Jean?" he asked suddenly.

She lowered her eyes.

"I will not tell you—now," she said, and ran into the house.

François stood gazing after her until she had disappeared, and then, like a man waking from a trance, he turned to the mundane business of filling his tank.

Chapter XXXV

Lydia was dressing for her journey when Mrs. Cole-Mortimer came into the saloon where Jean was writing.

"There's a telephone call from Monte Carlo," she said. "Somebody wants to speak to Lydia."

Jean jumped up.

"I'll answer it," she said.

The voice at the other end of the wire was harsh and unfamiliar to her.

"I want to speak to Mrs. Meredith."

"Who is it?" asked Jean.

"It is a friend of hers," said the voice. "Will you tell her? The business is rather urgent."

"I'm sorry," said Jean, "but she's just gone out."

She heard an exclamation of annoyance.

"Do you know where she's gone?" asked the voice.

"I think she's gone in to Monte Carlo," said Jean.

"If I miss her will you tell her not to go out again until I come to the house?"

"Certainly," said Jean politely, and hung up the telephone.

"Was that a call for me?"

It was Lydia's voice from the head of the stairs.

"Yes, dear. I think it was Marcus Stepney who wanted to speak to you. I told him you'd gone out," said Jean. "You didn't wish to speak to him?"

"Good heavens, no!" said Lydia. "You're sure you won't come with me?"

"I'd rather stay here," said Jean truthfully.

The car was at the door, and Mordon, looking unusually spruce in his white dust coat, stood by the open door.

"How long shall I be away?" asked Lydia.

"About two hours, dear, you'll be very hungry when you come back," said Jean, kissing her. "Now, mind you think of the right man," she warned her in mockery.

"I wonder if I shall," said Lydia quietly.

Jean watched the car out of sight, then went back to the saloon. She was hardly seated before the telephone rang again, and she anticipated Mrs. Cole-Mortimer, and answered it.

"Mrs. Meredith has not gone in to Monte Carlo," said the voice. "Her car has not been seen on the road."

"Is that Mr. Jaggs?" asked Jean sweetly.

"Yes, miss," was the reply.

"Mrs. Meredith has come back now. I'm dreadfully sorry, I thought she had gone into Monte Carlo. She's in her room with a bad headache. Will you come and see her?"

There was an interval of silence.

"Yes, I will come," said Jaggs.

Twenty minutes later a taxicab set down the old man at the door, and a maid admitted him and brought him into the saloon.

Jean rose to meet him. She looked at the bowed figure of old Jaggs. Took him all in, from his iron-grey hair to his dusty shoes, and then she pointed to a chair.

"Sit down," she said, and old Jaggs obeyed. "You've something very important to tell Mrs. Meredith, I suppose."

"I'll tell her that myself, miss," said the old man gruffly.

"Well, before you tell her anything, I want to make a confession," she smiled down on old Jaggs, and pulled up a chair so that she faced him.

He was sitting with his back to the light, holding his battered hat on his knees.

"I've really brought you up under false pretences," she said, "because Mrs. Meredith isn't here at all."

"Not here?" he said, half rising.

"No, she's gone for a ride with our chauffeur. But I wanted to see you, Mr. Jaggs, because—" she paused. "I realise that you're a dear friend of hers and have her best interests at heart. I don't know who you are," she said, shaking her head, "but I know, of course, that Mr. John Glover has employed you."

"What's all this about?" he asked gruffly. "What have you to tell me?"

"I don't know how to begin," she said, biting her lips. "It is such a delicate matter that I hate talking about it at all. But the attitude of Mrs. Meredith to our chauffeur Mordon, is distressing, and I think Mr. Glover should be told."

He did not speak and she went on.

"These things do happen, I know," she said, "but I am happy to say that nothing of that sort has come into my experience, and, of course, Mordon is a good-looking man and she is young——"

"What are you talking about?" His tone was dictatorial and commanding.

"I mean," she said, "that I fear poor Lydia is in love with Mordon."

He sprang to his feet.

"It's a damned lie!" he said, and she stared at him. "Now tell me what has happened to Lydia Meredith," he went on, "and let me tell you this, Jean Briggerland, that if one hair of that girl's head is harmed, I will finish the work I began out there," he pointed to the garden, "and strangle you with my own hands."

She lifted her eyes to his and dropped them again, and began to tremble, then turning suddenly on her heel, she fled to her room, locked the door and stood against it, white and shaking. For the second time in her life Jean Briggerland was afraid.

She heard his quick footsteps in the passage outside, and there came a tap on her door.

"Let me in," growled the man, and for a second she almost lost control of herself. She looked wildly round the room for some way of escape, and then as a thought struck her, she ran quickly into the bath-room, which opened from her room. A large sponge was set to dry by an open window, and this she seized; on a shelf by the side of the bath was a big bottle of ammonia, and averting her face, she poured its contents upon the sponge until it was sodden, then with the dripping sponge in her hand, she crept back, turned the key and opened the door.

The old man burst in, then, before he realised what was happening, the sponge was pressed against his face. The pungent drug almost blinded him, its paralysing fumes brought him on to his knees. He gripped her wrist and tried to press away her hand, but now her arm was round his neck, and he could not get the purchase.

With a groan of agony he collapsed on the floor. In that instant she was on him like a cat, her knee between his shoulders.

Half unconscious he felt his hands drawn to his back, and felt something lashing them together. She was using the silk girdle which had been about her waist, and her work was effective.

Presently she turned him over on his back. The ammonia was still in his eyes, and he could not open them. The agony was terrible, almost unendurable. With her hand under his arm he struggled to his feet. He felt her lead him somewhere, and suddenly he was pushed into a chair. She left him alone for a little while, but presently came back and began to tie his feet together. It was a most amazing single-handed capture—even Jean could never have imagined the ease with which she could gain her victory.

"I'm sorry to hurt an old man." There was a sneer in her voice which he had not heard before. "But if you promise not to shout, I will not gag you."

He heard the sound of running water, and presently with a wet cloth she began wiping his eyes gently.

"You will be able to see in a minute," said Jean's cool voice. "In the meantime you'll stay here until I send for the police."

For all his pain he was forced to chuckle.

"Until you send for the police, eh? You know me?"

"I only know you're a wicked old man who broke into this house whilst I was alone and the servants were out," she said.

"You know why I've come?" he insisted. "I've come to tell Mrs. Meredith that a hundred thousand pounds have been taken from her bank on a forged signature."

"How absurd," said Jean. She was sitting on the edge of the bath looking at the bedraggled figure. "How could anybody draw money from Mrs. Meredith's bank whilst her dear friend and guardian, Jack Glover, is in London to see that she is not robbed."

"Old Jaggs" glared up at her from his inflamed eyes.

"You know very well," he said distinctly, "that I am Jack Glover, and that I have not left Monte Carlo since Lydia Meredith arrived."

Chapter XXXVI

Mr. Briggerland did not enthuse over any form of sport or exercise. His hobbies were confined to the handsome motor-cycle, which not only provided him with recreation, but had, on occasion, been of assistance in the carrying out of important plans, formulated by his daughter.

He stopped at Mentone for breakfast and climbed the hill to Grimaldi after passing the frontier station at Pont St. Louis. He had all the morning before him, and there was no great hurry. At Ventimille he had a second breakfast, for the morning was keen and his appetite was good. He loafed through the little town, with a cigar between his teeth, bought some curios at a shop and continued his leisurely journey.

His objective was San Remo. There was a train at one o'clock which would bring him and his machine back to Monte Carlo, where it was his intention to spend the remainder of the afternoon. At Pont St. Louis he had had a talk with the Customs Officer.

"No, m'sieur, there are very few travellers on the road in the morning," said the official. "It is not until late in the afternoon that the traffic begins. Times have changed on the Riviera, and so many people go to Cannes. The old road is almost now deserted."

At eleven o'clock Mr. Briggerland came to a certain part of the road and found a hiding-place for his motor-cycle—a small plantation of olive trees on the hill side. Incidentally it was an admirable resting place, for from here he commanded an extensive view of the western road.

Lydia's journey had been no less enjoyable. She, too, had stopped at Mentone to explore the town, and had left Pont St. Louis an hour after Mr. Briggerland had passed.

The road to San Remo runs under the shadow of steep hills through a bleak stretch of country from which even the industrious peasantry of northern Italy cannot win a livelihood. Save for isolated patches of cultivated land, the hills are bare and menacing.

With these gaunt plateaux on one side and the rock-strewn seashore on the other, there was little to hold the eye save an occasional glimpse of the Italian town in the far distance. There was a wild uncouthness about the scenery which awed the girl. Sometimes the car would be running so near the sea level that the spray of the waves hit the windows; sometimes it would climb over an out-jutting headland and she would look down upon a bouldered beach a hundred feet below.

It was on the crest of a headland that the car stopped.

Here the road ran out in a semi-circle so that from where she sat she could not see its continuation either before or behind. Ahead it slipped round the shoulder of a high and over-hanging mass of rock, through which the road must have been cut. Behind it dipped down to a cove, hidden from sight.

"There is the Lovers' Chair, mademoiselle," said Mordon.

Half a dozen feet beneath the road level was a broad shelf of rock. A few stone steps led down and she followed them. The Lovers' Chair was carved in the face of the rock and she sat down to view the beauty of the scene. The solitude, the stillness which only the lazy waves broke, the majesty of the setting, brought a strange peace to her. Beyond the edge of the ledge the cliff fell sheer to the water, and she shivered as she stepped back from her inspection.

Mordon did not see her go. He sat on the running board of his car, his pale face between his hands, a prey to his own gloomy thoughts. There must be a development, he told himself. He was beginning to get uneasy, and for the first time he doubted the sincerity of the woman who had been to him as a goddess.

He did not hear Mr. Briggerland, for the dark man was light of foot, when he came round the shoulder of the hill. Mordon's back was toward him. Suddenly the chauffeur looked round.

"M'sieur," he stammered, and would have risen, but Briggerland laid his hand on his shoulder.

"Do not rise, François," he said pleasantly. "I am afraid I was hasty last night."

"M'sieur, it was I who was hasty," said Mordon huskily, "it was unpardonable...."

"Nonsense," Briggerland patted the man's shoulder. "What is that boat out there—a man o' war, François?"

François Mordon turned his head toward the sea, and Briggerland pointed the ivory-handled pistol he had held behind his back and shot him dead.

The report of the revolver thrown down by the rocks came to Lydia like a clap of thunder. At first she thought it was a tyre burst and hurried up the steps to see.

Mr. Briggerland was standing with his back to the car. At his feet was the tumbled body of Mordon.

"Mr.—Brig...!" she gasped, and saw the revolver in his hand. With a cry she almost flung herself down the steps as the revolver exploded. The bullet ripped her hat from her head, and she flung up her hands, thinking she had been struck.

Then the dark face showed over the parapet and again the revolver was presented. She stared for a second into his benevolent eyes, and then something hit her violently and she staggered back, and dropped over the edge of the shelf down, straight down into the sea below.

Chapter XXXVII

Probably Jean Briggerland never gave a more perfect representation of shocked surprise than when old Jaggs announced that he was Jack Glover.

"Mr. Glover," she said incredulously.

"If you'll be kind enough to release my hands," said Jack savagely, "I will convince you."

Jean, all meekness, obeyed, and presently he stood up with a groan.

"You've nearly blinded me," he said, turning to the glass.

"If I'd known it was you——"

"Don't make me laugh!" he snapped. "Of course you knew who it was!" He took off the wig and peeled the beard from his face.

"Was that very painful?" she asked, sympathetically, and Jack snorted.

"How was I to know that it was you?" she demanded, virtuously indignant, "I thought you were a wicked old man——"

"You thought nothing of the sort, Miss Briggerland," said Jack. "You knew who I was, and you guessed why I had taken on this disguise. I was not many yards from you when it suddenly dawned upon you that I could not sleep at Lydia Meredith's flat unless I went there in the guise of an old man."

"Why should you want to sleep at her flat at all?" she asked innocently. "It doesn't seem to me to be a very proper ambition."

"That is an unnecessary question, and I'm wasting my time when I answer you," said Jack sternly. "I went there to save her life, to protect her against your murderous plots!"

"My murderous plots?" she repeated aghast. "You surely don't know what you're saying."

"I know this," and his face was not pleasant to see. "I have sufficient evidence to secure the arrest of your father, and possibly yourself. For months I have been working on that first providential accident of yours—the rich Australian who died with such remarkable suddenness. I may not get you in the Meredith case, and I may not be able to jail you for your attacks on Mrs. Meredith, but I have enough evidence to hang your father for the earlier crime."

Her face was blank—expressionless. Never before had she been brought up short with such a threat as the man was uttering, nor had she ever been in danger of detection. And all the time she was eyeing him so steadily, not a muscle of her face moving, her mind was groping back into the past, examining every detail of the crime he had mentioned, seeking for some flaw in the carefully prepared plan which had brought a good man to a violent and untimely end.

"That kind of bluff doesn't impress me," she said at last. "You're in a poor way when you have to invent crimes to attach to me."

"We'll go into that later. Where is Lydia?" he said shortly.

"I tell you I don't know, except that she has gone out for a drive. I expect her back very soon."

"Is your father with her?"

She shook her head.

"No, father went out early. I don't know who gave you authority to cross-examine me. Why, Jack Glover, you have all the importance of a French examining magistrate," she smiled.

"You may learn how important they are soon," he said significantly. "Where is your chauffeur, Mordon?"

"He is gone, too—in fact, he is driving Lydia. Why?" she asked with a little tightening of heart. She had only just been in time, she thought. So they had associated Mordon with the forgery!

His first words confirmed this suspicion.

"There is a warrant for Mordon which will be executed as soon as he returns," said Jack. "We have been able to trace him in London and also the woman who presented the cheque. We know his movements from the time he left Nice by aeroplane for Paris to the time he returned to Nice. The people who changed the money for him will swear to his identity."

If he expected to startle her he was disappointed. She raised her eyebrows.

"I can't believe it is possible. Mordon was such an honest man," she said. "We trusted him implicitly, and never once did he betray our trust. Now, Mr. Glover," she said coolly, "might I suggest that an interview with a gentleman in my bedroom is not calculated to increase my servants' respect for me? Will you go downstairs and wait until I come?"

"You'll not attempt to leave this house?" he said, and she laughed.

"Really, you're going on like one of those infallible detectives one reads about in the popular magazines," she said a little contemptuously. "You have no authority whatever to keep me from leaving this house and nobody knows that better than you. But you needn't be afraid. Sit on the stairs if you like until I come down."

When he had gone she rang the bell for her maid and handed her an envelope.

"I shall be in the saloon, talking to Mr. Glover," she said in a low voice. "I want you to bring this in and say that you found it in the hall."

"Yes, miss," said the woman.

Jean proceeded leisurely to her toilet. In the struggle her dress had been torn, and she changed it for a pale green silk gown, and Jack, pacing in the hall below, was on the point of coming up to discover if she had made her escape, when she sailed serenely down the stairs.

"I should like to know one thing, Mr. Glover," she said as she went into the saloon. "What do you intend doing? What is your immediate plan? Are you going to spirit Lydia away from us? Of course, I know you're in love with her and all that sort of thing."

His face went pink.

"I am not in love with Mrs. Meredith," he lied.

"Don't be silly," she said practically, "of course you're in love with her."

"My first job is to get that money back, and you're going to help me," he said.

"Of course I'm going to help you," she agreed. "If Mordon has been such a scoundrel, he must suffer the consequence. I'm sure that you are too clever to have made any mistake. Poor Mordon. I wonder what made him do it, because he is such a good friend of Lydia's, and seriously, Mr. Glover, I do think Lydia is being indiscreet."

"You made that remark before," he said quietly. "Now perhaps you'll explain what you mean."

She shrugged her shoulders.

"They are always about together. I saw them strolling on the lawn last night till quite a late hour, and I was so scared lest Mrs. Cole-Mortimer noticed it too——"

"Which means that Mrs. Cole-Mortimer did not notice it. You're clever, Jean! Even as you invent you make preparations to refute any evidence that the other side can produce. I don't believe a word you say."

There was a knock at the door and the maid entered bearing a letter on a salver.

"This was addressed to you, miss," she said. "It was on the hall table—didn't you see it?"

"No," said Jean in surprise. She took the letter, looked down at the address and opened it.

He saw a look of amazement and horror come to her face.

"Good God!" gasped Jean.

"What is it?" he said, springing up.

She stared at the letter again and from the letter to him.

"Read it," she said in a hollow voice.

"Dear Mademoiselle,

"I have returned from London and have confessed to Madame Meredith that I have forged her name and have drawn £100,000 from her bank. And now I have learnt that Madame Meredith loves me. There is only one end to this—that which you see———"

Jack read the letter twice.

"It is in his writing, too," he muttered. "It's impossible, incredible! I tell you I've had Mrs. Meredith under my eyes all the time she has been here. Is there a letter from her?" he asked suddenly. "But no, it is impossible, impossible!"

"I haven't been into her room. Will you come up with me?"

He followed her up the stairs and into Lydia's big bedroom, and the first thing that caught his eye was a sealed letter on a table near the bed. He picked it up. It was addressed to him, in Lydia's handwriting, and feverishly he tore it open.

His face, when he had finished reading, was as white as hers had been.

"Where have they gone?" he asked.

"They went to San Remo."

"By car?"

"Of course."

Without a word he turned and ran down the stairs out of the house.

The taxi that had brought him in the role of Jaggs had gone, but down the road, a dozen yards away, was the car he had hired on the day he came to Monte Carlo. He gave instructions to the driver and jumped in. The car sped through Mentone, stopped only the briefest while at the Customs barrier whilst Jack pursued his inquiries.

Yes, a lady had passed, but she had not returned.

How long ago?

Perhaps an hour; perhaps less.

At top speed the big car thundered along the sea road, twisting and turning, diving into valleys and climbing steep headlands, and then rounding a corner, Jack saw the car and a little crowd about it. His heart turned to stone as he leapt to the road.

He saw the backs of two Italian gendarmes, and pushing aside the little knot of idlers, he came into the centre of the group and stopped. Mordon lay on his face in a pool of blood, and one of the policemen was holding an ivory-handled revolver.

"It was with this that the crime was committed," he said in florid Italian. "Three of the chambers are empty. Now, at whom were the other two discharged?"

Jack reeled and gripped the mud-guard of the car for support, then his eyes strayed to the opening in the wall which ran on the seaward side of the road.

He walked to the parapet and looked over, and the first thing he saw was a torn hat and veil, and he knew it was Lydia's.

Chapter XXXVIII

Mr. Briggerland, killing time on the quay at Monaco, saw the *Jungle Queen* come into harbour and watched Marcus land, carrying his lines in his hand.

As Marcus came abreast of him he called and Mr. Stepney looked round with a start.

"Hello, Briggerland," he said, swallowing something.

"Well, have you been fishing?" asked Mr. Briggerland in his most paternal manner.

"Yes," admitted Marcus.

"Did you catch anything?"

Stepney nodded.

"Only one," he said.

"Hard luck," said Mr. Briggerland, with a smile, "but where is Mrs. Meredith— I understood she was going out with you to-day?"

"She went to San Remo," said Stepney shortly, and the other nodded.

"To be sure," he said. "I had forgotten that."

Later he bought a copy of the *Nicoise* and learnt of the tragedy on the San Remo road. It brought him back to the house, a visibly agitated man.

"This is shocking news, my dear," he panted into the saloon and stood stock still at the sight of Mr. Jack Glover.

"Come in, Briggerland," said Jack, without ceremony. There was a man with him, a tall, keen Frenchman whom Briggerland recognised as the chief detective of the Préfecture. "We want you to give an account of your actions."

"My actions?" said Mr. Briggerland indignantly. "Do you associate me with this dreadful tragedy? A tragedy," he said, "which has stricken me almost dumb with horror and remorse. Why did I ever allow that villain even to speak to poor Lydia?"

"Nevertheless, m'sieur," said the tall man quietly, "you must tell us where you have been."

"That is easily explained. I went to San Remo."

"By road?"

"Yes, by road," said Mr. Briggerland, "on my motor-bicycle."

"What time did you arrive in San Remo?"

"At midday, or it may have been a quarter of an hour before."

"You know that the murder must have been committed at half-past eleven?" said Jack.

"So the newspapers tell me."

"Where did you go in San Remo?" asked the detective.

"I went to a café and had a glass of wine, then I strolled about the town and lunched at the Victoria. I caught the one o'clock train to Monte Carlo."

"Did you hear nothing of the murder?"

"Not a word," said Mr. Briggerland, "not a word."

"Did you see the car?"

Mr. Briggerland shook his head.

"I left some time before poor Lydia," he said softly.

"Did you know of any attachment between the chauffeur and your guest?"

"I had no idea such a thing existed. If I had," said Mr. Briggerland virtuously, "I should have taken immediate steps to have brought poor Lydia to her senses."

"Your daughter says that they were frequently together. Did you notice this?"

"Yes, I did notice it, but my daughter and I are very democratic. We have made a friend of Mordon and I suppose what would have seemed familiar to you, would pass unnoticed with us. Yes, I certainly do remember my poor friend and Mordon walking together in the garden."

"Is this yours?" The detective took from behind a curtain an old British rifle.

"Yes, that is mine," admitted Briggerland without a moment's hesitation. "It is one I bought in Amiens, a souvenir of our gallant soldiers———"

"I know, I quite understand your patriotic motive in purchasing it," said the detective dryly, "but will you tell us how this passed from your possession."

"I haven't the slightest notion," said Mr. Briggerland in surprise. "I had no idea it was lost—I'd lost sight of it for some weeks. Can it be that Mordon—but no, I must not think so evilly of him."

"What were you going to suggest?" asked Jack. "That Mordon fired at Mrs. Meredith when she was on the swimming raft? If you are, I can save you the trouble of telling that lie. It was you who fired, and it was I who knocked you out."

Mr. Briggerland's face was a study.

"I can't understand why you make such a wild and unfounded charge," he said gently. "Perhaps, my dear, you could elucidate this mystery."

Jean had not spoken since he entered. She sat bolt upright on a chair, her hands folded in her lap, her sad eyes fixed now upon Jack, now upon the detective. She shook her head.

"I know nothing about the rifle, and did not even know you possessed one," she said. "But please answer all their questions, father. I am as anxious as you are to get to the bottom of this dreadful tragedy. Have you told my father about the letters which were discovered?"

The detective shook his head.

"I have not seen your father until he arrived this moment," he said.

"Letters?" Mr. Briggerland looked at his daughter. "Did poor Lydia leave a letter?"

She nodded.

"I think Mr. Glover will tell you, father," she said. "Poor Lydia had an attachment for Mordon. It is very clear what happened. They went out to-day, never intending to return——"

"Mrs. Meredith had no intention of going to the Lovers' Chair until you suggested the trip to her," said Jack quietly. "Mrs. Cole-Mortimer is very emphatic on that point."

"Has the body been found?" asked Mr. Briggerland.

"Nothing has been found but the chauffeur," said the detective.

After a few more questions he took Jack outside.

"It looks very much to me as though it were one of those crimes of passion which are so frequent in this country," he said. "Mordon was a Frenchman and I have been able to identify him by tattoo marks on his arm, as a man who has been in the hands of the police many times."

"You think there is no hope?"

The detective shrugged his shoulders.

"We are dragging the pool. There is very deep water under the rock, but the chances are that the body has been washed out to sea. There is clearly no evidence against these people, except yours. The letters might, of course, have been forged, but you say you are certain that the writing is Mrs. Meredith's."

Jack nodded.

They were walking down the road towards the officers' waiting car, when Jack asked:

"May I see that letter again?"

The detective took it from his pocket book and Jack stopped and scanned it.

"Yes, it is her writing," he said and then uttered an exclamation.

"Do you see that?"

He pointed eagerly to two little marks before the words "Dear friend."

"Quotation marks," said the detective, puzzled. "Why did she write that?"

"I've got it," said Jack. "The story! Mademoiselle Briggerland told me she was writing a story, and I remember she said she had writer's cramp. Suppose she dictated a portion of the story to Mrs. Meredith, and suppose in that story there occurred this letter: Lydia would have put the quotation marks mechanically."

The detective took the letter from his hand.

"It is possible," he said. "The writing is very even—it shows no sign of agitation, and of course the character's initials might be 'L.M.' It is an ingenious hypothesis, and not wholly improbable, but if this were a part of the story, there would be other sheets. Would you like me to search the house?"

Jack shook his head.

"She's much too clever to have them in the house," he said. "More likely she's put them in the fire."

"What fire?" asked the detective dryly. "These houses have no fires, they're central heated—unless she went to the kitchen."

"Which she wouldn't do," said Jack thoughtfully. "No, she'd burn them in the garden."

The detective nodded, and they returned to the house.

Jean, deep in conversation with her father, saw them reappear, and watched them as they walked slowly across the lawn toward the trees, their eyes fixed on the ground.

"What are they looking for?" she asked with a frown.

"I'll go and see," said Briggerland, but she caught his arm.

"Do you think they'll tell you?" she asked sarcastically.

She ran up to her own room and watched them from behind a curtain. Presently they passed out of sight to the other side of the house, and she went into Lydia's room and overlooked them from there. Suddenly she saw the detective stoop and pick up something from the ground, and her teeth set.

"The burnt story," she said. "I never dreamt they'd look for that."

It was only a scrap they found, but it was in Lydia's writing, and the pencil mark was clearly visible on the charred ashes.

"'Laura Martin,'" read the detective. "'L. M.,' and there are the words 'tragic' and 'remorse'."

From the remainder of the charred fragments they collected nothing of importance. Jean watched them disappear along the avenue, and went down to her father.

"I had a fright," she said.

"You look as if you've still got it," he said. He eyed her keenly.

She shook her head.

"Father, you must understand that this adventure may end disastrously. There are ninety-nine chances against the truth being known, but it is the extra chance that is worrying me. We ought to have settled Lydia more quietly, more naturally. There was too much melodrama and shooting, but I don't see how we could have done anything else—Mordon was very tiresome."

"Where did Glover come from?" asked Mr. Briggerland.

"He's been here all the time," said the girl.

"What?"

She nodded.

"He was old Jaggs. I had an idea he was, but I was certain when I remembered that he had stayed at Lydia's flat."

He put down his tea cup and wiped his lips with a silk handkerchief.

"I wish this business was over," he said fretfully. "It looks as if we shall have trouble."

"Of course we shall," she said coldly. "You didn't expect to get a fortune of six hundred thousand pounds without trouble, did you? I dare say we shall be suspected. But it takes a lot of suspicion to worry me. We'll be in calm water soon, for the rest of our lives."

"I hope so," he said without any great conviction.

Mrs. Cole-Mortimer was prostrate and in bed, and Jean had no patience to see her.

She herself ordered the dinner, and they had finished when a visitor in the shape of Mr. Marcus Stepney came in.

It was unusual of Marcus to appear at the dinner hour, except in evening dress, and she remarked the fact wonderingly.

"Can I have a word with you, Jean?" he asked.

"What is it, what is it?" asked Mr. Briggerland testily. "Haven't we had enough mysteries?"

Marcus eyed him without favour.

"We'll have another one, if you don't mind," he said unpleasantly, and the girl, whose every sense was alert, picked up a wrap and walked into the garden, with Marcus following on her heels.

Ten minutes passed and they did not return, a quarter of an hour went by, and Mr. Briggerland grew uneasy. He got up from his chair, put down his book, and was half-way across the room when the door opened and Jack Glover came in, followed by the detective.

It was the Frenchman who spoke.

"M'sieur Briggerland, I have a warrant from the Préfect of the Alpes Maritimes for your arrest."

"My arrest?" spluttered the dark man, his teeth chattering. "What—what is the charge?"

"The wilful murder of François Mordon," said the officer.

"You lie—you lie," screamed Briggerland. "I have no knowledge of any——" his words sank into a throaty gurgle, and he stared past the detective. Lydia Meredith was standing in the doorway.

Chapter XXXIX

The morning for Mr. Stepney had been doubly disappointing; again and again he drew up an empty line, and at last he flung the tackle into the well of the launch.

"Even the damn fish won't bite," he said, and the humour of his remark cheered him. He was ten miles from the shore, and the blue coast was a dim, ragged line on the horizon. He pulled out a big luncheon basket from the cabin and eyed it with disfavour. It had cost him two hundred francs. He opened the basket, and at the sight of its contents, was inclined to reconsider his earlier view that he had wasted his money, the more so since the *maître d'hôtel* had thoughtfully included two quart bottles of champagne.

Mr. Marcus Stepney made a hearty meal, and by the time he had dropped an empty bottle into the sea, he was inclined to take a more cheerful view of life. He threw over the debris of the lunch, pushed the basket under one of the seats of the cabin, pulled up his anchor and started the engines running.

The sky was a brighter blue and the sea held a finer sparkle, and he was inclined to take a view of even Jean Briggerland, more generous than any he had held.

"Little devil," he smiled reminiscently, as he murmured the words.

He opened the second bottle of champagne in her honour—Mr. Marcus Stepney was usually an abstemious man—and drank solemnly, if not soberly, her health and happiness. As the sun grew warmer he began to feel an unaccountable sleepiness. He was sober enough to know that to fall asleep in the middle of the ocean was to ask for trouble, and he set the bow of the *Jungle Queen* for the nearest beach, hoping to find a landing place.

He found something better as he skirted the shore. The sea and the weather had scooped out a big hollow under a high cliff, a hollow just big enough to take the *Jungle Queen* and deep and still enough to ensure her a safe anchorage. A rock barrier interposed between the breakers and this deep pool which the waves had hollowed in the stony floor of the ocean. As he dropped his anchor he disturbed a school of fish, and his angling instincts re-awoke. He let down his line over the side, seated himself comfortable in one of the two big basket chairs, and was dozing comfortably....

It was the sound of a shot that woke him. It was followed by another, and a third. Almost immediately something dropped from the cliff, and fell with a mighty splash into the water.

Marcus was wide awake now, and almost sobered. He peered down into the clear depths, and saw a figure of a woman turning over and over. Then as it floated upwards it came on its back, and he saw the face. Without a moment's hesitation he dived into the water.

He would have been wiser if he had waited until she floated to the surface, for now he found a difficulty in regaining the boat. After a great deal of trouble, he managed to reach into the launch and pull out a rope, which he fastened round the girl's waist and drew tight to a small stanchion. Then he climbed into the boat himself, and pulled her after him.

He thought at first she was dead, but listening intently he heard the beating of her heart, and searched the luncheon basket for a small flask of liqueurs, which Alphonse, the head waiter, had packed. He put the bottle to her lips and poured a small quantity into her mouth. She choked convulsively, and presently opened her eyes.

"You're amongst friends," said Marcus unnecessarily.

She sat up and covered her face with her hands. It all came back to her in a flash, and the horror of it froze her blood.

"What has happened to you?" asked Marcus.

"I don't know exactly," she said faintly. And then: "Oh, it was dreadful, dreadful!"

Marcus Stepney offered her the flask of liqueurs, and when she shook her head, he helped himself liberally.

Lydia was conscious of a pain in her left shoulder. The sleeve was torn, and across the thick of the arm there was an ugly raw weal.

"It looks like a bullet mark to me," said Marcus Stepney, suddenly grave. "I heard a shot. Did somebody shoot at you?"

She nodded.

"Who?"

She tried to frame the word, but no sound came, and then she burst into a fit of weeping.

"Not Jean?" he asked hoarsely.

She shook her head.

"Briggerland?"

She nodded.

"Briggerland!" Mr. Stepney whistled, and as he whistled he shivered. "Let's get out of here," he said. "We shall catch our death of cold. The sun will warm us up."

He started the engines going, and safely navigated the narrow passage to the open sea. He had to get a long way out before he could catch a glimpse of the road, then he saw the car, and a cycling policeman dismounting and bending over something. He put away his telescope and turned to the girl.

"This is bad, Mrs. Meredith," he said. "Thank God I wasn't in it."

"Where are you taking me?" she asked.

"I'm taking you out to sea," said Marcus with a little smile. "Don't get scared, Mrs. Meredith. I want to hear that story of yours, and if it is anything like what I fear, then it would be better for you that Briggerland thinks you are dead."

She told the story as far as she knew it and he listened, not interrupting, until she had finished.

"Mordon dead, eh? That's bad. But how on earth are they going to explain it? I suppose," he said with a smile, "you didn't write a letter saying that you were going to run away with the chauffeur?"

She sat up at this.

"I did write a letter," she said slowly. "It wasn't a real letter, it was in a story which Jean was dictating."

She closed her eyes.

"How awful," she said. "I can't believe it even now."

"Tell me about the story," said the man quickly.

"It was a story she was writing for a London magazine, and her wrist hurt, and I wrote it down as she dictated. Only about three pages, but one of the pages was a letter supposed to have been written by the heroine saying that she was going away, as she loved somebody who was beneath her socially."

"Good God!" said Marcus, genuinely shocked. "Did Jean do that?"

He seemed absolutely crushed by the realisation of Jean Briggerland's deed, and he did not speak again for a long time.

"I'm glad I know," he said at last.

"Do you really think that all this time she has been trying to kill me?"

He nodded.

"She has used everybody, even me," he said bitterly. "I don't want you to think badly of me, Mrs. Meredith, but I'm going to tell you the truth. I'd provisioned this little yacht to-day for a twelve hundred mile trip, and you were to be my companion."

"I?" she said incredulously.

"It was Jean's idea, really, though I think she must have altered her view, or thought I had forgotten all she suggested. I intended taking you out to sea and keeping you out there until you agreed——" he shook his head. "I don't think I could have done it really," he said, speaking half to himself. "I'm not really built for a conspirator. None of that rough stuff ever appealed to me. Well, I didn't try, anyway."

"No, Mr. Stepney," she said quietly, "and I don't think, if you had, you would have succeeded."

He was in his frankest mood, and startled her later when he told her of his profession, without attempting to excuse or minimise the method by which he earned his livelihood.

"I was in a pretty bad way, and I thought there was easy money coming, and that rather tempted me," he said. "I know you will think I am a despicable cad, but you can't think too badly of me, really."

He surveyed the shore. Ahead of them the green tongue of Cap Martin jutted out into the sea.

"I think I'll take you to Nice," he said. "We'll attract less attention there, and probably I'll be able to get into touch with your old Mr. Jaggs. You've no idea where I can find him? At any rate, I can go to the Villa Casa and discover what sort of a yarn is being told."

"And probably I can get my clothes dry," she said with a little grimace. "I wonder if you know how uncomfortable I am?"

"Pretty well," he said calmly. "Every time I move a new stream of water runs down my back."

It was half-past three in the afternoon when they reached Nice, and Marcus saw the girl safely to an hotel, changed himself and brought the yacht back to Monaco, where Briggerland had seen him.

For two hours Marcus Stepney wrestled with his love for a girl who was plainly a murderess, and in the end love won. When darkness fell he provisioned the *Jungle Queen*, loaded her with petrol, and heading her out to sea made the swimming cove of Cap Martin. It was to the boat that Jean flew.

"What about my father?" she asked as she stepped aboard.

"I think they've caught him," said Marcus.

"He'll hate prison," said the girl complacently. "Hurry, Marcus, I'd hate it, too!"

Chapter XL

Lydia took up her quarters in a quiet hotel in Nice and Mrs. Cole-Mortimer agreed to stay on and chaperon her.

Though she had felt no effects from her terrifying experience on the first day, she found herself a nervous wreck when she woke in the morning, and wisely decided to stay in bed.

Jack, who had expected the relapse, called in a doctor, but Lydia refused to see him. The next day she received the lawyer.

She had only briefly outlined the part which Marcus Stepney had played in her rescue, but she had said enough to make Jack call at Stepney's hotel to thank him in person. Mr. Stepney, however, was not at home—he had not been home all night, but this information his discreet informant did not volunteer. Nor was the disappearance of the *Jungle Queen* noticed for two days. It was Mrs. Cole-Mortimer, in settling up her accounts with Jack, who mentioned the "yacht."

"The *Jungle Queen*," said Jack, "that's the motor-launch, isn't it? I've seen her lying in the harbour. I thought she was Stepney's property."

His suspicions aroused, he called again at Stepney's hotel, and this time his inquiry was backed by the presence of a detective. Then it was made known that Mr. Stepney had not been seen since the night of Briggerland's arrest.

"That is where they've gone. Stepney was very keen on the girl, I think," said Jack.

The detective was annoyed.

"If I'd known before we could have intercepted them. We have several destroyers in the harbour at Villafrance. Now I am afraid it is too late."

"Where would they make for?" asked Jack.

The officer shrugged his shoulders.

"God knows," he said. "They could get into Italy or into Spain, possibly Barcelona. I will telegraph the Chief of the Police there."

But the Barcelona police had no information to give. The *Jungle Queen* had not been sighted. The weather was calm, the sea smooth, and everything favourable for the escape.

Inquiries elicited the fact that Mr. Stepney had bought large quantities of petrol a few days before his departure, and had augmented his supply the evening he had left. Also he had bought provisions in considerable quantities.

The murder was a week old, and Mr. Briggerland had undergone his preliminary examination, when a wire came through from the Spanish police that a motor-boat answering the description of the *Jungle Queen* had called at Malaga, had provisioned, refilled, and put out to sea again, before the police authorities, who had a description of the pair, had time to investigate.

"You'll think I have a diseased mind," said Lydia, "but I hope she gets away."

Jack laughed.

"If you had been with her much longer, Lydia, she would have turned you into a first-class criminal," he said. "I hope you do not forget that she has exactly a hundred thousand pounds of yours—in other words, a sixth of your fortune."

Lydia shook her head.

"That is almost a comforting thought," she said. "I know she is what she is, Jack, but her greatest crime is that she was born six hundred years too late. If she had lived in the days of the Italian Renaissance she would have made history."

"Your sympathy is immoral," said Jack. "By the way, Briggerland has been handed over to the Italian authorities. The crime was committed on Italian soil and that saves his head from falling into the basket."

She shuddered.

"What will they do to him?"

"He'll be imprisoned for life," was the reply "and I rather think that's a little worse than the guillotine. You say you worry for Jean—I'm rather sorry for old man Briggerland. If he hadn't tried to live up to his daughter he might have been a most respectable member of society."

They were strolling through the quaint, narrow streets of Grasse, and Jack, who knew and loved the town, was showing her sights which made her forget that the Perfumerie Factory, the Mecca of the average tourist, had any existence.

"I suppose I'll have to settle down now," she said with an expression of distaste.

"I suppose you will," said Jack, "and you'll have to settle up, too; your legal expenses are something fierce."

"Why do you say that?" she asked, stopping in her walk and looking at him gravely.

"I am speaking as your mercenary lawyer," said Jack.

"You are trying to put your service on another level," she corrected. "I owe everything I have to you. My fortune is the least of these. I owe you my life three times over."

"Four," he corrected, "and to Marcus Stepney once."

"Why have you done so much for me? Were you interested?" she asked after a pause.

"Very," he replied. "I was interested in you from the moment I saw you step out of Mr. Mordon's taxi into the mud, but I was especially interested in you———"

"When?" she asked.

"When I sat outside your door night after night and discovered you didn't snore," he said shamelessly, and she went red.

"I hope you'll never refer to your old Jaggs's adventures. It was very———"

"What?"

"I was going to say horrid, but I shouldn't be telling the truth," she admitted frankly. "I liked having you there. Poor Mrs. Morgan will be disconsolate when she discovers that we've lost our lodger."

They walked into the cool of the ancient cathedral and sat down.

"There's something very soothing about a church, isn't there?" he whispered. "Look at that gorgeous window. If I were ever rich enough to marry the woman I loved, I should be married in a cathedral like this, full of old tombs and statues and stained glass."

"How rich would you have to be?" she asked.

"As rich as she is."

She bent over toward him, her lips against his ear.

"Tell me how much money you have," she whispered, "and I'll give away all I have in excess of that amount."

He caught her hand and held it fast, and they sat there before the altar of St. Catherine until the sun went down and the disapproving old woman who acted as the cathedral's caretaker tapped them on the shoulder.

Chapter XLI

"That is Gibraltar," said Marcus Stepney, pointing ahead to a grey shape that loomed up from the sea.

He was unshaven for he had forgotten to bring his razor and he was pinched with the cold. His overcoat was turned up to his ears, in spite of which he shivered.

Jean did not seem to be affected by the sudden change of temperature. She sat on the top of the cabin, her chin in the palm of her hand, her elbow on her crossed knee.

"You are not going into Gibraltar?" she asked.

He shook his head.

"I think not," he said, "nor to Algeciras. Did you see that fellow on the quay yelling for the craft to come back after we left Malaga? That was a bad sign. I expect the police have instructions to detain this boat, and most of the ports must have been notified."

"How long can we run?"

"We've got enough gas and grub to reach Dacca," he said. "That's roughly an eight-days' journey."

"On the African coast?"

He nodded, although she could not see him.

"Where could we get a ship to take us to South America?" she asked, turning round.

"Lisbon," he said thoughtfully. "Yes, we could reach Lisbon, but there are too many steamers about and we're certain to be sighted. We might run across to Las Palmas, most of the South American boats call there, but if I were you I should stick to Europe. Come and take this helm, Jean."

She obeyed without question, and he continued the work which had been interrupted by a late meal, the painting of the boat's hull, a difficult business, involving acrobatics, since it was necessary for him to lean over the side. He had bought the grey paint at Malaga, and happily there was not much surface that required attention. The stumpy mast of the *Jungle Queen* had already gone overboard—he had sawn it off with great labour the day after they had left Cap Martin.

She watched him with a speculative eye as he worked, and thought he had never looked quite so unattractive as he did with an eight-days' growth of beard, his shirt stained with paint and petrol. His hands were grimy and nobody would have recognised in this scarecrow the elegant habitué of those fashionable resorts which smart society frequents.

Yet she had reason to be grateful to him. His conduct toward her had been irreproachable. Not one word of love had been spoken, nor, until now, had their future plans, for it affected them both, been discussed.

"Suppose we reach South America safely?" she asked. "What happens then, Marcus?"

He looked round from his work in surprise.

"We'll get married," he said quietly, and she laughed.

"And what happens to the present Mrs. Stepney?"

"She has divorced me," said Stepney unexpectedly. "I got the papers the day we left."

"I see," said Jean softly. "We'll get married——" then stopped.

He looked at her and frowned.

"Isn't that your idea, too?" he asked.

"Married? Yes, that's my idea, too. It seems a queer uninteresting way of finishing things, doesn't it, and yet I suppose it isn't."

He had resumed his work and was leaning far over the bow intent upon his labour. Suddenly she spun the wheel round and the launch heeled over to starboard. For a second it seemed that Marcus Stepney could not maintain his balance against that unexpected impetus, but by a superhuman effort he kicked himself back to safety, and stared at her with a blanched face.

"Why did you do that?" he asked hoarsely. "You nearly had me overboard."

"There was a porpoise lying on the surface of the sea, asleep, I think," she said quietly. "I'm very sorry, Marcus, but I didn't know that it would throw you off your balance."

He looked round for the sleeping fish but it had disappeared.

"You told me to avoid them, you know," she said apologetically. "Did I really put you in any danger?"

He licked his dry lips, picked up the paint-pot, and threw it into the sea.

"We'll leave this," he said, "until we are beached. You gave me a scare, Jean."

"I'm dreadfully sorry. Come here, and sit by me."

She moved to allow him room, and he sat down by her, taking the wheel from her hand.

On the horizon the high lands of northern Africa were showing their saw-edge outlines.

"That is Morocco," he pointed out to her. "I propose giving Gibraltar a wide berth, and following the coast line to Tangier."

"Tangier wouldn't be a bad place to land if there weren't two of us," he went on. "It is our being together in this yacht that is likely to cause suspicion. You could easily pretend that you'd come over from Gibraltar, and the port authorities there are pretty slack."

"Or if we could land on the coast," he suggested. "There's a good landing, and we could follow the beach down, and turn up in Tangier in the morning—all sorts of oddments turn up in Tangier without exciting suspicion."

She was looking out over the sea with a queer expression in her face.

"Morocco!" she said softly. "Morocco—I hadn't thought of that!"

They had a fright soon after. A grey shape came racing out of the darkening east, and Stepney put his helm over as the destroyer smashed past on her way to Gibraltar.

He watched the stern light disappearing, then it suddenly turned and presented its side to them.

"They're looking for us," said Marcus.

The darkness had come down, and he headed straight for the east.

There was no question that the destroyer was on an errand of discovery. A white beam of light shot out from her decks, and began to feel along the sea. And then when they thought it had missed them, it dropped on the boat and held. A second later it missed them and began a search. Presently it lit the little boat, and it did something more—it revealed a thickening of the atmosphere. They were running into a sea fog, one of those thin white fogs that come down in the Mediterranean on windless days. The blinding glare of the searchlight blurred.

"*Bang!*"

"That's the gun to signal us to stop," said Marcus between his teeth.

He turned the nose of the boat southward, a hazardous proceeding, for he ran into clear water, and had only just got back into the shelter of the providential fog bank when the white beam came stealthily along the edge of the mist. Presently it died out, and they saw it no more.

"They're looking for us," said Marcus again.

"You said that before," said the girl calmly.

"They've probably warned them at Tangier. We dare not take the boat into the bay," said Stepney, whose nerves were now on edge.

He turned again westward, edging toward the rocky coast of northern Africa. They saw little clusters of lights on the shore, and he tried to remember what towns they were.

"I think that big one is Cutra, the Spanish convict station," he said.

He slowed down the boat, and they felt their way gingerly along the coast line, until the flick and flash of a lighthouse gave them an idea of their position.

"Cape Spartel," he identified the light. "We can land very soon. I was in Morocco for three months, and if I remember rightly the beach is good walking as far as Tangier."

She went into the cabin and changed, and as the nose of the *Jungle Queen* slid gently up the sandy beach she was ready.

He carried her ashore, and set her down, then he pushed off the nose of the boat, and manœuvred it so that the stern was against the beach, resting in three feet of water. He jumped on board, lashed the helm, and started the engines going, then wading back to the shore he stood staring into the gloom as the little *Jungle Queen* put out to sea.

"That's that," he said grimly. "Now my dear, we've got a ten mile walk before us."

But he had made a slight miscalculation. The distance between himself and Tangier was twenty-five miles, and involved several detours inland into country which was wholly uninhabited, save at that moment it held the camp of Muley Hafiz, who was engaged in negotiation with the Spanish Government for one of those "permanent peaces" which frequently last for years.

Muley Hafiz sat drinking his coffee at midnight, listening to the strains of an ornate gramophone, which stood in a corner of his square tent.

A voice outside the silken fold of his tent greeted him, and he stopped the machine.

"What is it?" he asked.

"Lord, we have captured a man and a woman walking along by the sea."

"They are Riffi people—let them go," said Muley in Arabic. "We are making peace, my man, not war."

"Lord, these are infidels; I think they are English."

Muley Hafiz twisted his trim little beard.

"Bring them," he said.

So they were brought to his presence, a dishevelled man and a girl at the sight of whose face, he gasped.

"My little friend of the Riviera," he said wonderingly, and the smile she gave him was like a ray of sunshine to his heart.

He stood up, a magnificent figure of a man, and she eyed him admiringly.

"I am sorry if my men have frightened you," he said. "You have nothing to fear, madame. I will send my soldiers to escort you to Tangier."

And then he frowned. "Where did you come from?"

She could not lie under the steady glance of those liquid eyes.

"We landed on the shore from a boat. We lost our way," she said.

He nodded.

"You must be she they are seeking," he said. "One of my spies came to me from Tangier to-night, and told me that the Spanish and the French police were waiting to arrest a lady who had committed some crime in France. I cannot believe it is you—or if it is, then I should say the crime was pardonable."

He glanced at Marcus.

"Or perhaps," he said slowly, "it is your companion they desire."

Jean shook her head.

"No, they do not want him," she said, "it is I they want."

He pointed to a cushion.

"Sit down," he said, and followed her example.

Marcus alone remained standing, wondering how this strange situation would develop.

"What will you do? If you go into Tangier I fear I could not protect you, but there is a city in the hills," he waved his hand, "many miles from here, a city where the hills are green, mademoiselle, and where beautiful springs gush out of the ground, and there I am lord."

She drew a long breath.

"I will go to the city of the hills," she said softly, "and this man," she shrugged her shoulders, "I do not care what happens to him," she said, with a smile of amusement at the pallid Marcus.

"Then he shall go to Tangier alone."

But Marcus Stepney did not go alone. For the last two miles of the journey he had carried a bag containing the greater part of five million francs that the girl had brought from the boat. Jean did not remember this until she was on her way to the city of the hills, and by that time money did not interest her.

THE END.

The edits and layout of this print version are Copyright © 2024 by Beauvale Publishing

Printed in Great Britain
by Amazon